"Shayla Black and Lexi B...... . page, and the Perfect Gentlemen series is no exception. Hot and edgy and laced with danger, the stories in the Perfect Gentlemen are just that—perfect."

—J. Kenner, *New York Times* and international bestselling author of the Stark series.

THE NOVELS OF SHAYLA BLACK ARE...

"Sizzling, romantic, and edgy!"

—Sylvia Day, #1 *New York Times* bestselling author

"Scorching, wrenching, suspenseful... A must-read."

—Lora Leigh, #1 *New York Times* bestselling author

"Wickedly seductive from start to finish."—

Jaci Burton, *New York Times* bestselling author

"The perfect combination of excitement, adventure, romance, and really hot sex."

—Smexy Books

"Full of steam, erotic love, and nonstop, page-turning action."

—Night Owl Reviews

THE NOVELS OF LEXI BLAKE ARE...

"A book to enjoy again and again... Captivating."

—Guilty Pleasures Book Reviews

"Utterly delightful."

—Night Owl Reviews

"A satisfying snack of love, romance, and hot, steamy sex."

—Sizzling Hot Books

"Hot and emotional."

—Two Lips Reviews

PRAISE FOR THE MASTERS OF MÉNAGE SERIES
BY SHAYLA BLACK AND LEXI BLAKE

"Smoking hot! Blake and Black know just when to turn up the burner to scorching."

—Under the Covers Book Blog

"Well done...full of spicy sex, and a quick read."

—Smart Bitches, Trashy Books

"Steamy, poignant, and captivating... A funny, touching, lively story that will capture the reader from page one and have them wishing for more when it ends."

—Guilty Pleasures Book Reviews

"Very well written. With just the right amount of love, sex, danger, and adventure... A fun, sexy, exciting, hot read."

—Girly Girl Book Reviews

SMOKE AND SIN

SHAYLA BLACK
AND LEXI BLAKE

Smoke and Sin
Perfect Gentlemen Book 4

Published by Black Oak Books

Copyright 2017 Black Oak Books LLC
Edited by Chloe Vale and Shayla Black
ISBN: 978-1-939673-90-1

Cover by Rachel Connolly

DEDICATION

To all the believers out there.

PROLOGUE

Yale University
Thirteen years before

Roman Calder rolled off the bed, not bothering to don the robe he'd slung over the desk. It lay in a heap, along with the rest of the clothes that had gone flying last night when Augustine Spencer had walked into his house.

"Have I told you that you have the most spectacular butt I've ever seen?" Gus lay on her side, the sheet only covering her below the waist. She cradled her head in one hand, the skeins of her caramel hair draping down to the mattress as she slid him the grin that never failed to tempt him. Sometimes Roman was sure Eve had used the same smile to tempt Adam when she'd offered him the apple and encouraged him to take a juicy bite.

That's exactly who Augustine Spencer was to him, Eve seducing him away from paradise with a desire he found almost impossible to resist.

It probably sounded crazy to most that his version of paradise was the grind of the political world. He would begin his first campaign in a few weeks, running Zack Hayes's bid to become a senator. They were young and taking a gamble by going big, but Zack's father—a political animal himself—had identified a district hungry for new leadership. If Roman did everything he should, this would be their first step on the road to the White House—straight to the money, power, fame, and control he'd always craved.

So why was it that all he wanted right now was to climb back in bed with Gus and shut out the world?

Unable to resist, he sat beside her and smiled her way, caressing the silky cascade of her hair. He loved when she looked sated and mussed. She was usually meticulous, hair in a chic bun or twist, but when he tugged on it and the curls came tumbling down, it was like a massive cloud around her. That hair went everywhere, touching him, brushing his skin. Arousing the hell out of him.

"Well, you know I work hard. A lawyer is only as good as his glute routine." He winked as he settled his palm on her lush hip. "But I need more cardio if I'm going to keep up with you." He winced. "I'll need it even more if your brother ever finds out about us. Why did Dax have to turn into such a badass?"

Daxton Spencer was one of his best friends. In fact, there were six in his group. They'd all met at Creighton Academy and remained close, despite anything and everything prep school—and life—had thrown at them. They'd finished Yale together. Recently, he and Zack had completed law school. Now they were at a crossroads. Gabriel Bond and Maddox Crawford were already in New York working at their family businesses, well on the way to taking over their respective multibillion-dollar birthrights. Dax had followed in his father's footsteps and joined the Navy after Yale, quickly rising through the ranks. Connor Sparks was at Langley, a valuable recruit of the CIA. He claimed he was an analyst. Roman deeply suspected otherwise.

It had been nearly a year since he'd fallen into bed with Augustine. She'd been in her last year of law school then. He'd known her since adolescence, of course. But she'd come over one night to help him prep for an exam…and wound up in his bed.

He'd hardly let her out of it since—not that he had to try hard to keep her there. Gus loved sex as much as he did.

They'd quickly fallen into a routine, but they shared nothing close to what he'd call normalcy. If Roman could count on anything in his relationship with Gus it was that if they weren't fighting, they were fucking. They fought about politics, heated arguments that would inevitably lead him to throw her over a sofa and thrust hard into her from behind. They argued about social issues. A disagreement about a Supreme Court decision had once led to them breaking the breakfast table. He hadn't even cared. They'd hit the ground with a bounce and he hadn't broken rhythm at all. He'd had to concoct a good excuse the next morning, and he still wasn't sure Zack had bought it.

"What do you mean? Dax is a sweetie," Gus said, rolling onto her back, a move that left her generous breasts totally available to him. "Besides, he's going to find out sometime."

God, he loved those breasts. They were full and soft,

with pretty pink nipples. And so responsive. Sometimes he could make her come simply by sucking on them. He palmed one, his brain only half on the conversation. "I don't see why. He's barely home now. When he comes back, we'll cool things off for a bit so he doesn't know anything."

She sat up abruptly. "That won't work forever, Roman."

The sudden flare in her eyes told Roman that he was on dangerous ground, that he'd stepped into something better left untouched.

He sighed and reached for her hand. "Let's not worry about that now, Gus. I don't have long before the bubble of school is over, when we'll have to move on. Can't we spend our time happy?"

He wanted peace with her. He wasn't sure why but she sometimes seemed to delight in pushing his every button, keeping him off-kilter. Yet he was drawn to her time and time again.

Maybe the distance would do them both good. He might get his head screwed on straight again.

So why did he ache at the thought of being apart from Gus?

"Move on?" She scooted away. Her eyes had gone blank, her voice small.

Gus was never, ever small.

"You know what I mean," he said, trying to wave his words off. "Your clerkship is almost done. You've got that job with the firm in New Orleans. I'll be on the road with Zack soon. We won't see each other often."

"Well, I've been thinking about that." She sat up, reaching for the robe he'd eschewed. She wrapped it around her body. There was no way to miss how tense she'd become. "I got another offer, this one at a firm in DC. Close to the Hill, lots of political work."

She was thinking about moving to DC? "The NOLA firm has some political work, too. Wait, are you talking about the job with Kleinman and Horne? That doesn't pay anything like the NOLA job, and you would be going in as a junior associate."

"Only for a year," she replied.

"Yes, and after that year they cut ninety percent of the class." He shook his head. What the hell was she thinking? The NOLA firm was old and respected, and she could grow her career quickly there. The DC firm was a recognized bloodbath. Yes, the two or three lawyers who made it tended to become sharks of the highest order, but they had to fight, teeth constantly bared.

She waved her manicured hand. "I'm not worried about that. I can handle the competition. Hell, I'll probably enjoy it. But if I stay in DC, we don't have to split up."

He strode to the dresser and grabbed a pair of sweats from a drawer, silently gaping. Were they really discussing the future of a relationship he'd never considered serious enough to warrant this conversation? Gus blew in and out of his life like a hurricane, and while he craved her constantly, he was smart enough to know all the reasons they wouldn't work.

He'd assumed she was, too.

Hell, he and Gus were oil and water. God, they were like his parents. Always fucking or fighting—with almost nothing in between.

Roman's childhood came rushing back. He'd often been grateful to return to Creighton where he didn't have to listen to the two of them scream at each other one minute, then behave as if they were the stars of the greatest love story ever the next.

How they'd stayed married all these years, he had no idea. But he refused to let that kind of bullshit drama overtake his life. Despite how crazy he was about Gus, he couldn't live constantly on the edge, always anxious about the next fight. Forever waiting for the other shoe to drop.

"I think you should take the NOLA job, Gus."

"Really?" Her gorgeous face went still with shock. She was quiet as she looked away. When she faced him again, her eyes sheened with tears. "You don't want to see me after you graduate, do you? You never intended to have any sort of a future with me."

Holy shit. Roman had never seen her cry. Not once. The sight threatened to tear out his heart. He moved into her space, reaching for her hand again. "I want what's best for you. I want you to have a happy life, and the next two years of mine are going to be a lot like hell, on the road, in one crappy motel after another. I'll be focused on Zack. I have to be."

"I understand that. Roman, I'm not some lovestruck teenager. I know how hard it's going to be and I could handle it." She squeezed his hand. "I'm tough. What I can't handle anymore is being the secret you shove in the closet. I hate that. We're good together. We challenge each other. We understand each other. I think we should give us a real shot."

He let go and took a step back. "I don't know where this is coming from, Augustine. You've never talked like this before."

"Because we haven't needed to," she replied. "I

know we started this whole thing on a lark, but don't you know I love you, Roman? I've been in love with you for a while. We're not kids anymore. Isn't it time to start thinking about the future?"

Every word felt like a punch to his gut. She loved him? He couldn't allow that. He'd worked too hard to give everything up for a woman, even one as amazing as Gus. When he married, his bride would be someone demure, someone who didn't yank his chain or push him, someone who would enjoy taking care of their house and would fully support his career. He would like his wife. He would never love her.

Unfortunately, he loved Gus. She was an aching pit in his soul, and if he stepped off the edge with her, there would be no climbing back up. His life would be a tumultuous hell, exactly like his parents'. Sure, he and Gus would be all right for the brief moments they sat at the top of the rollercoaster. But what went up always came down. Roman couldn't live with the lows. The fights. The desolation. It would be even worse between him and Gus. She was passionate—and stubborn—about everything. And they both knew exactly where to stick the knives in.

"Come on, Roman. Tell me you don't think about you and me together, and maybe a family someday? We would rule DC. I've already got some thoughts on Zack's campaign, actually." She was giving him that grin that threatened to melt his resolve.

He was teetering. He could practically feel the cliff crumbling beneath his feet. One step, and he would be falling over the precipice…and into the abyss.

"No," he managed.

"Ever?" She shook her head like she didn't

understand.

"I don't think about us in any way except naked. We've had fun, but I never intended for it to last. We've always had an expiration date, Gus, and I guess we've found ours. You're right about one thing, though. We're not kids anymore. I have to get serious."

"But not serious about me." It wasn't a question. She made the statement as though she needed to hear the words aloud.

Perhaps she did. Maybe a clean break would be best. Somewhere in the back of his head he'd imagined he could pop down to NOLA from time to time and see her, sleep with her, fill up that part of himself no one else could. Like she was a freaking gas station or something. How cruel was that of him? She deserved more. She deserved a good life with a man who would put her first, even if that thought killed him.

But no man could love her more. No one would ever love Augustine Spencer as completely as he did. Fucking no one. Too bad he was broken and couldn't give her his whole heart, the way she deserved.

Maybe it was better if she hated him.

"No, Augustine. I'm not serious about you. I never was. In fact, I have a date tomorrow night. Zack is meeting someone new, and I'm going with him."

"You mean Zack is auditioning political wives and you're going along to approve," Gus scoffed, no small amount of bite to her tone. "Don't look surprised. I've known for a while that Zack's father is sending 'proper' women his way. His date tomorrow night is a friend of mine, Joy. She's lovely, but she's no match for Zack. She's far too quiet. He needs some fire in his life. I love Joy, but Zack will squash her under his controlling thumb."

"I'm taking a date, too."

"Like…a double date with Zack and Joy? You've gone along on his dates in the past as the third wheel. Why wouldn't you… Oh." Something heartbroken crossed her face as she pressed her lips together in a grim line.

Yes, Gus was catching on. This was something he'd never intended to tell her, and watching her now hurt.

"You're auditioning, too." Her murmur sounded hoarse, strained.

He nodded. "Eventually, I'll need a wife."

"And that won't be me. So what you're telling me is that you *do* think about having a family, but you don't want one with me."

"Not exactly. I'm out on the family thing. I don't want kids. Ever." He wouldn't put his own offspring through the hell he'd endured. Even if he managed to find a woman he could live and build a proper partnership with, he refused to risk becoming a father and potentially fucking up some innocent kid's psyche.

"So I've been a convenience." She tossed off the robe, turned her back to him, and grabbed her clothes.

He leaned against the dresser. "I didn't say that. I thought we were just having fun since we never see each other outside of the bedroom."

"Really? So all those times I met you for a drink or drove over and we talked for hours, those don't count because they tended to end or begin with sex? When I helped you study for the bar, that didn't matter, either?"

"I didn't say we weren't friends." Actually, it hurt to think about how much she'd become a fixture in his life since his buddies had finished their undergraduate degrees and started their careers. He'd probably spent as much time with Gus as he had Zack. "I don't want us to not be friends."

That would be even worse.

She hooked her bra and shimmied her khakis over the silky underwear he'd damn near torn off in his haste to get inside her earlier. "I'm supposed to stand back and watch you find this dream wife of yours? And when the sex gets boring, maybe, just maybe you'll come and see the slut?"

Right on cue, the never-back-down goddess who knew exactly which buttons to push appeared, just in time for a rousing fight.

"I never called you that."

"But you thought it, didn't you? Gus is good enough to fuck but dear god, don't let my friends know I'm slumming it." Her hands were shaking as she buttoned her blouse. "So you thought it was okay to fuck your way through the entire female law school population, but somehow I'm not good enough to be your political wife. Is that right?"

"You want to know why you can't be my political wife? It has nothing to do with sex, baby. You are the be-all, end-all of sex for me and you damn well know it. It's that you can be a righteous bitch and you'll never learn how to play nice with others. That mouth of yours is a liability I can't afford, so yes, I'm ending the relationship because I've got to grow up and stop playing around. You're not the marrying type. Or the motherly type. So I don't understand why you're pissed at me when I'm merely being honest."

The flat of her palm cracked against the side of his face. His head snapped around, the jarring smack ringing between his ears. His jaw ached. He rubbed it with tense fingers.

Damn but that woman didn't hold back—not her opinions, not her advice, and definitely not when she decided to slap someone. Gus always gave as good as she got.

This was what they did. They pushed and poked each other until one of them backed down or broke. Then they always ended up in bed. Hell, angry sex had been a regular staple for them, and he hated to admit how much he loved it.

He had a feeling they wouldn't be having that anymore.

"I hope you enjoy the rest of your life, Roman, you fucking coward." She stepped back, grabbing her bag. "That's what you are. You and Zack have a lot in common. You both need women who won't challenge you." She scoffed. "Good luck with that."

She strode out of the room.

He let her go, watching every moment of the train wreck until she disappeared out of his bedroom.

It was done. They were over.

Well, they should be, but he followed her out, unable to find the slightest willpower to let her leave. "I'm a coward because I don't want to spend the rest of my life like this?"

She didn't turn around as she crossed the second-story landing and headed for the stairs. She merely raised her hand and gave him her middle finger. "Well, you can spend it kissing Zack's ass. That's what you've really prepped for all your life. Poor Roman. So terrified to have his own life, he needs to leech off Zack."

She was halfway down the steep stairs that led to the

main floor when he caught up to her. He reached out, intending to stop her because there was zero way they ended with this much ugliness between them. She could not have the last word.

The minute his hand touched her arm, she whirled around to face him with fire in her eyes and a curse on her lips.

That was the moment she slipped. Her eyes widened as she started to fall back.

Roman's heart nearly stopped in his chest. He reached frantically for her, desperate to stop her tumble.

Her blouse was silky. He couldn't grab on. She literally slipped through his fingers.

Gus crashed down the stairs, her body beating against the wood and the railing until she finally stopped at the bottom in a heap.

Roman raced down to her, so stunned he'd swear he had stopped breathing. "Oh, god, Gus. Are you all right?"

The door shot open, and Zack rushed in with Maddox right behind him.

"What the hell was that noise?" Zack asked, then saw Gus, who started to writhe and whimper. "Do I need to call an ambulance?"

"Yes!" Roman shouted, his only thought to get Augustine in his arms. To make sure she was all right. To fucking apologize to her and start this conversation over again. Because they couldn't be over. He'd feared that letting her go was a mistake the minute she'd started to fall. He'd seen a world without her, and it had been bleak as hell. Cold. He hadn't wanted any part of it.

She'd been right. He had been a coward. He had to own up to that, fix it.

"Don't touch me," she spat his way as she got to her knees with a groan.

"Augustine, please let me help you." He had to know that she was all right. She looked so pale, so unlike her. His Gus was ballsy and full of life. He'd forgotten that sometimes she could be fragile.

"I want to know what the fuck is happening and I want to know right fucking now." Maddox, the happy ne'er-do-well, stood at the bottom of the stairs like Gus's avenger, glaring at Roman with one of the single darkest looks he'd ever seen.

Gus held a hand out. "I fell, Mad. I came over to pick up something before I leave town and asshole here ran true to form." She sent a thumb in Roman's direction. "I took the stairs way too fast and I fell. Don't you dare call an ambulance. I'm fine with the exception of my pride. That's pretty busted up. So if you'll get out of the way, I'll say goodnight."

Mad was right beside her, taking her hand in his. "Let me help you to your car."

"I walked here," she said. "I'm fine."

Roman couldn't let her leave with things so broken between them. "Gus, we should talk."

"I don't want to speak to you, Roman. Not for a long time," she said without looking back. "And if you try to come anywhere near me before I'm ready, you should know that I can be every bit the bitch you accused me of being. I'll blow up your world and I'll enjoy it. So fuck off. And Zack? Joy is a sorority sister of mine. She's sweet and kind and good, and if you hurt her, I'll kill you. Do I make myself plain? You boys think you're the ultimate brotherhood. You have no idea what my sisterhood can do."

She headed out the door.

When Roman hurried after her, Zack put a hand on his chest, holding him back. "Don't. You will accomplish nothing except getting in another fight. You know Gus. She'll do everything she threatened. Mad?"

"I'll drive her home, take care of her." Mad frowned Roman's way. "If you keep your distance, I might not call Dax and let him know you fucked his sister over. I know you think she's some kind of warrior goddess whose vagina isn't attached to her heart, but she's way more delicate and caring than you give her credit for."

A chill went through Roman as Mad exited and slammed the door behind him.

"You knew?" Roman asked Zack. "Both of you?"

Zack sighed and walked over to the sideboard where they kept the good Scotch. He quickly poured out two glasses. "Did I know that you spent an enormous amount of time with Gus and it wasn't all studying and talking about former professors? Yeah. You didn't fool anyone. The two of you practically spark a fire when you're in the damn room together."

"Dax?"

"Is spectacularly unaware. And you'll have to forgive Mad. He loves Gus. He lost his virginity to her, and they've been close ever since."

Roman winced.

Zack pointed his way. "There it is. That's exactly why you should have left Gus the hell alone and never touched her."

Roman took the glass, his hand tightening around it. "What do you mean?"

After a long sip, Zack sank into the big leather chair he somehow always made look like a throne. "You'll never accept the fact Gus has more experience than you."

"That's not true." But maybe it was. He hated knowing that she'd slept with Mad. He loathed Zack for throwing it in his face right now. Though she hadn't gotten naked with that playboy Crawford in years, it still bugged him. Then there was that pesky rumor about her and Zack... At the thought, jealousy burned through him.

"It is," Zack replied. "And it's hypocritical. But I don't think it's something you'll be able to overcome. You resent anyone who looks at her twice, and she is one sexy woman. If you can't accept that, you'll make yourself insane. Then there's the fact that Gus is smarter than you are. She's funnier. She's a better lawyer. She's—"

"Could you stop? You know, if you want Gus to run your campaign, I can catch her for you."

"You've made my point brilliantly. You can't love a woman you're always in competition with. Sit down and make a decision here and now. You're either going to go after her and figure out how to make the two of you work, or you have to let her go."

He knew exactly what he should do. Zack was right. He didn't want to spend his life fighting with a woman. Or competing with her. Otherwise, his very existence would be a constant battle. As much as he lived for the political fight, he needed peace at home. Without that, he'd go insane.

He sank into the seat opposite Zack. This was how they ended most evenings—single glass of Scotch in hand, planning the future.

"So tell me about this new girl. Not Joy. I've read the dossier your father sent over. I'm talking about her friend." A hollow place gaped inside him, but maybe that was better than always being on tenterhooks. It might be boring and devoid of passion, but at least he wouldn't live in constant turmoil. He could think. He could breathe.

And he knew that made him weak. Zack was right.

"Are you sure?" his friend asked. "Maybe you should take a few days to think about this. I can handle the date with Joy alone. She's likely nothing more than one of my father's blindingly dull Jackie O wannabes. And now that I know Gus will murder me if I so much as lay a finger on this girl, I'll likely end this evening early."

"If Gus likes her, you should seriously consider her. Gus has good instincts." About most things, though apparently she had terrible taste in men. "And I need to look at this the way you are. Finding female companionship should be a logical choice. I need the right woman. I need someone who understands the job, who won't feel as though I'm ignoring her."

"Someone who doesn't care?"

Frustration slithered through him, a snake threatening to bite him. "Make up your mind, Zack. Either I'm an asshole for holding on to a woman who is clearly better than I deserve or I'm shit for being analytical and unemotional. Besides, you're one to talk. You're the one who's actively auditioning political wives."

Zack stared down at his glass, swirling the expensive amber liquid around. "Yes, but I've never once felt about a woman the way you do about Gus. I've never had one knock me on my ass, and I've realized it's never going to happen. I'm not capable of that sort of passion. It's best if I make a deal. I don't want to hurt whomever I marry because I'm incapable of love. I'm going to be upfront and honest, build a partnership with her."

That sounded so shallow and empty and…so easy. "What if you meet someone who knocks you on your ass?"

Zack shook his head. "Never going to happen. I'm too cold. I hate that about myself. I hate even more that my dad's trait in this matter seems to have prevailed. I try to connect to women but I never do. I would settle for a pleasant friendship. But I can only be passionate about one thing: The Oval."

That was something they agreed on—always. But Zack was wrong. He'd been passionate about his friends for years. He'd put himself and his career on the line for them more than once. Zack was nowhere near as cold as he thought.

But Roman felt a terrible chill envelop him. Without Gus to warm him, he had nothing left to do except embrace the cold.

Sucking back the pain, he raised his glass to Zack. "To the Oval."

* * * *

Augustine Spencer strode away from the townhouse, desperate to put distance between her and her Waterloo. That was how she would forever think of this night and this place. She had made her stand.

And she'd lost.

She wasn't going to cry. She refused to. She was a grown-ass woman. And she might be leaving with a broken heart, but at least she'd keep her dignity.

"Hey, Gus. Please let me drive you."

Damn it. Mad was on her tail, and she knew he wouldn't let her put him off. For all his charming ways, Mad was actually a bit like a tick when he wanted to be. He dug in and nothing would persuade him to let it go. She had to convince him that she was okay.

Gus stopped and turned, forcing a smile. "Mad, I'm good. You remember what they taught us in lacrosse. Walk it off, baby. My ankle actually feels much better."

She was worried about something else far more personal than her ankle, but she hoped the cramping pain would soon go away. After all, her baby had only been growing inside her for a few weeks. It would be so tiny nestled deep inside her right now.

The baby Roman had never, ever wanted. So it would be hers and hers alone.

"I hated all sports, Gus. You know that." He reached for her hand. "And I'm also not as unaware as you think. You love him."

Oh, but she couldn't anymore. She forced herself to laugh, although when she really thought about it, she should be laughing at how stupid she'd been. Roman Calder had never lied to her. He'd never promised her anything but a good time in bed. In the beginning, that had honestly been all she wanted anyway. She loved sex, and he was good at it. She made no apologies for her high-voltage libido.

But somewhere along the way, she'd fallen in love with him. She hadn't dated or taken another lover since the first time they'd gone to bed together, though she suspected he couldn't say the same.

"I don't love Roman. I'm not that girl." But she feared she wasn't fooling anyone, least of all Mad. He knew her better than she sometimes knew herself. They had a lot in common.

"Gus, don't bullshit me. I know."

She went still. "You know what?"

"Everything." He leaned against his Porsche, his eyes on her. The streetlight beamed a circle of light down on them, and she wished suddenly the street wasn't so well maintained. She would prefer shadows to Mad's probing stare. "I stopped by your place last week to drop off that book you loaned me. I let myself in with my key and before I left I used the bathroom."

She froze. It had been a terrible mistake to let Mad have a key to her place, but he stayed there sometimes when he was in town. She had an extra bedroom, and Zack and Roman often had too many things going on to spend time with him. Mad could be quite needy, though he hid it behind his party-boy image. He didn't like to be alone, so they spent platonic, friendly time together.

Panic tore through her. "You can't tell Roman."

Mad doubled over with a low groan. "Shit. I was hoping that pregnancy test wasn't yours. You're really pregnant, Gus?"

Well, she'd known it wasn't ideal. "That's my business and no one else's."

She turned to go. If Mad ratted her out, it wouldn't matter. In Roman's eyes, she was nothing but a convenient piece of ass. He probably wouldn't even think the baby was his. By morning, she would have her plans in place. She would quit the DC firm and go home to NOLA and beg the firm there to take her back.

She'd been such a stupid, naive girl. Now it was time to be a woman.

Mad caught up to her. "Nope. This is not just your business anymore. What are you going to do?"

"I'm going to have a baby." She'd thought about this every second of every day since she'd taken that pregnancy test she shouldn't have left on the bathroom counter. She should have thrown it out, but looking at it had filled her with excitement, knowing she was growing a tiny being that would forever be a blend of her and Roman.

She'd wanted to keep the proof that their child existed.

"You're having Roman's baby."

"No, I'm having mine. Not ten minutes ago, Roman made it clear that he has zero interest in either marrying me or having children. He's going to double down on the Zack Hayes method of arranged marriage."

"They're idiots, Gus. And he'll come around. He's probably in there right now realizing what a mistake he made."

"I don't see him running after me." She gestured toward Roman's house.

Yeah, some small part of her had wanted that, too. Her foolish heart had even believed he would dash out the door after her because that was what they did. They fought, someone stormed out, the other coaxed the first back in, and they ended up in bed. They'd always fixed everything with sex.

She'd thought she would already be in Roman's arms by now, that he'd be carrying her to his bed as he often did, whispering to her that everything would be all right. All they needed to do was to stop talking with their mouths and start talking with their bodies.

But he wasn't coming after her this time. He'd been plain. Now everything felt more wretched because she realized he hadn't been biding his time, waiting for the right moment to tell everyone about them. He'd never intended to tell anyone.

She'd been his dirty little secret.

"Well, he will after he finds out about the baby," Mad swore.

That was the last thing she needed. Well, almost. She needed this cramping in her stomach to end, too. But she didn't want a shotgun wedding. She'd always wanted a loving, stable marriage, like her mom and dad shared. She'd never get that kind of love from a man who was forced to marry her.

"Please, Mad. I don't want him to know."

He stared back at the house, and she could practically see the wheels in his brain turning and turning. Mad was the king of crazy plots. "All right, then. There's only one thing to do."

"I'm going home to New Orleans."

He frowned. "I thought you were taking the DC job."

She shook her head. "I can't as a single mother. The hours are too grueling. Believe me, I want that position more than ever. I need it to take my mind off Roman, but I have to think of my baby. I've got a great trust fund, but I don't want him or her raised by nannies. When I thought I'd have Roman by my side, I was willing to take the chance and try the family thing. Now I have to go home to New Orleans so my baby can have some kind of male role model I don't have to pay by the hour. My dad has been talking about retiring. Dax will be home every now and then. I'll tell him I don't know who the father is. He'll believe it."

"Tell him I'm the father. He'll believe that, too."

"What? Mad, this is not the time for one of your

schemes." She wanted to cry, but she needed to get away from here and regroup.

The trouble was Mad had truly become her friend, too. He was the only one of her brother's friends who had. Mad was special, and not because they'd so briefly had sex in high school. Mad reminded her so much of herself sometimes that it felt like looking into a mirror.

If only she could have fallen in love with him.

"It's not a scheme." He stepped close, tangling his fingers with hers. The saddest look crept across his face. "You need someone to help you out with the baby. I need purpose in my life because let me tell you, the days are getting long and the nights are even longer. I might be a crappy role model, but I promise I'll try. Come to New York and we'll do what Zack and Roman are doing. We'll build something together."

She shook her head, her heart so full. Why did everyone see him as some soulless party machine? Mad was one of the best men she'd ever met. What Roman hadn't managed with his rejection, Mad was doing with his sweet offer. Tears rolled down her cheeks because at least someone cared about her. Which was precisely why she couldn't take him up on it. "Mad, you're going to fall in love one day and I won't be the woman who keeps you from her."

Because no matter what anyone said about him, Mad would be faithful to his wife. If he had a family, it would take something terrible to make him break those vows.

He shook his head. "No. I fell in love once and I wasn't good enough for her."

"Sara was young back then." She knew all about the summer he'd spent trying to get Gabe Bond's sister to notice him. She also thought Sara had been too immature to see what Mad could offer. Or maybe too afraid to believe that sometimes love was worth the risk. "You don't know that she won't come around."

"Nah, she'll marry some nice guy with a nice job," he replied casually. "I'll be the dirty boy she kissed once and was smart enough to tell to go to hell. She told me I was the devil, believe it or not. So what do you say? I think we should just fuck 'em all. Let's show them how two badasses do life."

That was Mad. Arrogant. Sweet. Rebellious. Loving.

She couldn't let him do it. And she couldn't marry another man when Roman the bastard was still in her heart. Sadly, he might always be.

A pain low in her body started stabbing in earnest. Damn it. She was going to be sore in the morning. At least she hoped that was all. She should have been more careful, but she'd been so angry, and when she'd realized Roman was behind her, she'd lashed out.

"Gus?" Mad had gone pale.

She straightened up, forcing her shoulders back and her head high. It was time to go home and cozy up to ice cream, lay down and take care of herself and her baby. Tomorrow she would face a world without Roman. She could do it. She was strong. She would do whatever necessary to protect herself and her child.

Then the world seemed to tilt, her equilibrium shifting. She felt nauseous. Maybe she should sit down.

"Gus, baby, you're bleeding. I have to get you to a hospital."

One minute she was thinking about how strong she was and the next, Mad was lifting her up and shoving her in his car.

She was bleeding? The world was spinning. And all

she could think about was that if she lost this baby, she'd be utterly and completely alone.

She could hear Mad's voice from seemingly far away, telling her everything would be all right.

But it wouldn't. As she passed out, all she wanted was to hear Roman's voice, to feel his hand in hers.

But she feared in her heart that she never would again.

CHAPTER ONE

Air Force Two
Somewhere over Canada

Augustine Spencer glanced out the window. No lights sparkled from this altitude, high above the cloud cover. Only inky blackness stretched across the sky. In a few hours the sun would rise, and they would be in London. She hoped the new day would illuminate everything necessary. But for now, she found comfort in the shrouding darkness. In it, she could feel without prying eyes. And in it, she could plot her next move because she had a job to do and she wouldn't allow anything or anyone to stop her.

Not even Roman Calder.

"Is this seat taken?"

She glanced up to find Connor Sparks standing over

her. Ah, the most dangerous of the Perfect Gentlemen, as her brother and his besties had become known. Not that they would ever call themselves anything so silly as BFFs, but that's what they were. If pressed, they might call themselves bros for life or something they'd deem appropriately masculine. They certainly believed in bros before 'hos.

Or they had until recently.

"I don't think I can stop you," she answered with what she hoped was a magnanimous smile.

Connor sank down beside her, an earnest expression on his face. It wasn't a look she normally saw the former CIA agent wear. "All you have to do is tell me to go and I will. I hope you won't though. I'd like to talk to you about something."

Damn it. Whatever Connor had to say would almost certainly be about Roman. "Now that you're working for Zack, I'm sure you have more than a few things to say."

And she would take whatever shit Connor or his pals dished out because she couldn't afford to get fired now. She was so close to the truth.

"It's about Lara."

The unexpected topic made her sit up slightly, though she tried not to betray how much he'd surprised her. Lara Armstrong Sparks was Connor's new bride. She was vibrant and adorable, if a bit of a naive crusader. At least that had been Gus's first impression of the girl. Instantly, she'd wanted to wrap Lara up so she couldn't get brutalized by the real, cold world. Gus had been skeptical the brunette would actually find her happy ending. But maybe she'd underestimated Connor's bookish wife. So far, this little Belle seemed to have tamed her dangerous Beast of a husband.

Under Connor's watchful eye, Gus glanced over to find Lara in one of the seats typically used by the aides, all curled up with a blanket, eyes closed.

"Why didn't she use the suite?" Air Force Two was smaller but still had the trappings of a luxury jet. This particular modified 747 had a presidential suite located under the cockpit, where the president and First Lady would shower, dress, and sleep—even hit the small gym, if they were so inclined. "Zack's not here, and Roman never sleeps anyway. I'm fairly certain he made a deal with the devil for that advantage."

Connor flushed slightly. "She thinks it's wrong that the aides are forced to sleep in their seats while the president of the United States slumbers in luxury at the taxpayers' expense. So she's sleeping upright and hunched over in solidarity with the working man."

Gus had to smile. Some of those aides came from the wealthiest families in the world. Oh, many of them were super-hard workers, but they were also the elite of the elite.

And Lara Sparks thought she would stand up for their rights. Sheltered little girl.

But even if Lara's protest was a bit silly, nothing in the world softened Gus up quite like the underdog or someone willing to stand up for them. "Good for her. It's refreshing to see someone give a damn about something other than politics around here."

"My wife is different. She genuinely cares, but she hasn't figured out that the world doesn't work the way she wants it to. I know I should have left her at home, but she wanted to come with me and I…"

"Couldn't say no." She felt her lips tug up into a smile. The mighty Connor Sparks had been felled by a quirky, big-hearted girl. It was almost too much to fathom...and yet from what Gus had seen, they were perfect together. Balanced each other. Deep down, she was a bit envious.

Then she realized why Connor Sparks was probably sitting in front of her. Why he would take time from his solemn duty to talk to her. He was warning her off his wife. "Well, I hope you both have fun in London. I've got a crazy schedule, so I won't have much time to socialize. You don't have to worry about me."

His intentions bothered her more than she'd imagined. Hurt, actually. She'd grown up with Connor. He'd always been Dax's best of the besties. Then again, she'd also drifted away from everyone but Mad after... Well, after Roman.

In fact, she'd surprised herself by taking the job with the White House. Sure, she'd helped with the campaign. But when she'd been offered the position as second in command at the press office—working so closely beside Roman—her first thought had been to tell Zack to fuck himself, then suggest he fuck Roman, too. But they had been way too smart to ask her themselves. No, the bastards had sent Joy, knowing that Gus had never, ever been able to say no to her sweet friend. Joy, one of her best friends. Joy, who would have been First Lady if she hadn't been killed. Joy, whom she suspected Roman had truly loved.

"Of course you have a full schedule," Connor conceded. "But I was hoping Lara could help you. I've got some things to do and I can't take Lara along. Can she...I don't know, act as your assistant?"

Gus let out a breath of surprise. So he wasn't warning her away? "What?"

"Hear me out. She's incredibly smart. And...I'm worried that some of the aides are going to be mean to her. She doesn't keep her opinions to herself and her politics don't exactly align with the others around here."

Because this world was cutthroat and ruthless, and every single one of those aides would rip a heart out if they thought it would get them one step higher on the ladder.

Suddenly, Gus felt a little more protective and determined to preserve Lara's illusions.

"Is it true she runs Capitol Scandals?"

Connor's eyes flared, then he chuckled. "I should have known you would figure that out. Yes."

That adorkable girl ran one of the trashiest rags in DC. Of course, it also published some real, in-depth stories. Likely, Lara tried to clickbait people in by posting stories on the president's love life in the hopes she could educate them on more pressing matters once she'd lured them to the site. Gus doubted the ploy worked, but she admired Lara's hustle. "If she wants to follow me around, I can use the company most days, but I do have a few...plans that require privacy."

He frowned. "You're meeting a man?"

Nope. She was doing something far more important. She was going to avenge a friend—even if that meant bringing down her boss. But she couldn't exactly tell Connor that. "You know I have friends in lots of places."

Gus also had a reputation, so she knew what Connor would assume. In this case, it worked to her advantage. If she had a twinge about the fact that Dax's bestie assumed she was blithely hopping into bed with a random guy, Gus shoved it down. Her friends knew who she was. Her mom and her brother accepted her. She refused to give a shit what anyone else thought. They could get on board or go to hell.

"I understand." He was quiet for a moment, his eyes lingering somewhere on the floor as though he was trying to decide how to proceed. "Have you ever thought about cutting Roman some slack?"

Before she could think to temper the response, she shot back at him. "Every day. I think about how much rope it would take for that man to hang himself."

Connor grimaced. "Wow. Okay. Look, I know something happened between you two a long time ago. But I think he's still attracted to you."

She scoffed, laughing hard at those words. A few heads popped up around her, disgruntled expressions crossing the faces of sleepy aides nearby.

Gus lowered her tone. "I seriously doubt that. Roman and I had a fling a long time ago. He's over it. I'm over it. He made it plain that I wasn't the kind of woman he wanted for more than a good time. He's searching for a shy flower who will tend his home fires, never raise her voice to express an opinion of her own, and accept the fact that he's married to Zack in all ways but sexually."

"You think so? I wonder how he hasn't managed to find his beacon of virtue yet."

"Oh, he did. Unfortunately, she married his best friend, got shot, and died."

A long moment passed, and Gus felt her stomach turn. She'd loved Joy. The truth was already ugly enough, so why had she added such a biting tone? Stress and having Roman so close…but so far away. He always brought out the worst in her.

She looked Connor's way, not even trying to stop

the tears that flooded her eyes. That was one thing she'd learned after all the bad stuff. Some tears were simply unstoppable. Rather than trying to save face, it was better to worry about things that truly mattered. She was kind and loving, even if most people didn't know that. And she'd treasured Joy's friendship. She would never again give others a cold shoulder because Joy's death had taught her that life was short. She especially refused to bristle over some asshole who couldn't love her.

"I'm sorry," she murmured. "That was terrible and I didn't mean it. I loved Joy very much. Please forgive me."

He leaned over and patted her hand. "There's the Gus I remember. You know, one of the things I always adored about you was that you could be a bitch from hell when necessary, but you have a sweet, gooey center. It's why I want you to look after Lara. She's a bit lost."

Having her gooey center on display was uncomfortable, but she also wouldn't take it back. She refused to change who she was.

But she did have some tough choices to make. Long ago she'd decided that action was better than reaction. Action was a step taken, based on who else was in the situation and how much she knew or trusted that person. Reaction was dependent solely on how someone else made her feel in a given moment, which was rarely ever wise or a proper representation of herself.

Therefore, she acted. She did not react.

Connor's slip of a wife rose and stretched, then shuffled beside her husband, her ridiculously lush dark hair flowing all around her shoulders as she yawned. "Connor? Are we there yet?"

Action. The woman in front of her, though

misguided, seemed kind and well-intentioned. That meant something to Gus. And in truth, Connor had never wronged her. Her beef was solely with Roman.

"We're still hours away, Connor's Beauty. You should totally throw the patriarchy out of the presidential suite and get some sleep for the proletariat." Gus winked. She could speak liberal.

Lara's eyes had widened. "I hadn't thought of it that way."

She looked so tired and she obviously wasn't used to this fast-paced lifestyle. If Gus could say a few well-placed words and get the girl comfy enough to sleep, all the better. "Well, no woman has slept in that taxpayer-enabled suite since Zack took office." She leaned in. "At least not one he didn't pay. You should take it for all the sisters. And come to think of it, Connor here has been an underpaid warrior for our country for years, and what did he get? Craptastic motel rooms all across the Third World. You haven't seen a shit-hole until you've been to the Sudan."

"Then we have to claim that space for America," Lara said with a grin, looking her husband's way. "I'll meet you there."

Connor smiled as Lara strode toward the front of the plane, then disappeared. "You want to give me notes on how to handle my wife?"

He was happy. She missed the cocky, unapologetic Perfect Gentlemen sometimes, but it was good to see so many of them in love. It made her ache for the future Mad would never have. The hole his absence left was a hollow, gaping pang every day.

It also made her wonder if Roman would choose a wife and settle down soon. Gus didn't know how or if she could handle it.

"Sure," she teased Connor. "I'll even type them up for you. And don't worry about a thing in London. I know Roman thinks I'm going to cause trouble, but I really do have other things to do besides hang around and give him a hard time. Besides, he's seeing that chick from the British Embassy while we're here anyway. She'll keep him plenty busy." Gus tried to ignore the burn in her belly. "So if you're worried I'll play the jilted lover, the last place I want to be is on his radar."

"You both say things like that, yet neither one of you has ever married," Connor mused.

"Well, Roman has impossible standards, and I have a demanding career." If there was one thing she'd learned early, it was that men didn't like women with demanding careers, especially if the woman was smarter than their testosterone-laden counterpart. So she'd taken to viewing the men around her as chess pieces. Or if they were excellent in bed, playthings. That's all. "I'm afraid I'm married to the White House."

"And when Zack moves on?" Connor asked quietly.

She was always a girl with a plan. "Then I take on consulting work and make an incredible amount of money. Why the sudden interest in my future?"

Connor sat back. "You know, I suppose a man gets to a certain age or a certain place in his life, and he looks back, wonders where things went wrong. You know what I'm talking about, right? I've been reflecting, trying to pinpoint where things turned. We were friends, Gus. And then we weren't."

She didn't like the sudden turn of this conversation. "It's hard to be friends with a man who spends most of his time in classified locations doing things I'm not allowed to know about."

"Don't bullshit me, Gus. I would come home—and yes, by home I mean your home in New Orleans. One Thanksgiving we were fine, and the next you were cold and rebuffed my every attempt to talk to you. At the time I thought you disapproved of my job, but then I realized you'd stopped talking to all of us for about four years. Except Mad. Eventually, we started seeing you again, slowly and in small doses. But I'm not really sure what happened."

Okay, so maybe she didn't appreciate the softer, more caring Connor Sparks after all. The hardened spy had at least stayed out of her business.

She gave him a smile because the drama of all that tragedy was behind her, and sometimes the truth was the best way to hide a secret. "I'm sure you know that Roman and I spent a hot year together. When he finished law school, I suggested we make it official. He declined. We argued. It wasn't pretty." She shrugged as if age and wisdom had given her immense perspective, so she could dismiss that girl of her past. "I struggled with my embarrassment."

Connor's eyes widened. "I did not expect you to admit that."

But he'd known, of course. It was there in his expression. He'd only been surprised she'd confessed to being cast aside, not that it had happened.

Dealing with any of the Perfect Gentlemen was always an intricate game of chess. Thankfully, she'd had a lifetime to become a master.

Then again, they'd had equally as long to figure her out. Did Connor have any idea what she actually planned on doing in London? Is that why he'd taken this sudden interest in her and her visit? Had Zack sent Connor to find out how close she was getting to the truth?

"It happened a long time ago. I assumed Roman had told you. If not, there's your grand mystery. Getting dumped sucked, and I didn't want to face any of his friends."

"But you stayed close to Mad." Connor shook his head, his jaw tightening. "Damn it. Of course, you did. The two of you had a thing for a long time. Mad was damn good at taking advantage of a situation."

"Don't," she bit out with gritted teeth. "Don't you talk that way about Maddox. He wasn't like that." Yes, it would be smarter to let Connor think whatever he wanted to, but Mad was no longer here to defend himself, and she couldn't let anyone, even Connor, malign the one friend who had stood by her side when no one else had. "He never took advantage of me. What we had was mutual and friendly. My relationship with Mad was probably the healthiest of my life, so do *not* say another bad word about him."

During that terrible first year, Mad would show up at her DC apartment some weekends with a bottle of tequila, a stash of movies, and a pizza, and he would get her through. She had no idea how she would have survived that first year without the grueling work schedule and Maddox Crawford. Taking the DC job had saved her in so many ways. If she'd gone back home, her mother would have known something was wrong and meddled.

After the pain had subsided and Gus had gotten some distance, Mad still appeared occasionally, but instead of crying her way through ridiculous chick flicks, she and Mad had fucked like bunnies, both of them secure in the knowledge that they were friends and nothing more.

Then Mad had finally lost his heart and won over Sara Bond, the girl he'd wanted for so long. Gus had let him go and fondly wished him well.

"Hey. He was my friend, too. I wasn't maligning him," Connor promised, staring at her like she'd given him some important information. "I was only worried about you. And I miss Mad, too." He stood. "Thanks for whatever you can do to take Lara under your wing."

"Of course." She would probably have fun getting to know the woman who had conquered Connor's cynical heart. Everly, Gabe Bond's wife, loved her. So did Holland, Gus's new sister-in-law. That made Lara a part of the sisterhood, and Gus took that seriously. "And you can tell Roman he has nothing to worry about. He doesn't need to tense whenever I walk in a room. I'll do my job and stay completely out of his way. Everything will be ready when Zack lands in four days. I'll make sure of that. So Roman can simply broker deals and smoke cigars in the good-old-boys' clubs and take credit for everything, as usual."

"Your claws are showing, Gus."

"My claws are always on display. It's why I'm so effective at what I do."

"Have you thought about the fact that being close to you is hard on him, too?"

Not once. "He hired me because I'm the best and he needs me. That does not mean he doesn't find it distasteful to deal with me. I know the score and exactly what he thinks of me. He views me as...let me see if I can remember the description verbatim... Ah, yes, a man-eating anaconda who squeezes the life out of her victims before she swallows them whole."

"Jesus," Connor breathed. "All I'm saying is that maybe this is a great opportunity for you two to give each other a second chance."

She frowned at him. "I can't think of anything I want less."

With a sigh, Connor walked away, shaking his head and muttering something she probably didn't want to hear.

Gus reached up and turned off the overhead light, then lost her gaze in the vast darkness out the window once more. There was no such thing as a second chance. She'd learned that when she'd miscarried her baby. When her father had perished. When she'd lost her dear friend to a bullet. When she'd realized Mad had gone down with his plane.

But there was something she could do for the kindest, most misunderstood member of the Perfect Gentlemen, one thing she could offer Mad even now.

Revenge.

* * * *

"I don't know why she didn't wait and come with the rest of the press office." A man's murmur reached Roman's ears.

He stopped at the sound. It was late and the plane was quiet, but there was always a hum of activity. These were people who never really slept. Roman had taken the plane's office, locking himself away to get some work done—and to stop himself from doing something stupid like reaching out for Gus. Like pulling her body against his to see if the perfection he remembered had merely been a dream.

Thirteen years had passed, and he wanted to know if foolish youth or a faulty memory made him compare every single woman in the world to Augustine Spencer and come up lacking—even the one woman he'd thought he could marry, the one woman he'd thought he could love.

"Probably because the Ice Queen has a plan to be someone's pain in the ass."

"Well, I'm staying out of her way."

Roman knew precisely who they were talking about. Among the White House staffers, Gus was known as the Ice Queen. Elizabeth Matthews, Zack's press secretary, was Glinda the Good Witch. What none of the fuckers understood was Liz was every bit as ruthless as Gus. She simply ruled her kingdom with a soft smile and easy words. But none of that charm would work if she didn't have Gus as her enforcer.

Just like Roman was Zack's. While Gus's moniker had become the Ice Queen, Roman was known as the Hitman. He did the dirty work so Zack could keep his hands clean. The funny thing was, if he and Gus didn't share such a shitty history, they would probably be good friends. They would certainly understand each other. They played the same role and should be good about helping each other out, laughing at the trash talk they endured.

"It just chaps me. Bitch thinks she's better than us. I bet that whore got her job by spreading her legs for Hayes."

Roman saw red. It was a sad fact that politics could still be a good-old-boys' network, and because she was female, Gus had to hear the kind of slurs no one would ever have dared to speak about him.

He refused to listen to anyone malign her now.

Roman stepped out of the shadows and was damn happy to see both aides turn pasty white. "What did you say?"

"Mr. Calder, I didn't realize you were still awake." The kid with the nasty mouth couldn't be more than twenty-eight years old. A fucking baby who was about to learn the world didn't revolve around him.

"I'm always awake and I'm always listening. And I would very much like for you to repeat what you just said."

The second little asshole proved that he was smarter, but merely a kiss ass. "Mr. Calder, Austin was only joking around. It's late and we haven't slept. We say stupid shit when we're tired."

"I'm not tired. In fact, I'm quite energetic and my mind is working overtime. But if Austin is that weak, he's not cut out for this job. Since that's the case, I'm wondering how he's going to get home because he certainly won't be on a plane with me." Sometimes it was good to be the Hitman. He had no idea how Zack ever juggled everyone's fucking feelings. "Austin should understand that when we land, he needs to find his way back to the States, go directly to his office, clean it out, and hope we never cross paths again because I'm being patient right now. If we meet again, I won't be."

"Mr. Calder..." the friend began.

Roman turned to him. "I don't know your name. Do you want me to know it?"

The aide shook his head. "No. No, I'm good."

Austin opened his mouth to speak, but suddenly they weren't alone.

Connor put a hand on Austin's shoulder. "You should keep your mouth shut or we'll give you another way off this plane, and it will likely not include a parachute. And if your father, the senator, has a problem with the fact that Roman fired you, please let him know that Air Force Two has security features that include cameras in this cabin. What you said was recorded and we'll release it if necessary. Your father's progressive views on women's issues are well known. How will his constituents feel about his son being a misogynist douchebag?"

That shut Austin up and fast. His nameless friend was smart enough to ease the fired aide away from what could become the killing zone. Because Roman wanted to wrap his hands around the fucker's throat and see how blue he could turn.

"Do you have any idea how crazy-eyed you look right now?" Connor asked once the two young fucks were gone, glancing around the now empty area. "You made that dude piss himself and managed to send all the other aides huddling together at the back of the plane. Oddly enough, all on one side because I think they're too afraid to go near Gus."

Good. He didn't feel like company anyway, at least not theirs. The only person he wanted to see was the one person he wouldn't let himself be near.

"If I ever hear the aides talking about any of our female employees like that again, I'll do the same. That kind of talk will not be tolerated here."

"I think they get that now. But if you think the outrage in your expression is for any random female employee, you're in even deeper denial than I thought." Connor nodded toward the office. "We should talk."

That's the last thing he wanted, but Connor could be stubborn, like a dog with a meaty bone. He stepped back into the large office reserved for the president. "Lara walked by fifteen minutes ago. She said something about the patriarchy and how she was taking over the presidential suite in the people's name or some shit. Shouldn't you join her? It isn't like that room has seen any action in years. The president before Zack was five hundred and fifty years old and Zack…well, he's a monk these days."

"That's not what the press thinks." Connor shut the door, closing them away from prying ears and surveillance. He crossed to the bar and poured himself a glass of Scotch. Two fingers. Neat. Like they'd managed to find ways to drink it since before they could purchase the stuff legally. "I noticed Zack's been out on the town a lot lately. You, too."

"You know why he's doing that," he muttered, almost under his breath. For Elizabeth. He had to sell the illusion that she was nothing more than an employee.

Someone was manipulating Zack Hayes's presidency and had been even before he'd been elected. Mad's death a few months ago had brought the conspiracy to light. Now they had uncovered the fact that the Russian mob had woven tendrils into the very fabric of Zack's life, perhaps even from birth. They'd already discerned that Joy's death hadn't been a botched assassination attempt by some lone lunatic to off then-candidate Zack Hayes. No, a network of criminals had actually murdered his wife in cold blood to ensure the sympathy vote landed him in the White House. Now high-level officials in his administration jetted to London, and Roman intended to use this official trip to find out if the conspiracy included the death of Zack's mother eight years ago. Roman's gut was telling him that Constance's car wreck in the British countryside hadn't been an accident at all. That the woman, alcoholic or not, had known far more about this possible conspiracy than anyone had guessed.

In the midst of all the chaos, Zack had realized he had one weakness his enemies could use against him. Elizabeth Matthews, his press secretary—and the only woman who'd ever truly both knocked him on his ass...and stolen his heart.

After seeing the evidence that his wife had been murdered, Zack had shoved distance between himself and the fiery blonde. Then he'd started dating a string of well-known actresses. The fallout between Zack and Liz had been silent and chilly...but ugly. Then the gossip had begun, and some of the cattier circles of the press had dubbed Zack the Playboy President. Roman had joined him, going on empty double dates that ended in polite goodnights because he was getting too old for casual sex.

These days, he wanted sex to mean something, to fill some emptiness inside him. To make him feel whole again, as he hadn't in over a dozen years.

God, he fucking craved Gus. How could the woman be more beautiful all these years later? Sexier? More magnetic?

"I think he's hurting Liz in ways he didn't count on," Connor said solemnly. "What is any of this worth if he can't be happy when we untangle the plot?"

"What's any of it worth if Liz dies? Like Joy and Mad?" He slumped back against the fine leather of the seat, feeling a headache coming on. "It's better if she's alive and unhappy at the end of this. At least then Zack has a shot at explaining everything to her. She's a smart woman. She might understand."

"Maybe. But smart women can also hold mean grudges," Connor pointed out. "I think Liz might take exception to being kept out of the decision-making process."

"He's doing it to protect her."

"Think she'll care? Women often have different ideas about how relationships should work. By the way, are you planning on introducing Gus to your British girlfriend?"

Roman stared at his friend. "What the fuck are you talking about?"

Connor's lips curled up in a secretive smile. "The little blonde, Darcy Hildebrandt? She seems pretty damn determined to get her hooks in you."

"We've been planning the president's state visit together. I don't intend to date her."

"Yeah? She can't stop telling everyone how late into the night your meetings run, especially Gus."

"Gus is smart enough to know when another woman is trying to get a leg up by shoving the knife in. I'm not foolish enough to think no one knows Gus and I used to have a thing. Darcy is just playing the game."

Though strategically speaking, he should actually consider dating Darcy. She fulfilled every item on his list. Competent and logical. Check. Sexual attraction. He hadn't taken it for a test drive, but he could see the appeal. Educated and familiar with the grind of life in politics. Check and check. Married to her career. Absolute check.

Yet he couldn't bring himself to even think about moving them beyond a simple working relationship. He

blamed Gus. Did she think he was sleeping with Darcy?
Was that why she'd been so testy lately? Was she
jealous?

Connor waved him off. "Yes, they're all smart
women, which is precisely why I'm worried about Gus.
That's what I wanted to talk to you about. Did you know
she's been investigating a member of Zack's detail? A
guy named Matthew Kemp?"

"What do you mean by investigating?" Roman
scowled.

Gus worked in the press office. She was known for
her spot-on oppo research. Gus was excellent at digging
up dirt, even when it was buried super deep. But
someone in Zack's detail should hardly be construed as
the opposition.

"I mean someone requested all the personnel records
on Agent Kemp. Zack brought me in to take a look at the
procedures and see if anything stood out," Connor
explained. "Sometimes the devil is in the details, and a
sleeper agent will make mistakes that can be found by
looking at the minutiae of his or her job. The press office
asked for the records. I tracked it down to Gus."

"Are you telling me that Zack thinks Gus is a
fucking sleeper?" Maybe he would exorcise his rage by
getting his buddy on the phone, and if Connor's
accusation was true, he would cuss out the president.
Then he might have to quit. But there was no way he
would investigate Gus as a freaking spy.

Connor rolled his dark eyes and knocked back half
his drink. "Don't be so dramatic. Of course he doesn't.
It's simply something I found while looking for potential
spies. But I can't figure out a reason for the press office
to sniff around a Secret Service agent. Naturally Gus had

a perfectly logical reason for requesting the records. She's working with an author on a 'profiles in courage' style media campaign. No details about the actual agents, of course, but she wanted to get the backgrounds right."

"I've heard nothing about this." What game was Gus playing? He frowned as he realized what her intent most likely was. He knew Matthew, one of the strong silent types. He was also thirty-two and movie-star gorgeous. He was the kind of man who thought leg days were a thing. "Is she running a check on one of her boy toys?"

She had plenty of them. Gus could rip through a group of men with the voracity of a Valkyrie in battle. She left them all whining and mooning after her because she didn't often go back for seconds. The two times she'd kept a lover for more than a few nights, she'd carefully vetted the man. Did she have her eye on Matthew now?

Could he find a viable reason to fire the guy?

"I don't know. I suspect that's what she wants me to believe," Connor admitted. "I'm worried though. Gus isn't an idiot. Neither is Elizabeth. Have you thought about the fact that if we don't bring them into our investigations, they might start their own?"

Connor was high. "You think she's starting an investigation into a Secret Service agent as a service to her country? C'mon…. He's younger, and according to other women in the White House, as Secret Service agents go, he's the hottest. How could he be wrapped up in our conspiracy? You do realize he wasn't even born when some of this crap likely started."

"That doesn't mean he's not involved. I only found this out yesterday. I haven't had time to go through his records myself yet, but I will. Did you know he's come in with the advance team?"

"Another sign that Gus is scratching an itch." It explained why she'd been so set on getting on this plane instead of coming to London in a few days with Zack and Elizabeth. She wanted to get to know Matthew better, and he would be on call 24/7 once Zack got to town.

"Did you know she's made five trips to the City in the last year?" Connor asked.

What was he trying to imply? "I'm sure I have, too. New York isn't far. We all go in from time to time."

"Gus tends to go home to visit her mother when she has time off. Instead, she's been taking trips to New York, and I can't tell who she's meeting."

Because she was probably meeting a lover. Or shopping a book deal. "Damn it. I bet she's talking to publishers. We've all been asked to write about Mad. We've all turned them down."

"Why do you always think the worst of her? She couldn't possibly be a spy, but she'll sell out her friends?" Connor asked. "Don't get me wrong. The feeling is mutual. She totally thinks the worst of you, too, but I'm surprised you would accuse her of doing something like that. She loved Mad."

Her relationship with Mad had been one of the sore spots between him and his long-time friend. Roman and Mad got along right up to the point that Gus's name would come up. Mad had never forgiven him for the night he'd taken Gus home after her fall down the stairs. He hadn't shown back up, hadn't even called for weeks afterward. Once he finally had, he'd been cool. Roman had always wondered if Gus and Mad had started their "fun times" up again that very night. "She and Mad were fuck buddies."

"I knew they were friends with benefits, but I think their sex was about comfort, not just orgasm. And not love."

"When did you get into pop psychology, Connor? Look, I'm sorry. I'm wound up and having Gus around doesn't help things."

"So fire her or reposition her."

Fire Gus? He'd just found a way to get back into her life…even if she tied him up in knots. He was so fucked up. "She's too good at her job. I can't move her. We need her."

"Then suck it up, buttercup, because I'm telling you she and Liz are up to something and we need to figure out what before it bites us all in the ass."

"You really think so?" A plotting Gus was a dangerous Gus. And a sexy one. She was never hotter than when she was playing the game.

"I do." Connor seemed to relax now that Roman was taking him seriously. "I'm sending Lara in. Gus is going to let Lara follow her. I told her it's because I'm worried about how the other aides will treat her."

"Ah, you're appealing to Gus's underdog syndrome. She can't stand it when the bullies show up. She tends to prove she's the biggest, baddest bully of them all."

"Yes, and you know she'll love Lara."

"She'll view Lara as a wide-eyed baby bird she needs to protect from predators." But there was something Connor wasn't thinking about. "What exactly do you expect Lara to do? Spy?"

Connor laughed, a deeply amused sound. "No. I wouldn't send my princess in to do that. She would be terrible. I'm going to let nature take its course, then carefully question Lara about what's going on with Gus.

She'll never know what I'm doing. We'll simply be talking about her new friend. Lara loves to talk about her friends."

And she made them quickly. She also tended to be loyal, something Gus could use against them. "I think this is going to backfire on you. Gus is excellent at getting baby birds to follow her. And I'm worried about getting the women together in one room."

"Why?"

Revolution. A coup d'état. Gus taking over and steamrolling everyone. "Up until now the women have been mostly low key, but—"

"BS, my brother. Everly and Lara can cause some serious trouble. There's still an APB out for Everly, I'm fairly certain. They managed to nearly start an international incident at the Lincoln Memorial."

"My point exactly. They can be dangerous." Roman nodded. "Now imagine adding Gus to that mix."

Connor breathed out. "Wow. I need another drink."

He wasn't alone. "Pour me one, too."

It was going to be a long week.

CHAPTER TWO

Normally Regent's Park was a placid ocean of green, and the manor house with its soaring neo-Georgian architecture gave Roman a sense of staid peace. Not today. He stared out an upper-floor window, over the sea of impatient reporters covering the president's imminent visit to London. The crowd of them was so thick he couldn't see the damn lawn.

Of course, all those cameras and questions weren't the only reasons Roman couldn't find any calm.

"I'm surprised you didn't go to the airport to meet Zack. You know I truly can hold things down here. Nothing would have burned to the ground." Gus stared out, her eyes on the crowd rather than him.

She'd refused to look him in the eyes since their arrival. In some women, he would have interpreted her downturned gaze as a form of submission. And he would probably have relished it. With Gus, the lack of visual contact was merely her way of telling him he wasn't worth her time. All week long, even when they'd been forced to work side by side, she'd made him feel as if there was massive chasm between them.

It was driving Roman insane.

"I didn't want to fight all that London traffic to the airport. Connor is making sure Zack's arrival runs smoothly. That gives me a few moments to find some peace and quiet before the storm begins." Before he could quietly sneak away because all eyes would be on the president.

"Ah, well, I'll leave you to it, then," she murmured as she stepped back.

He was so weary of her interpreting every word he said in the worst possible way. "I wasn't telling you to leave. I was answering your question."

She stopped, turning on those ridiculously sexy heels he would swear she wore twenty-four seven. Even when she dressed down, those red-soled shoes would poke out from the hem of her jeans and make her legs look a million miles long. It was even worse when she paired those stilettos with shorts so teeny-tiny they should be outlawed. When she wore them, Roman couldn't think straight.

"But you're after peace, and we all know I'm not conducive to that." Her lips turned down in a frown, but she was still one of the most gorgeous women he'd ever seen.

She also looked at home amidst all the luxury. Normally the president would stay at Winfield House, but it was under renovations so they'd been offered this jewel of a mansion in the heart of London. He could practically see Augustine in one of those Victorian gowns, all buttoned up and proper, like her name. But he knew how hot she could get underneath that prim exterior. Lately, he'd been wondering if he could make her hot again. If he could melt the ice between them.

Dangerous thoughts.

"That's not true. Do you think I don't see all the effort you put in to make everything run without a hitch? You've worked your ass off all week so that Zack will be comfortable when he gets here. I know that." Did she think he didn't see her at all?

"Ah, but I didn't do that for Zack."

Of course not. Zack might be the authority figure, but technically that wasn't who Gus worked for. "You did it for Liz."

Her hair was piled on her head in a perfectly mussed bun. On other women it might look messy, but the soft tendrils perfectly framed her face, drawing attention to her eyes and those bee-stung lips. "Yes. She's my boss. I did my job. Don't think it was anything more than that."

Why did she have to play the tough chick around him? If any realization had come out of the last few months of secrets and lies and death, it was that he missed Augustine. He missed her in bed, missed the passion that had once been a conflagration between them, but most of all, he missed her friendship. He knew they weren't good together in the long term, but were either of them looking for forever? They were married to their jobs. "So you watching after Lara was just your job? You taking on the Number 10 chef was your job?"

Number 10 was the colloquial term for Number 10 Downing Street, the residence of the prime minister of Great Britain. They'd been in and out of Number 10 several times for preliminary meetings and to ensure that everything was ready for the president's visit. Naturally

Gus had made friends. If by friends, one meant someone powerful who wanted to murder her.

Her jaw firmed and she pointed a finger his way. "That fucking chef made one of my girls cry for asking if she could get some ranch dressing on the side. I get it. He's some kind of wizard with twenty culinary degrees, but the girl only wanted some damn dip. Pretentious ass." She took a deep breath. "Did you have to deal with the aftermath? I'm sorry. I honestly didn't think about the fact that the prime minister might get involved."

The chef had been caught shouting at one of the aides and threatening to quit if she wasn't shown off the premises. Watching Gus put the incredibly rude man in his place had gotten his dick hard. Seeing her put an arm around the thirty-year-old Harvard grad she called one of her "girls" had softened up his...did he have a heart? Oh, he knew he had one in the physical sense. He had a whole report from his physician on how his dietary habits would kill his heart someday. But did he have one that felt things?

Roman shook his head. "I told the prime minister that we would bring our own ranch next time if it was too much trouble to stock his pantry with his guests' preferences. It wasn't his fault, per se, but he needs to understand I won't see any member of our staff treated that poorly, even by a celebrity chef."

Her lips turned up from a frown to a sexy-as-hell smirk. "I wish I could have seen that. And thanks for backing me up. You know how I get when I see an injustice done."

She couldn't allow it to pass. She had to fight, not only for herself but for those around her. Augustine, The Ice Queen. "I know." He glanced down at his watch and sighed. "In another ten minutes, Zack will arrive. And the world around us will explode."

She grinned, the first real, honest smile she'd given him in years. That expression kicked him in the gut. "Oh, it might explode in more ways than you know. Mommy and Daddy are still fighting."

"What? Zack claims that everything is fine. Did something happen that I'm unaware of?"

Gus moved into his space, her hand wrapping around his tie. "Hang on. You've got this knotted wrong. It's too short for this suit. Can't have the great Roman Calder looking less than perfect."

Yes, there was his heart. It was thudding in his chest because she was touching him for the first time in years. Gus was always careful. Even when they worked together long into the night, she made a concerted effort to keep distance between them. Now she moved in close and he could feel the brush of her breasts against his chest as she righted his tie.

"What's happening with Zack and Liz?" he reiterated, staying perfectly still under Gus's hands. He didn't want to give her any reason to stop. Being so close to her, he could feel the heat of her body, smell the delicate scent of citrus that clung to her. Desire warmed his blood.

She twisted the tie with an expert hand. "Well, after years of flirtation your boy suddenly decided that he no longer wanted my girl. It's like getting dumped—and hard—when you least expect it, and you didn't even get the fun stuff that might have made the upset worthwhile."

Roman had to defend his best friend. He also had to keep up the pretense to prevent Gus from guessing the real reason Zack had put distance between him and his press secretary. "I'm sorry Liz is hurt, but I doubt Zack meant to make her feel as if their relationship was anything more than professional. I should probably be less surprised that Liz developed feelings for him. Zack has a certain charm, I suppose, and I know many women view him as a challenge. Still, for him they've always shared a strictly working rapport."

Her hands didn't stop working, but her eyes suddenly lifted, met his. Roman worried Gus could see right through him.

"Really? I find that interesting since I've watched them together for the last few years. He tends to her as often as she does to him. But then I suppose my instincts aren't the best when it comes to the Perfect Gentlemen." She released his tie and tried to step back.

Gritting his teeth, Roman caught her hands gently in his. "It's not the same, Augustine. What's happening between Zack and Liz is nothing like what happened between us. Zack's never touched her. Don't paint him with the same brush. He's not a bad guy."

"But you are? Somehow, I don't think you see things that way."

He knew he should let her go, knew touching her, being this close, was dangerous, but he couldn't force himself to step back. For the first time in thirteen years, she was looking at him. She was giving him an opportunity to explain himself.

Had he been waiting all these years to do exactly that? He'd tried to call her over and over after that night. She'd changed her number, and he'd convinced himself it was for the best. The very next time he'd seen her, she'd been so cold that he'd sworn the memories of her warm smiles and hot embraces couldn't possibly have been real. He'd let more than a dozen years slide by since then. He thought he'd gotten over their affair. He'd even convinced himself that he'd fallen for another woman. Later, he'd pondered marriage. Having a family had actually crossed his mind once or twice. Inevitable as he'd gotten older, he supposed. Maybe parenting wouldn't be so terrible. Maybe he'd matured enough to be a decent father. Roman didn't know.

What he knew for damn sure was that he was right back here with Augustine. Full circle.

"I see myself as the man who hurt you when I didn't mean to."

She backed away, ending the contact with a laugh that didn't sound even vaguely happy. "Roman, that was forever ago. I don't think about it."

That was his cue to puff up and toss back the "fact" that he thought about her even less. At least that's what he would have done in the past. Before Joy died. Before they'd lost Mad. Somehow enduring all that, knowing that life guaranteed no tomorrows, had made him less combative. "I think about it a lot. All the time lately."

Her eyes flared, a sure sign he'd surprised her. It was good to know he could still do that. "Why?"

He moved in again, like a moth to her never-ending flame. "I suppose I feel the years weigh on me. I never meant to hurt you."

She wouldn't quite meet his gaze. "It's okay. I was fine."

But now that he was standing so close, Roman saw plainly that wasn't true. She hadn't been all right then and her armor was even stronger now. "Gus, we were so young. Definitely ambitious. If we'd tried anything more permanent, I'm sure it would have been a disaster. We weren't ready for commitment."

A single, perfectly manicured eyebrow arched up. "We?"

He sensed the danger, but didn't know how to avoid stepping in it. "Yes, Augustine. *We* had no idea what we were doing. But we had fun and learned a lot. In the long run, no one honestly got hurt. At that age, feelings mend easily, right? So shouldn't we forgive ourselves for whatever mistakes we made and move on?"

She pulled away, her whole demeanor turning chilly. "Sure. No one got hurt. All is forgiven. Consider me moved on."

Frustration welled, sharp and unexpected. "What did I say wrong now?"

Her face went blank, smoothing into the same impersonal expression he'd seen for the last thirteen years. "Nothing at all. The past is in the past, and we should leave it there. But now I should make sure the sitting room is ready for Liz. I'm sure she'll need some quiet time after all that press. Oh, I meant to ask... Is Zack bringing a date? He's got a lot of appearances planned. Lately, he shows up for every occasion with some bimbo on his arm."

Roman saw two things clearly: he wasn't forgiven, and the past wasn't just an ancient memory. "He's not seeing other people to hurt Liz."

"And yet, he's managing to do so beautifully. But then he learned from the best."

He could feel his frustration simmering. At her tight, acidic smile, it bubbled and spilled over into anger. "What is that supposed to mean? Damn it, Gus. In one breath, you tell me you're over everything that happened between us, then the next you throw our past back in my face. Which is it? What do you want from me?"

"The truth would be nice," she shot back. "If Zack only cares about Liz professionally, why won't he let her quit? Maybe she has other opportunities she'd like to explore."

"That's between the two of them."

She stepped in his path again, ready to fight. "No, it isn't. That play has Roman Calder written all over it. You think I don't know your moves?"

"I get blamed for everything, don't I? Everything that goes wrong, every nasty political move, you lay all that at my feet. In your eyes, no one else could possibly be as bad as me. But you're totally over what happened between us."

"I am. I don't care about you. I don't think about you."

She was a liar. The stubborn tilt of her head all but shouted that her bravado was an act—one he'd believed for years. "Is that right?"

"Not unless it's work, and then I'm usually trying to get through it so I don't have to deal with you."

He moved closer, knowing damn well she wouldn't back up. That wasn't how Augustine operated. No retreats for her. She would hold her ground until the bitter end.

Awareness flared through him at the light in her eyes. "Never? You haven't once stopped to remember how good we were together?"

"I'm good with a lot of men," she shot back.

No one ever challenged him the way she did. She got his blood pumping in a way it hadn't in well over a decade. In the past, this kind of anticipation had been reserved for election night, but fighting with Gus right before he shoved her on the bed to begin the real battle ranked right up there. He remembered.

Roman loomed over her. "Oh, I think you forget how I could make you scream my name, baby."

"I don't forget anything, Calder. It's just that nothing between us was particularly worth remembering," she replied, her head tilting back to maintain their eye contact. Her shoulders squared and he could practically hear her growl. "In fact, neither were you."

The barb hurt, but that was her anger talking. Roman let it go. "Then let me show you all over again."

He slid a hand behind her neck, giving her precious seconds to oppose him. If she said no, he might be able to walk away. It would kill him, but he'd do it.

"This won't change a thing," she whispered, her face guarded.

But he saw the anticipation gleaming in her eyes.

Roman held in his shock. Her reply was not a no. She didn't hate the thought of him touching her.

That was all he'd needed to hear. The time for talk was done. Not recognizing those moments in the past had been his mistake. Talking had never been their strong suit, but this… Oh, this had been everything. He could feel her body pressing against his as though she couldn't quite help herself. As though she felt the same magnetic pull.

Breath held, he lowered his mouth to hers, ready to taste her for the first time in well over a decade.

"Roman? Roman, are you in there?"

Gus stepped back quickly, her face flushed as she turned toward the door that led to the hallway. The French doors opened, and Darcy Hildebrandt strode in.

The attaché to the prime minister was lovely and young as she smiled his way. She was wearing a perfectly respectable but feminine business suit, her blonde hair artfully styled. She had a charming upper-crust British accent and the worst timing in the world.

She ignored Gus altogether and strode right to him, hands outstretched in welcome. "There you are. I've been looking everywhere for you. Good morning, Roman. You look completely dashing."

She moved into his personal space, offering her cheek.

He tilted his body away, pecking her lightly and wishing he didn't have to deal with all the European affectations. He had a stupid erection because whenever Augustine was around his dick stood and saluted. "Sorry. I was trying to have a few moments of peace and quiet before the president arrives."

She stepped back. "Well, I'm sorry you were interrupted, then." She finally turned toward Gus. "Is there something I can help you with, Ms. Spencer? Mr. Calder's job is extremely important. We should give him this time alone so he can be rested when the president needs him."

"Wow, did you also earn a master's of kiss assery while you attended Oxford?" Gus asked.

Yep. There was the Augustine he knew and admired the hell out of.

Roman moved into damage repair mode. Darcy was sweet—and no match at all for Gus. Maybe he'd been too relaxed about letting the pretty Brit flirt with him. She'd seemed like a balm to his ego, but he certainly wasn't going to shift their relationship from professional to personal. "Augustine, you mentioned something about making sure there was tea served in the ladies' parlor?"

"Nope. I didn't mention tea at all," Gus replied. "But I've got a full bar in there. After six hours on a plane with Zack, Liz is going to need a drink. In fact, I think we all are." She glanced down at her phone. "And they're pulling in. I'll go and greet them in the drive. You and Darcy can have the room."

She strode out as if she didn't care whether she saw him again.

Damn it.

Darcy frowned up at him, lingering entirely too close for his comfort. "Your tie is all wrong. It's far more fashionable to wear it a bit shorter now."

She started to reach for it, but he caught her hands. "I prefer it as is."

He didn't care, honestly, but Gus had fixed his tie the way she wanted it. He wouldn't let someone else change it. Not that she was paying any attention to him at the moment. Instead, he turned to see her walking out to the drive.

"Of course. You look smashing either way. Shall I go and fix the ladies' parlor, then? It won't take a moment. I've seen to the president's library myself. You have appetizers and a fully stocked bar. I'll switch the ladies to a lovely high tea. We wouldn't want the gossip to get out that the women in the American party are less than ladylike."

What the hell did that mean? "I think you should leave the ladies to Augustine. Dear god, don't take their booze. They'll come after ours." He switched topics, letting her know this one was closed. "I'm rethinking tonight's gathering. Maybe we should have a single greeting party and host it here. All of us together."

She wrinkled her nose and put her hand on his arm as he started outside. He suspected Darcy had read one too many Jane Austen novels. She had very Victorian ideas about how women should behave. It wasn't a representation of most of the British ladies he knew. At first, he'd found her approach rather cultured. Interesting, even. Now it bugged the hell out of him.

"Perhaps we should discuss that at length," she argued. "Oh, and you asked for theater tickets. I reserved a box at one of the West End's most historic theaters. It's good publicity. There will be six of us. The prime minster and his wife, the president and his date, and you. I'll come along to ensure everything runs properly and to handle the press on our end. I know them quite well. I thought that since you don't have a date, my idea would be most logical. The arrangement would be all work, of course, but leaving that seat open seemed a bit sad."

He shook his head. "I'll let Gabe and his wife go."

"Oh, no. I've let everyone know to expect Roman Calder. You must go."

Damn it. One of the reasons he had insisted that the other couples come along was to give him some cover. And for a visit. It had also been an awfully long time since they'd all been together for more than a few hours.

Roman opened the door, holding it for her like a gentleman. "I'm sure the prime minister will find Gabe and Everly charming."

She looked back at him, tears glimmering in her eyes. "I promised him you would come." She stopped and visibly shook off her sadness, discreetly wiping her eyes. "But I'm sure it will be all right. He can be a demanding man, but I'll make him see reason."

Or the PM might fire her because she'd vowed to

deliver time with the president and his right hand. The last thing he needed to deal with from Darcy was an anxiety attack. "All right. I'll go."

Her smile turned brilliant and she reached for his arm again as they strolled into the anemic London sunlight. "Excellent. We'll have a lovely time. I've got the prettiest dress. I'll ring Mimi to make certain we won't clash. We can't have that when we're arm candy for two of the most powerful men in the world."

"Mimi? The British model?" Gus asked. "The one who's far too skinny to even manage carrying a last name? That's who Zack's dating now?"

If Darcy heard the sarcasm in Gus's voice, she didn't show it. She simply smiled and squeezed his arm. "Yes, she's quite lovely. She and the president will make the most stunning couple. But Roman and I won't be far behind. I'll go and talk to the housekeeper now, darling. Don't worry. I'll make certain everything is exactly the way you like it."

She turned on her heels and hurried away.

Gus stared at him, looking all but ready to roll her eyes.

"It's not a date."

Her gaze slid away as the big black SUV pulled up. Suddenly they were surrounded by men in black suits. The Secret Service was damn good at keeping a low profile until the moment they were needed. Every square inch of the big manor home they were staying in had been checked and rechecked, security on high alert for this visit.

Flashes began flaring the moment the door opened. As a second SUV stopped behind the first, Zack stepped out, buttoning his suit coat and waving at the crowd. He looked cool and collected, nodding toward the reporters even as he completely ignored their shouted questions. Surprisingly, he moved around the SUV and stood stoically as Liz emerged, his hand outstretched to help her down.

"What is he doing?" They'd talked about this. Liz was supposed to ride in the second SUV, staying as inconspicuous and removed from the president as possible. Gabe and Connor were meant to occupy the lead car with Zack.

Gus's lips turned up in a smile. "Something right for once in his life."

Zack helped Liz down, one hand steadying hers and the other on the small of her back. She tried to pull away the second she stood on solid ground.

What the hell was going on? Gabe and Connor were smiling and waving to the crowd, obviously providing cover. But why?

Liz started up the stairs and stumbled. Zack caught her, helping her back up and whispering something in her ear. Liz's whole body stiffened but she allowed Zack to hustle her inside the house.

Roman looked over at Gus. Her face didn't show it exactly but he knew her well enough to realize she was as surprised as he felt. In silent answer, she shook her head. She had no damn idea what was going on either. As they followed the party, Roman gave her a little shrug, holding the door open for her.

"Don't touch me again." Liz turned on Zack, her normally perfect blonde hair mussed.

Zack's face was a mask of frustration as he faced her down. "If you don't want me to touch you, then how about you stay away from the vodka, baby?"

Zack was always calm. Always cool. Holy shit.

"Holy shit," Gus said under her breath.

Yes, they always had been in sync.

Liz bent over, pulling off her high heels. "I'm not drunk, you asshole. You try walking around in five-inch heels!"

Liz drew her hand back and Gus went into action.

"Nope, we're not taking our frustration out on the Louboutins. They are innocent." Gus looked back at Zack. "Unlike you."

Zack seemed to deflate. "Gus, I…"

She was already turning her boss toward the east wing where she'd set up the ladies' parlor, one palm held in his direction. "Talk to the hand, Mr. President."

Yep, there was his Augustine. Proper when she needed to be…but otherwise quick to send a guy her proverbial middle finger.

Once the two ladies were gone, Roman turned to Zack. "What the fuck?"

Zack held up his hands. "You do not want to know. Where is the Scotch?"

The door opened again and the rest of the party streamed in.

"She had no right to say those things," Gabe muttered.

"Oh, really?" Everly faced off with her husband. "After everything he's done? Screw you, Gabe."

When she turned and flounced out of the room after Gus and Liz, Gabe shook his head, looking incredulous. "I don't get why she's so angry. Everly knows why Zack has to distance himself from Liz."

Lara stood next to Connor, her eyes wide. She looked down the long hall as the other women walked away.

Zack turned to the only remaining female in the room. "Lara, you talked to Liz. Could you please tell me what's going through her head? And Gus. I know Gus is planning something."

Lara's lips formed a stubborn line.

Connor put a hand on his wife's hair. "Princess, it's okay. You're helping your friends by talking to us. We simply want to make sure they're all right."

Connor was high if he thought that woman was going to talk.

Lara broke away. "I'm so sorry, babe. Down with the patriarchy!"

Lara turned and jogged after her friends.

"I told you. Augustine is a terrible influence," Roman reminded. "We're damn lucky Dax took Holland on a honeymoon to that bed and breakfast in Maui or she would be right there with the other women. Lara's lost to the dark side now. Accept it and move on, buddy. No one's getting any tonight." He put a hand on Zack's shoulder. "Let's get you a drink and catch you up. I think we'll be safe in the study."

"Call it what it really is. The doghouse. We're all sharing it," Zack pointed out. "I'm the most powerful man in the freaking world and one blonde can still make me tuck my tail between my legs."

Roman leaned in. "Well, you wanted to know what it's like when a woman knocks you on your ass. This is it."

Zack marched to the study, holding up his middle finger and muttering how badly he needed a drink.

Roman sighed and prayed they would all survive the next few days.

CHAPTER THREE

Two hours later, Gus hugged Everly as she and Lara prepared to return to their rooms—and their husbands.

"Why don't you come to the dinner thing tonight?" Everly asked. "Gabe would love to spend time with you."

And then she would have to watch Darcy the Ever Perky plaster herself to Roman's side. No, thanks. "Liz and I need to finish some work tonight. I've got details for a morning meeting to prep and review with her. But tell Gabe I expect some time with the two of you."

Everly glanced back to the cluster of comfortable chairs where Liz and Lara were talking with hand gestures and frowns. "Is she all right?"

Gus doubted that very much. Oh, Liz put on a big smile because they hadn't been alone, but she rather thought her friend was running on pure Southern charm and old-fashioned gumption. "She's a professional."

"Zack is..." Everly began, then stopped and her jaw

tightened. "Well, he's being a stubborn ass, but I'm sure Zack thinks he's doing the right thing by not letting her quit."

Gus agreed since no reasonable man would want to keep an angry woman around. Normally, she'd snoop until she could confirm her suspicion, but she couldn't call Holland and ask her sister-in-law to break trust with her brother, especially during their honeymoon. She hated to ask Lara for roughly the same reason. Her affection for the quirky girl had grown over the last few days, so she hated to put Lara in a position that might threaten her marriage. Everly understood something else was going on behind the scenes, but she wasn't talking. Gus gave Gabe's wife the side eye. She might be able to break Everly, massage and maneuver her into coughing up whatever information she had. Maybe. But she didn't try. Not only was she getting soft, Gus was beginning to wonder if she could live with the answers.

It was precisely why she held back from everyone except Liz. She couldn't risk them, couldn't ask those women to choose between her investigation and their husbands.

She was fairly certain Roman wouldn't give an inch. He'd press whomever until he got exactly what he wanted, but she'd decided a long time ago that she would never sell her damn soul the way he had.

After a pause, she gave Everly her blandest smile. "I'm sure that's exactly what Zack thinks. Of course you know that's not true, right? Liz has offers from some of the best PR firms in the country, so holding her back is actually hurting her bottom line, and I don't understand what possible reasoning he could have."

She studied Everly, watching the way the redhead

tensed. Everly was good, but she was also emotionally invested. She squeezed Gus's hand in a way that told Gus she hated being less than honest. But Everly, Lara, and even Holland knew something she and Liz didn't. Gus had been certain of that for months, and it probably had everything to do with the men they were married to.

The Perfect Gentlemen loved to keep their secrets.

"There might be a lot going on behind the scenes you don't understand," Everly hedged.

Yes, there obviously was. "But it's nothing you can talk about. I understand and I'm not going to ask any of you to break trust with your husband. But Liz and I aren't married to a man from the inner circle. I know everyone would love for us to have blind faith, but I've been burned by one of them before. Tell Zack it would be better for everyone if he let Liz go. I don't know what he's up to, but all his caveman power play will accomplish is to crush her, and I won't stand for that. Tell him he can deal with Liz fairly or he'll be dealing with me."

Everly cursed under her breath. "If I hadn't promised…"

Gus held up a hand. "I know. Believe me, I do."

Everly and Lara left the parlor to get ready for dinner. And perhaps to yell at a couple of men.

Gus handed Liz her Grey Goose gimlet and started to pour one for herself. She was damn happy she was a planner because she wasn't sure what she would do if she had to mix the drinks herself right now.

Even hours after her encounter with Roman her hands were still shaking, her body still hot. What the hell had almost happened? She could still feel the heat from his big form brushing hers, making her nipples hard and aching. He'd come so close to meshing their mouths together again after so many long, empty years. Even after she'd promised herself that she'd never let him close again.

But had she pushed him away? No. She'd stood there and almost let him kiss her.

Nope. She wasn't going to lie to herself. If Darcy hadn't barged in, she would have welcomed him. Her brain had switched off in that moment, and all that had mattered was being close to him once more. The years had melted away and she hadn't cared that he was an ass of massive proportions who didn't deserve her.

Ugh, her female parts had no sense when it came to that ruthless, disgusting, no-good, dickless bastard. Well, that wasn't exactly true. She'd felt the brush of his cock against her earlier and had never quite forgotten what he could do to her with it... But the rest of her assessment? Spot on. Roman Calder hadn't changed one bit. He still had the whole Madonna/whore view of women. He wanted the whore in his bed, tucked away from prying eyes. That would be her role. And he'd obviously selected the annoying, way-too-perky Darcy as the perfect arm candy to show off to the world.

Fucker.

"I hate him," Liz said, staring into her glass.

"I do, too." Both of them. Normally she adored Zack, but Roman was finally proving to be a terrible influence on him. His chief of staff and bestie had taught him how to take something good, crap all over it, set it on fire, then have the gall to wonder what the hell had gone wrong.

"I didn't drink too much on the plane." Liz sighed and sat back. "Oh, I have now and I'm sure I'll pay for it tomorrow, but I had one vodka on the flight right before we landed. He decided that was some kind of sign that he couldn't let me out of his sight. He forced me into his car and gave me the most ridiculous lecture about being professional and…let's just say the man is not professional. He's insane and he can't keep doing this to me. I quit."

"You know you can't."

"I sure as hell can." Liz sat back. "I won't work again, according to that asshole, but maybe I don't have to. Maybe I can take up the hobo life. I like trains."

"You like trains that have first-class accommodations." This was not their first conversation about Liz's professional future. "Sweetie, I don't think they have a bar in hobo-class seating."

"Okay, that's terrible," Liz admitted. "Maybe I can marry an incredibly wealthy foreign leader and get him to nuke Zack. Only Zack though."

"Throw Roman in. It won't be hard. They're always together. I swear those men would have been far happier if their sexuality had permitted them to marry."

"I called Zack a spineless moron in front of the whole staff."

Shit. "And what brought that on?"

"I was testing a theory."

"He's not going to fire you." They'd been over this before.

Liz groaned. "I know. What is he doing and why?"

"I suspect he's hiding something. This is likely a way to keep you close so he can watch after you, all the while maintaining distance in the world's prying eyes. Zack thinks he's in danger and he's trying to both protect you and stay clear."

"Why wouldn't he just tell me that? We've been friends for years, Gus. Years. I've been his advisor on everything from campaigning to dealing with his father to how to avoid war with North Korea. I don't understand why he would stop talking to me. It makes no sense at all."

"Because he's male and that means his brain is unfortunately wrapped up in his dick, and his thought process depends on which one is getting the most blood flow."

"Well, I'm sure it's his dick that's making all the decisions right now."

She knew what Liz thought. Gus wasn't so sure. "I find it interesting that he's gone from being dateless to taking out more single girls than The Bachelor in a few weeks."

Liz's face fell. "He told me he was sick of not having a love life. He was ready to move on from Joy, and waiting until after he left office would be too much of a hardship. He also said he never meant to hurt me, but he doesn't have romantic feelings for me. I'm apparently like a sister to him." She gritted her teeth. "A sister."

Bullshit. "Do you want me to push this? I can fix this if you need me to. I might have to burn a bridge or two...but I can." She had some sway with Zack. Of course, if he was covering up the secret she suspected, then she didn't really know Zack at all.

Zack couldn't be the one who had Mad killed. God, she prayed he hadn't.

If she was wrong, if her faith in him was misplaced, it would rock everyone and shatter everything she and her loved ones had held dear for decades.

Liz shook her head. "No. Leave it. I'm going to stop fighting him and simply do my job. I'm not going to hate him. And one day I won't feel anything for him at all. That's the goal."

"And if he's doing all of this to protect you?"

"Then he can't possibly trust me," Liz said sadly. "And something more meaningful between us would never have worked. Zack was a stupid, girlish dream on my part. I need to wake up. I don't know who he's turned me into. A shrew. I can't believe I yelled at him like that."

Maybe what Liz needed was a distraction. "You could help me out."

Liz leaned forward, her voice going low. "You're still looking into Maddox Crawford's death?"

Gus glanced behind her, making sure they were alone. "Yes."

"Okay. Tell me what you have. You know I thought this was a wild-goose chase, but I have to wonder. So much is happening behind closed doors now."

"It's like they've battened down the hatches and we're left on the outside," Gus agreed. It wasn't the first time she'd found herself watching that door close with Roman and her brother and their friends on the other side. Now their wives were part of their inner circle, too. Somehow that hurt more than it should.

Liz sat up suddenly. "We don't need them. And you know what? We can't trust them anyway. Share what you know and we'll figure out the rest. Did my source at the FAA give you anything?"

Gus hesitated. Maybe this was a mistake. This investigation could get dangerous, and she wasn't sure Liz could handle more proof that Zack might be dirty.

She sighed. Break her friend's heart or provide the distraction Liz needed? Not an easy choice.

"Don't you hold out on me, Gus. If I'm going to stay here and survive, I have to be able to help someone. You're my closest friend. Don't push me away, too."

Damn it. Liz knew exactly how to get to her. "All right. Yes, I've been looking into Mad's crash and I've found a few things that don't add up. Did you know Zack personally asked for all the details of the FAA investigation? While it was active?"

"Mad was one of his best friends. I know it doesn't look good to have the president stick his nose into an active investigation, but it's understandable."

"Twenty-four hours later, the FAA abruptly changed their initial determination from likely criminal action to pilot error." She switched seats to move closer to Liz. The Secret Service was always around somewhere, and unfortunately they played a part in creating this complicated web. "I talked, off the record, with your friend there and she says the unofficial gossip is that Zack requested that they close the investigation."

"Why?" Liz looked stunned. "I know that Mad called Zack's private line the day before he died. They were arguing about something. I didn't hear much, but I think it was about Gabe's sister. She worked for Mad for a while or something."

Or something was right. She knew what the rest of them were trying so hard to keep from the public. Gus had known all along because she'd played fairy godmother to those two. "I convinced Mad to give Sara a job at Crawford. She needed some intern hours to finish her MBA and I convinced her that working at Crawford would be more impressive than working at Bond

Aeronautics."

"The rumor is she's pregnant," Liz murmured quietly. "I suppose Mad was… Well, Mad had earned his reputation, maybe even more than the rest of his friends."

"Mad was in love with Sara for fifteen years. And his reputation might have been well earned, but there was so much more to him. He was such a good friend. I've never known anyone more loyal than Mad."

"You had an affair with him, right?"

Ah, the gossip mill. "I wouldn't call it an affair. Mad and I understood each other. We were close friends and when we weren't involved with anyone else, we would go to bed together. I enjoyed Mad a lot, but I wasn't in love with him. And he wasn't in love with me. We cared about each other. Mad helped me through some dark times."

"That's why you're so determined to figure out what happened."

"Yes. Even if I don't like the answer."

"I might hate Zack right now, but I still find it hard to believe he had anything to do with Crawford's death. And why would Zack kill Mad over Sara? I would think he would rather have had a shotgun wedding than a funeral. He wasn't even seeing her at the end of his life, was he?"

"No. He'd broken it off with her a couple of weeks earlier. I was out of the country at the time. I called him, and he wouldn't say anything except that their split was for the best and he would talk to me when I came home. He died before I got back." Gus wished every single day that she'd cut her trip short and raced to his side. "The last couple of times we talked, he seemed on edge. He was definitely more secretive than usual. Maybe even a little paranoid."

"But he didn't tell you why?"

"No. He refused to go in depth over the phone, even to discuss why he'd broken things off with Sara. He just kept reiterating that their relationship hadn't worked out. But I didn't believe him because I'd seen them together. And I know something no one else knows. Something I haven't told anyone, so I expect you to keep it secret, too."

Liz nodded. "My loyalty is all to you now, Gus. We're in this together."

They were the outsiders. Despite the fact that she hated how Liz had been made to feel, it was good to have someone she could count on. "I helped Mad pick an engagement ring for Sara two weeks before he broke up with her. He wasn't even thinking about separating from her then. He was in love and he was planning a lavish proposal. Something changed, and it wasn't his heart."

"That sounds familiar," Liz muttered in frustration.

"Yes, I think whatever caused Mad to dump Sara is what caused everything else to turn upside down. If we figure out why Mad was killed, I suspect we'll figure out what Zack and the others are hiding. And why he's suddenly decided you're like a sister." Gus rolled her eyes.

"I can't go down that path," Liz insisted. "I'll be your investigative right hand because I want to help you, but I won't keep gnashing my teeth about why Zack no longer wants me. The answer to that question is meaningless, but I'll work with you however necessary to find the truth about Mad's death. I know how it feels to lose a friend, one I had complicated feelings about."

Joy. Like everyone who knew the woman, Liz had

loved her, but she'd also loved Zack. Hell, Gus had complicated feelings about Joy herself.

Joy might have married Zack, but their union had been more of a friendly partnership. The man Joy had really loved was Roman.

I'm the world's worst wife. I can't stop thinking about him. He makes me feel special.

Liz slid a hand over hers. "I'm sorry. I shouldn't have mentioned Joy. I know how hard it is for you to think about her."

Gus let the sorrow wash over her. Embracing that and shoving aside her jealousy was the only way to deal with her complicated feelings. "I loved her. She was like my sister."

"And yet you never told her about you and Roman."

By then, it hadn't mattered. She'd seen how madly in love her friend was. "I think she suspected. But the information would have done nothing to help her. It would only have made things between the two of us difficult. And you know I wouldn't want to come between lovers."

Liz shook her head, blonde hair tumbling. "Never lovers. I know for a fact they never even kissed."

Like she suspected that Liz and Zack had never kissed. But the pretty blonde didn't understand what Roman's platonic adoration had meant. "He respected Joy. He thought she would be his perfect wife, which meant never giving into passion because the woman on his pedestal is some fifties housewife with perfect hair, a placid smile, lovely pearls, and a voice she never raised above conversational tones. I loved Joy, but if she'd ever married Roman it would have been a disaster. He would have walked all over her and she wouldn't have liked keeping up with him in bed."

"I'm sorry I brought it up. I guess I thought that since so much time has gone by, maybe you and Roman would get close again."

Oh, they'd gotten close, and she'd needed the reminder about why he was suddenly willing to get close to her again. He was horny and she was convenient. That was all she'd ever been to him—an easy lay within easy reach. Joy had been the Madonna. Gus had no illusion; she was always going to be the whore.

Roman hadn't wanted her child. Would he have welcomed Joy's?

She shook off that thought. She didn't think about the night she'd miscarried. Not ever. Except once a year when she got drunk off her ass and Mad held her hand while she cried.

Who would hold her hand this year?

"There's nothing between me and Roman. There wasn't anything back then, either. It was all hormones and forbidden thrills."

Liz raised a brow at her. "Maybe for him, but not for you." When Gus didn't reply, the other woman accepted the subject change with grace. "So, what's our plan? What can we do to investigate while we're in the UK? Don't we have to wait until we're back in the States?"

Gus was relieved she had something other than Roman to focus on. "No, we definitely have details to dig up while we're here. I visited the airport Mad used on his last flight." She pulled out her phone, flipping through some of the files she kept there. "There was nothing in the security footage from the airport itself. Shockingly, the CCTV footage was taken by the FAA and now it's mysteriously gone missing."

"Shit."

"But I'm smarter than that. That airfield is remote and there's only one gas station near it. So I paid to get their security footage for the twenty-four-hour period preceding Mad's crash. There were three cameras. I found this on the one that covers the cash register. Look familiar?"

She showed Liz the slightly grainy photo. It showed a young man wearing a baseball cap, pulled low on his head, but the camera angle was perfect to reveal his insanely chiseled jawline and those eyes no one could mistake.

Liz gasped. "That's Matthew Kemp. He's on Zack's detail."

She'd double-checked her assumption, using facial recognition to verify the match. "It is. So what was a Secret Service agent doing in close proximity to that airplane not four hours before Mad took off? Especially when the records show that Matthew Kemp was in DC that day working on pre-security for a fund raiser?"

"That's a great question. Tell me what I can do to help you find the answer."

"Well, I heard a rumor that Mr. Kemp and one of his peers have the night off and that they plan on hitting a nearby pub." Gus had intended to go alone, but it would be so much easier if she had a wingwoman with her. "I thought I might arrange to bump into Kemp, get to know him a bit, figure out some way to look at his phone and see who he's been calling."

"That could be dangerous." Liz looked nervous about that possibility.

"Absolutely, but I only need you to distract him while I download his device. I have spiffy items from my friend in the NSA. The kind of gadgets that probably won't ever hit the marketplace, if you know what I mean. And if he catches me..." Gus knew she was no ninja, so she'd given this some thought. "Well, I'll tell him that I was so interested, I couldn't wait to leave my contact info on his phone in the hopes he'd call. I'll bat my lashes and flash cleavage, if I need to. He's a man with an ego; he'll believe it."

"Zack and the others have a dinner tonight. I was told to stay here." Her lips curled up and a stubborn light hit her pale eyes. "But I think a change of clothes and a touch-up of the hair is in order. We should definitely have some fun tonight."

And maybe catch a killer.

CHAPTER FOUR

Roman paced the library at the manor house, looking out the window over the empty front drive before glancing again at the clock. Three o'clock in the fucking morning. Three! Did the woman sleep? Gus had been up early this morning for a critical meeting, so she should be pretty fucking tired, and yet she wasn't tucked in her bed like a good girl. Nope, Augustine Spencer was traipsing around London—no idea exactly where—partying the night away. Goddamn it.

"I'm going to put a tracking chip in her." Zack paced the room. If he kept it up, he'd wear out the carpet. "I can do it, too. I'm the motherfucking president of the United States. If I want someone's location pinpointed at any hour of any given day, I'll make that happen. And if I tell someone to stay put, she'd goddamn better stay put." He stared out the window, his face tight with worry. "I'm only trying to protect her."

He'd never seen Zack quite so angry and off balance. If he hadn't been horrifically pissed at Gus, Roman might have found the situation amusing. It wasn't often his pal dropped his presidential demeanor, but when Liz was involved it seemed to happen more and more lately.

"I know. When all of this is over and she's happy, healthy, and alive, she'll thank you."

"I suspect after the past few days that we might be done." Zack's laugh held no humor at all. "I've loved that woman for years, and now she hates me. I'll never get to kiss her even once."

"Well, I know what that's like."

Zack turned, his eyes narrowing. "No, you don't."

He should let it go. Zack was on the edge, and Roman knew now wasn't the time to poke at a touchy topic likely to lead to a verbal brawl. But he wasn't in the mood to swallow the argument down. "Of course I do. You know I loved Joy."

"Are we finally going to do this?" Zack took a long drink and then set the crystal glass down with a smack. "Maybe we should. Fucking honesty is long overdue."

Was Zack tipsy? He rarely had more than one drink. Perhaps two, if the day was almost over and he knew he could go straight to bed. Tonight he'd had several. Roman had watched him all night at the dinner with the American ambassador and several of the PM's senior aides. He'd been seated next to a gorgeous woman and hadn't paid a bit of attention to her. He'd spent the entire night sipping Scotch and checking his phone as though waiting for some vital communication.

Had he been trying to text Elizabeth all night? Was the president of the United States behaving like a lovesick schoolboy?

"I think we should get you to bed. I'll call Connor. He and I will find Liz and Gus."

Zack sighed. "You didn't love Joy, you big moron. Oh, I know you would have married her if I hadn't, but you didn't love her and that was exactly *why* you would have married her."

Roman gritted his teeth. "That's not true."

"Oh, face it, man. This is your last chance and you're fucking it up."

"Last chance?" But he knew deep down what Zack meant, and Roman didn't want to talk about it. Hell, he didn't even want to think about it.

"With Gus, damn it." Zack kept coming at him verbally, glaring at him as if he'd turned part idiot. "I loved Joy as much as I could. But she was not the woman for me. Or for you. She was smart and kind and patient—everything most men could want from a wife. And I didn't feel any passion for her at all. She didn't feel any for me. I don't know if Joy was even capable of that." Zack clammed up, then glanced down at the table where his drink sat. "This woman is going to drive me crazy."

So Zack was back to mooning over his press secretary. Little surprise. Roman tried to refocus his friend. "What is that supposed to mean?"

"It means Liz is driving me to drink."

Roman sighed, searching for patience. "That wasn't what I was asking."

Zack slanted him a challenging stare. "Tell me you ever felt an ounce of true passion for Joy."

"Of course I did."

"Bullshit. You had a hard-on for the *idea* of her, not the woman herself. And even that's a crock of crap."

Zack tossed his hands in the air and resumed pacing. "God, how are we still here? How are we still stuck staring into our Scotches with long faces, denying ourselves everything our hearts want?"

Roman tried to hold on to his temper. Zack didn't understand. He probably never would. "You might be. But you're wrong about my feelings for Joy. You don't really grasp what I want."

"Is that what you think?" Zack scoffed. "You want a marriage that's the polar opposite of your parents'. You want a wife who won't fight with you, who never turns your gut inside out. You want to spend your life with a woman who's incapable of making you wish you hadn't met her one minute, and then forces you to realize that you can't live without her in the next. You, my dense friend, want to feel nothing. You want a housekeeper, hostess, and cook you have sex with, one who wears your ring on her finger like a trophy and doesn't tug on your heart at all."

"That's pretty fucking hypocritical coming from a man who chose the same path."

"I did, and you know what? I regret it. I didn't wait long enough. I wasn't patient, or maybe I just didn't believe in love. Life is all about perspective, isn't it? I know you hated the seemingly endless cycle of your parents' breakups and makeups. Their fighting and the resulting upheaval. But I saw something different. I saw passion. I saw two people who loved each other so much they were willing to fight every day and never give up the struggle to make their marriage work. My parents never did that. My father was the head of the household and when my mother became a problem, he decided she was no longer an asset. So he sent her to a mental ward.

Tidy and clinical. Cold. Ruthless."

Roman conceded that Zack's father had been downright arctic where Constance was concerned, but his friend didn't understand what it was like to grow up with constant bellowing and shrieking rattling the walls. To this day, he had recurring nightmares about the stairs vibrating under his feet with the thunder of his parents' shouted obscenities and slurs while he sat praying they wouldn't kill each other. The next morning, he'd often creep from his room, expecting another bloody battle in World War III, only to find them sharing a kiss so fiery they'd forgotten he even existed.

"You and Joy were never chilly strangers."

"No, we were friends. We cared deeply for each other and shared common interests. We were compatible because we had one mutual goal to bind us together: the White House. That was all we talked about, all we planned for. We had sex maybe twenty times our entire marriage."

Roman felt his jaw drop. They'd been married for six years before her death. "Are you kidding me?"

"I'm pretty sure you and Gus went at it more than that the first week you started sleeping together. You can discount that kind of passion all you like, but I can't live without it anymore. I can't be this hollow on the inside for the rest of my life. I need Liz to come back." Zack cast an agitated glance out the window again.

Roman watched numbly. Oh, his first week with Gus. He remembered those golden days with perfect clarity, as if they had just happened yesterday. The two of them had gotten into a horrible argument about politics. One minute she'd been calling him a blind nationalist who couldn't see the future because his head was too far up Zack's ass...and the next he was tearing off her clothes and thrusting as deep into her as he could manage on the kitchen table.

He'd been so desperate. He hadn't wanted sex with Augustine. He'd *needed* it. He'd had to have it or he would fucking die.

And that had scared the shit out of him.

Roman stood. "I didn't know about you and Joy."

Zack took a deep breath and turned. "I didn't want anyone to know. I went into the marriage knowing exactly what it would be. I expected peace. What I didn't expect was the emptiness. I truly loved her, but I was never *in* love with her. Then, when I met Elizabeth, I knew I'd made a terrible mistake."

"Augustine isn't Elizabeth," Roman insisted.

"And you aren't me. But Elizabeth drives me crazy."

"The way Gus makes me insane," he admitted.

"But in a good way...if you'd let her." Zack shook his head. "I see you making the same mistakes over and over. It damn near kills me. What the hell are you doing with Darcy Hildebrandt? A woman like that would put you to sleep for the rest of your life."

"I'm not doing anything with her except working and being polite. Why does everyone assume there's something going on between us?"

"Because I watched you with her tonight."

Roman couldn't BS Zack—or himself. He'd paid careful attention to Darcy. The woman had been nice to a fault. She never raised her voice and she knew how to make a man feel as if he was in control, powerful. She checked a lot of the boxes on his list.

Damn it. Even listening to his own thoughts, he sounded like he needed therapy. Or a swift kick. He didn't want to be this asshole.

"Are you going to date her?"

"No." Roman couldn't. While he admitted that Darcy interested him on some level, she didn't intrigue him. She didn't tie him in knots and make him sweat. She certainly didn't make him hard, like Augustine, who was so close he could almost taste her. "I want Gus. I know I shouldn't, but I can't seem to stop myself."

"Why the fuck should you stop yourself? I understand the past. We were all young and stupid and ambitious, but I'm going to ask the only question that matters now. Are you happy?"

"Of course." Wasn't he? He'd accomplished everything he'd promised his ladder-climbing twenty-something self he would. He'd reached the pinnacle of power.

"Well, I'm not. I'm done. When we get back to the States next week, I'm going to announce that I won't seek a second term. Maybe if the Russians figure out I'm not going to play these games anymore, they'll let up."

Roman stopped, his whole world tilting askew. All of their lives, they'd worked to be here. When other kids had dreamed about being baseball players or rock stars, he and Zack had dreamed of the White House. Now Zack intended to throw it all away without a fight? "How could you make a decision like this without consulting me?"

Zack slumped back on the couch. "I don't know what to do, Roman. Some moments I think that's the right move. Others…I'm not sure if announcing I won't seek a second term would launch the conspirators' plans into more rapid motion. The not knowing is killing me."

Roman sat beside him. There was zero chance he

would allow Zack to give up his second term. They still had a lot of work to do for the people, policies to implement that would make a difference in Americans' lives. Zack was a popular president who knew how to get things done. And Roman would protect his friend's legacy, as always. That meant dealing with the situation they found themselves mired in now.

"I'll figure this out and take care of everything," he promised Zack. "I leave for Homewood Sanatorium the day after tomorrow. I've got myself set up at a B and B. It's way out in the country. I doubt anyone there will know who I am. I'm going to figure out what happened to your mother. Maybe then we'll know who's coming for you."

"And why. I want to know why." Zack looked older than his years, a deep crease of worry furrowing his brow. "I want to know why all these people around me had to die. What do these assholes want? Why did they put me here? Roman, what if I'm not Zack Hayes?"

His stomach flipped. He'd looked at the problem from all angles, and this was one of the ugliest scenarios he'd considered. "You are. I don't care what happens or what comes out of this investigation. You've got to be Zack Hayes."

"What if I'm really Sergei?" He finally voiced the question, his tone strained and hollow.

This was the possibility they'd all begun to fear. "You're Zack."

"Natalia Kuilikov gave birth to a son around the same time I was born. Her child died, according to all the records. And yet when Connor and Lara talked to her, she still spoke fondly about her Sergei, as if he was still alive."

This was the most compelling evidence they had to support the conclusion that Zack was actually the son of his former Russian nanny, but it was all circumstantial. With one bullet, the Russians had ensured that Natalia would never talk to anyone ever again.

The only other way to know for certain, comparing DNA samples, was impossible. The president of the United States couldn't demand the genetic material of a dead Russian citizen who'd cared for him as an infant without raising brows and setting chins wagging. And since Franklin had given away everything of Constance's shortly after her death, Zack had no hairs from a brush or the like with which to compare her genetic material to his. Nor could he exhume her body for answers since she'd been cremated. Even if he could, turning up graves wouldn't go unnoticed—either by the press or his enemies. "We don't know for certain if that was her son's name."

"We don't know it wasn't, either. I remember my mother babbling about a baby dying. She did that when she was drunk. She'd also weep, apologize. I didn't understand. My father never explained. When Mom got on a jag, he'd hustle her out of the room before I could ask questions. But recalling those times got me thinking. What if Constance's baby died and I'm the one they replaced him with?"

"No." It wasn't possible. It couldn't be. That would make Zack a non-American born on Russian soil, and thus constitutionally unable to serve as POTUS. He'd be impeached. Dishonored. The repercussions of that were too horrible for Roman to even contemplate. "Impossible. You look so much like your father."

"We both know my father likely had an affair with

Natalia Kuilikov. God knows he was never faithful or even terribly discreet. Maybe he got her pregnant, and I'm the result. It would explain so much. If that's true, the Russians would have the perfect reason to ensure I made it to the White House. Once I was sworn in, they had a nearly foolproof way to blackmail me into doing whatever they want. Which could be anything. We have sanctions against Russia right now. Putin is looking to expand his power base. They could ask me to look the other way as he annexes another part of the old Soviet block. They might want me to pull out of NATO altogether. I won't do it. They'll have to kill me before I'll betray my country."

Roman clenched his fists. Zack had been thinking about this possibility a lot, and he hated to admit it...but this theory made far too much sense. "Have you asked your father?"

"Asked him what?" He laughed, the sound bitter. "He's not in his right mind. Hell, most days I'm the only person he remembers."

Once it was clear the dementia had completely overtaken Frank Hayes's mind, they'd tried to put him in a memory care facility. But the man was a master of escape. Once he slipped out and tasted freedom, he inevitably found himself surrounded by the press. Or maybe the scumsuckers found him and took advantage of the old man's state. Either way, reporters snapped pictures of him walking the streets in his robe and slippers, ranting that his son was never around.

Whenever he and Zack secured Frank in the White House, the man was calmer, as though proximity to the son he'd invested his life in quieted the demons ravaging his brain. He still had moments of lucidity. Not many, but every so often Roman would hear Frank talk about how proud he was of his son and share a fond memory or two. "But there are times he remembers the past."

"They're getting fewer and further between. Let's see what we can find out while we're in the UK," Zack replied. "If we come up short, once we're Stateside again I'll try to probe him about the past. Maybe he'll have useful information, if he can recall anything. I spoke to his nurse earlier tonight. Seems he's okay right now. He thinks I'm in another part of the White House working."

Frank could be difficult when his son was gone. They'd catch him roaming the halls, looking for Zack—his last link to a normal life.

The gravity of the political tangle they were in sucked the air from the room. Roman shifted and glanced at the clock again. Worrying about Gus was far preferable to worrying about Zack's future as the leader of the free world. Not that he could keep his mind off the vixen for more than a minute or two.

"Where the fuck are they?" Zack asked, in sync with him as always. "I should have left her at home."

"If you had, you wouldn't have been able to watch over her. We shouldn't let Gus too far out of our sight, either. Her father already lost his life over this plot. I can't lose her too." He sat back, realizing how possessive and protective his words had come out. "I mean, Dax… He couldn't handle losing his sister."

"Sure you did, buddy. Let me give you some advice. Ditch the Brit for tomorrow's event. Take Gus instead. Bend a little. You know you want her. You're both older and wiser. Try again."

He shook his head. "I can't. Even if I do, it's got to be kept quiet. The last thing we need is the scandal pages

making a big deal out of me dating someone who...
Well, we all know the rumors."

"Are you serious? Fuck the rumors. You know damn
well they aren't true."

"Some of them are. She *did* sleep with Mad. And
everyone in the free world thinks she had sex with you,
too. Do you want some rag putting together one of those
maps connecting us with a million and one lines running
through Augustine's square?"

"So we're back to me being a whore. Nice."

Roman whipped around to the sound of her voice.
Naturally Gus chose that moment to stroll in. Liz
followed her. Both women looked stunning in low-cut
designer cocktail dresses made to catch the attention of
any heterosexual man with freaking eyes. Liz's blonde
hair flowed around her like a halo while Gus's sun-
stroked brown curls and vampy lipstick made her look
like sultry sin personified. The angel and the she-devil.
They'd likely had every man in London panting after
them.

"Elizabeth, I thought I made myself clear." Zack
stood, his eyes turning steely. "You were to stay here
unless you're working, and then you are only allowed to
leave if someone I approve of accompanies you."

"They were out having a few drinks." Connor
sauntered in behind them with an easy smile, waving a
hand as though telling them to cool off. "And they
weren't alone. They had three Secret Service agents with
them. They weren't even far, just a couple of blocks
away."

Roman could bet they'd had a Secret Service escort.
He knew a few of the detail would have had time off
tonight. Had Augustine gone looking for Matthew

Kemp? Had she spent the evening flirting with him? Making arrangements to meet up with him later for a hot fuck?

"Then why the hell didn't you find them more quickly?" Zack asked. "You've been gone for hours."

"I spotted them about an hour ago. I thought they deserved some time out, like the rest of us. As neither one of these lovely ladies is attached, I didn't see any reason I should play dad and drag them home like wayward girls. So I watched over them and let them have some fun," Connor replied, his tone even.

"That wasn't what I asked you to do. I asked you to find them and bring them back immediately," Zack spit out. "And Elizabeth, if you disobey me one more time, you'll find yourself in custody."

Liz frowned. "With the same hot Secret Service guys we just spent the evening with? Count me in, Mr. President." She gave him a terribly sarcastic salute. "And I'll be up bright and early. I know you have a date tomorrow night. We'll need to make sure your tux is pressed and you're presentable. You've clearly done some drinking tonight. I'll make sure the cook brings you my momma's patented hangover cure."

"I'm not drunk," Zack shot back.

It didn't slip past Roman that this was the same argument Zack and Liz had earlier, the roles merely reversed.

"Still, your date tomorrow night is barely twenty-two. We'll need to work overtime to ensure you don't look like a creepy old man next to her. You getting so little sleep won't help the cause." Liz turned to Gus with a hug. "Thanks for tonight. I had a blast. I'll see you in a few hours, and we'll go over our schedule."

Gus winked her way. "Bright and early, sister."

Liz stopped when she reached Connor. "Thank you for giving us breathing room and time. It was good for me to see some of the world and realize how many possibilities are out there. I appreciate it very much."

"I meant what I said, Elizabeth." Zack seemed determined to get the last word.

"You always do, Mr. President. Right up until the moment your words become an inconvenience. Don't worry. I won't give you trouble and I'm done making a fool of myself. I thank you for being so concerned about my and Augustine's welfare that you would send your friend after us. I'm so sorry you had to wait up. Bless your heart." With that parting shot, Liz turned on her heels and strode away.

Roman winced and glanced at Zack. Yeah, he knew Liz's last words were the Deep South's equivalent of fuck you.

Gus smoothed out her skirt, using the gesture to smother a laugh. "On that happy note, I'll go to bed myself. You two can continue plotting world domination or whatever."

"No, you're going to stay right here because we're having a talk," Roman insisted. It was time to put his foot down. He couldn't tell her why they were acting this way, but he could damn straight let her know he wouldn't put up with her rebellion anymore.

"Zack, I think you should go to bed. Liz is right about that woman you're seeing tomorrow. She's really young. You're going to need stamina to keep up with her," Connor said.

"I don't need fucking stamina and you know it. I'm not touching that girl. Cancel the whole thing." Zack started out the door, Connor hard on his heels explaining why that plan wouldn't work.

"Darcy will be super sad if you cancel," Gus pointed out. "You wouldn't want to disappoint that sweet little thing."

He wasn't taking the bait. "Since that party tomorrow night is meant to welcome us to England, you know we can't cancel. So let's skip that subject and get to something worth discussing. What kind of stunt were you up to tonight, sneaking away?"

"Why is Zack acting like a massive ass? You answer my question and I'll answer yours." She tossed him a saucy glance over her shoulder as she approached the bar.

Roman gaped. "Are you kidding me? Connor just dragged you out of one bar and here you are pouring yourself another drink?"

"Is it hard to be that sanctimonious?" Gus mused as she filled her glass with two fingers of Scotch. "Do you have to shove the two by four up your ass all by yourself or do you have an aide do it for you?"

"I'm not joking, Gus."

"I can leave, if you'd rather. I won't be near a bar then."

"Stop being such a smart ass. Why did you and Liz pull that disappearing act tonight?"

"What are you worried about, Roman? Two single women painting the town without—gasp—male escorts. I mean, our female minds could have gotten us into all kinds of trouble..."

"That's not what I meant. Don't play coy or stupid. And don't pretend you're innocent."

She stood there, crystal glass in hand, all those

gorgeous curves barely encased by the silk of her cocktail dress. "Of course I'm not. We both know what you think of me. I might as well wear a scarlet *A* on my chest. And if I keep this scandalous behavior up, I'll ruin poor virginal Elizabeth."

Why did she have to take everything he said or did and twist it in the darkest way? "I didn't say that. That's certainly not what I meant. And I'm sorry for what you overheard when you walked into the room. I simply don't want all our personal issues aired in the press. I hate that."

"You're embarrassed to have slept with me. I know. You made yourself plain years ago."

"Damn it, Gus, that is not what I said or what I'm trying to convey. I only insisted that I don't want someone drafting a chart with lines drawn to show whom we've all slept with. If that makes me some kind of prude, then so be it. Hell, the last few years I have been a damn prude." He needed to get back to the point. "But you can't take Liz out like that."

"Why?"

"It's not safe," he hedged.

She shook her head, her expression telling him she found his assertion terrifically stupid. "We were two blocks away, talking to Secret Service agents. We had a couple of drinks and some dinner with them. Apparently most of the time we had Connor watching over us, as well. How exactly were we not safe?"

"Did it occur to you at all that you're a high-value target?" He had to try something. He couldn't spend the entire visit running after her to make sure she wasn't getting into trouble...or Matthew Kemp's bed.

She snorted. "No. That did not occur to me. What's

smacking me between the eyes right now, however, is your paranoia. Again, we were with Secret Service agents."

He couldn't trust anyone who wasn't a part of Zack's inner circle. If this conspiracy had been going on for as long as he suspected, the Russians would most assuredly have a sleeper agent inside the president's detail.

"Is that why you went out, to get close to those boys? Gus, please don't make me fire them."

"Why would you do that? As far as I can tell, they're perfectly competent."

"Yes, but I swear to god if I catch one of them looking at you twice, I will strip his credentials and march his ass out in a heartbeat."

Gus slammed down her glass. It clattered against the bar. "Nice. You don't want me but you damn sure don't want anyone else to have me, either."

That was where she was wrong. "Who said I didn't want you? I wish I could stop wanting you. I want you every minute of every day, and I have since the moment I laid eyes on you."

She shook her head at him. "So I'm like heroin? You know I'm bad for you but sometimes you just need a fix?"

"I didn't say that, either, Gus." He was so tired. Why did they always fight?

Roman sank down to the seat Zack had vacated and wished he could tell her everything. He'd give almost anything to stop keeping secrets that put him on one side of the fence and her squarely on the other. But he couldn't do that without risking her safety. The more she knew, the more the Russians might see her as a target.

Hell, he'd even settle for telling her that one of the reasons he'd convinced Zack to hire her three years ago had been simply because he missed her so fucking much after all these years. If he did, the way things were now between them, Gus would never believe it. Or she'd laugh in his face. Or maybe they'd fall into bed.

He wasn't sure which outcome to fear most.

Even as he'd fallen in love with Joy, some part of him had ached for Gus. Sometimes he was sure he'd convinced himself he was in love with Joy because she was Gus's opposite, and if his heart belonged to Joy then he couldn't possibly still be hung up on his sexy, sassy Louisiana beauty. Because Joy had never once made him angry. She'd never challenged him. He had never yelled at her because she'd never given him a reason to. Joy certainly had never made him want to rip his own heart out so he didn't have to feel so fucking much for her.

He was a coward.

"Go to bed, Roman. You're tired. You can yell at me again in the morning," Gus said with a sigh.

"I don't want to yell at you." He debated the wisdom of his words, then realized he couldn't help himself. "I want us to be friends again."

She sank down on the sofa beside him, leaving plenty of space between them. "I don't know that we were ever friends. I think we were lovers, and I thought we could be something more at one time. But that's long over. Now, we need to try to be good coworkers."

Bland. Boring. He didn't want to be her coworker. He wanted the right to touch her, make love to her, call her his. So dangerous... "And when we're not working together?"

"Then we see each other at weddings and birthdays.

We wish one another well." She shrugged. "We send Christmas cards if we ever find the time to and think about that crazy year we spent together with fondness."

"Is that how you remember us? Do you feel any affection at all?"

A wistful smile crept across her lips before it fell away. "Sometimes, but not often. I usually recall it as a cautionary tale."

He didn't like the sound of that. "I never meant to hurt you."

"And yet you did it so well. I think what you truly mean is you never thought I could be hurt at all."

"I thought I was one of your many boy toys," he admitted because they were finally talking about the past. Even more surprising, no one was yelling. "There was a part of me that worried you viewed our year together as nothing more than my turn with you."

She stared at him, rearing back for an instant. He felt the heavy weight of her judgment. "Of course. Because I'm something to be passed around, like a joint at a party. All your friends get a hit, right?"

"I didn't mean it that way." How could he make her understand? Everything between them was fucked up. He knew that, just like he knew he probably couldn't change it. But that was also a year of his life he wouldn't take back. "I knew you'd been with Mad. I heard the rumor you'd been with Zack, too. I rather thought you were working your way through us all. I know that sounds like I'm some misogynistic prick, but by that time there were women trying their damnedest to do it. Women who viewed us as trophies."

"Oh, believe me. I knew some of them. Not a one of you argued with them or protested their ill treatment of you."

Because they'd been young and stupid, and he'd never imagined the consequences. "You're right. Back in those days, they were lovely, and we really only thought about fun while we plotted our futures. I admit I happily sent a few of those women right down the line. But not you. Never you. That should tell you something."

"Yes, it tells me you didn't want to upset Dax by shoving his sister in the same lot with the good-time girls."

There it was, the frustration. Why couldn't they have a straightforward conversation? She never listened to him. She always told him what he must be feeling—and she usually made it some insult he'd never intended at all. This was how their fights started, damn it. Roman was tired of the pattern.

"No. Listen to the truth instead of inventing your own. I was jealous. Brutally, blindingly jealous that Mad had you first, and when I heard about Zack, I wanted to kill him. My best friend."

Her eyes softened and so did the tone of her voice. "You know, I spread those rumors about Zack to save a friend, right? She was a preacher's daughter, and he would have been very upset to find out the scooter he'd gifted her with on her sixteenth birthday had been used as a prop in the first sexual encounter of the future president of the United States. When the whispers started and everything nearly went to hell, she called me and I saved both their asses."

He nodded, thrilled with her honesty. In the past she would have flipped him the bird and told him to fuck himself. That nasty well of resentment inside him cooled from a boil to a simmer.

"Yeah, Zack admitted as much later on." Roman couldn't help but laugh. "He was never any good at physics. If he'd paid attention in class, he would have known that scooter wasn't going to hold the two of them while they fucked."

Gus's lips turned up in a brilliant grin. "He also should have turned it off. I hear he still has scars on his ass from the scooter taking off and him falling buck naked into the dirt."

"Oh, don't forget the poison ivy he got, too." He turned to her, their knees brushing. It felt good to sit and talk with her, just be with her, nothing but laughter between them for this sweet moment. "Why did you do it? Why did you take the fall for her?"

"Well, it was fun to watch Dax make that terrible face he always does when he thinks he's about to throw up. He goes green. I live for that." When he raised a brow, she caught his stare and sighed. "Fine. I did it because I didn't care what other people thought of me. Because I learned at a young age that the people who love me won't stop, despite the silly antics I get into. They'll still embrace me even if I don't conform to what society thinks a good girl should be. And the people who don't love me don't matter, Roman. Ally was raised to believe that her father was the be-all, end-all authority figure and there were strict rules she had to abide by in order to keep his affection. By taking the blame, I spared her that lesson...though not forever. She married a man her father didn't approve of and he cut her off. I believe his crime was being Jewish, and Daddy wouldn't stand for that. So much for his 'love.' I don't think Ally has seen her father in years."

"But she's seen you." He could guess. Gus collected

strays. She was that person who everyone communicated through because she cared enough to reach out. She kept all her friends together.

"Of course."

Friendship meant something to Augustine. She was loyal and kind. And she was fierce. If she thought a friend was in trouble, she would send in armies to save them. Or Secret Service agents. She'd done that with her brother and Holland. When he'd found out how carefully she'd plotted to watch over Holland, he'd been blown away by the lengths the woman had gone to.

She was also no damsel in distress. Augustine Spencer waited for no one to save her when she could so competently save herself.

It used to make him feel small. When he was younger, he'd so desperately wanted to be the one who saved the girl. Now that he was older, he could see how nice it would be to have a woman who didn't need to cling, who saw a potential disaster and simply handled it.

God, he wanted to talk to her about what was happening with Zack and the other Perfect Gentlemen. She'd probably be an asset. But he and the other guys had all agreed to keep the circle closed.

"But you can't be friends with me?" he asked. "You still talk to people you haven't seen in years, but we can't be friendly?"

"You don't honestly like me, Roman. You can cast any light you like on our year together, but I know the truth. People who are merely having fun don't sleep together for an entire year," she pointed out. "They don't make up any excuse to see other. They don't sneak in and out of each other's beds so often they lose track and can't remember whose house they're at. If I'd been anyone else in the world, you would have called me your girlfriend. You would have introduced me around and openly dated me."

Was she right? It had only been after she'd left him that Roman wished he had made more of their relationship than writing it off as a year-long hurricane of lust, sex, and anger. No one brought out the fight in him quite like Gus. At the time, that had seemed like such a destructive force.

"Do you know much about my parents?"

"Only what Dax and Mad told me. I know they fought a lot. Lots of couples fight. I also know they're still married."

They'd mellowed some over the years. Now his father was retired and they seemed to lead a more peaceful life. "They would fight like cats and dogs, so viciously I was actually afraid they might kill each other."

"I'm sorry to hear that. Was it an abusive relationship?"

"Only when there was alcohol involved…but that was often. My mom would slap my dad then he would slap her back. And then after more screaming that would rattle the house, they would end up having unavoidably loud sex. In the morning, they'd act as if nothing had happened. They're better now. Mom doesn't drink at all and Dad limits himself to a beer or two, but when I'm with them all I can remember is how hard it was to sleep at night not knowing if they would both be alive when I woke up. I wondered a lot about how that cycle started. Did it begin when my father reached out in the middle of a fight and somehow threw my mom off balance? Maybe the next time he did it on purpose. I worry that I learned something terrible from him I never meant to."

"Roman, that was forever ago. It was an accident. Believe me, if I'd thought for a second what happened on those stairs wasn't a mishap, you would have felt my wrath." Some unnamed emotion crossed her face and he could have sworn he saw a sheen of tears blanket her eyes before she blinked them away. She reached out, patting his arm. "So you're saying you dumped me because we fought a lot?"

How long had he waited to have this conversation? "I didn't dump you at all. I mean, I didn't intend to."

She huffed, an indignant sound. "Please. You were going on a double date with Zack the next night."

He'd forgotten about that. How? That was the night he'd met Joy. Yet he couldn't summon up a single memory of how the introduction—or the evening—had gone. He couldn't remember her friend's name or what restaurant they'd gone to. All he could remember about that night was how miserable he was knowing he wouldn't see Augustine again. "I never intended that date to lead to anything meaningful. I was helping out Zack."

"By your own admission, you were auditioning wives, Roman."

"Well, I didn't do a particularly good job, did I? Here I am, all these years later with absolutely no one at my side."

She stood up abruptly, her movements stiff. "Yeah, well, you found your perfect woman and you let her marry your best friend."

He felt his stomach knot. She knew about that? "I cared about Joy. I won't lie, but it's been pointed out to me lately that I had underlying reasons for the attraction."

"She was the opposite of me, I suppose."

He stood, unable to hold back another minute. He hated the distance she was putting between them. The distance he'd put between them long ago. "Damn it, Augustine. Yes. She wasn't like you and I was trying my hardest to forget you. I was trying so hard not to remember how it felt to touch you, to have your body against mine, because nothing in my entire life has ever been as exciting as fucking you. Not winning the election. Not running the Oval. Nothing has ever made me feel as alive as you."

Her eyes had gone cold. "And no one has ever broken me the way you did, Roman."

No one had ever made her feel small the way he had. No one had ever made her feel used. He was the only one who could bring Augustine down, and he hated that. But didn't she understand he could do the opposite, too? They were older now. He was better able to handle the kind of relationship they'd have together.

He reached for her. He couldn't let her walk out on him. Not again. It killed him every single time she left a room because he always felt as if he'd squandered another opportunity to bring her back into his arms again. In persuading Zack to hire her, he'd managed to draw her into his life once more, but she maintained strict distance between. Now he couldn't let her leave without saying the one thing he should have said all those years ago.

He moved into her space, letting their bodies brush. "Don't walk away."

"There's no reason to stay," she replied. But her words sounded a little breathless. She wasn't struggling against him and she wasn't stepping back. Her cheeks had flushed, her eyes had darkened, the color turning deep.

"There is." They'd left so much unsaid, undone. It had taken him years, but he'd finally figured out that what he'd had with Gus was good. This might be all he was capable of having with a woman. Moments of pleasure. If he worked it right, they could have a private and a professional relationship, keep the entanglements and the fights to a minimum. "I'm so sorry for the way things ended. I'm sorry for making you feel less than extraordinary because you are, Augustine. You are an amazing woman and I've missed you. I've missed this. Tell me you don't feel the same and I'll let you go."

"I haven't missed you."

But that wasn't what he'd asked. He leaned in, his lips hovering oh so close to hers. "But did you miss the way you and I feel together? No other woman ever fit me the way you did. They felt awkward in my arms because you were the one I wanted there. I'm not asking if I was your best lover. I'm sure I wasn't. But don't tell me you fit together with anyone else the way you did with me. We were built for each other. I can't stay away from you. I don't want to hurt you again, but I can't be in a room with you and not want to touch you. Kiss you. Fuck you."

Her head tilted slightly and he felt her hands drift to his waist. Her lids fluttered shut. That was all the invitation he needed. He let his mouth find hers and the world seemed to explode.

CHAPTER FIVE

Gus melted as Roman's mouth found her own. It was wrong. She knew it even as she felt the electric heat burn through her system. She should tell him to fuck off. She should tell him that she wouldn't touch him with a ten-foot pole.

Her brain tried to convince her to refuse him. But it was no longer in control. Her body was, and it knew what it wanted.

Roman Calder.

His mouth covered hers, destroying her resistance and ramping up her need in a way no other man ever could. Or ever had. She wasn't a petite thing, but Roman made her feel that way. His big, muscular body blanketed hers, and she loved the way he crushed her to his chest, as though he was afraid to even let her breathe in case she slipped through his fingers. He made her feel feminine and soft against him.

"So long. Too damn long," he whispered against her mouth before running his tongue over her bottom lip, demanding she let him inside.

Gus did what came naturally with Roman. She softened and gave in. Instantly, he devoured her with his kiss again. She began to unravel.

The danger this man posed to her was real. When they were close, she couldn't think about anything except how it felt to be wrapped up in his embrace, how good it was to be the center of all that ruthless attention.

His arms banded more tightly around her. One hand gently grasped the back of her neck, guiding her to move with him as he plundered her mouth. His tongue dominated, the silky glide igniting sparks through her system.

His other hand slid to the curve of her ass and hauled her closer, pressing her against him. There. She felt his cock already stiff and ready and rubbing against her in need.

"Feel that? I hope you do because I haven't in months, baby. No women. No sex. Because all I can think about is you," he muttered thickly against her lips. "Even when I slept with other women in the past, it took forever to get me half as hot as you make me simply by walking in a room. I told myself I was getting older, that this jolt of pure lust was only the hormone high of youth. Then I caught sight of you again. And I knew I'd been lying to myself."

Months? He'd been celibate for months? She knew he'd dated because he and Zack had been out on the town with actresses and models galore. But he wanted her instead?

She sank into his kiss, his mouth enveloping hers

utterly. He had the most gorgeous lips for a man. Lush and sensual. There had been a time when her whole world had turned on whether those lips were smiling or scowling or flipped up in that half smirk that let her know he was thinking about sex. "Don't lie to me, Roman. I know who you've been dating."

He sank his fingers into her hair, twisting lightly until her scalp tingled. "I'm not lying to you. All of those women are for show. This…this is fucking real."

He slammed his mouth down on hers once more, tongue delving deep. Heat flashed through her.

Could he be telling the truth? Gus hated to admit that it had been a long time for her, too. Her sex drive had been healthy since adolescence, but after Mad died, grief had pressed down on her. Her world had felt shriveled and smaller than before. Coupled with Roman's daily presence in her life, she hadn't been able to think about climbing into bed with anyone.

She needed what Roman offered her now. She needed to feel like herself again. Maybe she hadn't felt like herself for years because only one man could truly make her feel this alive.

Gus clawed at his shirt, desperate to feel his hot, hair-roughened skin against hers. All thoughts of fighting him, of wondering whether this was right and if she'd regret it tomorrow, were gone. She surrendered.

Roman turned her, flipping her around so her back pressed against his chest. He'd done it easily, using those beefy arms of his to maneuver her. He held her close. The heat of his breath blew against her ear. "No. Not yet. I've been waiting forever and I want to fucking touch you. Savor you. I won't let you rush me."

"But I want to touch you, too." She had to admit this

was something about Roman that had always gotten her hot and bothered. He didn't play in the bedroom. He might compromise on pizza toppings or a movie selection, but when it came to sex he didn't budge. He simply took control.

"You'll touch me after I get what I want. I intend to relearn every inch of your body. I want to run my hands over every curve and valley. I want to use my fingers and my tongue." He licked around the shell of her ear, making her shiver. "And I want to kiss and taste every fucking inch of you."

This was what she'd been missing for thirteen damn years. Sex with other men had been nice. She'd enjoyed herself, but nothing had shaken the foundation of her soul. Nothing had come close to the times she'd let Roman deep into her body and heart.

It was hard to call what they'd done years ago mere sex because when Roman had maneuvered her beneath him and demanded she yield everything to him with a touch, the sensations had encompassed so much more than her body. Then—like now—she could feel how much he wanted her. As if no other woman in the world could satisfy him.

He caressed his way up her torso until he cupped her breasts. "God, I've missed these. You have the most gorgeous breasts. I dream about them at night."

She couldn't help but breathe with him, into him. Her hard nipples pressed against the silk of her dress. Even that almost created too much sensation, but the needy woman in her wished his hands covered her bare, aching tips instead. "Take my dress off."

His teeth scraped over her sensitive earlobe as he dragged the sleeves of her dress and bra down. As usual,

Roman did what he wanted, freeing only her breasts. The fabric also pinned her arms to her sides. Cool air hit her peaks, followed by pure heat as his greedy hands enveloped them, fingers working them. She shivered, writhed, caught up completely, unable to shove him away. She knew damn well he would respect any refusal she voiced.

But she had no intention of speaking one.

"Tell me you didn't miss this," he growled in her ear as he rolled her nipples between his thumbs and forefingers.

She couldn't help but rub her ass against him. His cock was right there, long and thick and hard as hell. Still, she couldn't make this easy for him. She didn't want to risk too much of her heart. "I didn't."

He pinched down, making her groan. "Bullshit. I can tell. What would happen if I pulled your skirt up and ran my hand up your thigh? If I found your pussy, would it be wet and ready for me? That was one of the things that always drove me crazy, Gus. You responded so readily to me. All I had to do was touch you and you went wild."

She felt wild. For the first time in years, pure lust thrummed through her blood. This wasn't some itch any man could scratch. Only Roman could make her this hungry, then slake her need to sighing satisfaction. Only Roman and his rough, dirty mouth could take her to these heights.

"Maybe I go wild for everyone." She couldn't give in without a fight. She couldn't give him everything. She couldn't let him know how terribly he was unraveling her with every touch. She especially couldn't admit after all these years that she still dreamed of him, too. She was constantly haunted by what they could have had, by what she'd lost that terrible day.

She stiffened. Damn it. She wasn't going there. She couldn't.

"No, you don't." His voice was softer now and she felt his mouth on the curve of her throat. "Maybe I'm fooling myself, but in my mind I will always be the man for you. I'm convinced you're like me, desperate to feel young and wild, the way I did when the world was still wide open to me. That's what I feel when I think of you."

Youthful and carefree and brimming with possibilities. That's what he sought. No wonder they'd been doomed. All she'd wanted during her year with Roman was him. "Don't talk or I'll walk away. I want this. Hell, I might even need this, but I can't play these games with you again."

He growled in her ear and she found herself being hauled into his arms, against his chest. As if she weighed nothing. As if she was some tiny waif he could play with at will.

He crossed the room to the couch that had played host to several presidents and world leaders over the years. Roman dropped her on the antique and moved between her legs, like a general consolidating a victory.

With his hands on her knees, he slowly pushed her thighs apart, watching as her skirt slid up. "It's not a game. No games this time."

But everything was a game with Roman. Even when he didn't know he was playing, there were always possibilities to dissect, moves to be considered and made. Even knowing that, she couldn't turn him away, not when he was so close. Not when the last few months had been so devoid of joy or pleasure. She'd lost Mad, and now she had so many questions about Zack. She would have to interrogate him, subtly of course.

At some point, she'd have to interrogate Roman about his best friend, too. But not tonight. Now she wanted to believe that it was all a hideous mistake and Roman was exactly the noble—if complicated—man she'd always believed him to be. That he was strong and ruthless but damn loyal. The kind of man who would never hurt his country…or one of his childhood friends.

"I told you I don't want to talk." Otherwise, she couldn't pretend. If they kept talking, she would have to remember why she was in London. And she would have to walk away from this brief moment of heaven.

"Then I'll have to do something else to keep my mouth occupied, won't I?" As he gave her a crooked smile, his hands slid farther up her thighs, making her shiver.

"Yes," she breathed.

He stared at her breasts. His jawline tightened and his eyes went pitch black with desire. Gus could feel her heart thudding against her chest. Every inch of her skin had come alive as he moved with slow, purposeful grace.

She couldn't look away, could barely breathe. She was half naked in front of the only man she'd ever loved and he was so, so close to touching her where she needed him most.

"You'll have to tell me what to do, Augustine. If you don't want me to talk, how can I possibly occupy my mouth?"

She hated her full name. It made her sound like some fainting Victorian heroine. And yet when Roman caressed the syllables with his deep-as-sin voice, she loved it. He made her name sound like sex and need and pure woman.

"You know what I want." She wanted his mouth on her needy flesh, licking her, sucking her. Making her forget about everything except this man and the pleasure they could share.

"I can do that." He leaned over and kissed her knee with a soft brush of his lips. "Here?"

Bastard. "No."

"So you're going to be picky, are you? I should have known. I can think of a place to put my mouth." He leaned closer, bracing his hands on either side of her and lifting more of his body over her own.

Then he sucked her nipple into his mouth, and Gus nearly screamed. His tongue rolled around her sensitive peak as he pressed her against the sofa cushions. The hard edge of his teeth nipped her. She gasped, her body flashing hot in an instant. God, she was getting ripe and wet, as though there was a direct line from her nipple straight to her pussy. Each suck and lick and swipe of his tongue made her swell with need.

"This is a good occupation for my mouth." He kissed his way to her other breast, giving it the same lavish attention. "I'm sure we can find something to do with my hands, too. Tell me where I should touch you, Augustine."

She lifted her hips to him, moaning as she searched for the relief only he could provide. "Touch my pussy, Roman. Suck my nipples while you fuck me with your fingers."

"God, you have the filthiest mouth." For a moment, he tilted up so he could cover her lips with his. His kiss told her that he loved everything about her mouth, including how dirty it could be.

He caressed her with his tongue. She parried back,

drowning in the sensation while he shifted to one side and slid his hand between her legs. Gently, he bit her bottom lip, sucking it behind his teeth as his fingers eased under the edge of her barely there thong.

Gus couldn't move. Roman pinned her legs open with his big body. He'd trapped her arms with the sleeves of her dress. He'd tied her up as neatly as if he'd had a rope. "I want to touch you."

"You are," he whispered. "Your lips are touching mine. Give me your tongue again."

She opened her mouth and drank him in. It wasn't enough. "I want to touch you with my hands. I want to touch you the way you're touching me."

He slipped the pad of one finger over her clit. "Later. If you touch me now, I might come in your hand, and that's not how I see this evening ending. Tell me you don't want this."

He rubbed her, his fingers moving easily over her sensitive button because she was wetter than she'd been in forever. He sank one finger inside her, teasing her inner walls while his thumb on her clit did terrible, destructive things to her self-control.

"You know I do." She couldn't lie about that. Later, she could make up some excuse about not having sex in forever, but right now she couldn't turn him away. "Are you going to give it to me, Roman?"

She didn't merely want it. She *needed* it, had to have it. If he pulled away now, she would freaking scream in frustration. She might lose her mind.

"Fuck, yes. I'm going to give it to you. Then you're going to give me something." He kissed her again, their mouths merging in a hot dance.

With perfect precision, he shifted his hand. He added

another finger, fucking deep inside her and hooking up to find her sweet spot. He pressed down on her clitoris. Sensations clawed. Gus couldn't catch her breath. God, she'd been waiting for this—for him—for half a lifetime. And when he rubbed her insistently, silently demanding she surrender her pleasure to him, she could do nothing but close her eyes, give in to him, and hurtle over the sharp, sweet edge.

Gus let the orgasm crash through her system. Her body pulsed. She bit her lip to keep from crying out as the release overtook her, wracking her, undoing her.

This was what she needed. Not simply the sex, but the overwhelming dominance Roman brought to the bedroom. She didn't have to think, just follow his lead. No one else in the world gave her that. In everyone else's bed, she'd always been the leader. In their work lives, Gus would never even think about giving in to Roman, but in his arms? Here she could just let go and take the pleasure he gave her. All she had to do in return was give him everything he wanted.

She was beyond ready.

"Fuck, Augustine. Oh, you feel so good. You're so damn hot. Gorgeous. Look at you," he whispered. "Give me more. Give me what I want. Scream for me all night."

She was too far gone to reply, much less argue. She wasn't going to send him to bed alone, not when she could be with him. His fingers had provided relief, but she knew that climax would be nothing compared to the heights his glorious cock could take her. She ached to spend the rest of the night underneath him, his body working over hers, connecting them in a way they hadn't been for too many years. "I will, Roman. You know I can."

"Good," he said slowly, his hand still gently working over all her tingling spots, creating pleasurable aftershocks. "Don't talk to that Secret Service agent again. Tell me you'll stay away from him entirely and you'll keep Liz out of trouble."

His soft words washed over her like a bucket of freezing water. She turned them over again in her head. Had he just used her desire against her to get something he wanted out of bed? "What?"

He nuzzled her neck, his tone still low and seductive. "That's all I want. You and Liz safe and out of trouble. You don't need to hang out with Kemp. Keep your distance from him and I'll take care of you whenever you need something."

When she needed sex.

Damn it. She'd been naive to assume that Roman could—or would—put aside his scheming simply to be with her. Bitterness welled. She knew the sort of man he was, but the minute he'd touched her, her brain had flown out the door. She'd let herself become his pawn.

Stupid.

"Get off me." What had felt like a decadent, wonderful miracle moments ago had become a chilling reminder of all the ways Roman could exploit her—if she let him. She struggled to wriggle her arms free from her sleeves so she could push the bastard away.

Roman's head lifted, his stare zeroing in on her. "Come on, Augustine. I'm not asking for much. Stay away from that asshole and watch over Liz. How does that make me the bad guy?"

She struggled harder. She heard the dress tear, but it didn't matter. At least she now could put her hands on his shoulders and force some distance between them. "I forgot that everything is transactional with you, Mr. Calder. I thought our exchange here was mere pleasure, but you're far too cold for that, aren't you?"

His jaw formed a stubborn line, his eyes hardening. "You think I'm not hot right now? What the hell do you call this?"

He ground his hips against her thigh, letting her feel just how hard his cock was.

Two minutes before that was all she'd wanted from him. She'd wanted to end the evening with him buried deep inside her, but now she realized his entire come-on had been bullshit. He wanted to give her just enough to persuade her away from another man. The old I-don't-want-you-but-no-one-else-can-have-you crap. And why? Because he needed to be in control? Or something deeper?

Tears threatened. She felt exposed, raw. Everyone believed she was a strong, independent woman. And she was...but not when it came to Roman Calder. He made her feel young and dumb and heedless again, so hopeful that if she gave him enough of herself, he would love her back.

Ridiculous.

"I call that something you likely get when there's a stiff breeze in the room. Get off me." She gave him another shove.

His expression changed as though he'd realized her rebuff wasn't some coy ploy to heighten his anticipation and amp up the sex. "What are you talking about? I told you how it's been for me. Augustine, why are you so angry?"

He knew the answer. "I'm going to scream if you don't get off me right this second. Don't think I won't.

We all know how much you don't want to get caught fucking the office slut, so you should move quickly or this scandal will go front page."

He practically leapt off her. "I never said that. Never fucking once, and I have a real problem with you calling yourself that. Did someone else say it? Because I'll take off his fucking head."

Gus had to hand it to Roman. He was so damn good she almost believed his indignant reply. Maybe he'd missed his calling and should have been an actor, instead of the White House chief of staff.

She rose quickly, shoving her skirt down and pulling the bodice of her dress up until she was covered. Yet somehow, standing in front of Roman, she still felt undressed. "You've got better things to do with your time than try to defend my honor, especially when you've always thought mine was questionable."

He shoved a hand through his hair, pacing like a caged lion. "What's wrong? Come on. Tonight does not have to end like this. It shouldn't."

"You ended this the minute you thought you could exchange sex for a 'favor.' Maybe you've decided sex is a good way to control me, but you're wrong. I won't let you, Roman. No matter how good you feel. I learned my lesson with you a long time ago. All I could ever get out of you is a good time in bed. You're not built for anything else. And now the price is too high."

"Is it so hard for you to understand that I would be jealous about you with another guy? Do you have to have us all on your string? How many men do you need at once? That was all I was asking for. As long as you're in my bed, you're only with me."

"And I suppose you'll be breaking off your date with

Darcy tomorrow night?"

"That's not the same."

She laughed. "Of course. When you see someone else, it's all for your job. When I do, it's cheating. Your moral relativism is showing, Roman." She'd worked with him for a few years now, and only when she'd shown interest in Matthew Kemp had he decided to crawl back between her legs. If she didn't know Roman and Zack and the rest of the Perfect Gentlemen were keeping secrets, she might have been fooled. But she did. He was trying to keep her from investigating whatever the hell was going on.

What did Roman know about Mad's death? She didn't want to believe for an instant that he could have something to do with it, but why else would he insist that she leave another man alone? He might claim jealousy, but it seemed thin and convenient. He only seemed to care who she might be fucking when she showed interest in the very man who'd been at the airport the day of Mad's death. Gus doubted that was a coincidence.

He took a deep breath and anchored himself in front of her, then reached out as though he meant to take her by the shoulders. When she jerked away from him, he stepped back. "Damn it, Gus. Is that what you want? I'll call Darcy, end the whole thing. Hell, Zack basically told me to do it."

She gave him what she hoped was a chilly smile. "I wouldn't dream of interfering in your social life, Roman. After all, you have a job to do."

And so did she. It was time she remembered that. The evening had gotten her closer to Matthew Kemp. They'd had a couple of drinks, shared some flirtation. Tomorrow, she would find a way into his room. Then she would damn sure discover whatever he might know about the reason Mad was killed. No forbidden, middle-of-the-night thrill with the best lover she'd ever had was going to derail her from solving Mad's murder.

Because a thrill was all Roman would ever give her. He would take her so high she'd swear she was floating on clouds and singing with the angels. But the minute the sex ended, he'd let her crash back to earth and she would end up in the dirt, feeling battered and bruised and forgotten.

"Please. I don't want to fight. I should have chosen my words more carefully," Roman began. "Sit with me. Let's talk. Nothing but talk, I swear. I'll keep my hands to myself."

But now she knew his game. It would *not* work again. Talking would lead right back to his hands all over her and him trying to manipulate her to get what he wanted, which wasn't really sex. It was her willing silence.

"Goodnight, Roman. Have fun on your date." She grabbed her purse and turned to go.

He reached out, gripped her elbow, and for a second she was falling down those stairs again. Her knees knocked against the wood and jarred her entire body. Her world had gone off-kilter and tumbled. Ended.

She couldn't forget how she'd lost her baby.

Gus whirled around without thinking. One minute she was walking out the door and the next she was thrashing against Roman. Fighting. Hitting. "Don't touch me!"

He caught her in his arms. "Baby? Baby, what's wrong? You're crying. Oh, my god. Please tell me why you're crying."

"Let her go, Roman."

She went completely still at the sound of Connor's voice. What had happened? She didn't cry. She especially didn't let anyone see her tears. Yet she could feel them now running down her cheeks.

"Let her go." Connor stepped into the room.

Roman released her, dropping his arms to his sides with a curse. He'd gone stark white as he turned to answer Connor. "I wasn't trying to hurt her."

The former CIA operative's voice went low. "I'm sorry but I was walking back to my room and you two didn't close the door. I thought I should make sure no one walked in. Gus, let me walk you back to your room. Roman, go to bed. Don't make me assign someone to guard her door."

"What the hell do you think I would do to her?" Roman gaped, then turned her way. "Baby, I'm sorry. I screwed everything up. Please, just talk to me. Tell me what happened, because a moment ago you weren't here with me. You were somewhere else bad."

Yes, she'd gone back to that night. She'd thought she was over the hurt and pain of her loss, but tonight had proven that Roman could bring it all back. Without another word, she turned and walked out, trying to pull familiar numbness over her heart like a blanket. Hopefully by tomorrow she'd have her defenses shored up and emotions under control again.

She knew Connor was following her, but it didn't matter. She managed to nod his way when she made it to her room.

"Gus, whatever happened in there, he didn't mean to hurt you," Connor said.

Yes, she'd heard that over and over again. "He never

does, I'm sure."

Connor put a hand on the wall, as though he was too tired to entirely hold himself up. "Do you want me to beat him up for you?"

She rolled her eyes. "Sure. You do that."

"Gus, Dax isn't here. If he hurt you, I'll deal with him. He might be one of my best friends, but you are the closest thing I have to a sister. Don't think I'll let him take advantage of you."

Clearly, she hadn't managed numb yet, because all the feelings she tried to quiet screamed just under the surface, scraped her raw. Damn it, she was not going to cry again. "I'm fine, Connor."

"Do you want to talk? Because it really did look like you mentally disappeared somewhere else. Do you know what PTSD is?"

"Of course. I'm fine. It was a momentary thing. I honestly thought I was over the past. I guess Roman brings out the worst in me. Thank you for being there. I promise I'm going to stay away from him. You won't have to save me again."

"If you need me for anything, all you have to do is call." Connor reached up and wiped his thumb over her cheek, brushing away the tears she hadn't known were falling again. "I know you used to talk to Mad, but he's gone. So if you need someone, you can open up to me. I'll be on your side," he vowed. "Goodnight, Gus."

"I'm fine, but thanks. Goodnight."

She said the words, but when the door closed, she couldn't hold back another torrent of scalding tears a second longer.

CHAPTER SIX

The following evening, Gus felt stronger as she sat across from Liz in the office they'd taken over. It was in the east wing of the house, far from the temporary offices Zack and Roman worked from. Gus was certain Darcy Hildebrandt had something to do with that, but this evening she couldn't say she wasn't grateful.

She'd slept fitfully and managed to avoid the boys all day. She'd had one text from Roman asking if he could come down and talk to her. She'd replied that she needed some time and he'd relented.

Perhaps what she needed was more space. Lots of it. Maybe she should consider finding another job and moving on. But not until she'd accomplished her goal.

"Is there anything else I can get for you, Ms. Spencer?"

She looked up from her laptop. Vanessa Jones was one of the admins in the press office. She'd worked her way through the campaign's ranks and become a press office right hand. Liz relied on her implicitly, and when they traveled, she offered to assist Gus as well. Luckily for Vanessa, Gus preferred to do most of her own work.

And many of the items on her list for this trip were far too private to entrust to anyone else.

"I think I have everything, thank you." She looked up at the clock. It was far later than she'd suspected. The afternoon had flown by as she'd answered e-mail and approved press releases. Work was good for the soul. "Did everything go all right with the paparazzi?"

Vanessa frowned. "Do you mean did they get lots of pictures of the president and the stick he's dating? Yes."

"That stick is one of the world's most photographed models," Gus corrected with a grin. It was good to know Vanessa was sticking to the girls' side. "And she has to be that thin. The camera really does add a bunch of pounds. She's quite lovely in photos."

Vanessa wrinkled her nose. "She's like a scarecrow in person. Don't get me wrong. I like a slender girl when it's natural. I don't get the world today. I wear a size two and I get called fat. They can keep it coming. I'm not giving up pizza night."

Vanessa was a lovely young woman, vibrant and still full of hope. She made Gus feel old sometimes. "Don't you dare. You're gorgeous."

Vanessa smiled, showing perfect white teeth. "Thank you. I need that sometimes. None of the boys around here want to play with me. Or the girls. Makes me sad. You're all far too involved in each other. You know it's like watching a foreign-language soap opera. I get it...but I don't quite understand."

"What have you heard?" Gus knew that tone of

voice. Vanessa was fishing.

She leaned against the desk. "The rumor is the president told the Secret Service to stop you and Liz from leaving the grounds. Why would he do that?"

Because something was going on that she did not understand, and she had to guess it all came back to Mad. She'd been turning the situation over in her head all morning. It was far easier to think about the mystery of Mad's death than to remember the terrible drama of last night.

What if Mad had known something? Something bad. Something Zack had felt the need to cover up at all costs. Or what if Mad had gotten into the sort of trouble that had gotten him killed, and Zack was hell bent on protecting the rest of them? But then why the hell wouldn't he simply tell Liz that he was trying to save her from an eminent threat? She would comply with reasonable requests.

But Zack was a man. And men believed they were noble saviors. Really, they could be so stupid.

The possibilities kept chasing each other around in her head. The truth was, she would only solve this conundrum if she figured out what had happened to Mad.

"I'm not sure. I guess the president knows something we don't. He's still getting intelligence briefings," she replied. There was no reason to bring anyone but Liz in on her sleuthing. Except maybe Zack. Damn but she wanted to demand he answer her questions. Of course if she did and Zack *had* done something wrong, she could find herself in a concrete bunker ten feet underground in Gitmo. Going up against the most powerful man in the world had its risks.

"Still, it's odd since the president's schedule hasn't

changed at all. Just Liz's."

Oh, Gus was sure she would be stopped if she tried to leave, too. But tonight, that might be helpful…

"Anyway, here's the itinerary Liz asked for." Vanessa handed her a folder. "Did she meet a guy last night? I heard you two went out with some Secret Service hotties. Come on, Gus. Give a girl a heads-up when we're going to party."

Oh, but it hadn't been a party. It had been a very careful laying of groundwork to get close to someone she needed to steal from. She hadn't gotten hold of Matthew Kemp's phone and she wasn't certain that would even be possible at this point. He had probably been warned away from her. And he was a super-careful man.

Then again, a potential assassin would have to be.

"I promise the next time we're allowed off the leash, I'll send you an invite." The door eased open and Liz slipped in, wearing a black Chanel suit and sky-high Louboutins. "Speak of the devil. Vanessa says our fun evening out is already making the gossip rounds."

Luckily, the way the evening had ended wasn't. Gus likely had Connor Sparks to thank for that small blessing.

Liz gave Vanessa a smile that didn't reach her baby blues. "It was fun, but now we're in full lockdown mode. I'll be surprised if I leave this house until we go home, so everyone settle in for the week. I sent you both a briefing on what the president and prime minister are scheduled to discuss on Wednesday. I'm up to date on ninety percent of this stuff, but I need some information on the situation with Russia and the gas pipelines. Apparently we're talking to the PM about the possibility of designing a way to bring American natural gas to Europe and circumventing Russia. I know next to nothing about the topic. Please get me the details before the press starts asking questions."

"I'll talk to some friends in Energy. They can send you tons of super-boring reports." Vanessa breezed to the doorway. "I'm heading out. I've got tickets to a show in the West End. Maybe I can find a hot Brit to spend some time with. Bye, you two."

"Sounds like everyone's going to the theater." Liz glanced up at the television on the left wall. Twenty-four-hour cable news flashed on the screen, sound muted.

There was Zack, looking perfect in a tuxedo as he stepped out of a limo. He waved to the reporters as he took the hand of the stunningly gorgeous Mimi. Yes, she was thin, but there was no denying how beautiful she was. Roman walked behind Zack and Mimi, his hand on Darcy's back as he escorted her. Roman looked grim, but he nodded down at something she said.

Gus stared at the blonde, the woman he wasn't embarrassed to be seen with. The woman he likely wouldn't finger fuck on a couch in an attempt to control. No, Gus was sure the extraordinarily uptight Ms. Hildebrandt would be offered the comfort of a bed when Roman fucked her. It would be oh so polite. There would be no shouting or fighting, only gentle moaning—maybe. They would be considerate.

How was your orgasm, my dear?

Perfect, darling. Please pass the tea. I require refreshment after that strenuous episode of sexual congress.

"You have a super-evil look on your face. Are you thinking about murdering someone?" Liz asked the question with pure curiosity. "Because I want in. I've got some aggression to work through."

"No, I was thinking about how well Roman and Ms. Hildebrandt seem to get along." She slanted an acidic smile Liz's way. "And I'm wondering a tiny bit how hard it would be to replace the lube in his condoms with icy hot. I think I can make that work."

"Oh, I want in on that, too." Liz sank into the chair in front of Gus's desk and stared at Zack, who stood beside his date wearing a wide smile. "They look good together."

"Nope. She looks way too young for him." That was the truth. Mimi was nearly twenty years younger than Zack. She also had vacant eyes. "I read an article about her recently. The interviewer asked her what her favorite political cause was. She said Jackie O because she dressed so beautifully. Yep. That's your potential First Lady right there."

Liz groaned as she picked up the remote and clicked the monitor off. "I think I'll stay away from the news for a few hours. I got some of the information you requested. It looks like Matthew's next break is the day after tomorrow. He's requested permission to do some sightseeing. But I also did a little digging and discovered that he rented a car."

"Why rent a car in London?" It was one of the easiest cities in the world to get around. The London Tube was famously accessible to even newbie travelers.

"Maybe because he's leaving London for the day," Liz mused. "The question is, where is he going? You didn't come close to swiping his phone last night, did you?"

The whole evening had been frustrating. Worse, not accomplishing her goal had actually been the least irritating event of the night. "No, and I'm starting to wonder if I'll be able to dupe it at all. He never let it out of his sight and I'm not even going to pretend I'm skilled enough to lift it out of his pocket. I think I'd have better luck trying to follow him when he leaves London."

"If you're allowed to leave the house," Liz pointed out. "How do you feel about searching his room?"

"Like I might get murdered if he catches me." After all, if she was right, Matthew Kemp had already killed one of her closest friends. "But if I get the chance, I'll probably take it anyway. I can always come up with some excuse."

A brief rap sounded at the door seconds before it opened. As though she'd conjured him up, Matthew Kemp stood in the doorway, along with his equally well-built partner, Clint Gates. Both men had changed into street clothes, showing off their muscular bodies in jeans and T-shirts. Neither one held a candle to Roman, though they were younger and obviously hit the gym on a daily basis. Somehow Roman in a three-piece suit was the height of sexiness to her. She needed to retrain her libido to focus on younger men. Absolutely no one over thirty. Any lover she took from now on would also have to be easy on the eyes—and without a brain in his head.

Unlike Mr. Kemp. Nobody joined the Secret Service on looks alone.

"Hello, Special Agent. What can I do for you today?" *Besides steal your phone and illegally search your room and pray you don't find out?*

He sent her a truly sexy smile as he strode into the room. "You and the gorgeous Ms. Matthews can grace us with your presence tonight. We enjoyed talking to you two last night."

How could she say no when that might give her

another shot at his phone? "Well, we've been asked to stay in this evening."

Clint backed his partner up. "We know. We're supposed to keep a quiet watch on you, make sure you don't get into any trouble. It's like asking the fox to watch the henhouse, really. Look, ladies, we're not trying to get you into trouble. We simply want to spend a little more time with you." He looked Liz's way. "Unless I misunderstand, and whatever is between you and the president is serious. Then I'll back off."

She watched Liz shake off her sorrow as she stood with a smile. "There's nothing at all between me and the president except the fact that he's my boss. So if we can't leave, what do you two suggest?"

"Well, we brought in some dinner. A guy from the PM's detail gave us a tip about the best takeout in London. We've got it set up in the kitchen, so it's informal," Matthew explained. "We might have also gotten some beer and wine and requested to use the theater room. We scored an early copy of that new spy film all the girls are crazy about."

Liz squealed a little. "*Love After Death*? I read that book a hundred times. I'm so excited to see the movie. It's the new *Fifty Shades*. I think we can make this work, gentlemen." She sent Gus a wink. "There's a brief call with a small newspaper here in Ohio I need Gus to take in about an hour. But I'll make sure you guys aren't too bored while she's gone. Other than that, we're all yours."

Stroke of brilliance. Liz could keep the boys occupied while Gus wandered up and searched the room Matthew shared with Clint. It was the perfect cover. Liz was always on her phone. If something started going sideways, she would send Gus a 911, advising her to hightail it out of there.

"What do you think?" Liz was smiling her way but Gus saw the challenge in her eyes.

The woman knew exactly what she was doing and she was a perfect partner in crime. Gus gave Matthew the once-over. He was a gorgeous hunk. Too bad he might have killed her best friend. "I think that sounds lovely. When do you want to start?"

Matthew held a hand out to her. "No time like the present."

She gave him a wide, totally fake smile and let him lead her out of the office, more than ready to start her real work.

* * * *

An hour later, Gus stood up and stretched. "Time for my press call. Don't pause the movie. I'll be back as soon as I can."

Matthew looked up at her, his eyes gleaming in the darkness. "Are you sure? I don't mind waiting."

She shook her head. "I've actually already seen it. I was invited to the premiere. It's so good. There's a scene in the elevator coming up that's hysterical. Be back soon."

Liz looked over from the screen and winked. She had her phone by her side.

They'd come up with a protocol. If Matthew left the room, Liz would text a single emoji to let Gus know he was on the loose. Gus would then hightail it out of his room and run as fast as she could back to the theater. It would be okay. She wouldn't get caught and she would have at least a few solid minutes alone in his room.

It wasn't as good as downloading his phone, but she had to try something. She needed information, and beggars couldn't be choosers.

Gus picked up the pace the minute she left the theater room, finding the stairs and rushing down one flight, followed by another until she reached the basement where the servants' quarters were. Lara had been quite vocal when she'd discovered there was a whole floor nowhere near as lovely as the rest of the manor merely housing the help. Luckily, everyone was out on the town this evening, so the actual servants had the night off. The remaining people—the security staff—were concentrated outside the building.

Gus knew this was her one shot. She wouldn't get another.

The floor beneath her squeaked. Wincing, she paused, hearing the house moan again. Was that sound a door opening?

She shook off the worry. Time was limited, so she forced herself forward once more. If she got caught, she had an easy lie on the tip of her tongue: she'd gotten lost after receiving a text from one of her staffers who needed to find a working printer. Since the one in the office wasn't functioning, she'd had to go looking for another. Actually, that wasn't a total prevarication. The printer in the office truly wasn't working. She'd loosened a cord personally before they'd gone to the kitchen for dinner. If she got caught, she would bat her eyes at Matthew or Clint and ask them to fix the infernal machine for her. When they discovered the dangling cord, she would laugh at herself and pretend embarrassment with her abysmal technological shortcomings. They would believe it because they were men and she had boobs.

The ploy would work.

Her heart fluttered with every creep forward. She would have been an awful spy.

As quietly as she could, she turned the handle on the door to the room Matthew shared with Clint and entered, thanking whatever higher power deserved credit for the miracle of having a door without a lock. She waited until she quietly eased the door closed to turn on the light.

The room was Spartan. Nothing but two twin beds, matching nightstands, a dresser, and a mirror.

There was a small notebook and pen on the nightstand. She picked it up, flipping through it, but all it seemed to have was a list of names. Darcy Hildebrandt was the first name on the list, along with a few others. She pulled out her phone. It was likely nothing more than a list of people who would be in and out of the house while the president was in town, but Gus didn't recognize some of the names. She took a picture of the list and thumbed through the rest of the notebook.

The agent liked to doodle and he was fairly good at it. There was a sketch of Marine One, the helicopter that took the president to the airport. She flipped another page. The president was frowning, his brows furrowed, and a caption under him. *No white socks with your suit, Matthew. Are we barbarians?*

She smothered a giggle.

There was a sketch of herself and Liz in the White House pressroom. Instead of their normal designer business suits, he'd drawn them as superheroes, with skimpy costumes and knee-high boots. It might have been insulting if not for the caption. *Badass Bitches are the Best.*

Men. Even when they were complimenting a girl,

they were looking at her boobs. With a little smile, she flipped the page.

When she caught sight of the next image, her entire body went cold.

Maddox Crawford. He was wearing jeans and a collared shirt, and he was standing by his airplane, giving the artist the thumbs-up sign.

How long had Matthew stood there? Had he watched Mad go through his preflight check to make sure the bomb he'd placed on the plane hadn't been discovered? Had he hidden in the shadows and drawn the man he was about to murder?

She closed the notebook and noticed a small pad of sticky notes by the phone. There were indentations, as though someone had written a note, the pressure of the pen leaving the details on the page beneath. She pulled off the top three and shoved them in her pocket.

Where was his luggage? She opened the closet door, ready to go through anything she could find.

How much time had passed? Four, maybe five minutes?

The closet was divided into two sections, but oddly looked exactly the same. Four black suits and white dress shirts hung on either side. There were loafers below, again the same, though one set was slightly larger than the other. The standard Secret Service uniform.

There was a duffel bag to her right that she thought she recognized as Matthew's. She dropped to her knees, ready to rifle through it. Behind her, the bedroom door opened.

Gus went stock-still and prayed she wasn't discovered by someone who had no qualms about murder.

CHAPTER SEVEN

"I had the loveliest evening," Darcy said, leaning into Roman as the limo pulled into the drive. "Are you sure it has to end?" Her voice dropped to a whisper. "Just because the president and Mimi lacked chemistry doesn't mean our evening has to be over."

Zack snorted slightly, letting Roman know he'd heard Darcy's murmured come-on.

Roman doubted Zack had spoken more than three sentences to his date all night long. They'd already left Mimi at her townhouse earlier, after Zack sent her off with a very dispassionate good-bye. The woman had been stunningly beautiful, but his friend hadn't noticed one whit. He'd spent the entire evening on his phone, texting back and forth with Thomas, the head of his detail, who was in touch with the agents left behind. He'd gotten real-time, moment-to-moment details of what Liz and Gus were doing with their evening. Once

Zack had learned their women were having an intimate meal in the kitchen with the same agents they'd spent the previous evening with, he'd decided to cut the evening with his supermodel short. Roman seconded the decision. Kemp and Gates were hunky…and younger. They hadn't tried to control the women's comings and goings without any real explanation why. Gus and Liz didn't think those guys were assholes.

In fact, right this minute Gus was probably cozied up with Matthew Kemp, whom she'd likely never fought with—or stared at with that expression of horrified heartbreak twisting her face.

Roman didn't know why she'd looked at him that way last night, but it had felt like a punch to the gut. Gus had been out of her head when she'd turned on him. He'd seen her eyes. Fear, followed by utter despair, had lurked there.

What had been racing through her mind? Mere moments earlier she'd told him she didn't blame him for her fall that fateful, long-ago night, but something had happened. Roman knew it. But he had no idea what Gus had endured in the years they'd been apart.

In the years since he'd abandoned her.

He'd bet Mad had known. It boiled Roman's blood as much as it hurt. Worse, he had no one to blame but himself.

"Roman?" Darcy prompted.

"The president and I need to confer about tomorrow's conversation with the prime minister," he said finally.

They didn't. They were as prepped for this meeting as they could possibly be. Reaffirmation of NATO ties. Check. Delicate conversation about a new trade deal after

Brexit. Check. Pushing a pipeline that could make America a mega shit ton of cash and stick it to Russia? Check and high-five. But he would do or say almost anything to wrap up this date now.

Because while Darcy Hildebrandt was sweet and polite in most everyone's view, with him she'd shown that she possessed at least ten hands, all of which she liked to put in places that violated his modesty. She'd been surprisingly aggressive, and he'd tried a hundred subtle ways to suggest she back off. She wasn't getting the clue, and he wasn't sure how else to handle her. He'd never bothered to develop more than a trick or two to ward off overeager women.

But Roman also knew he had to be diplomatic. Darcy worked for the prime minister. Zack needed these talks to go well. They encompassed some of his most important negotiations, but Roman wasn't willing to sleep with Darcy to ensure their success.

Funny, his younger self would have looked at the woman's graceful curves and pert breasts and said *what the hell*. Today, he only wanted to be intimate with Gus.

For a while, it seemed she'd wanted sex with him, too. If he thought it would work, he'd sic Gus on Darcy. Except Gus would flip him off and tell him she couldn't care less if he was molested by a five-foot-nothing attaché to the British prime minister. But after the way things ended between them last night, she would likely hand him over to Darcy on a silver platter and turn her attention to fucking Matthew Kemp again.

Darcy slid one of her many hands up his arm. "I could help you with that. I know the agenda backward and forward."

The waiting Secret Service agent stepped toward the

car door to open it. Roman needed to make sure Darcy the ambidextrous didn't follow him. "The president and I should talk about the meeting in private."

"But I really could help you." Darcy leaned into him, plastering herself against his side. "With the prep, I mean. I'd be happy to assist if that sets your mind at ease—or help with anything else if it relaxes you enough to rest. Even if it takes all night."

"Do you think it's proper for an attaché to the prime minister of England to advise the president of the United States on how to handle your own leader?" Zack challenged. "Because I think your boss will question your loyalty if you cross that line."

Darcy's eyes went wide, like a frightened deer in some big-ass headlights. "Oh, no. Sir, I was only offering to have a little…fun."

Zack didn't let up one second. "This isn't a party, Ms. Hildebrandt. This is a serious negotiation so our countries can work effectively together. If the press found out you spent the night with my right-hand man, they would likely question where Roman's loyalties lie as well, not to mention precisely which of his heads is doing the thinking. Their conclusion would probably be that he doesn't care about serving the best interests of the American people. That opinion could extend to me, since they would also speculate very publicly that I don't have control of my staff. Those optics are unacceptable. I need the press to see you heading home while Roman and I return together so there's no question about anyone's allegiance."

She hung onto his arm and sniffed. "With all due respect, I'm not hurting my country by establishing a friendly relationship with your chief of staff."

Roman tried hard not to roll his eyes. The woman clearly had more than a handshake in mind. And after being chastised by the president of the United States, he couldn't believe that she seemed completely unfazed.

He'd been wrong about Darcy. A complete idiot, in fact. She wasn't sweet and polite. Whether she was genuinely hot for him or merely looking to climb the political ladder, she was up to something. "I appreciate that, but Zack and I really do need to have a private conversation. Our countries are friendly, but we all need to make sure there's no appearance of collusion."

She pouted, her lower lip sticking out slightly. "Fine. I'll see you tomorrow. Perhaps we can have lunch."

"I'll check my schedule. I'm extremely busy for the next few days, but I'm sure I'll see you at Number Ten," Roman hedged, willing to say pretty much anything to put distance between himself and her at this point.

So he could find out what Gus was doing and wrest her from Kemp's company.

The door opened to the sight of a man in a black suit. "Mr. President, welcome back."

Zack nodded his way. "You ready?"

More than. "Yes, we should handle that issue we didn't have the opportunity to finish discussing earlier."

"You're right," Zack agreed, knowing no such issue existed. He turned to Darcy. "Good evening. I'll see you tomorrow."

The second the president left the car, Roman turned to Darcy. "Thanks for being a lovely escort. It was enjoyable."

That was a goddamn lie, but he managed a semblance of a smile her way just before he unfolded himself from the car.

Darcy reached for him, but Roman was faster, intent on escaping little Miss Tentacles. He had no hesitation about where he was going next. Straight to wherever Augustine was. Maybe he could talk to her, get her to tell him what she'd been thinking or going through the night before.

As the fresh evening air hit him, Roman was gratified to hear the car door shut in Darcy's face. Then finally, he was breathing for the first time in hours.

Zack moved in beside him. "So you get it now, huh? That woman is after you, and she's only going to get more insistent until you explain to her that it isn't happening. You have to be firm."

He put out a hand, holding off the lecture. "I get it. I'll deal with her tomorrow. Let's go and figure out what Liz is doing. You've been worried about her all night. We won't be able to have a reasonable conversation until you're assured."

Zack stopped, his brow raising. "Are you fucking kidding me?"

Obviously, Roman wasn't fooling anyone. There was nothing like the person who knew you best calling you out on your shit. "Fine. Let's figure out what Gus is doing."

"That I can do. And if we figure out what Elizabeth is doing as well, then that's what happens." Zack started for the door.

This would hardly be the first time he gave Zack's attachment to his press secretary plausible deniability.

Roman followed as the car took off, shuttling Darcy back to her apartment. "So they're having dinner with Kemp and Gates? Maybe they were merely all in the kitchen at the same time."

He had no doubt Gus was with Liz. If Liz was stuck and miserable, then Gus would be right beside her, plotting workarounds and revenge.

"Sure they did. It was all coincidence," Zack complained. "Now they've moved to the theater room. Apparently one of my Secret Service guys got an early Blu-ray of that thing all the girls want to watch. Do you think that was coincidental, too?"

So Gus was sitting in a cozy, dark room with the man of her choice, watching a film that had been dubbed by some critics as a bare step above porn. His first instinct was to stride right in that room and drag her the hell out.

But under what pretext? She'd followed his rules. She was safe and sound right where he'd left her, while he'd done exactly what she'd accused him of doing the night before: dating someone else. Of course, he hadn't considered it a date, but after careful reflection and numerous attempts at evading Darcy's grabby hands, he realized Gus had a point.

Did he have any right to barge in and interrupt her? That was his instinct, urged on by his hunger to possess her. Roman wanted her away from Kemp right now so he could set firm boundaries...and have her all to himself. But what would that accomplish except pissing her off, especially since he couldn't offer her anything more than his devotion in bed? Even that was dangerous until he, Zack, and the others figured out what complicated web of international espionage they were embroiled in.

And if they did put an end to the suspense and murder? What could he offer Gus then, besides great sex when she wanted some? He couldn't see them working long term. What had changed? Sure, they were older. But wiser? He wasn't convinced. They were still incendiary, still prone to argue as much as fuck.

He didn't know if he could live like that.

"What's going on in that brain of yours, Roman?" Zack tugged at his bowtie as they were ushered into the house.

He knew what should be going on—the negotiations that would begin tomorrow. He should be plotting and maneuvering, doing his utmost to make the absolute best deal possible. He needed to go over the plans for a transatlantic pipeline that could mean billions for the US and be a nice chunk of Zack's enduring legacy.

Instead he was thinking about a woman.

"Maybe we should leave Liz and Gus in peace." Roman wasn't sure he could handle it if she looked at him again like he was a monster.

Yeah, and maybe you're being a coward.

Zack glanced at the stairs that led to the recreation rooms, and his jaw firmed. "I think I would like to see that film."

"The only thing you're going to accomplish is to rile her more. Unless you're willing to truly talk to her, tell her what's going on, you should leave her alone."

Zack turned, his eyes heated. "What are you trying to say? You think I should walk away and let her revenge fuck a glorified security guard assigned to *my* detail?"

"He's hardly a security guard who'd be working the local mall. He's a Secret Service agent, and I seriously doubt it would be a revenge fuck. That's not Liz's style." But he might not say the same thing of Gus. She was more than capable of extracting her pound of flesh, and if she found the experience pleasurable, so much the better.

He and Gus were so very alike.

"I don't give a damn. I won't have it. She needs to trust me." Eschewing all further conversation, he started up the stairs.

Roman hesitated. What should he do? Would Gus be any less annoyed with him if he gave her space tonight? Or would he simply be crushed if he woke to discover that she hadn't slept alone the night before?

He stood there, feeling paralyzed. Finally, he realized that he had no idea how to handle Gus. He never had. Was it even possible to handle her? How wise was it to try? How stupid was it not to?

Maybe the better question was, did he intend to simply stand by and watch her play around with some younger guy?

Hell, no. But even if he and Gus really tried to make a go of it, even if they could make it work, how did he commit? Roman wasn't sure what he would be doing in a few years. Sure, he would throw himself into Zack's reelection campaign, followed hopefully by a second term...and then what? After Zack left office, Roman would be closing in on fifty with no job. Sure, he'd have achieved all his goals, but he had no idea where life would take him next. Or where he'd want to go.

On the other hand, did he want to be that sad fuck who had sacrificed any shred of a personal life to make his professional dreams a reality? The older he got, the more he thought about family, about a wife and kids, about a future that wasn't purely political. He'd always thought of those guys as dumb fuckers with kids hanging all over them. Now... Connor and Lara were actively trying to get pregnant, and he suspected Gabe and Everly wouldn't be far behind. Dax was already talking about having a family with Holland. Hell, even though Mad wasn't with them anymore, he'd have a kid running around in the world soon.

Did he really want to spend his entire life clawing his way through politics, assuring Zack's presidential legacy while leaving nothing personal as his own?

The question slammed him between the eyes.

Roman frowned. His child didn't have to grow up the way he did. He could choose a different path, right? He didn't have to send his kid away to some boarding school. He could settle down close to his friends and they could be his family of choice. Yeah, that sounded great...but he couldn't see himself having a family with anyone except the only woman he actually wanted. The one who drove him crazy.

Speaking of Gus, he spotted her sneaking down the stairs. She must have missed Zack as he'd headed up. He almost called out to her, but she stopped to give a worried glance over her shoulder. Even more curiously, she flattened her body against the wall next.

As though trying not to be seen. As though she was up to something.

Roman sidestepped to his left, ducking behind one of the graceful columns that dotted the mansion. She couldn't see him from this vantage point, but he could watch her through the large mirror on his right.

Maybe she was sneaking back to her room because she was sick of spending all her time with an overly muscled himbo who couldn't form more than a few sentences without interjecting the word "bro." If so, he might follow her, see if he could persuade her to talk to him. Not in possessive anger, but to apologize for the night before.

He waited, expecting her to turn down the second

floor corridor that led to the wing she shared with Liz, Gabe and Everly, as well as Connor and Lara.

Instead, she looked around carefully before heading down. On light feet, he followed just enough to see her turn again to creep down to the lower level.

Where Matthew Kemp's room was located.

Fuck. All thoughts of not being a possessive caveman evaporated. What the hell did she think she was doing? He'd turned down a very willing, decent-looking woman earlier because it was the professional thing to do. Also because he wasn't that into Darcy, and he'd been scared at the thought of how many arms she might have hidden under her clothes. But he was going with the professional argument. He was both good at his job and a patriot, too, damn it.

Roman waited a moment and followed her down, sticking to the side of the staircase where the likelihood of his footsteps causing a telltale creaking was the least. He turned down the hall in time to see her slip into one of the small rooms the agents shared and quietly shut the door behind her. He didn't remember offhand, but he'd bet that one belonged to Matthew Kemp.

Frozen, he stared at the solid wooden surface. What would happen if he opened it, just barged in and stared? Would he see her in that asshole's arms, offering up her gorgeous body to a guy who couldn't possibly appreciate it because he was far too uncomplicated to understand her? Roman had a vision of the jerk kissing her, running his hands all over her bare curves.

Logic and reason flew straight out the window. Rage took over.

He yanked the knob and flung the door wide open, sending it crashing against the wall.

"Augustine!"

He heard her gasp from another part of the room. Not the bathroom, since that was down the hall. No, she was in the closet.

Roman scowled. What the hell was she doing there? A million and one kinky scenarios ran through his head. He wanted to take Kemp apart in numerous and violent ways. He wouldn't even have to do it himself. His connections were far better than that fucker's. He could have the agent labeled a traitor and renditioned someplace nasty where he would be tortured by artisans who excelled at their craft. Only the best for Gus's boy toy. The best waterboarding. The best beatings. The best of everything for his ass.

But in that moment, Roman was looking forward to personally getting his hands on Kemp and making him pay.

He marched to the closet and wrenched the door open to find Gus staring down at her phone. Her face was pale, her eyes a bit wild. He could only guess that her fling of the moment was in the dark corner, waiting for her.

In some ways, that made him even angrier.

"What the hell do you think you're doing?" Roman damn well knew the answer, but he was going to make her admit out loud that she was seducing Kemp in order to shove a knife in his own back.

And what would he say if she told him she was screwing Kemp because he had a really big dick and was good in bed?

"We need to get out of here." She shouldered past him, grabbed his arm, and gave him a frantic tug toward the door.

Because Kemp was still in the closest? Roman refused to go anywhere until he said a few words to the asshole. "You're" and "fired" came to mind. He wouldn't give a damn about the inevitable lawsuit. He could handle that. He'd gone to Yale Law School, after all. He could certainly fire one dipshit who behaved unprofessionally on a critical visit abroad.

"Kemp, get your ass out here," he growled.

Gus tugged at him again, putting her whole body into it and clutching her cell with her free hand. "We have to go now!"

Oh, hell no. He wasn't leaving without letting this prick know the score.

Damn, Roman hated to go into a fight unprepared. What did he know about the guy so he could use the information against him? Sure Kemp had clearance to protect the president, but what if he was part of the deep state? Or a traitor working with a foreign government to bring his own down? Maybe this guy was getting close to Gus because she was Dax's sister? Yes. That was the way to spin this. Gus was too important to the president to allow her to fall under the influence of someone they couldn't trust.

For a moment, Roman feared he wasn't making sense…but that moment was fleeting. His brain wasn't in charge. Nope, his cock was.

And his cock was pissed.

He pulled away from Gus and thrust his head into the closet, peering into the shadows. "Do you even understand how unprof—"

But no one was inside. Certainly he didn't see anyone panting and half dressed with his junk hanging out. He only saw a row of neatly hung suits and loafers.

Suddenly, Gus shoved him into the closet. He gaped at her as she killed the dim light inside and shut the door with a barely audible click. The only illumination was the screen of her phone. He could see her face in the ghostly light.

"Get in the corner and be quiet," she whispered. "Please, Roman. Please. He's coming and he can't find us here."

Kemp? Didn't she want him here with her? Undressing her? Pleasuring her? Roman would have thought so…but the quiver in Gus's voice said no. If not, what was she doing here? He had a million questions, but then he heard the bedroom door open. Gus shut off her phone, wrapping them in darkness.

She backed up against him, and he could feel her shiver. He edged to the other side of the closet, finding a little extra space so he could pull her deeper into shadow. Obviously, she wasn't pulling some prank. Had she been scheduled to meet Kemp here? Roman wondered if his sudden appearance had thrown her plans for seduction for a loop.

Maybe she didn't want her lover to see her with him. On second thought, no. Gus would simply tell Roman— or anyone who butted in—that she and her guy were going to have hot sexy time and they should get lost pronto. But Gus would never willingly hide her desire.

Gus was hiding now. She was scared.

He wrapped his arms around her and whispered, "Get behind me."

She shrank back against him, rolling her head onto his chest. "Stay quiet."

"Hey, I've got a minute. I thought I'd touch base." Matthew's voice was clear and strong on the other side of the closet door.

She stiffened and strained against his hold, working to get closer to the sliver of light filtering through the cracks. Holy hell, she was trying to listen in. Was she trying to see if her latest fling was cheating? Otherwise committed?

"Yes, everything seems fairly normal except for the fight with the woman," Kemp muttered. "I believe so. He knows something. I don't know what, but he's definitely keeping her out of the loop. He's nervous. Something spooked the hell out of him a few months ago. He went somewhere in DC on a secret meeting and when he came back, I noticed the change."

Now Roman was listening—and listening hard. Who the hell was Kemp spilling these details to?

What the hell had Gus gotten herself into?

"Yes. I've got it all set up. Something different this time. Keep 'em on their toes." A long pause followed, and Roman could hear the shuffle of Kemp's feet as he paced. "You know I will. And I'll get the information to you as soon as possible. I think I've identified who I need to talk to and who I need to take out. Yes, we're getting close. I'll know more after I return from my trip to the countryside. Everything will be quiet until then. I've made sure of it. You're going to owe me everything you promised very soon." He chuckled. "I'll hold you to that. And no promises on the other thing. She's pretty delicious. If I can get my hands on her, it might be worth it." There was a low groan. "Yeah, I hear you. Fine. I'll do my job. Spoilsport. I'll call in after I get back to London."

A long sigh resounded, followed by the slide of a drawer opening. The twisted sounds of metal and plastic being smashed filled the air next.

Gus smothered a gasp. Kemp was destroying something, probably that phone. Damn.

A moment later, they heard the efficient click of a magazine sliding into a gun. She stiffened, and Roman wrapped his arms around her again, pulling her back against him as quietly as he could. He didn't have a gun, didn't carry one, but now he saw the benefits. His heart thudded wildly as he realized this might be a fight he couldn't win. If Matthew Kemp opened the closet and found them here, Roman could do nothing to protect Gus except step in front of her and offer to die first. Kemp was highly trained and heavily armed.

Gus trembled in his arms. Roman held his breath.

A moment later, the sliver of light filtering inside the small space shuttered. They heard the bedroom door open and close again.

He held her for another long moment as he listened for the sound of Kemp's footsteps fading in the distance.

Finally, they were alone.

Roman dragged a calming breath in and released her.

Gus flipped the overhead light on and turned to him. "What are you doing down here?"

He felt his eyes narrow at her tone. "You're asking me that question? No, baby. I want to know what the hell *you* were doing, searching a Secret Service agent's room and eavesdropping on his phone call. And I want to know right now."

Because Augustine wasn't worried about whether her lover had someone on the side. She was spying. He had to find out how deep she was in.

When he took her hand and reached for the doorknob, she resisted with a forced chuckle and her head held high. "You're imagining things, Roman. I was just looking for something I left here the other night."

Ah, her queenly pose. How many times had he seen her use that very tactic when she was in a corner? She wouldn't back down, merely send whatever fool chose to question her a haughty look and say something cutting in that how-dare-you-question-me tone. This was how she'd become such a popular surrogate for Zack on the news shows. She could stare down and tear down even the best argument from her most able opponents.

Roman shook his head at her because if she was going to play the queen, he would show her who the damn king was. He wasn't allowing her the upper hand now. "No, Gus. You have two seconds to tell me what's going on."

She held his gaze with a little shrug, as if she didn't have a care in the world. "If you have to know, I lost my best thong in Matthew's room last night. I was looking for it."

She was lying. Connor had sworn to him that he'd walked Gus back to her room last night, then waited until she had shut her door and turned out the lights. He'd hung around another few minutes to be absolutely certain she'd gone to sleep. What she hadn't done was sneak out to have a little nookie with Kemp at four a.m., especially when Gates was lying in the twin bed beside his.

If Roman couldn't get answers out of her, he would get them from the only other person who could shed some light. "All right, then. You keep looking, baby. Maybe Kemp will help you, though I don't know why you didn't ask him when he was here a few minutes ago. But if you've got this under control, I've got something else to do."

He opened the closet door and strode out.

She followed right behind him. "Roman, let it alone. This is none of your business."

He glanced down at the nearby trashcan. Nothing there except a couple of tissues. So where had he taken the remnants of the phone he'd destroyed? Roman knew damn well what he'd heard. Kemp had smashed that device, then probably taken the SIM card with him. Little wonder. Based on that conversation, the man was up to no good where the country—and Gus—were concerned.

But Roman had to hand it to the agent; he was good. He hadn't left a single trace of the device behind.

He pulled out his phone, ready to call Zack. They would need to advise Connor, develop a strategy. He wanted a quiet interrogation, and that meant keeping the Agency and the FBI out of this. Until he could prove what was going on, Roman refused to bring in anyone he couldn't absolutely trust. They could say Connor had been promoted and was now filling the role of the president's acting advisor on sensitive security matters. It was good to be chief of staff. He could make up jobs on the fly.

"What are you doing?" Gus followed him, hot on his heels.

He was happy to toss her own words right back. "It's none of your business. You go your way and I'll go mine."

But he would circle right back to her because he intended to discover whatever secrets she was keeping—one way or another. Gus would learn she couldn't hide from him.

"Roman, stop."

He paused mid-stride. He would give her a chance.

One. She'd better tell him the damn truth or the gloves were coming off. He wasn't taking risks where her safety—or their president—was concerned.

Brow raised, he turned and faced her, laying one hand on the railing to the stairs so she would understand fully that he was *thisclose* to walking away. "Yes, Augustine?"

Her face flushed to a pretty pink, and for a moment he could see the wheels of her brain working, trying desperately to find a way out of the trap he hadn't meant to catch her in. Nevertheless, he'd keep the cage door shut tight. Her hands fisted at her sides. "Please, Roman. I think he did something that hurt a friend, and I'm investigating him. I'm asking you to drop this and let me handle the incident myself. Please. Just walk away."

He moved into her space, looming over her. She was poking into the business of a highly trained killer, had walked into his room and attempted to search it. Gus made the crime against her friend sound more like a minor transgression against one of her girls, not a potential crime against his country. Roman wasn't buying her tale. If he hadn't come along, she would have been in the room all alone when Kemp unexpectedly strolled in and quietly plotted something insidious with an unknown caller. If she'd been caught, Kemp could have done anything at all to her. And no one would have been the wiser.

"Not on your life, baby. You're involved in something incredibly dangerous. I'm taking over. I heard every word he said. He's spying on Zack, and that means he's mine."

"Is he spying on Zack? Or working for him?"

He stared at her for a moment. "What do you mean?

Of course he works for Zack, at least in theory. That's why I have a problem with Kemp spying on him." Some of what she'd said was beginning to sink in, but he still pressed her. "Who is the friend of yours Kemp hurt?"

"I told you, it's none of your business."

"If you want to play it that way, I'll have Kemp arrested and find out myself."

"What will it take to get you to back off, Roman?"

She didn't understand him at all.

He stared down at her, letting one hand drift up to find the back of her neck. "There is nothing you can give me that could possibly make me walk away from you and potentially allow that asshole to hurt you. No amount of money. No amount of power. No amount of sex, even with you. I'm not walking away from this."

"Tell me you didn't have Mad killed." Her voice sounded hoarse and low. Anguish twisted her face.

He felt his jaw drop. "What?"

Tears filled her eyes as she looked up at him. "I think I have proof that Matthew Kemp is the one who put the bomb on Mad's plane. I *need* to prove it. I owe him that much. But I have to know if Zack made the call to take him out…and if you helped. So help me god, if you walk away from me and spill all of this to Zack before I get answers, I'll never, ever forgive you. Do you understand me?"

Not that she ever had. Obviously, if she thought he was low enough to have had one of his best friends killed.

He could spill everything to Zack and do his job…or he could try to calm her down and make her believe that neither he nor Zack had anything to do with Mad's murder. He didn't like her threat, but he understood it.

Roman's thoughts raced. How could he maintain his loyalty to Zack while not testing Augustine's vow to cut him out of her life forever? The perfect, simple solution presented itself. Connor was already on full alert, and Roman hadn't promised Gus that he wouldn't give Connor a heads-up about Kemp's possible plot. When Roman told Connor there might be a threat, he wouldn't ask for explanations. He would simply protect his president and friend.

And all the while, he could also shield Gus by making certain that fucker Kemp understood he couldn't use her for his own ends. "All right, but I have some demands of my own, and they aren't negotiable."

"I thought nothing would make you walk away," she replied with a bitter laugh.

How little she knew. "Oh, I'm not about to walk away. That's the first demand, baby. You're stuck with me. You will stay with me, sleep in my room, act like my lover until we figure this thing out. You will not be alone with him, and if he asks, all you were trying to do with him was make me jealous. Is that understood?"

She shot him a cynical glance. "I thought I couldn't buy you with sex."

"You can't, but I didn't say you couldn't rent me out for a while," he shot back.

Damn it, this always happened. He ended up saying things he didn't mean because she pushed him. "I didn't say you had to have sex with me, but you will be in my bed tonight. I will be by your side for the remainder of this investigation, and you will obey me implicitly when it comes to anything I deem important to your safety. Do I make myself clear?"

"You make yourself into a massive asshole, Calder,"

she hissed back. "What do I get out of this? Except being made to look like your complete doe-eyed idiot."

"You get the privilege of not being in protective custody. Don't think I can't do it. You know I can, and I'll have Dax on my side. I'll tell your brother absolutely everything you've been doing, and I might even make some shit up, and he will believe me. He'll cut his honeymoon short so he can protect you. I'll call your mother, too. Fill her in on what's happening. If that's not enough, I'll call every friend you have and either beg or threaten them—whichever works—not to enable you because I'm the man who's desperate to save you. You won't see the light of day for a long time, baby. It's me or a lovely gilded cage."

She shook her head. "We can be partners, but I won't pretend to be your lover."

The little shudder in her voice told Roman that he had her. A thrill wound through him. This was his in, how he got her. This was how he kept her for however long he could. "No one will believe that you and I can be in the same bedroom night after night without fucking our brains out. Not for a second. Besides, I don't trust Kemp to keep his hands off you unless he understands that someone bigger and badder has dibs."

"Don't be juvenile."

"I'm not. I'm being possessive, and he'll understand that. Did you sneak away from him to come down here?" Suddenly, he could almost see her whole plan. She'd gone out the night before with the singular intent to get close to Kemp. She would have flirted and made it clear she was interested, and all to put herself in the position to be closer to him, maybe get into his room. She might have thought she could do something stupid like get a look at his phone. When that hadn't panned out, she'd decided to search his room instead.

"Yes." Her mouth flattened into a mulish line.

Still, she was so sexy in his eyes. She always had been.

"Think about what I'm doing." He took her hand. "If you fight or double-cross me, I'll have Kemp arrested and I'll bring Zack up to speed on everything. That's not a threat. But right now I'm choosing you, Gus. Over my best friend and my president, I'm choosing you. Do you understand?"

She scoffed as she followed him up the stairs. "You're blackmailing me."

He came to a grinding halt on the second floor landing when he heard some commotion above.

"And I need everything you have on the meeting tomorrow," Zack was saying, his voice hard.

"I've already e-mailed it to you," Liz shot back. "Mr. President."

"I want you to personally review it with me." Zack stomped his way down the stairs. He stopped and glared up at Kemp and Gates, who were peering down from the railing. "And you two should find something better to do with your time."

"My apologies. We had the evening off, as did Ms. Matthews and Ms. Spencer," Kemp spoke. "We were simply spending it together, watching a movie."

This was his moment. Roman leaned over and pulled Gus against his body, his arms wrapping around her tight. "Last chance, Gus. Don't fight me."

Her eyes widened and she gasped as she seemed to realize what he planned to do.

He slanted his lips over hers and kissed her long and

hard. He hauled her against him and cupped her ass with his big hands. Roman wasn't playing. He intended to leave Kemp—and everyone else—absolutely no question about what was happening between he and Gus. So he dominated her mouth, and the moment he felt her soften, he let his tongue surge inside.

God, she tasted like heaven, like something sweet and forbidden. Like precious memories he'd forgotten. Like perfection.

After a suspended moment, she lifted her arms and encircled his neck. Primal thrill filled him when she kissed him back with a hunger he hadn't expected. And she melted into him with a soft sound of need.

From above, someone cleared his throat. Roman figured he'd made his point and released Gus. It was the last thing he wanted to do but if he kept drowning in her lips, he feared she would kill his resolve.

When Roman eased away from her, he saw with satisfaction that everyone had been watching them. Good. That had been the point of his display. Liz looked dumbstruck. Zack's blank stare would have told anyone else absolutely nothing, but Roman knew the man's minute expressions. Zack was wondering what the hell was going on; Roman had no doubt he'd have to dodge plenty of questions later.

But Roman had one far more specific target, and he found the blond hunk grilling him with a blue-eyed glare from the third floor landing. Roman merely smiled in return. "Special Agent Kemp, thank you for entertaining my girl while I was out, but I think we're going to head to bed."

Gus's hand tightened in his, almost to the point of pain. Oh, she was pissed, but she wasn't giving away the game. Yep, he had her.

"And Ms. Matthews has work to do," Zack said. "She won't be getting any more nights off. I think it's important that she's by my side so she can deal with the press properly."

Clint Gates held his hands up. "Of course, Mr. President. We were only relaxing with friends."

"Ms. Spencer, are you all right? Is there anything you want to say?" It looked like Kemp wasn't backing down even as his friend gave him an elbow to the side. "Because if you do, you should understand that while I'm here to protect the president, I'll protect you, too."

Gus gave him a brilliant smile. "Protect me? From Roman? I'm afraid he's the one who needs some protection. I'm sorry if you feel I've misled you, Special Agent. I was trying to get this one's attention. You know, after a while they stop trying, get a little complacent, and start thinking three minutes is a marathon."

"And we're going to bed." He should have known Gus would find a way to bust his balls, even when he had her firmly in his grasp. She would never cry prettily as she asked for his mercy. She would have none on him when they were alone again. Of that he had no doubt.

Why did he find that so damn arousing?

"You're dismissed, gentlemen," Zack told Kemp and Gates.

Neither looked happy—Matthew much less thrilled than his counterpart—but they retreated.

"Gus?" Liz asked, her stare falling to where his hand gripped her elbow.

"I'm fine. I'll talk to you in the morning. You okay? If you don't feel like working, you could tell Connor. He's very much on our side when it comes to manageable working hours."

Zack frowned. "When did Connor get so interested in your schedules?"

Sometimes Zack was slow to catch social cues.

Roman moved in close so the boys above couldn't hear. "She's talking about you being alone with Liz. Connor's offered to babysit…just in case."

"What does he think I'll do?" Zack asked, sounding outraged.

"I can tell him it won't be anything at all interesting," Liz replied. "I don't need Connor to save me. President Hayes is completely harmless except for boring me to death." She turned to Zack. "If you'd like to review our talking points for the press, I'll follow you. I wouldn't want you to not know the names of every member of the British press circuit. I've made flashcards. It'll be fun."

Zack watched Liz walk away. "I wouldn't hurt her."

"You already have," Gus said under her breath.

"*Et tu*, Augustine?" Zack asked with a sad twist of his mouth.

"You have no idea, Mr. President. None. I'm going to Roman's room now where we're going to have violent hate sex and he might tattoo his name on my ass so that when he tosses me out like garbage again, no other man will want me." Gus turned and stomped her way to the stairs, but not before she pointed his way. "And don't forget our deal. You don't want to cross me on this, Calder. It won't be pretty."

With that, she was gone. He and Zack were alone, looking in different directions as the objects of their affections/irritations sauntered away.

"What the hell was all of that?" Zack demanded.

"Nothing I can't handle. I'll take care of Gus.

Zack scowled, obviously not liking it, but equally baffled by the woman. "All right. What the hell are we going to do?"

"No idea." But he knew he'd better come up with one—and fast. Gus would sleep in his bed tonight. She might stab him, too. Or, if he played his cards right, she just might fill his arms again.

He had the closest thing to a second chance he'd ever had with her. The question was, should he take it?

CHAPTER EIGHT

Gus strode up the stairs, ignoring Roman behind her. Nothing he could say would make her stop this death march to his room. Once they reached his quarters, she knew they would have one hell of a fight.

Then what?

She worried a bit about that answer. It would be so easy to fall into bed with Roman, just like losing herself in that damn kiss had been. Gus didn't want to think about that.

"Augustine," he called after her, his voice full of demand.

She kept right on walking. She had zero reason to start a conversation before they reached his quarters. Otherwise, they'd only argue sooner, where anyone could hear.

When they turned down the west wing hall, Roman right on her heels, the doors to the two largest suites came into view. Naturally Zack had the best, but Roman's digs weren't far behind. Yes, she understood custom dictated that the officials with the most important positions in the administration were given the most lavish quarters. Hell, they were like small luxury apartments. And neither man could defer or refuse for fear of insulting their host country. But Roman and Zack were single. Why did either of them need multiple rooms and a king-sized bed?

On the other hand, Gus intended to make damn sure Roman would be happy his room had a sofa tonight.

"Augustine, stop. I found something."

She paused mid-stride. Okay. He could say words that would make her talk before they were behind closed doors. No idea what he might have found, maybe his good sense. Or perhaps some decency. That would be nice.

Schooling her expression, she spun around and found him holding up something plastic. Awesome. He'd found trash. That would help them so much.

Responding with only a sigh, she turned again and headed for his room. They couldn't have this out until they had privacy. Then she would explain the world to him.

Her phone buzzed in her hand. Liz was texting her, likely asking what the hell was going on. Or asking Gus to save her from Zack.

Zack. Damn it. She needed to know if her brother's friend, the president, was involved in this tangle. She'd looked into Roman's eyes when she'd asked about his involvement in Mad's death and she'd seen his shock. And hurt, too.

Had Roman become a good actor? Years ago, he'd

been terrible. But since then, he'd cultivated that blank poker face she'd come to associate with him stonewalling. He did it to the press all the time. Tonight, however, his face hadn't been blank at all. He'd been open in that moment. And seemingly stunned.

Did she dare believe him?

He rushed to catch up, his long legs now striding in sync with hers. "You're an impossible mule."

Took one to know one. "You didn't have to humiliate me."

He nodded to the Secret Service agents standing guard outside the president's room. The whole house was full of them. There would be one or two shadowing Zack...and overhearing his latest fight with Liz. But despite the black suits crawling everywhere, Roman had ensured she couldn't get close to the only one who mattered.

"I wasn't trying to humiliate you," he said under his breath as they passed by the agents. "I was trying to keep you safe. How was that humiliating?"

He was supposed to be so smart, but sometimes she swore he had the emotional IQ of a turtle. "You treated me like a piece of property."

He sighed and rushed ahead of her, using his key to unlock his door. He held it open and hustled her in, then shut them away from the rest of the world. Despite her anger, Gus knew all too well how dangerous it was to be alone with him. Five minutes after that kiss he'd used to brand her as his, her body still thrummed, her blood still coursed, and her pussy still ached.

He turned on her. "I treated you like a woman who doesn't have the sense to protect herself. You were in his room. If he'd caught you there, he could have killed you."

She rolled her eyes. At the time, it had been terrifying, and she'd been oddly relieved to have Roman huddled in that closet with her, his arms wrapped around her as if she was precious and he meant to protect her at all costs. Then he'd ruined everything with his caveman kiss. He hadn't pressed his lips to hers because he wanted to be closer to her or because he wanted to pleasure her. He'd done it simply to prove his ownership.

"I doubt he would have killed me. He could only get away with that while surrounded by this much security if everyone is involved. Are you telling me the entire Secret Service would look the other way? Were they all involved in Mad's death, too?"

"You're deliberately twisting my words. Of course, I'm not saying that. But if Kemp was involved in Mad's murder, that's one more reason you shouldn't put yourself in danger, especially without any kind of backup or protection."

"I'm not an idiot. I had backup."

"Who?"

Maybe she shouldn't have opened her mouth. "None of your business. What we should be talking about is what to do now that you've ruined my entire investigation."

His eyes had narrowed. "It damn well is my business. Who are you working with? You had someone helping you since you knew Kemp was coming before—" He shook his head, running a tense hand through his hair. "Liz, of course. She was monitoring Kemp's position and texted you when she'd lost track of him. You honestly believe that Liz, who's never without her stilettos and can barely handle a broken nail, is up to battling agents with a proven track record?"

When he put it like that, her plan sounded silly. Liz was a badass when it came to dealing with the press pool, but she wasn't exactly a ninja. "I was perfectly safe. I would have sneaked out of the room with no one the wiser if you hadn't barged in." And that brought up a good question. "And why exactly were you following me, Roman? You were supposed to be on a date."

"It wasn't a date," he insisted as he shrugged out of his jacket and laid it over the back of the sofa. "I never intended it to be one. Zack and I decided to call it a night after the play. When we arrived, I saw you sneaking down to the bottom floor and I was curious."

Oh, she could guess exactly what he thought. "You mean you were curious to know whose bed I meant to hop into."

He shrugged one muscled shoulder. "All right, I was jealous. I can't help how I feel, Augustine. But once we were stuffed in Kemp's closet, I realized the situation was so much worse."

"You have no right to be jealous."

"I know that. Believe me, I realize my feelings about you are complex and perverse, but I can't change them. I've tried." He pulled at his tie. "And I'm sorry you felt as if I humiliated you. I had to make a point."

"Somehow I think telling Special Agent Kemp to back off might have worked. He seems to understand English quite well."

"No, baby. He's a man, so he doesn't actually understand anything except pure caveman dibs. That's what you don't get about Kemp and his ilk. He wasn't about to back off unless I gave him a reason to. So I did. After all, men understand visuals far better than words."

He tossed the tie beside his jacket and undid the first couple of buttons of his crisp white dress shirt. "Now, after dealing with a woman who seemed to have eight arms tonight, I need a drink. How about you?"

She had to laugh. If he thought she didn't understand men, she could point out all the ways he didn't grasp the female psyche. "Darcy finally made herself plain, did she?"

He groaned, and the tension in the room ratcheted down as he poured two glasses of what was probably Scotch old enough to apply for its own AARP card. "Fine. I was wrong. You were right. I spent the entire night trying not to be molested."

The thought of big, sexy Roman Calder swatting feminine hands away from his silky boxers was definitely the highlight of the evening. "So you decided to retreat here. Did Zack not like his supermodel?"

Roman passed her a glass. "Go easy on him. He's having a hard time. And you know precisely why I didn't go back to Darcy's place. She's not the woman I want."

Gus didn't say a word, just ignored the thrill in her belly.

He scowled. "The woman I want is complicated, but now she's going to listen to me. Do you know what this is?" From his pocket, he pulled out the plastic he'd flashed her earlier.

When she glanced down at the scrap in his hand, the puzzle pieces slid into place and she realized what Kemp had done after he'd hung up with his mysterious caller. "Matthew talks on the burners and destroys them once he's done. How is he getting his hands on those devices? Everyone's luggage should have been carefully checked. If he'd been carrying a bunch of disposable phones, someone would have flagged his bag."

"You're right. Which tells me he's getting them from someplace—or someone—here." Roman paced, clearly thinking through the problem. "But I doubt he's sneaking out to buy them. Too risky. And anything he brought into this house would be checked. So he's working with someone else, likely someone who was already here."

He sounded almost calm now. Logical. It irritated her. How could he be so even-keeled when absolutely nothing was settled between them? But if he wanted to sweep their shit under the rug, she would help him. "I'll start looking into it. I can have Vanessa ask the local staff a few subtle questions. Fish a bit for any helpful gossip."

His eyes went hard, his hand tightening on the glass, but he spoke in tones both measured and soft. "You will leave this to me, Augustine. I don't want you or Liz or Vanessa putting yourselves in danger."

She glared at him for a moment. She'd avoided Roman for personal reasons, but she'd also been unsure whether Zack was involved in Mad's death. And by association, his best friend and chief of staff. A Secret Service agent on the president's detail murdering one of his long-time pals for shits and giggles seemed like an awful big coincidence to her. No, Mad had been eliminated for a reason. If Kemp had planted the bomb on Mad's plane, then the plot somehow connected back to Zack.

On the other hand, Gus had known the Perfect Gentlemen for the majority of her life. They might be ruthless as hell, but they were loyal to each other. She couldn't picture Zack or Roman wanting Mad dead. Or maybe she just didn't want to.

"Did Mad know something he wasn't supposed to?" Gus asked quietly. Mad had been cunning at times, but also reckless as hell. "Something that could hurt Zack? In his last few days, he seemed upset. Agitated. He wouldn't talk to me over the phone. I thought it was about Sara, but... Was it something else? Something that those loyal to Zack didn't want anyone to know?"

Roman slammed his glass onto the table, sloshing liquid over the sides. "Are you really asking me if Zack ordered Maddox Crawford's death? Again? Goddamn it, Gus. What do you think of me? How could you even imagine for a second that Zack or I had Mad murdered?"

"If he knew something he shouldn't..." she started. Maybe there was an explanation. She wasn't sure she could accept it, but she was willing to listen. She had to know.

Roman shook his head, his gaze steady on her. "Even if Mad knew a secret that could bring down Zack's whole presidency or somehow send Zack and me to jail, we wouldn't have killed one of our best friends. We would have talked to him, reasoned with him. But I would rather be behind bars for life than have Mad's blood on my hands. We've lost more than enough." He frowned. "Why would you imagine I'm capable of murder? I know I hurt you, but do you really think so little of me?"

Gus heard the genuine pain in his voice. In Kemp's closet she'd been wondering if Roman was acting. Now she knew better. Her instincts screamed that he was being completely honest. Her head might want proof, but if she really wanted to know who'd cut Mad's life short, it was time to get smart. Time to stop blaming Roman for everything simply because she didn't trust him with her heart.

"Tell me why Zack had the FAA call off the investigation into Mad's crash. I don't buy a single sentence of that report they released. Mad was an excellent pilot."

He hesitated, and she thought he would clam up on her. When she contemplated her path to the door, he sighed. "Zack didn't have anything to do with the FAA report. But I'll be honest, we didn't fight it too hard because Gabe was in a bad position. He still could be if the report were somehow reversed, even worse now because it would appear as if Zack had been trying to cover for him. You know Gabe was originally a suspect."

Yes, she'd seen the video of him and Mad arguing just before the crash. Yet not once had she ever suspected Gabe would hurt Mad. Yes, she had her reasons for thinking the worst of Roman, but if she took herself out of the equation, she knew he was a decent man...just not right for her.

That fact was still a deep-seated ache.

"I wondered if that was the reason Zack didn't fight the FAA report. But I suppose he would rather have Mad alive and married to Sara than dead for revenge." At Roman's nod, she pressed on. "Then we have a murder to solve. Kemp was at the airport the day Mad died. Well, nearby. I don't have pictures of him there, but I have surveillance video of him at a convenience store mere blocks away. And then there was this sketch he drew."

"Sketch?"

The memory of it still chilled Gus. "Kemp had this notebook on his nightstand. Apparently he draws. He's freehanded a bunch of White House staffers. Mostly cute images. But this one scared me. If anyone saw it, I don't think they'd realize what they were looking at. It's a picture of Mad giving a thumbs-up. He's standing by his airplane, the one that went down. Why would Kemp be anywhere near Mad just before takeoff unless he was involved in murder?"

"Son of a bitch." Roman turned and headed for the door.

She should have known he would freak out. Roman was cool as ice on the job, but he'd never been good at controlling his temper when someone stirred his emotions, as they were now. She ran to catch up to him, snagging him by the arm. "Roman, you promised."

Fist clenched, he whirled around. "I promised not to talk to Zack when you suspected he was a part of this scheme. Now you know he's not, so we'll bring him in. On second thought, we'll take it from here. You get back to your normal life and regularly scheduled duties."

"You bastard! You never meant to investigate this with me. You know something, and even after I've shared information, you're not going to tell me squat, are you?" She cursed, wishing she could punch something— like his caveman ego. "I'm not an idiot, you know. Zack didn't wake up one day and decide he wanted to be Liz's surrogate big brother. Something happened. Something's been happening since Mad's death. You and the rest of your pack are covering it up. Since you didn't have anything to do with Mad's death, that means you're protecting Zack from something. Aren't you?"

Roman's face iced over. "Leave it, Gus. Don't get involved."

She was right back where she'd been at the

beginning of her investigation, only now Kemp wouldn't touch her with a fifteen-foot pole because Roman had seemingly staked his claim. He'd shoved her in a corner, expecting her to be a good girl and accept it.

He didn't know her at all.

Gus scoffed. She still had a few aces up her sleeve. At least she hadn't given Roman everything she'd collected. She still had the top few slips from the sticky pad he'd written on. At her first glance, it looked as if he'd jotted down numbers and an address. She would run a pencil over the indentions and see if she could find out where Kemp intended to go. Roman could go hang.

But the fact that Roman was cutting her out left her even more bitter.

"Tell me something. Does Everly know what's going on? Is Lara involved? Is Holland even now being taught the club's secret handshake since she's married to my brother and therefore 'trustworthy?'" That hurt, too. She'd known these men for far longer, but apparently until a female fucked one and promised undying devotion in her wedding vows, she wasn't part of the family.

It didn't matter that, under different circumstances, Gus would have given birth to the group's first baby. No one cared that she'd loved Roman for far longer than anyone else had even known their spouse.

"It's not like that," he insisted.

"Then what's it like? Tell me, oh mighty and grand Roman Calder, what does it take to get on the inside? I grew up with you guys, protected you. Hell, I introduced a couple of you to sex, but that doesn't buy me a damn thing, does it?"

His face flushed. His jaw tightened. She realized

she'd finally scored a direct hit.

"This isn't a game."

"Everything's a game with you, and you don't care how much you have to cheat to win. You promised me." She retreated a step. "But hey, if we're reneging on our promises, then let's go back on all of them. You go and talk to Zack, and I'll deal with Mad's murder my own way. I'm sure you'll have Kemp in custody, interrogating the hell out of him in the next five minutes, so you don't have to protect me anymore. Bye."

While Roman was distracted by Kemp's questioning, she would try whatever address she could lift from the notes on that sticky pad and see if she could determine what Kemp might have sought there.

Roman's shoulders squared and he glared. "You will stay in this room, right here with me. That's the end of the conversation."

"The hell I will. You can't keep me a prisoner here."

He leaned into her personal space, dark eyes delving and menacing. "Watch me."

"Fuck you." She stormed toward the door, threw it open, and ran into a massive mountain of muscle in a designer suit.

"Can I help you with something, Ms. Spencer?" the Secret Service agent asked.

She gave him her sweetest smile. "You could escort me back to my room, Special Agent Johnson. I would appreciate that very much."

The enormous man frowned and looked back to Roman, obviously for permission. Not surprisingly, he addressed her a moment later with resolution on his face. "The president would prefer you stay here, so this is your room now. He's concerned about some dangerous elements in the city. Our intelligence briefing earlier this evening has everyone concerned, so we're upping security around the core team. Don't worry, though. We'll keep you safe. Could I have the staff bring you something? Some tea perhaps?"

She didn't need tea. "I'd like a sharp knife—serrated would be nice—and a tarp, please. There's no reason to ruin a perfectly good Aubusson rug. It's innocent. The rug, that is. My victim isn't. He deserves to feel a lot of pain."

Roman rushed over and nudged her from the doorway. "Don't mind her. She's upset because *The Bachelor* isn't airing here in the UK and I spoiled the ending for her. Please let Sandra inside the living area when she arrives with Ms. Spencer's luggage."

With a saccharine smile, he closed the door. Then he backed her against the frame.

"You're really having Sandra bring my stuff to your room?" Gus demanded.

If he was serious about locking her in his room, she was going to need that knife.

"I told you. You're staying here until we head back to the States and that's the end of it. You can try to get around me but, as you've seen, I'll ensure you stay here tonight and every night we're in London."

"You fucking bas—"

"This doesn't have to be contentious." He moved closer. "What if I promise I'll keep you up to speed on everything I find out about Special Agent Kemp?"

She could see exactly how that would go. He would tell her what he wanted her to know, nothing more. He would ensure that everything else would be classified out of her reach. "And you expect me to trust you? Go fuck yourself, Roman."

"That's not the way I planned tonight to end, baby." His voice had gone low, his gaze dark with desire as he braced his palm on the doorframe above her head and leaned close.

She couldn't ignore his heat and pull.

Her whole body went rogue. Traitorous. She had a very, very stupid vagina because all he had to do was say a few words in that gravelly voice and send her a seductive stare, and she softened up. Her hormones—also very foolish—started pumping through her blood, making their demands known. Her nipples perked up.

Gus crossed her arms over her chest. "You have got to be kidding me."

"I can't stay away from you. I know you hate me, but you have to admit we do one thing together exceptionally well."

She didn't argue with him and she didn't retreat. She refused to give him the satisfaction of knowing he unnerved her. "I thought you were going to talk to Zack."

He closed his eyes, jaw clenched. "Give me one good reason I shouldn't. I'm trying to do what's right for you. What's right for Mad. Give me one good reason not to tell Zack everything right now. What if Kemp is supposed to kill him in London and we didn't speak up? Could you live with yourself if he succeeds? I can't."

Was he giving her a chance to play this game her way? Did she dare trust him? Maybe not, but he'd backed her into a corner, and her options were limited. She could either roll the dice with the sexy bastard who had once burned her or stay in the dark, never avenging Mad's murder.

Shitty choices.

"All right. Kemp is going somewhere day after tomorrow. He requested leave. Do you remember what he said when he was talking on the phone? He seemed to think everything would be quiet until he got back. If you go to Zack and have Kemp arrested, he can't do whatever he's planned. Which may tell us what the hell he's up to. And good luck getting him to talk."

"We have experts," Roman murmured. But his words were offhanded. Instead, his attention—and his stare—had wandered to her chest. He sidled even closer.

Why did every cell of her body heat up the minute she was alone with Roman? Irrelevant. She had to focus, work with him or sit this investigation out. She could do it...even if he had seduction on his mind. Seriously, two could play that game. Yes, he'd manipulated her before, was probably trying to do it again. Why couldn't she do the same to him?

She wasn't making this choice because she wanted him. Or because she loved how he aroused her whole body with a mere glance. It wasn't at all because he could make her feel the press of her nipples against her bra without touching her even once. That had absolutely nothing to do with it.

"What if they can't break him?" she challenged. "What if he manages to kill himself before you take him in?"

"I know what you're doing," he objected even as his hands dropped to her hips and his mouth hovered, his nose brushing against hers in a sweet touch. "And I know what I should do, but you have a point. All right. We'll follow him. We'll find out where he's going, who he's meeting—and why."

She nodded, but her gaze was caught up with

Roman's. She couldn't look away, didn't want to think about the fact her heart rate had tripled. "You and me. We can't trust anyone else. We can watch each other's backs."

It wouldn't be bad to have a partner, especially one who could call the CIA if they got into real trouble.

"Gus." He moaned her name long and low. "There's so much you don't know."

"Then tell me. You can trust me."

He fisted a hand in her hair, tugging lightly. "It's not about trust. I have to protect you."

She bit back a groan because she loved the sensation that lit up her scalp every time he gently pulled. "If you leave me out, I'll find a way to do this. I won't sit around and wait. And don't think the Secret Service can keep me here indefinitely, Roman. I will quit my job and walk out the door if you make me."

His hand tightened, making her shiver. "You're such a bitch."

Gus knew he meant that as a compliment. Roman got off on being challenged. She sent him a saucy smile.

"That's why I'll be an excellent partner." She let him yank her hair softly again, drawing her head slightly back and exposing the line of her neck.

"So it doesn't matter if I promise I'll handle everything?" He kissed her throat from her clavicle up to the lobe of her ear. "If I take care of everything so you'll be safe?"

"I owe Maddox Crawford. He was my friend when I didn't have one."

He gritted his teeth, leaning his forehead against hers with a sigh. "Did he take care of you that night?"

Tears threatened. They trembled on her lashes

suddenly, waiting to be shed. The words were there, too, but she shoved them back. "Yes. He took care of me. Not sexually."

He shook his head against hers. "I wasn't asking that. Please don't always make me the bad guy, Gus. I don't want to be that man in your eyes. I have no idea what I can give you, but I also know I can't walk away. I don't have it in me right now."

"Then promise you'll take me with you or I'm gone."

He dipped his head, his mouth covering hers, peppering her lips with shallow kisses that made her long for more. "I shouldn't. I know I shouldn't. I shouldn't do this at all. Damn it, I'm not good for you. I can't give you what you need."

Maybe this was exactly what she needed. Maybe she needed to be with him again so she could prove that he wasn't good for her, that her head was playing tricks on her. If she spent a handful of days in his bed, knowing they had an expiration date, she could work him out of her system. Then she would be sure that whatever they'd shared years ago was definitely over. And she would finally be able to move on.

"I just need for you to let me come with you when you track Kemp. I'll stay with you for however long it takes to sort his intentions out. And we can be together. We'll both know this isn't going anywhere this time. No expectations. No unrealistic hopes. Nothing but pleasure and comfort and some closure we both need to move on."

He hesitated, his eyes going hard. "You'll stay with me until my investigation is over."

She had no idea how long that could take since she didn't know the entire scope of his probe. "But you won't let me in on it?"

He groaned. "I will as much as I possibly can. But don't push me. I told you I was choosing you when I didn't spill all of this to Zack immediately. I'm not betraying your confidence. Don't make me betray his."

It was the best she was going to get. And the closer she stayed, the better chance she had to figure out what was going on.

"Keep your secrets, Calder. Just don't leave me behind. I'm going to solve this with you or without you." She lifted her arms around his shoulders, giving over to the need he roused inside her. She couldn't turn him away anymore. Not when she ached for him so badly, not when he'd bent for her in a way she'd never expected him to.

"You always put me in a goddamn corner, but this time I swear I'm keeping you there with me."

He didn't give her a chance to reply. His mouth simply swooped over hers, crashing down until she forgot about everything. He crumbled her barriers, and for the first time in forever, Gus simply let herself feel. Tomorrow would be soon enough to deal with the inevitable and terrible fallout.

CHAPTER NINE

Roman felt the instant she surrendered. It wouldn't last long. Tomorrow, her defenses would be up and she'd fight him again. But tonight she was his, and he didn't have to think any further than their next touch, their next kiss, the next slow slide of his tongue against hers.

His body pinged electric, as though being with Gus had flipped some switch. He felt more alive than he had in a decade.

Touching her was like running his hands over the finest silk, smooth and perfect. Soft and yet so damn strong. She was wearing far too many clothes, but he couldn't get her naked here. Any minute now Sandra would walk into the outer rooms of the suite, hauling Gus's things.

He'd moved quickly to consolidate his victory—before Gus found some way to maneuver around him. After she'd turned haughtily and strode away from him, he'd used the time to call a staffer and explain that Augustine needed a quick move for security purposes. Of course, no one believed the White House chief of staff needed to personally see to the safety of the second in command in the press office, but that didn't matter. Gus would be moved to his room officially, and no one would ever publicly question why they were together.

And they would remain together until the danger had passed. Until he said otherwise.

He leaned over and slid an arm under Gus's knees, hauling her high against his chest. No more dancing around their incendiary chemistry. He needed her in his bed, naked and laid out for him like a gorgeous feminine feast he could see and smell and taste over and over again.

He hadn't gotten his mouth on her pussy the night before. He'd been thinking about that lapse in judgment all day. Merely touching her hadn't been enough. Yes, he'd slid his fingers through her slick arousal and given her pleasure. But damn it, he wanted his tongue there. Years and years had gone by. He'd had countless women since then. Yet he remembered her—and her alone—this sharply, as if he'd last had his mouth on her just yesterday, not over a decade ago.

He strode through the door that led to the bedroom, kicking it closed behind them. Then he set her on her feet and immediately started unfastening the buttons of his shirt. "Take your clothes off."

She stood there, hands on hips, like a goddess, staring him down. "You're bossy, but then you always were. Why don't you undress me?"

He could do that. He tossed his shirt aside before yanking the sides of her blouse apart. The buttons pinged every which way. The scrap of stylish gray silk joined his shirt somewhere on the floor. He had the front clasp of her bra undone in a heartbeat. Her breasts sprang free into his waiting hands. She gasped. Yeah, she hadn't been expecting him to act quite so decisively.

He was just getting started.

Roman whirled her around, flattening her back to his chest. He palmed her breasts, planted his face in her neck, and inhaled. Now that he'd decided he would damn well have her, he refused to wait another moment to start staking a claim on what was his.

At least for now.

He shoved the thought aside and concentrated on the feel of her body against his. Her nipples were already hard, poking sweetly against his palms. He pinched them and breathed in her scent, something citrus and jasmine mingled with her own arousal. He let her intoxicate him, and his mind buzzed with her nearness. It was like being drunk on the very best Scotch. He remembered getting high on Augustine. He'd never felt the dizzy, sweltering need again after her. Never imagined he would. But it was back—with a vengeance.

"I liked that shirt, Roman," she complained, but her words sounded more like a breathy moan.

"I needed it off your body. I need this gone, too." He skimmed his palms down to the waist of her skirt, tore through the button, yanked down the zipper, then shoved it over her hips. It pooled at her feet, and Roman admired his handiwork. In mere seconds, he'd stripped her down to a pair of barely there undies and fuck-me heels. She could leave those on, but the pretty bit of lace was in his way. It would have to go. He didn't really care if that was in one piece...or two.

Roman caught sight of her in the mirrored armoire that dominated one side of the bedroom. She looked like sin. In the tussle, her hair had come undone and now flowed loose around her shoulders, thick and wild. Some would call it brown, but it was a mix of chestnut and red with sun-streaked gold. A long curl brushed against her ribs, luring his gaze to her curves tucked against him. Her breasts were perfect, round and topped with blushing nipples he intended to suck until she squirmed and begged for mercy. He might show her some...but probably not.

He rolled the hard tips and watched as her lips parted and desire filled her face. Her breasts swelled in his hands.

That wasn't the only thing swelling...

Roman pinched the sensitive nubs again, squeezing a little harder. This gasp sounded more like a moan. She squirmed against him, letting him know she was every bit as aroused as he was.

Raw possessiveness raced through him. The way he wanted her now, he'd been a fool to think he could truly want anyone else. Augustine had always been the only woman who could make him lose his mind, let go of everything but the thought of being with her. Though time had changed them both, she was still the most beautiful woman he'd ever seen.

Gus was definitely more lush than she'd been in her twenties, her hips wider, her thighs thicker, waist seemingly smaller. All of that only made her more gorgeous to him. Her curves complemented the confidence her youth had only hinted at. Now, it had come to fruition. She stared right back at him in the mirror, her lips curled up. Yes, she knew exactly how beautiful she was. He wanted her even more for it.

He felt his way down her body, to the lace of her white panties.

"I'd almost forgotten how beautiful you are naked. And you're more stunning now than you were then." No denying he'd dreamed of her at night, but now that he was here with her in the flesh, reality was shockingly better. She was so vibrant and warm that it hurt.

How long had he been cold inside?

"I swear if you pull the same trick on me you did last night, you won't enjoy the rest of your evening, Roman," she warned as he slipped his fingers under the waistband of her panties and drifted toward her pussy.

He'd been an ass, even if he'd been trying to protect her. But now they had an agreement. He didn't need to negotiate with her, try to exchange pleasure for her compliance. No, now he had control. He could simply enjoy her.

"I won't." He wasn't letting her go tonight. She was in his room and she would spend the night in his bed. She would wake up in the morning and find herself wrapped around him while he pounded inside her. He only had a few weeks. He intended to make the most of them. When he wasn't working, he would be fucking her until he'd purged her from his system.

"Everyone is going to know about this. You can say you're watching after me, but everyone with half a brain will know we're having sex. The rumor mill won't stop at this shore, either. People in DC will hear all about it, too."

"Let them gossip. I don't care. Do you really give a damn, Augustine?"

Before she answered, he slid his fingers over her

pussy. She was already slick and ready for him. The way she responded so totally, it was as if she'd been made for him. And when he skimmed over her clitoris, her head fell back against his shoulder with a groan.

"Roman…"

"I'm here. I'm the only one with you. All those busybodies can go to hell if they have a problem with us. I'll fire anyone who says anything other than 'Congratulations. The two of you are great together.'"

Until now, he would have shared her concerns. Appearances were everything in politics. Reality didn't matter half as much as perception. He'd preached that to the rest of the White House staff. But now that he had Gus's bare curves against him, he couldn't remember what the hell he'd been so worried about. He was single. She was single. There was nothing to stop them from falling into bed and staying there as long as they damn well wanted. If someone wanted to gossip about them, why should he give a shit? He was one of the most powerful men in the world. If he wanted to fuck the most beautiful woman he'd ever known, he would.

"That's the Roman I remembered. The one I dreamed of," she admitted, her voice low.

"And this is what I dreamed of." He let his fingers slide through her pussy as he rubbed her slowly, soaking his skin in her sweet arousal.

So wet and ripe. She was slick enough to take him now, but he wanted more. He wanted her writhing, needy, begging…

With a groan, she moved against him, her backside rubbing against his cock in a silent plea. Arousal gripped Roman by the throat. He couldn't breathe through the need without inhaling her and wanting more. But he still held back, watching in the mirror as her pleasure unfurled. He loved the sight of her in his arms, so feminine and wild. And right now, all his.

Gus bit her bottom lip as he eased the pad of his finger over her clit again, pressing down lightly. Then a bit harder. Her body bucked, pelvis pressing up. Her breathing turned choppy. He smiled.

"Roman!" Augustine didn't pretend she was unaffected or play coy. After all, she was a sensual creature. That open, honest sexuality had always made his pulse pound and his cock ache. Nothing had changed in the last thirteen years except that she'd ratcheted up her effect on him.

Her stare tangled with his as she slid one of her arms up and around his neck, anchoring her closer to him. The other she slid to his thigh, then around his body to cup one cheek of his ass.

Gritting his teeth, Roman held her in his strong grip. If he let her go, he would shove his cock inside her before he'd explored her body as thoroughly as he ached to. The temptation to bend her over, shove his slacks and boxers down, and fuck her until they both screamed out and found relief was strong. He'd done that plenty of times in their past. But after waiting so long for her again, he didn't want this over fast. He intended to drag it out, make her feel every sensation he could heap on her. He wanted more.

Shooting her a cocky grin, he withdrew his fingers and took a step back. "No orgasm yet, Augustine. I want to taste you. I didn't get my mouth on you last night. I want you to come all over my tongue. Panties off. Lay on the bed. Spread your legs for me."

"I shouldn't. I know how this ends but..." She

pushed the tiny scrap of silk off her hips as if she didn't have an insecurity in the world and strode to the bed, sending him a come-hither glance over her shoulder. "I want to see if this is as good as I remember."

God, he wanted that, too. He needed to know for his sanity.

She did his bidding, sliding her gorgeous body across the bed and spreading her legs for him. Roman stared for a moment, taking in the sight of the best pussy he'd ever had. He'd wanted to live between her legs when he was younger. Despite the years and reaching the pinnacle of power, he still couldn't think of any place he'd rather be.

On the other hand, he recognized their old pattern. They'd always fought, then fucked, only to start the cycle all over again. Sometimes it had happened so fast he hadn't even recalled what they'd been fighting about. One minute he'd been yelling about something he would have sworn was vital. The next he would have his tongue deep inside her, lapping her up and soaking in her taste, dizzy with her scent, right before he plunged into her with every ounce of his strength. But he wasn't twenty-five anymore. He didn't want to hurry their foreplay just to get inside her tonight; he also didn't want to revert to screaming, then patching things up in bed.

He wrapped his hands around her ankles and removed her shoes. Those fuck-me heels were a crutch for her, a shield that showed the world how powerful she was, but she didn't need them while she was with him. If he was careful, if he showed her that he could be good to her, she wouldn't feel the urge to protect herself from him, just surrender everything that made her the woman he'd never been able to forget.

Surprise widened her eyes. "I thought you liked the shoes."

Something he'd never felt before gripped him: pure possessiveness. The moment that had seemed merely sexy seconds before now felt precious. He didn't know why but he damn well intended to experience her even as he imprinted himself on her indelibly.

He drew her foot to his lips, kissing the pretty, painted tips of her toes. "I like *you* more. I like you even better when you're completely naked and open to me."

He dragged his lips across her arch, up to her ankles. Odd that he found her feet so pretty. But everything about Augustine lured him. Her calves were firm and round, her knees dimpled and lovely. Why hadn't he taken this kind of time with her before? He'd spent a year in her bed, but every encounter had been fraught with urgency, with stirred anger and whipped passion. And fear. He'd both been afraid of getting caught with her and being caught up in her.

No, he'd been most fearful of how completely he lost himself in her.

He smoothed his fingertips up her legs, loving how velvety her skin felt under his palm. What would have happened way back when if he'd slowed down? Would he have felt this searing need? Would he have felt then how right it was to touch her, like he did right now? Would he have fallen even more in love?

"What's wrong?"

Not even realizing he'd paused, Roman had been turning the questions over in his head. But he had no answers. So he diverted his attention back to her silken flesh.

Leaning closer, he kissed her knee before tightening

his grip on her ankles and flipping her over. Damn, that was a beautiful ass. Heart-shaped and perfect, the globes of her backside were made to fill his hands.

"There's absolutely nothing wrong with this." He cupped her lush derrière. "You're beautiful, woman."

"Roman, if you've changed your mind..." She pushed up to her elbows and turned her head to face him.

Oh, no. She wasn't getting away. He moved in between her splayed legs, using his body to hold her down. Once he had her pinned, he bent to whisper in her ear. "The only thing I've changed my mind about is how this will go down. You know what I've decided, Gus? I don't care what our sex life was like back then. We were horny kids who couldn't wait for orgasm. Now I'm a man. I want more. I need it. I intend to have everything from you."

She ducked her head, resting it against the bed. "It wasn't so bad back then."

"It was the best sex I've ever had," he admitted. "It was the sex I've compared encounters with every other woman to. All of them came up lacking. But I think you and I can do even better this time. We're stronger. We can go higher."

She slid a seductive grin his way. "I like how you think. Why don't you show me how much better this Roman is, because the younger version was pretty good."

Faint praise, but he would prove that he was right.

He licked the shell of her ear. She'd always been sensitive there. Had any of her other lovers known that? How well had she been loved during the years they'd been apart? Had her other lovers been more tender? Had they taken the time to worship her properly?

Water under the bridge. Their sex in the past might

have been hurried, but he'd definitely learned to please her in small ways. She liked a little nip. And when she was really hot, she could do some damage with teeth and claws. Roman hadn't minded one bit. In fact, he hoped to feel that again. The fresh, raw scratches down his back used to fill him with confidence, make him feel like such a man.

"Now I need time with you. We're not hiding from anyone anymore. We've got no reason for quickies. We have all night, Gus. I'm going to use every minute of it."

"You're going to kill me, Calder." Her voice sounded throaty, rough. Aroused.

"Roman," he corrected. "I'm Roman. And you're my Augustine."

She used last names to force distance, and he refused to allow that tonight. Inevitably, it would come, but not until later. For now, he wanted absolutely nothing between them. Not their past. Not the uncertain future. Just the glorious now.

"All right. You know Dax will likely find out," she murmured.

Yes, he did, but she wasn't fighting him. He considered that a win. He had no idea what his old pal would think. In fact, Roman wasn't entirely sure Dax hadn't known about them back then. He'd never said anything, but the odd tension he'd noticed between them had evaporated after Gus had taken the shark-in-training job in DC. At the time, Roman had thought it was a mistake, but she'd proven herself. Her stubborn choice to do exactly the opposite of what he had wanted was the reason they were together now. If she'd gone back to New Orleans all those years ago, she wouldn't have been as versed in politics and wouldn't have been qualified for the job that brought her close to him again.

Thank god she was so willful.

"I'll handle your brother." He wasn't sure how, but he would. He hated strife between him and any of his remaining brothers, but in that moment he knew that even if being with Gus again cost him Dax's friendship, he wouldn't make any other choice.

Maybe being willing to lose a dear friend for a woman made him a selfish ass. She seemed willing to risk her relationships for the chance to touch him, too. Of course he could protect Gus without getting into her bed. But he was determined to have this time with her. Most likely, it would never come again.

And if Dax showed up with a shotgun...well, he wouldn't have much choice, would he? He'd do what he had to.

Roman wrapped his hand around her hair, drew it away from her neck, then brushed his lips over the sensitive skin at her nape. "I'll handle everyone. All you have to do is let me stroke you. Let me kiss you. Fuck you. Let me show you everything I should have before. Affection. Need."

She shivered beneath him as he kissed his way down her spine. "You're going to torture me, aren't you?"

He loved the curve at the small of her back and the twin indentations there. "Think of it as anticipation. My dick is so hard right now and I can smell how ready you are for me, but that doesn't mean we should throw down with no preliminaries. I'm sick of quick and empty. I want this to mean something."

She stiffened. "It always meant something to me, Roman."

He soothed her with kisses down the curve of her ass

before shifting down her legs, licking the back of her knee and loving the way she squirmed. "Then that was my mistake, baby. I still don't have anything to offer you except pleasure. I'll give you all I can. I'll make it so good for you."

They weren't fighting right now, but they would. For the moment, he needed this truce afforded by arousal, the blissful respite.

Why was it the only woman in the world who could bring him such peace was also the only one who could rev his temper and turn him into a blind hothead he swore he'd never be?

Roman forced the thoughts aside. There was only now. Only this. Only Gus.

Slowly, he wandered back to her feet and her perfectly kept toes, gratified to see her shiver under his touch. When was the last time he found a woman's toes and ankles fascinating? Never. In fact, not once. But he wanted to inspect every inch of Augustine, like a man memorizing something precious, something he knew he would eventually lose so he needed a picture in his mind of its perfection.

He flipped her over again. She gasped up at him. Then a frown flattened her gorgeous lips, and she fisted her hands at her sides, as though she didn't trust herself not to reach for him. Or because she was thinking of punching him. With Gus it could be either.

"When did you take to manhandling me?" she demanded.

He grinned. So she'd noticed that he could still lift her and carry her around. Daily workouts had kept him strong, but he might need to up his cardio if he was going to spend a few weeks in her bed.

He yanked her down the mattress so her backside perched on the edge—and her pussy was splayed wide open to him. Her skin had flushed a pretty pink, and her nipples were straining for attention. Already, Roman could tell she liked being aroused slowly, being kissed and caressed and adored as if he had all night long. She might not want to admit it, but her body didn't lie.

He urged her to bend her legs and place her feet flat on the bed. "I don't know if you noticed, but I like being in charge."

Her eyes flashed. "You are *so* not in charge of me."

Another challenge, but then he should have expected that.

He laid his right hand on the tiny curve of her belly. Frustratingly close to the flesh he wanted to touch...but he would get there soon. "Do you want to bet me? How about I won't give you my cock until you admit I'm the boss in the bedroom?"

"You'll give in before I will," she vowed. "I'm in control, Roman. Always. I have to be. This is all nice, but I can handle you."

So she could take him or leave him? That's what she implied. That pretty mouth could BS him all day long if she needed to protect her ego. The old him would have been hurt by her tart words and started a fight. Now, he simply shut his mouth and vowed he wouldn't give up until she'd surrendered everything to him.

He smiled down at her, satisfied when unease crept across her face. "I will take that deal, baby. Let's see who gives in first."

* * * *

"We'll see." Gus dug her nails into her palms. If she didn't, she might do exactly what she'd sworn not to. She would beg.

She wasn't sure who the hell Roman had turned into, but this new version was infinitely more devastating than the previous one. This Roman was slowly driving her mad with his long caresses, deliberate kisses. If he'd missed an inch of her skin, she wasn't sure where. Well, besides the one place she needed him most.

"Why are you still dressed while I'm naked?" She bit back the need to ask when he would stop this torture and put his damn sexy mouth on her pussy.

But she couldn't give him that kind of power over her. He already had enough. Begging was totally out of the question.

He lowered his head, his mouth hovering above hers. "Because you're so pretty naked, Augustine. I don't think you should ever wear clothes."

Yep, he was making her crazy. The Roman she remembered didn't talk and tease during sex. That Roman had fucked. Oh, he'd fucked well, and for the blissful moments she'd been with him, she'd felt as if he truly needed her—at least for his orgasm. But the way he made her feel like the center of his world now was totally new.

And so dangerous.

She wasn't about to tell him that she liked being naked for him. Something about the way the fabric of his slacks gently abraded the skin between her legs made her feel wanton and sexy, like she was a treat he'd rushed to unwrap because he couldn't wait another second. "I think the press pool would find me walking around naked amusing."

His mouth played lightly over hers, his tongue teasing her before retreating in a frustrating dance. "I think I would have to kill a couple of those reporters, but your nudity would be an easy way to change the narrative of the twenty-four-hour news cycle. Maybe we should consider that the next time Zack steps in it. We'll send you out all pretty and bare. At least half those asses won't be able to think long enough to ask questions."

Who the hell was this? Roman didn't joke during sex. He single-mindedly forged ahead until he was inside her, pounding away at her. She'd thought it was so passionate at the time, so romantic that he couldn't wait another second to have her. But this…this was something more than sex. He was taking the time to make a connection with her.

It scared the hell out of Gus, but she'd ached for him so much and for so long, she couldn't find the will to fight him.

He kissed her again, drugging her. She slid her hands over the smooth skin and rippling muscles of his back. That hadn't changed. If anything, he was stronger now than he'd been then. More manly. And more tempting. When he'd picked her up, she'd actually felt light and dainty, and for a woman who was taller than most of the men she knew, that was saying something. She wouldn't admit it to Roman, but when he turned or twisted her at will into whatever position he wanted, her heart raced. She loved the way he could press her down into the mattress and hold her still so he could ravage her mouth with his.

He raised his head again, staring down into her face, seemingly trying to read her. "But you should understand that the first one who touches you will never see the light of day again. I'll charge him with treason and turn him over to those bloodthirsty boys at the CIA."

Before she could respond, he kissed her into silence, then began working his way down her body. His lips brushed her neck, sending electric thrills through her. She bit back a moan when his mouth wandered to her breasts. He teased her, his tongue licking around her areola in long, unhurried laps—first one, then the other. More blood rushed to the untouched tips. Gus bit her lip to hold in a whimper.

"Need something, baby?"

He was taunting her. And he probably relished how hard she fought not to beg. Damn sexy bastard.

Gus meant to assuage some of the ache without his help, so she raised her hands to pinch her aching nipples. Roman was having none of that. He grabbed her wrists and pinned them to the mattress on either side of her.

"Bad girl. All you had to do was ask."

Beg, he meant. But thankfully, he didn't make her, he merely showed her mercy and sucked one nipple into the heat of his mouth. His teeth grazed her, approaching the right side of pain. Searing tingles sizzled, and she could feel her pussy clenching and pulsing with an arousal so fierce it was almost painful.

He shifted to her other breast, lavishing it with affection. Like the first, he engulfed the tip into his hot mouth while he cradled the straining globe, seemingly more than content to worship her body. As she arched up to him, he groaned and wended farther down her body. He settled his hips between her legs, looking as if he intended to stay and torment her until he was good and ready for more.

This was something she hadn't counted on. Over the

years, she'd thought a lot about what it would be like to sleep with Roman again. The idea had danced through her fantasies, but in every scenario, the sex had been quick, furtive. He would haul her into his office, growling and grabbing her as he bent her over his desk before taking her hard and fast, hurtling her to a screaming orgasm. The sex would be good, sure. But more important, she would have solved the mystery of what it would feel like to be Roman's lover again. Then she could tell herself that, since their youth, she'd had better. And she could walk away after satisfying her curiosity and need, knowing she'd gotten all he was capable of giving her.

But never in all her daydreams had he laid her out and made a decadent feast of her. Never had he teased her and taunted her. Never had he joked with her. And never had she imagined that he could make her want something more from him again beyond mere sex.

Gus didn't like the realization, but she couldn't spare the brainpower to stamp it out now. She couldn't think about anything, except the fact that Roman shimmied his way down her body, his exploring mouth inching closer and closer to where she needed him most.

Callused fingertips skimmed over her ribs, drifted across the indentation of her waist, then settled on her hips. His hands were so big, so masculine, so talented as they held her in thrall. A shiver raced through her as he eased lower, showing her just how good he was with his lips, too. They skated over her abdomen before he dipped into her navel, awakening nerve endings she hadn't known existed, giving her a preview of what his tongue could do elsewhere.

When he edged down her body once more, he

stopped just short of planting his mouth on the spot that would give her relief. A whimper slipped free from her throat. He was so close. The heat of his breath on her needy flesh wracked her. He palmed her thighs, spreading them even wider, and gazed up her body. His dark eyes flared when their stares tangled.

A single lock of inky hair had fallen over his forehead. He was usually so meticulously groomed. When he was in his pressed three-piece designer suits with his hair tamed and neat, he was the president's strong right hand. But now, with his shirt off, his eyes hot, and his hair tumbled, he was a dangerous predator. Gus couldn't wait for him to eat her up.

"You still shave." His voice rang with satisfaction.

She shook her head. "I got the kitty lasered a long time ago."

His stare held hers as he lowered his mouth and brushed his lips over the fleshy pad of her pussy. "So fucking soft. That's what makes me crazy about you. You're so strong and still soft. And this is beautiful."

Gus tried to give him an offhanded smile, as if his adoration didn't matter. But she couldn't stop herself from clutching the comforter in her fists. She didn't know how else she could keep herself from tangling her fingers in his hair. Because if she did, she would tug on the strands and try to force him to fuck her with that mouth of his. Not only would he torment her by doing the opposite because the man was contrary, but she couldn't let him know how much she needed him and the pleasure he could give her.

Any power she gave him, Roman would use with ruthless intent.

"Do you know how much I want this, Augustine?

How often I think I can still taste you on my tongue? I'll be sitting in a meeting and see you walk by, and I'll swear your flavor is still lingering. Do you have any idea how often I get a hard-on in the middle of an intelligence briefing at the thought of getting my mouth on you again?"

He still thought about her? No matter how much she'd tried not to, she'd thought about him, too. She'd told herself she'd moved on, but her longest relationship had been the ten months she'd dated a JAG lawyer Dax had introduced her to. It had ended when she'd taken the job at the White House. She'd told him her schedule was too insane, but not missing him at all had been her first clue he wasn't the man for her. Now she had to wonder if being near Roman day in and day out had forced her to acknowledge that, deep down, no one could compare to him.

"Do you?" He lifted his hand to her folds, gently pulling back the hood of her clitoris.

Oh, god. What was he doing to her?

"No," she managed to breathe out.

"I do," he whispered softly against her pussy. "Oh, baby."

He licked her with a slow stroke of his tongue. Soft. Barely there. Gus closed her eyes and shuddered, fighting not to thrash against him. It felt so good, but it wasn't enough. Not nearly enough.

She pressed her lips together so she didn't beg him for more. He wanted this, too. She had to remember that. Just like she had to remember that she was with Roman. He would eventually take what he wanted. It was his nature.

"Hmm," he groaned. "That's exactly the flavor I

remember. Tell me, Augustine. Do you want me to give you more?"

"I do, but I won't beg you."

"Baby, we're not there yet. Not even close." He leaned closer and licked her once more, drawing his tongue over her sensitive button and engulfing her whole body in heat. It swamped her, searing her skin, making her sweat. "I'll let you know when you can beg."

Bastard. Even his arrogance aroused her. It was a new thing. Not that he hadn't been arrogant before, but he'd kept it to the classroom and the office. In bed, she'd suspected he felt less than secure because she'd had more experience. He'd been touchy about her showing him how she liked a caress or wanted his mouth on her at times. Oh, he'd learned, but in his time and in his way. Now all that seemed gone, replaced with a confidence that fit him like the custom-made suits he wore.

"But until then…" An unholy grin flashed across his face before he parted her labia and covered her with his mouth.

At the electric sensations, she nearly came off the bed. She gripped the comforter tighter, mashed her lips together even harder.

With a demanding grunt, he settled in, licking and sucking and making her throat ache with the repressed scream. He was relentless, laving her with his affection and plaguing her with his tongue. He drove her up, up, almost letting her soar. But he always pulled back when she trembled against her will, breath held, thin seconds from climax.

"Gus?"

She knew what he was asking. Nope, she still wasn't begging.

Then she felt a single finger tracing her entrance, teasing her. Her hips jerked toward him. She tried to regain control of her body, tamp down her reaction. But it was too late. He knew. He rewarded her lapse of restraint when a second finger breached her.

Roman moved the digits inside her with slow strokes. Against her will, her body tightened again. He licked, sucked, and stroked her with his mouth all while heaping more agony on her with his thick fingers. They fucked her deep, hooking upward to the perfect spot.

Oh, god. She could barely breathe. Satisfaction shimmered right there, closer than ever…but still out of reach. All she needed was another few seconds—another lick, another stroke of his fingers against her G-spot—and she would go flying. But Roman held her satisfaction in his grip. She had to wrest it back, without letting him know how close she was to going over the edge. Then he would never have to know how deeply he affected her. She could steal this orgasm without begging.

His lifted his head and withdrew his fingers. "You know, I was thinking about the upcoming G7 meeting. What's your take on it?"

"I am going to kill you."

He chuckled, a deep rumble that rolled over her skin. "I'm not really thinking about that, baby. I'm thinking about how my cock is going to revolt if you don't give in soon. Come on, Gus. Give me this one thing. I won't even make you beg tonight. Just tell me you want me. Tell me you're not here merely because we made a bargain."

Gus swallowed. That was surprisingly vulnerable for him. And she wasn't immune to it.

In some ways, she longed for the previous Roman.

He would never have opened himself up. It would have been so easy to get revenge on that man. A few well-placed words vowing that she didn't give a damn about anything except their bargain and that, when it came to orgasm, any man would do... That would have crushed the twenty-something Roman. Then he would ache exactly the way she had all those years ago. But he was no longer the self-absorbed asshole who'd spurned her callously without regard for her feelings, who had never asked why she wanted to change her plans for the future, who had been way too ambitious to notice her missed period.

If she could trust his words, he'd broken off their relationship back then not because he hadn't cared, but because he'd cared too much. Because she made him feel.

Maybe it wasn't witty or worldly or even smart, but she wouldn't hurt this Roman.

"I want this, Roman. I don't want the boy I once had. I want the man. I want you." It wasn't begging. She could never do that, not with him. But she could give him the truth.

Besides, she wanted to feel this Roman, even if he was more dangerous than the younger version. Even if he broke her heart again.

"Then let go. I want you to come all over my tongue, baby." He lowered his head again, mouth finding just the right spot while he held her gaze. Electricity arced between them.

Finally, he groaned and his eyes slid shut. Gus gave in too, letting her hands sink into his hair. No, she wouldn't beg with words, but her body had different ideas. Her hips tilted up in silent entreaty, thrusting against his mouth as he suckled her clit. He eased his fingers inside again, curling them up to press and rub against her sweet spot. The man was going to kill her.

The heat built again until the cataclysm felt imminent. Lightning flashed through her, singeing, coiling, burning, rolling up under her. The powerful clap of thunder was right there... Finally, the shattering pleasure crashed through her, pummeling her, nearly destroying her. She couldn't stop the shout that gathered deep inside. It began in her heart and burst from her lips.

She called Roman's name as she thrashed and panted and scratched in satisfaction.

As she caught her breath, he gave her one last savoring lick, accompanied by a low moan, then dragged himself to his feet. When his hands paused at the fly of his slacks, he raked his gaze over her body. "Tell me I can have you, Augustine. I need to hear it again before I go on."

He was giving her a loophole out of their bargain. She could send him away, end everything between them, just as he'd unwittingly done the night before. But like her last gut check, she couldn't make herself hurt him. In fact, the thought of wounding him upset her even more now, especially when all she wanted to do was wrap her arms around him and welcome him inside her body. There were no walls between them now. No boundaries or barriers. It was everything she'd wanted back then. She knew she should protect herself, but she couldn't say anything to disrupt this golden moment. Though he'd shattered her once before, here she was again, addicted and hoping for more from him than was wise.

Still, she held her arms out to him. "Don't leave me, Roman. I don't want to be alone tonight. I need you."

His gaze softened. "I don't want you alone. I want you happy. Hell, I want to make you happy. But I have to get a condom first, baby. I didn't take one with me when I went out earlier. I didn't even think about it because I wasn't touching that woman with a ten-foot pole."

He looked so sincere that she believed he had no designs on Darcy. Something inside her melted even more.

"I'm on birth control, Roman. And believe it or not, I actually haven't had sex since my last checkup three months ago. But you should—"

"Fuck, Gus." He shoved his slacks down, followed immediately by his boxers. His cock, big and thick, sprang free, standing proud against his abdomen, almost touching his navel. "I haven't had sex since my last checkup a year ago. I'm totally clean. Tell me I can have you now."

He might have hurt her in the past, but he would never lie about this. She normally didn't have sex without a condom because she would never trust a man with something this important. Only Roman. He was the only man she'd ever conceived a baby with, even if accidentally. And somewhere in the back of her mind…maybe she was mulling the idea of doing it again. Not to trap him, but some part of her wanted so desperately to get back what she'd lost.

She couldn't let her mind wander there. Instead, she reached for Roman, wanting this moment with him. She was safe. She'd had her contraceptive shot. There was no reason to make him stop now. "Yes."

That was all she had to say. He toed off his loafers, peeled off his socks, and kicked his slacks away before he turned back to her, wide shoulders lifting with every harsh breath as he stood between her legs and aligned his cock against her. Gus froze, waiting eagerly. This moment was real. He was here. They were finally going to make love.

Roman pushed inside her in one long thrust, gliding through her sensitive flesh and submerging deep until he filled her. Gus gasped as sensation flowed over her. She clamped around him with a cry, feeling stuffed tightly and desperate for more. But she also felt open and unfettered by their past. Having him inside now seemed right.

"Damn you feel good." Roman stood over her, jaw clenched, holding himself still as though he needed a moment to regain his self-control. "This I definitely remember, feeling like a teenaged boy fucking a goddess for the first time."

He made her feel like a goddess. At least he always had when they were in bed together. Now, he made her feel important, too. A woman he wanted more than a trophy he felt compelled to win.

She wrapped her legs around his waist, drawing him down until he covered her chest with his and they rested overheated skin to skin. "I remember this part, too. This is where you make me crazy. Don't hold back on me, Roman. Don't you dare."

She wanted everything he had to give. If they only had a few weeks, she would damn well make the most of them. No more hiding pieces of herself from him. At least when they were in bed, she intended to give him her all. Yes, she would be shattered when he walked away again, but maybe that was better than being numb. She hated how gray her days had become. She needed some sunshine, even if it was only for a short time.

"I can't hold back, not even if I tried. Not with you." He gripped her waist and dragged his cock back out before plunging in again.

He set a ruthless rhythm, shuttling in and out, testing his angles until he found just the right one to have her tensing and gasping, clawing at him as he sent her closer and closer to the edge. The pleasure built, a hot, destructive force threatening to break her—and tear down all the walls she'd erected against him at any moment.

Over and over he slammed into her, ratcheting up her senses. He bellowed out each breath. The bed rattled. Gus dug her fingers into his shoulders, nails in his skin. When her thoughts evaporated and she clawed her way down his back, he tossed back his head with a groan.

"I remember that, too. Oh, fuck. Baby, I can't stop. Feels too good," he panted as he surged inside her again, somehow even deeper. "Why the hell did we wait this long?"

She didn't know how to answer him.

Then she couldn't because he settled his thumb over her clitoris and pressed down while his cock shuttled in and out, picking up speed and prodding her most tender spot over and over.

The explosion built and swelled, climbing, growing, overwhelming. Then he sent her soaring toward heaven.

Gus clutched him. He felt like the only solid anchor left in her world. Everything else was violent sensation. Pure emotion and energy flowed through her as her body jolted, her hips crashing into his, and she keened out in agonized satisfaction.

Roman's head fell back and he gave up all semblance of control, following her into orgasm. He slammed into her again before she felt the heat of his climax jetting deep inside her.

He slowed his strokes before stopping altogether. But he remained inside her, still connected to her. Roman's chest heaved as if he'd sprinted hard for the finish line. Then Gus realized she was breathing hard herself.

The younger Roman would have immediately withdrawn from her and either left the bed or talked about something deeply unromantic. Through the lens of maturity, Gus wondered now if he'd intentionally put walls between them because he'd been afraid not to. This Roman caressed her cheek, his stare delving into hers. He didn't need words now. His expression told her that he was just as amazed by the pleasure and connection as she was.

"You good?" he murmured, thumb trailing over her temple as if he didn't want to let her go yet. As if he wanted to savor their joining a moment longer.

"Yeah." Gus wasn't sure what else to say. Anything more would have told him that feeling him deep inside her again had opened some part of her heart closed for more than a dozen years, some part that belonged to him alone.

He smiled her way, then groaned as he withdrew and stepped back, stretching his big body. Gus shifted closer to the headboard but didn't try to cover herself. It was nice to be naked with him. Her body was still pulsing with the gentle aftershocks of orgasm. She tried not to wonder if the two of them having lived more and now being less immature could mean anything to their future. A nice blanket of peace began to settle over her thoughts instead. Later, she'd think about the ramifications of tonight. Now, she intended to wrap herself in bliss.

"Wow. We should be happy you're on the pill because there's no doubt in my mind that episode would have ended in an unwanted pregnancy." Roman sighed. "I've never come so hard in my life."

His words yanked the peaceful blanket away and punched her in the gut. She jolted upright. He was joking, of course. He had no way of knowing what had happened the terrible night they'd split up. She'd never told him. But it didn't matter. One word rang in her head over and over: unwanted. That was all she needed to hear.

She remembered why she'd never intended to be with him again.

His expression shifted from satisfied to concerned in an instant. "Augustine? Baby, are you all right?"

She sat up, scanning the room for anything she could use to cover up. She refused to look his way. "I'm good. I need a shower before I get in bed." She rolled off, grabbing the robe the staff had obviously left behind for him. It was far too big, but she needed the cover it provided now. "Are you sure you want me to sleep here? It's been forever since I slept with someone. For actual sleep, anyway. I might snore."

Roman blocked her path to the shower, wrapping her face in his big hands and tilting her up to meet his stare. "What did I say wrong? That's the second time I've seen you turn pale and haunted. What am I doing, Augustine? Talk to me."

She couldn't. She wasn't ready. Panic started to creep in. God, she felt so vulnerable. And now that he wasn't showering her with ecstasy, now that she knew he still felt the same way about any child they might have conceived, she couldn't stand it. Rose-colored thoughts of the future aside, she and Roman didn't need to share more than sex. She didn't need to give him the power to hurt her again.

"I don't have to talk to you. That wasn't part of our deal. I only have to fuck you and I did that."

His face flushed as he dropped his arms to his sides, stepping back. "Are you kidding me? That's such bullshit and you know it."

She opened her mouth to fight back when a knock sounded on the door and a masculine voice called out. "I'm sorry to interrupt, Mr. Calder," one of the Secret Service agents murmured. "The president needs you in his suite now. You and Ms. Spencer. He says it's an emergency."

"Understood. We'll be there in a moment," Roman barked before looking back to her, his eyes narrowed. "Get dressed. And in case you were wondering about the answer to your last question, yes. You will stay in that bed with me tonight. And if you think this conversation is over, think again. I'm not done. Not with the conversation. Not with the sex. Not with you."

He stalked off toward the bathroom. She was left clutching the robe and wondering how the hell she could stop him from bulldozing her heart again.

CHAPTER TEN

Roman ushered Gus into the presidential suite before him, studying the stiff set of her shoulders and the haughty way she held her head. The questions rolled through him like a storm. What the hell had he done to suddenly put her in that bitchy, closed-off mood? He'd watched her change. One minute she'd been a happy little sex kitten, all curled up and ready to be cuddled. The next she'd gone cold as ice.

Was it because he'd joked about getting her pregnant? Was Gus's biological clock ticking? Had he poked at some sore spot?

He wasn't about to tell her that when he'd thrust inside her without a condom, his first and arousing-as-fuck thought had been that he could get her pregnant. They weren't kids. They could handle it. Plus, a baby would bind them together. It would mean a permanent connection to her. They would have to work something out, then. They would both have to think about the child they shared first.

Not that his parents had. They hadn't changed at all once they'd had a kid. In fact, they might have gotten worse. That was why he'd made the joke. His desire for a kid whose life they would probably ruin scared the hell out of him.

But…was his life really ruined? Or was he holding on to that thinking as a defense against the terrifying possibility that he cared about a woman and might want a future with her? That he was falling for Gus again?

He couldn't love her.

Roman stopped at the scene that greeted him. Liz sat on the couch, wearing a set of lounge pajamas. Because she was Liz, she looked elegant even though she was barefaced and clearly ready for bed. Zack was still clad in his tuxedo slacks and shirt, his tie and jacket gone. He paced behind Liz as he held what looked like a file folder in his hands, reading in a silent, grim fury. Lara sat beside Liz while Gabe and Everly had taken up the desk in the corner. She clicked away on her laptop. Everyone was tense.

Something was wrong.

"The gang's all here." He kept his tone bland since not everyone was in the loop about the conspiracy around Zack. He nodded Lara and Liz's way, noting Gus immediately sat down beside her friend. When he was close enough to be certain the women couldn't hear him, he leaned toward Zack. "It looks like a party, not a family gathering. Should I get us some beers?"

Zack sighed. "I can't leave Liz out of this now, and since I knew Gus was with you, I saw no reason not to bring her in, either."

Roman wasn't pleased. "And we couldn't leave them out why?"

Zack held the folder up, his voice a harsh whisper. "This is the reason. Liz?"

"I found that folder laying on my bed. I guess my room was easier to get into." The press secretary might look casually elegant, but her hands shook as she clutched them together in her lap. "The president and I had a long talk about tomorrow's discussion with the prime minister and the press conference that will happen at the end of the week. Then I got ready for bed. When I came out of the shower, that folder was waiting."

Zack closed the folder, his face icy and closed. "She brought it straight to me. I've got Connor trying to figure out how the bastard left the folder behind. Liz locked her door."

"Is she sure?" Roman knew sometimes he forgot even habitual things.

Zack flushed slightly. "I'm sure. Trust me. I heard that sucker lock."

Ah, she'd slammed the door in his face. Zack's night hadn't turned out as well as his had. If one didn't count the fact that Gus refused to look his way now. "What did the security cameras catch?"

There might not have been one trained specifically on the room Liz was occupying, but there would surely be one in the hall.

"I'm pulling the feed right now," Everly explained. "Zack wants us to handle this in-house. Secret Service knows something is happening, but they don't know what. We intend to let them think this is a personal issue, some squabble going on between friends and staff that Zack has decided to fix. They'll believe it."

It was a smart play. There was a ton of drama going on between them right now, and there was no way the sharp, trained agents hadn't noticed. This kind of late-night gathering wouldn't come as a surprise, especially if everyone seemed calm and on the same page in the morning.

"Why aren't we calling them in?" Liz wrung her hands again. "I should have gone straight to Thomas, but after what I read, I thought the president should see it first."

Or more likely, she'd been scared and wanted to walk straight into Zack's room so she could feel safe again. Poor bastard. Zack couldn't afford to keep Liz as close as Roman intended to keep Gus. Liz's safety depended on everyone believing she was merely an employee, nothing more.

Gus sent Roman a pointed look. "I would also like to know why the Secret Service isn't involved. It's almost as if you guys know something we don't."

Of course, keeping Gus close had its disadvantages, too. He cursed under his breath.

"What's in the folder, Zack?" Sometimes it was best to ignore her jabs. If Zack was comfortable with Liz and Gus knowing what was in the letter, then he had to be as well. If the contents were as serious as it seemed, he had no choice.

The door opened again, and Connor strode through. "Well, I figured out how they snuck that package in."

Gabe looked up from the screen. "Did someone have the key to her room?"

Connor shook his head. "Didn't need it. I found a hidden passage. The whole place has been renovated a few times over the centuries, but those secret passages the servants used to get food quietly from the kitchen to the guests still exist. Liz's room is easily accessible. No key required and no cameras recording. I would bet Everly's going to come up with nothing."

"Someone can come into my room at any time?" Liz asked, her voice shaking.

"Obviously I'll have you moved." Zack had his encrypted cell in hand. "I want a secure room and I want to know the name of every single person who's been in this house today. There must be a security log."

Connor held up a hand. "I can get that for you, but you should know one of the tunnels I followed went out to a storage shed on the grounds. It looks as if it was bricked up in the past, but someone took a sledgehammer to it. I crawled through the opening and only had a moment or two where I thought I might have to grease myself up to get through. That was a tight space."

Everly looked up from the screen. "I'll see if anything gets picked up on the CCTV right off the grounds. At this time of night there can't be too many people milling around. If I can get enough to run through facial recognition software, we might get lucky."

"It's London," Zack pointed out. "It's always busy, but you should definitely try. Now that we're all here, we should talk about what Liz found. This is a piece of blackmail intended to force me to change the way I negotiate with European leaders."

Roman felt his heart squeeze. This was the drop of the shoe they'd been waiting for. "What are they blackmailing you with?"

Zack was quiet for a moment. "You, my friends. If I don't downplay the transatlantic pipeline, the person who delivered this intends to ruin all of you. Every one of you in this room."

"How?" Roman didn't quite understand. He'd expected whoever was out there to come directly at Zack.

Then again, Zack would throw himself on the sword, but he would fight to the death to save his friends. The enemy was obviously smart enough to know that.

Liz sniffled. "I read it, but I didn't understand it all. Some of it doesn't make sense. I get the part about Gabe and the FAA."

Gabe groaned. "They want to bring up that shit again? I thought we were done with that. I didn't have a reason to kill Mad. I wanted him alive. And the NYPD now believe that Mad's own employee brought that plane down because he was going to expose her human trafficking operation."

"I've never quite believed that was the only reason," Roman murmured under his breath, along with a curse. "How exactly do they intend to revive the scandal? What's the angle?"

"They claim they have proof that I shut down the investigation and instructed the head of the FAA to rule that it was pilot error," Zack replied.

"You didn't do that. You merely requested that you be kept up to date." They had been relieved when the agency had ruled the way they had—not because they agreed with their findings, but because it kept Gabe out of jail.

"This person claims to have documentation between my office and the head of the FAA," Zack explained. "They'll leak it to the press if the prime minister and I reach an agreement to bring American natural gas to Europe in the next ten years."

"You said us." Gus perched on the edge of her seat.

222 Shayla Black and Lexi Blake

"What exactly is he threatening the rest of us with?"

Zack opened the folder. "You apparently made a sex tape, Augustine."

Gus scoffed. "Probably several. Let it out. I don't care as long as my butt looks good."

"Augustine," Roman growled.

She shrugged. "Seriously, if that's the best they've got on me, it's no threat at all. I don't give two shits."

Roman clenched his jaw. "This isn't a joke. It could hurt your career."

"Or I'll be the Kim Kardashian of DC and grow my Twitter following by millions," Gus shot back. "Look, I'll weather this just fine. Dax and my mom will be upset, but not exactly surprised. Kind of like you." She addressed Zack again. "So take me out of the equation. What about everyone else?"

She was right, and once Roman stopped looking at a possible sex tape like a jealous lover, he realized it wasn't a very strong threat. He shouldn't be terribly upset by it. He didn't like it, of course...but Gus had been a bit wild in her younger years. Probably now, too. Still, she wouldn't be ashamed. She wouldn't let a sex tape throw her for a loop. She would likely take a bow and wait for the spotlight to fade.

Because she was tough. Because she knew what she wanted and she didn't let anything stand in her way.

Damn, he admired her.

"What about Connor and Lara? Do they know about Capitol Scandals?" Roman asked.

Liz turned to look at Lara. "Wait. Are you sincerely telling me that the biggest rag in the Beltway is run by Connor's Disney princess?"

Connor folded his arms over his chest. "How do you

know it's not me? You immediately go to Lara. I can run a website, you know."

A brilliant smile crossed Gus's face. It was one of the things he found fascinating about her. She could find the absurd or ironic in almost anything. "She knows because you have no sense of humor whatsoever, Connor. You are the single dourest man in the world besides Roman. You couldn't come up with even one of those headlines."

"My favorite was the article titled *If the President's Penis Could Talk*," Liz said, putting her hand over her mouth as if to stop herself from squealing. "I'm fangirling so hard right now. You have a lot of fans in the press office."

Lara had flushed a deep red. "In my defense, his penis had some extremely intelligent things to say about environmental law."

"Could we stop talking about my…junk," Zack growled, then took a deep breath. "No, there is nothing in here about Capitol Scandals, but thanks for outing Lara."

Gus flashed a superior smile. "I knew."

"You did?" Liz groused. "Damn, I'm always the last to hear anything."

"No one told me. I figured it out a long time ago and kept it to myself. Sorry," Gus murmured to her friend.

Zack waved the conversation off. "Capitol Scandals isn't mentioned at all. No, this is a different threat. It's about Connor and an operation he was responsible for in South America that led to the deaths of three civilians."

"Shit." Connor reached out for his wife's hand, tangling their fingers together. "I know what you're talking about. That op was beyond complex, and we got some bad intelligence about a narcoterrorist group.

Things went wrong. And yes, some civilians died, but I stand by that mission. We saved a lot of lives by breaking up that group."

"Apparently new information has come to light. One of those civilians was the son of a cartel kingpin." Zack was looking down at the information he'd been given. "The man known only as El Guapo has no idea the CIA was behind that raid, and he's been looking for someone to blame for his loss. If this classified information came out, you and Lara would be in grave danger."

"Where is this asshole getting his information?" Roman found the threats to his friends and brothers maddening. "How does he know these things?"

"And why does he think a bunch of e-mails between Roman and Joy would be a problem?" Liz asked. "That's the one I don't understand."

The whole room went quiet. Roman froze when he saw Gus's face flush. She seemed to turn in on herself.

He'd never really discussed Joy with Gus, but he knew Joy had talked about him to Gus. She had talked to Gus about their odd relationship. How hard had it been for Gus to stand quietly while her friend had purged her conflicted feelings about Gus's own ex? He would bet she'd never once told Joy about their history, or she'd made it all sound like a long-ago fling that simply hadn't worked out. She would never have made Joy feel guilty for her feelings or as if they were in competition. She would have been a steadfast friend.

"Joy and I had a flirtation," he admitted to everyone in the room. "Some of the e-mails could be considered scandalous since she was married to Zack at the time. I should have been smarter, but it seemed innocent. It certainly started that way. Most of the e-mails are merely friendly. But later ones talk about things that would be interpreted salaciously."

Liz hadn't known, and the surprise on her face told him she found his admission shocking. In truth, admitting it out loud felt wrong. Saying it in front of Augustine, not an hour after he'd been inside her, made him feel somewhere close to ashamed.

Liz turned to Zack. "What does he have on me? I haven't had any affairs. I've basically been a nun for years."

"Your sister," Zack replied quietly.

She shook her head. "What about her? Annie's in the middle of a divorce. She's too busy fighting for custody of her kids to get naked with anyone and have a fling."

"Your sister spent two weeks in a mental hospital when she was seventeen," Zack said quietly.

"Because she had PTSD. She was in a car accident and lost her best friend. Six months later she was still struggling and she thought about hurting herself. My mother got scared and took her in for an evaluation," Liz explained quickly. "She was a minor. That information is supposed to be private."

"Nothing is private," Connor said with a sigh. "Even sealed records can be found, opened, and exposed. They could have hacked the hospital or gotten the information through insurance records. And I'm sure your brother-in-law's lawyer would use that against her."

"So we have to figure out who sent this to us and how I can mitigate the damage as much as possible," Zack said. "I don't want to hurt my friends, but I can't give in to blackmail. The future of the country is too important."

Gus stood. "Don't worry about me. I'm a big girl.

I'll let my mom and Dax know what's coming, but if I had a copy I would release it myself so it couldn't be used against you. And if having a sexually adventurous woman on your press team is too tawdry, then I'll happily turn in my resignation."

"Absolutely not," Roman said quickly. "You're not quitting."

Zack grinned, the first time he'd shown any amusement all evening. "And I would decline to accept that resignation. As for Liz's sister, let's hire the best lawyer we can and dig up some dirt on her soon-to-be ex. We'll give her as much ammo as possible."

"My vote is to release the e-mails between Joy and me." Roman hated the thought of those secrets becoming public. But he hated Zack giving into blackmail even more.

He remembered the day he'd received the first personal missive from Joy, roughly a year before the campaign for the White House had begun. All their previous exchanges had been purely business, though Roman had occasionally sent comics or absurd news items to make her laugh. Her responses until then had been like the woman herself—seemingly shy and quiet, even in e-mail. But she'd broken the barrier between them by sending him a message that asked if he ever thought about her.

Roman shifted his gaze to Gus. She would have boldly walked into his office and told him she wanted him. She wouldn't have played around or written him so she didn't have to face him in person. She would have been upfront. Then again, if Gus had been married, she would have divorced her husband before she flirted with another man. "It only hurts me. I was the one in an emotional relationship with my best friend's wife. Not you. It makes you look like a freaking saint."

"Or an idiot, but I can live with that, too. Not anything the press hasn't said before," Zack quipped.

His friend had been much more careful. Despite the fact that he'd planned all along to be with Liz after his presidency ended, he'd never sent her e-mails anyone could use against him.

"Besides, they have no idea what I was thinking at the time," Zack murmured obliquely, though Roman knew the yearning for Liz he implied. "That leaves us with two problems. The FAA scandal coming back will hurt me, and it could definitely have an effect on Gabe and Everly. It could send both Bond Aeronautics and Crawford stock down."

"We'll be fine." Gabe put a hand on his wife's shoulder. "I've got excellent lawyers, and the NYPD considers the matter very much closed. Without any proof to refute them or criminal charges forthcoming, the story will go the way of gossip and blow over."

"I'm not so sure about that." Roman knew conspiracy theories could haunt a presidency. He needed to talk to Zack and the guys alone. "But we're all tired tonight, so why don't we reconvene in the morning? Does Liz have a new room? A secure one?"

"Gus's room is secure," Connor offered. "The tunnel was blocked to that suite. I'm having her things moved in there. They can share for a bit."

Gus helped Liz up. "Yes, I think Liz will feel safer with a roommate."

"No." They had a deal, and Roman knew if he let up for a second, getting her back in his bed would be one hell of an uphill battle. "By all means, help her settle in.

But you're staying with me. We're not done, not by a long shot. Unless you've changed your mind."

Unless she was willing to reveal everything about her investigation to everyone in the room here and now. He knew he was being a bastard and he was planning on telling Connor anyway, but after waiting so many years to touch her again, he wasn't giving her up until he was good and ready, despite the fact they'd all been threatened tonight.

And if he didn't like the dirt the conspirators dangled over her head, well…that was his problem. After all, he'd let her go. Anything she'd done with another man after their split had been consensual and none of his business. He'd hardly been a saint, either. Of course, he fully intended to find the unscrupulous bastard who'd taped her and make him pay. She didn't deserve either the scorn or blame that might come with the video being released. Despite everything, she was behaving in a very Gus-like fashion, being bold and brave about the possibility. No one took her down. No one made his baby feel small.

No one except him.

A vision of her expression that night thirteen years ago hit him square in the gut. Her righteous fury, yes. But he remembered her pain most. He hadn't been kind that night, hadn't been the man he should have been.

In fact, her expression tonight had looked hauntingly similar. Why?

Roman didn't know.

"No, I haven't changed my mind," she snapped. "I suppose I'll go to bed, then. If I had to guess, the good-old-boys' network has an emergency meeting and once again, we're not invited. Come on, Liz. I'll help you get settled in my old room."

Lara stood up as well, shaking her head. "I can't attend good-old-boys' clubs, so I'm going to call my dad and check on Lincoln. Zack, you do what you need to. Connor will handle this. If someone comes after us, we'll deal with it in a calm and humane way."

Connor cupped his wife's shoulders, looking down into her eyes, their connection a palpable thing. "I am not going to sit down for a conflict-resolution summit with a crazed drug dealer who wants to murder you."

"Of course not. You're going to very humanely put him down," Lara agreed. "You can kill him, but it can't hurt."

"Quick and easy, baby. I promise." He kissed her lightly.

"We've both learned to compromise. It's so important in marriage." She turned and followed Gus and Liz out the door.

Everly closed the lid of her laptop. "I'm going to our room. It could take a while to run all the facial recognition software, and I'm afraid I'm still pretty jet-lagged. You boys don't stay up too late plotting." She turned to Roman when she reached the door. "And you should seriously think about what you're doing with Gus. I know she seems invulnerable, but she's just a woman when it comes to you. You can take her apart with a harsh word."

"I'm not trying to hurt her," he insisted. "I'm trying to protect her."

Everly clutched the laptop to her chest. "See that you do or you'll answer to the rest of us. I hate leaving her out of this. You think she could be a weak link, but I think she would be an amazing asset. She's smart. She thinks outside the box. She's good at damage control. Consider it at least. Lara's right—compromise is important."

Once the door closed behind her, all the women had gone. Roman found himself with three of the five men he'd considered his brothers for the majority of his life. Dax was missing, but for the best of reasons. No doubt, he was enjoying his honeymoon at that little bed and breakfast in Maui.

But Mad would always be a hollow space in their lives—and their hearts.

"When did the women get so scary?" Connor asked.

Gabe held his hands up. "Mine has always been scary. Let's face facts—we have a type. Even Lara's got claws. Oh, I'm sure they're organic, cruelty-free claws, but they are claws all the same."

Zack sank down to one of the ornate chairs, weariness plain on his face. "Can we all agree this is likely the shit we've been waiting to hit the fan?"

"I think that's clear." Gabe nodded.

"But it's not the tactic I expected," Roman mused. "If this Sergei person is out there and he's been pulling the strings the entire time, why come at the president's friends? Why not the president himself? Certainly he didn't think Zack would betray his country to spare us some embarrassment."

"Whoever is behind this plot has been working for a long time to ensure Zack got into office. Now that they're clearly demanding that we stay out of the European energy market, we have some specific ideas why they might have gone to so much trouble. We're talking billions of dollars," Connor explained. "But none of the dirt they dug up on us is terribly compelling. This strategy doesn't make sense."

"I suspect this is only the beginning." Zack sat back. "They're testing my resolve and our defenses. Right now, they're only making demands about delaying a pipeline that could eventually make America one of the world's leading energy exporters and deal a major blow to the floundering Russian economy, since they're Europe's primary supplier of heating oil. That's the reason Russia 'annexed' Crimea. The line about protecting Russian citizens was BS. They wanted control of that natural gas pipeline to Europe."

"So now they want to ensure we don't build one that would connect our resources to their number one customer," Connor agreed.

That made perfect sense to Roman. The Russians had always been involved. At first he'd thought the threat merely stemmed from the *Bratva*, the Russian mob. But he'd realized a while back that the conspirators were pushing Russian interests and merely using the *Bratva* to eliminate anyone who got in their way.

Like Admiral Spencer, Dax and Augustine's father.

Like Maddox.

Like Joy.

He'd come to England to find out if he should add Constance Hayes to that list. He'd hoped to see if he could pull the string that would unravel the conspiracy so they could finally understand what they were dealing with. And hopefully figure out how to stop it.

"The pipeline is a long-term project," Zack mused. "It's at least a decade out. We're not even certain it can be done."

"But simply announcing it could undermine some of Russia's plans and further destabilize their economy,"

Gabe observed, sitting opposite Zack.

"I agree. It's a test to manipulate you," Connor said quietly. "To see how quickly they push you into a corner. If they can get you to delay the pipeline for a few years, they'll know they can influence your decision, maybe even force you to change your stance on world issues and eventually make you a puppet for Russian interests."

"You're right," Roman murmured, horror and fury raging through him.

Connor shrugged. "In their shoes, I would slow play every move. Coming at Zack too fast could cause him to quit the game altogether, like the old anecdote about the frog being boiled alive. If you toss the frog in hot water, he'll jump out quickly. So instead, you put the frog in the pot of nice, cool water. You give him some time to get used to his new environment, get comfortable. And when he's certain everything's normal again, that's when you turn up the heat. You do it slowly, so the frog doesn't even realize he's boiling alive until it's far too late. This is the first adjustment. They've come after your friends because they perceive us to be your weak spot. They give you an easy fix to the problem. Don't talk about the pipeline, simply make it clear to the prime minister and other European leaders that any American policy on this topic is something we'll deal with down the line. Which is easy because we're not ready yet."

Roman could see exactly where this was going. "So Zack figures it's easy to concentrate on other negotiations. After all, there's plenty of time. We're not killing the deal, merely downplaying it, while saving his friends some heartache. But the conspirators have won the round, and the heat soon goes up. They realize Zack is vulnerable, so they aim higher next time, maybe ask

Zack to ease up on the sanctions of Russian goods. And if he does, that gives them more dirt on him. Little by little, they chip away at him until, one day, he's completely in their pocket without any way out. He won't even be able to quit because they'll have so much blackmail material on him. And probably us, too."

"Has anyone considered that they could turn all these mysterious deaths over the years back on us? If I look at this rationally, examine all the evidence and try to figure out who profits the most from their silence, I can only come to one conclusion." Gabe looked grim.

Roman knew the answer because he'd thought the same thing. "Zack."

Gabe nodded slowly. "Yes. Mad knew too much, so Zack had him eliminated."

"Admiral Spencer knew too much so he had to die as well." Both had perished at a politically expedient time for Zack.

"I was losing the election by three points." Zack's voice was hollow. "So I had my wife take a bullet that everyone believes should have been for me. Mourning and sympathy swept me right into the White House. Even the pollsters said the election swung in that one moment."

They had Zack in check, and none of them had even realized the game swirling around them.

Roman winced. He felt like hell about betraying Augustine's confidence, but he couldn't not tell his brothers what he knew. The stakes were far higher than anyone's feelings. "Augustine believes that one of your Secret Service agents was in on Mad's murder. She's got proof he was at the airport the day Mad died."

Zack sat up straight. "Are you kidding me?"

"I wish I was."

Zack sent him a steely gaze. "Who? Connor, I want him arrested and questioned."

This was everything Augustine had feared. Roman held out a hand. "Wait. The man in question is still working. If he's a sleeper agent and you pull him now, we'll lose the chance to figure out what he's doing here in England. We could also lose the opportunity to see who he meets with and if there are any other traitors among the staff."

Gus was right about that. She simply didn't know how dangerous the game was.

"Connor can make him talk," Zack said, his voice tight.

Connor hesitated. "Yes, but I think Roman's right. I think I should follow him. Tell me it's not Thomas. We have to have someone we can trust with Zack."

Zack laughed, but it was a bitter sound. "It's either Matt or Clint. I should have seen it. Am I right? That's why Gus and Liz had a sudden desire to flirt with them. Damn Gus and her plots. She cannot bring Liz into her reckless antics."

Anger sparked through Roman's system. Zack didn't get to criticize Gus...even if he'd thought the same thing at one point. "Hey, she's trying to find out who killed Mad and you're going to back off her. She loves Liz and wouldn't put her in danger. And don't confront her about this. She didn't come to us because we've been assholes. We've kept secrets and she's smart enough to know something's going on. What is she supposed to think? She finds out a Secret Service agent was prowling around the airport before Mad's plane exploded? We're hiding something and won't talk to her? Take the logic leap there, Zack."

Zack had turned a sufficient shade of pale. "She can't think I sent him."

"Oh, I bet she can," Gabe murmured. "At one point, I even wondered about that, and I'm one of your best friends. I know better now, but Gus has never been one of the inner circle. Without information to disprove her theory, how is she supposed to allay her suspicions?"

"I'm only trying to protect them. Right now, Liz has plausible deniability. She's got to talk to the press on a daily basis. I do not want her to have to knowingly lie. And Gus is in roughly the same position," Zack argued. "If I thought for a second they would be safer away from the White House and us, I would send them in a heartbeat."

"But the conspirators already know how close we are to them," Roman surmised. "If they didn't, they wouldn't have bothered to include either in the blackmail. That letter was also a statement of intent. He knows who we care about, and if we don't acquiesce to whatever they demand, they will come after Gus and Liz. Pushing those two away won't fool him. I understand you're trying to ensure Liz's job and integrity, but you need to rethink. I'm not pushing Gus away. I made a deal with her and I'm going to honor it. Well, after I've totally broken it by telling you all about Kemp."

"Your secret is safe with me," Zack promised. "And the truth is, if Gus has it in her head to investigate, she'll do it one way or another and she'll bring Liz in, too." He slapped at the table and stood up straight. "All right, then. You have a job to do, Roman."

Keep Gus contained…somehow.

"Yes, I'm scheduled to go out to the sanatorium

tomorrow while you're meeting with the prime minister. Kemp has time off the day after, and Gus wants to follow him."

"I'll stay on top of the esteemed agent," Connor offered, voice acidic. "And I'll keep you in the loop. I will sit Gus down in the morning and let her know she's important to this operation. Then you can sneak away, and she'll think you're in meetings with Zack and the PM. If you run late, that's how it goes."

But he must be back by bedtime or Gus would know he'd lied. The hospital was two hours outside London. He had a room at a local bed and breakfast, but if he had to he could drive back and be in bed with Augustine that night. She didn't have to know a thing. He could keep the spirit of his promise and protect her at the same time. She would understand that Connor was the better bet to follow Kemp, especially now that the agent knew she wasn't currently single. As long as they kept her updated, she should accept that. He would even let her research the man from the safety of Everly's suite. Since Gabe's wife was a hacker and had long ties to law enforcement, she would be an excellent resource for Gus.

It also didn't hurt that Everly was a badass who knew Krav Maga—and her way around a gun.

Yes, this could work. "Excellent. I'll get what we need from the hospital in the morning and return tomorrow night."

"Liz will keep Gus busy and out of danger," Zack said. "I'll make sure they've got a lot to do over the next few days. She won't have time to notice you're gone."

"All right. That gives us time to see what other stones we can upturn before we have to deal with any announcement about a potential pipeline. No one will expect anything on that before the end of the week. Tomorrow, all you're scheduled to discuss is European relations and the reaffirmation of NATO ties."

"I'll look into the FAA problem and see if there's anything we're unaware of that could bite us in the ass," Connor promised. "And I'll enlist Thomas's help to keep an eye on Kemp. I don't have to tell him why. He won't ask and he won't confront the guy." He turned to Zack. "We'll get through this week. Once we get back to DC, we'll sit down and decide how to move forward."

They would decide *if* they could move forward. He could see it in Zack's eyes. He was already wondering if his smartest move was to simply step down before these bastards had too much on him and he no longer could.

"Connor's right. Stop overthinking this, Zack. Concentrate on the next few days and leave the rest to us. The water's not boiling yet. We have time," Roman promised. "But for tonight, I need to go and make sure Gus isn't enlisting Liz in some plot against us."

Zack huffed out a laugh. "Yes, you should do that. She could incite a rebellion." Then he frowned. "Does she still suspect I killed Mad?"

"No. She knows better now. Don't worry. I'll take care of her," Roman swore.

Zack nodded his way. "It's about damn time."

He turned and walked out, hoping he could untangle this situation and keep all his promises.

CHAPTER ELEVEN

Gus closed the door to the room she previously occupied and glanced back at Liz. "Did something else happen? Did you see anything odd before you got that envelope? Or after I left you?"

Liz sat on the bed with a sigh. "No. I had an incredibly awkward meeting with the president. I kept it as unemotional as I could. When we finished, he walked me back to my room and I slammed the door in his face. I definitely locked it, too. As for the secret tunnels, I had no idea. This is my first trip here."

"Do you think the Secret Service knows?" The Secret Service didn't change with the presidency. As far as she knew, Matthew Kemp had been working on a presidential detail for four years. Zack had only been the president for three. "Did the prior administration come here in the last two years of his presidency?"

Liz took a deep breath. "I doubt it, but I can find out

for sure. Do you think Kemp left that folder on my bed?"

"It makes sense. I really think he's involved in this mess. I want to know in what way and how deep. Now that you and I are away from prying male stares, let's find out what he jotted on the notepad on his nightstand. Do you have a pencil?" When she'd gotten dressed, Gus had shoved the sticky notes she'd taken from the stack in Kemp's room into the pocket of her jeans.

Liz crossed the room and dug through her purse. "What happened earlier? When you didn't come back, I was terrified. Then a few minutes later Kemp got up and said he was going to the bathroom. I texted you like crazy."

Gus rolled her eyes. "Roman happened. He and Zack returned while I was sneaking down. He spotted me, got suspicious, and followed. We were stuck in the closet while Kemp made a phone call. We were damn lucky he didn't catch us hiding under his suits."

"I knew something had gone wrong when Zack showed up and acted like a caveman. He doesn't want me but no one else can even look my way. Asshole." She approached, a slender pencil in her hand.

"I don't think it's a case of Zack not wanting you. My emotional radar isn't faulty. He's always been interested. I'm telling you, something is going on with these men. We got a taste of it tonight, but I guarantee there's more. I've been around that group long enough to know when they're plotting or covering up something." Gus gripped the pencil. "Now I have to wonder if it isn't related to Mad's murder. It would be so like Mad to have stumbled into a situation he shouldn't have just before it exploded. Is your computer up?"

Gus pulled the sticky notes from her pocket and

lightly traced the indentations with the soft side of the pencil. What Kemp had written with a somewhat heavy hand slowly became clear as she jimmied the pencil back and forth.

"No, but I've got my phone and I've got a browser open, if you're trying to look something up." Liz tapped to unlock the device. "What is it?"

"An address. Kemp wrote this down in his room. Can you look this place up for me?" She handed Liz the note. "I'm starting to think everything going on is connected, and I don't like the intersecting lines."

"You think the blackmail is only part of the story? That Zack and the others are hiding the rest?" Her face was illuminated by the glow of the phone's screen as she typed with her thumbs.

"Yeah, there's more. Something bigger. I suspect someone is trying to manipulate Zack. Why else do you blackmail the president? And did you notice that no one else in the room seemed terribly surprised by the fact that someone sneaked into your room?" At Liz's nod, Gus charged on. "But whatever's happening is deep, insidious. When Kemp was on the phone, he muttered something about getting information and eliminating a target. I think his destination is that address, and if I follow him I might get some answers."

Liz frowned. "It's a mental hospital two hours north of London."

Gus nearly groaned. "Homewood Sanatorium, right?"

"Yeah. Why does that sound so familiar?"

Gus tried not to shiver at the implications. "Because it was in our oppo research."

During Zack's campaign, one of the first things

she'd been in charge of was finding any and all dirt the opposition would likely dig up on Zack and use against him. She'd compiled a file on Constance Hayes.

All their problems pointed to Zack. That meant trouble. Serious trouble. What kind of dangerous game were the boys playing?

Liz set the phone down. "That's right. Frank Hayes stashed his wife there when she had her breakdown. They registered her under an assumed name, Jane Downing. The information never came out during the campaign, but I remember everyone worrying that someone would question Zack's fitness for office, given his mother's history of mental illness." She frowned. "But why bring this up now? The next election is over a year away, and why wouldn't the opposition save this for an October surprise just before voters hit the polls?"

"They're looking for more fodder for blackmail? Because they want Zack to do something now? I don't know. But you're right. Why now? Dirt like this doesn't matter as much in a reelection campaign. Zack's already proven he can handle the job." Gus's mind was whirling. "If Kemp is planning a visit to the sanatorium during his leave day after tomorrow, I need to get there first. I need to figure out who he's talking to and why."

"How are you going to do that?" Liz asked. "Roman appears to have you on a short leash now. Or did I read things wrong and you moving into his room is about something other than him crawling back into your bed."

"He says he's protecting me."

And right up to the moment he'd joked about getting her pregnant, she'd felt perfectly happy with their arrangement. In fact, she'd felt something close to precious and protected and content. Making love with

Roman had been a revelation. He'd been tender and even a little funny. It had felt so good and right to be with him.

She couldn't think that way. They'd had sex, period. All Roman had been doing was scratching an itch. Nothing had really changed between them.

"Or he's watching you. Did you tell him what you've discovered?" Liz asked.

"I told him pretty much everything." She'd given it all up like a girl with a crush on a boy. Didn't that burn? "In my defense, he threatened to blow up my entire investigation, so I had to play along. He intends to go with me when I follow Kemp, but I think we should definitely beat the agent to the hospital. It's too coincidental that just when Zack is blackmailed, someone on his security detail decides to visit the hospital where his mother was treated for mental health issues, in the town where she mysteriously died. He's looking for more dirt."

"Haven't they found enough on all of us already?" Liz squeezed her shoulder. "Are you okay?"

Gus waved her off. "Please, a sex tape is so passé. I'm a little surprised that hasn't happened to me before. I guess revenge porn is all the rage, and you know I can piss off a man like no one else."

"I wasn't talking about that. I meant the bombshell about Joy and Roman."

It made Gus a little queasy to know Roman had given the other woman his heart, which she'd once wanted so desperately. But she pasted on a smile to pacify Liz. "I already knew about that. Joy told me. I'm fine."

Liz's eyes narrowed. "The minute you use the word *fine* I know you're not. You knew Roman and Joy were having an affair but you never mentioned it?"

"It wasn't an affair. It was...a flirtation. Zack knew about it, too. By the time Joy admitted to me that she felt much closer to Roman, she and Zack had already been married for a few years. They'd moved into a friendly partnership by then. I thought you might have noticed during the campaign." Gus always wondered if Zack had ever talked to Liz about Roman and Joy in an attempt to set the stage for their own relationship. Apparently not.

"I knew they weren't the most affectionate couple, but they liked each other. I guess now that I look back, Joy did prefer to spend time with Roman. They had a lot of meetings and lunches I didn't quite see they needed, but it wasn't my place to question. I knew Joy had a lot of pull with Roman. Did you know Roman didn't want to do the Midwest campaign the last week before the election? He considered it totally lost and wanted to concentrate on Virginia and Colorado. Zack was willing to do whatever Roman thought best. It was Joy who convinced him to reconsider. I sometimes think that if Roman had followed his instincts, she would be alive today."

Gus hadn't known Joy had quietly changed Roman's mind. When her dear friend had discussed Roman, she'd mostly gushed that he was amazing, strong, and thoughtful. But Joy was smart, too. Gus wasn't terribly surprised she'd influenced the outcome of the election— in more ways than one.

"Joy might have seemed passive, but she wasn't. She was actually quite ambitious, though not in the same way you and I are. When I met her in college, she went out of her way to be friends with me. I didn't get her at first, but we were in the same sorority, and I eventually understood that we were just different. She was raised to be a powerful man's wife. I was raised to be powerful myself. Marrying well was her goal. When she hooked Zack, she knew she'd caught the great white whale. I actually tried to talk her out of it because I knew they didn't suit."

"But she shared his aspirations and she wanted the chance to be the First Lady." Liz sighed. "Then I suppose it's not surprising she would look for love and affection with someone else. I'm just surprised she gravitated to Roman. He can be intimidating. There's a reason he's called the Hitman."

"Yeah, but he's always had a thing for quiet, demure women. I remember telling Joy that she would probably be a better match for Roman. I was pissed at the time. So angry with him."

Liz grimaced. "I can't see them together at all, if that helps. She would have utterly bored him."

"Well, Roman could see it, and that's exactly why I need to be careful with him. I'm not his type. Never have been. Never will be."

Gus heard a soft knock. The door, which had been slightly ajar, opened wide. Roman stood on the other side. Damn it, how much had he overheard? His expression gave nothing away.

"Hey, let's go to bed. It's late and we've got a lot to do tomorrow," he said, his voice soft.

So he wasn't backing off. An hour before, she'd thought the two of them sharing a room might be a good thing, a way to get him out of her system. Now she wondered. But she couldn't back out of their deal unless she wanted him to spill everything about her investigation to Zack.

Gus gave Roman a tight smile as she stood. At least she had a plan...one she had to proceed with tomorrow, while he was tied up with Zack and the prime minister. She'd tell him what she found afterward. After all, she'd merely promised to share her information. She hadn't specified when.

"I'll see you in the morning," she said to Liz.

Liz nodded. "See you then. We'll handle everything beautifully, like we always do. Don't worry about a thing."

Liz was telling her that if she needed to leave to investigate the sanatorium before Kemp, she could.

"'Night."

At the thought of running around the English countryside, retracing the footsteps of a potential killer, Gus wondered what she was getting herself into.

When he held out his hand, she took it and allowed him to lead her into the hallway. He nodded to the dark-suited Secret Service agent stationed in the hall as he tangled his fingers in hers, warming her skin. Then he headed toward his room—and the bed they would share.

"Augustine, I want you to know that I don't care about the sex tape, but you should understand that I'll beat the holy shit out of whoever recorded you," he said quietly. "I'll do everything I can to make sure it doesn't get out."

"You don't care?" Gus frowned. He expected her to believe that?

He stopped in the middle of the quiet hall and glanced down the narrow space, as though trying to figure out if they were alone and could talk. "I don't give a damn what you've done in the past."

"Hmm. I've done some crazy shit, Roman, and we

both know it. It's always bothered you before, despite the fact that you're friends with a couple of men who put me to shame in the sexcapades department."

"Could you allow that thirteen years might have mellowed me? That maybe I learned something in the time we've been apart?"

Maybe…but did a leopard really change his spots? "Like I said, Zack should worry about the others. I'll be fine."

He dropped her hand, frowning. "But *I'm* worried. I don't want you involved in this, and before you accuse me of leaving you out, I don't want you involved because I care about you. You're one of my oldest friends and I never want you hurt."

Friends. Of course he would use that language, even though they'd never really been friends.

Was that entirely his fault? Had she treated him like a friend in return? He'd called her after their breakup. And every time, she'd rebuffed him. She needed to stop being so angry with him for a tragedy he couldn't apologize for because she hadn't told him a thing.

Could they actually be friends? They couldn't if she never tried, never softened even a bit around him. Maybe the better question was, after losing Mad, could she afford to lose anyone else close to her?

Roman started walking again, his shoulders slumping wearily. She could see how tired he was.

Gus hurried to catch up, her palms feeling cold without his touch. She'd been warmer, felt safer when he'd held her hand and given her his strength. What was wrong with being affectionate? Even if they wouldn't be together forever, couldn't they enjoy each other for now? He'd compromised. He'd promised to keep her secret, and she knew how much that had cost him. He was treating her like a true partner. So he'd made a joke he couldn't possibly have known would wound her. It wasn't his fault.

She dashed to his side and slipped her hand into his. He stopped, looking down at her in surprise before he locked their fingers together and continued down the hall, past the stoic Secret Service agents.

"I thought we were going to fight," he said as they approached his door.

"We can do that later. You're tired tonight. Let's go to bed and deal with everything in the morning."

He used his free hand to open the door and usher her in. Once he closed it again, he pulled her close and wrapped her in his arms. His mouth descended quickly. "I'm not that tired."

He kissed her and she forgot about everything except how good it felt to be with him.

* * * *

Gus curled up in bed an hour later, her body still pulsing with the most recent orgasm Roman had given her. Her fourth of the night. It was surprising she could still move. The man hadn't lost a bit of his athleticism.

The light went out, plunging the room into warm darkness. Roman crawled back into bed and skated a hand up her leg, settling on her hip. He hooked his arm around her waist, pulling her against his body. Such delicious heat. She couldn't help but wriggle against him, getting as close as their bodies allowed. Funny, after he'd been gone from her life, his nearness was one of the things she'd missed most.

"I set the alarm," he assured in a whisper. "I'm going to be totally useless tomorrow."

"Me, too. But we have to talk. Kemp is going to be on the move after tomorrow." Perhaps after sex was the time to bring up her plan, rather than following her investigative jaunt to the country. He'd be sated, easygoing now. She wasn't trying to manipulate him, just ease the conversation. Besides, if she didn't bring this up now, he'd be gone by sunrise.

"I know. I already took care of the Kemp issue." He kissed her shoulder.

She had to force herself to sound calm. "Took care of it how?"

"Connor's going to follow him."

"We agreed we'd do that together."

"Too much to do, and it's getting really dangerous. So I talked to Connor about it tonight. This is his wheelhouse. He spent a lifetime as a spy, so he'll be better at staying under the radar of a trained agent than either of us. He'll keep you in the loop. Don't worry about a thing. I've got this. All you have to do is work with Liz and let me take care of you."

The warmth Gus had been feeling moments earlier vanished, and she realized she wasn't the one using sex to manipulate.

Roman had gotten smarter over the years. He'd almost figured out how to play her.

Connor would keep her in the "loop," huh? She was certain Connor's loop would only include what Roman and Zack wanted her to know. She wasn't a complete idiot. If Roman had talked to Connor tonight, he'd done it with Zack present. After all that blackmail talk, he wouldn't have told one and not the other about her plans to investigate Kemp. Gabe probably knew her secret, too. They'd likely sent the women away, then plotted how to keep them out of it, how to keep all the information to themselves and use it to their benefit.

They wouldn't allow themselves to think about Mad. They would think of the living. Gus was the only one who gave a shit about her oldest friend not having died in vain and resting in peace.

But it also told her that her bargain with Roman, the sex they'd had, and his flimsy assurances had been mere strategy meant to soften her attitude and persuade her compliance.

Fuck that.

"You all right, baby?"

If she fought him now, he would simply reassess and come at her another way, like put so many security guards on her she couldn't sneeze without him knowing. Maybe even send her immediately back to DC. Gus couldn't risk that.

"I'm fine. I'm thinking about tomorrow. Lots of meetings."

"You're not upset about me handing this over to Connor? Zack needs me in these meetings and I don't want you doing this on your own, baby. It's too dangerous. After tonight, you must see that." His arm tightened around her as though he was afraid she might bolt from the bed.

She saw that he was a snake in the grass. He wanted Connor to take over the investigation so he could control everything. If she'd been in their last good-old-boys powwow, she would have found out how all these seemingly random facts and events were connected. But no, she'd been sent away like a bad little girl so the big boys could plot without the women worrying their pretty heads.

Gus also feared he'd never meant to keep any of his promises.

"You're right. When you've got a former CIA agent in your pocket, you should probably use him." And she would. She would let him trail Kemp and never once complain because tomorrow morning, she would go to the hospital herself and find the answers she needed.

Then tomorrow night, once she had the information she sought, she would tell Roman exactly where he could shove his deal.

"It's going to be okay. I'll make sure of it," he murmured with an absent kiss.

After a few minutes, she heard his breathing slow and the arm around her midsection went lax with sleep.

Gus stayed awake, her mind whirling. She had to deal with everything—Mad's murder, the sudden blackmail, whatever trouble Zack was up to his eyeballs in—on her own. She was alone again.

And nothing between her and Roman had really changed. Now she was pretty sure it never would.

CHAPTER TWELVE

Roman glanced down at his phone. Still no response from Gus. He'd texted her a couple of times to say hi and ask her how the day was going. And...maybe to keep track of her a little. He didn't like the fact that she was in London and he was hours away at the sanatorium. If she got into trouble, he couldn't reach her quickly.

Of course, Connor was there, keeping an eye on Kemp. Still, Roman wanted to call her and hear her voice, but he was supposed to be in a series of meetings. He'd thought of joining them via phone while he'd been driving up, but the line had to be absolutely secure. And he didn't need anyone else asking where he was going or why, especially if Gus overheard.

They had reunited less than twenty-four hours ago, and he was already lying to her.

"You the man who's come about some old records?" The receptionist was dressed in soft scrubs, her dark hair pulled into a tight bun. Her name tag merely read *Yolanda*, with none of the designations that explained an employee's function around a place like this.

He slipped his phone back in his pocket. Gus was probably consumed with her work. Putting together a press conference that included the prime minister of Great Britain and the president of the United States was no small feat. "Yes, I made an appointment to talk to the director of the hospital."

"He's in a meeting right now, but he should be available soon," she replied. "That one didn't have an appointment at all, but she's damn fine at talking her way in, if you know what I mean. Don't hurt none that she's a looker. Dr. Billings took one look at that and he no longer cared about his by-appointment-only policy. Sorry."

So he was getting sidelined because the doctor was horny.

"If it doesn't take too long, fine. I'm a busy man," Roman said, then remembered that his usual "I'm the White House chief of staff and you will do my bidding" routine wouldn't work here. Besides, he needed to keep this trip on the down low or he'd run the risk of having reporters on his ass. He had to operate under the radar until he got his hands on whatever information he could and returned to London. "But I can wait a few minutes."

He also needed to be back with Augustine.

The nurse nodded his way. "I'll go and interrupt him shortly. I don't mind doing that none at all. He's a bit high on his own self, if you know what I mean."

"I work with a lot of people like that, so yes," he replied. "I probably am a person like that. Or at least my girlfriend would likely say so."

Wow. He'd called Gus his girlfriend. And he'd liked it.

It had occurred to Roman this morning as he and Gus were getting dressed that they didn't have to stop seeing each other when the danger passed. Having a quiet breakfast with her, passing the newspaper back and forth, and talking about the headlines had been a nice way to start the day.

Yolanda laughed. "I say that about my husband, too, but I'm telling you he ain't got nothing on these doctors. You treat one or two celebs and suddenly they think they're god's gift to clean living."

It occurred to him that he could put his wait to good use. Yolanda looked to be in her late thirties, perhaps early forties, and she had the eager look of a gossip. The waiting room was empty, and when he'd walked up she'd been filing her nails. No wonder she was happy for the chat.

"How long has Dr. Billings been the director here?" he asked.

"A couple of years now, but he's worked here for ages. He's the worst of 'em. Calls hisself the doctor to the stars and all."

"Do you get to meet them? The stars, that is?"

She shrugged. "Not really, but I don't mind. They're usually all drugged up when they first arrive. And when they leave, they tend to go quietly. No one wants to admit they've been here. Except the druggies. They want to pat themselves on the back about how they got clean, but the others, the ones who have come because they're supposedly not right in the head... I wonder."

"About?"

"Maybe I shouldn't say nothing, but sometimes I

think this place is just an expensive babysitting service. It certainly was a few years ago. Before they opened the addiction wing, this was where rich men sent their inconvenient women. Now, I'm not saying anything loads of others haven't. It was a well-known fact all through the country in polite circles that if a man was tired of his wife, he could send her to Homewood."

"So you don't think the patients had real mental health issues?"

"Mental health issues can be defined in lots of ways. That's the trouble, isn't it? No definitive test for lunacy like there is for cancer. What one person calls a quirk another calls a mental disorder. If you look back a hundred years or so, you'll see plenty of men used that excuse to shed troublesome wives. Back then they didn't divorce, you know. So they said lots of things made to make their woman a candidate for the asylum. Novel reading. Yeah, that was one. How ridiculous is that?"

"In the Victorian era, and even the early twentieth century, any woman with a high spirit and half an opinion could be considered crazy," he agreed. Gus would likely have been tossed into an asylum back then if she'd married the wrong man. She definitely would have been on the front lines of the suffrage movement. "But surely we've improved as a society. That sort of groundless institutionalization hasn't happened much in the last fifty years, right?"

She laughed, the sound reverberating through the quiet lobby. "It still goes on all the time. It's just done a lot quieter than before. And sometimes the ones that come in for drugs and alcohol stay for other things. Standard treatment is twenty-eight days, but if the husbands don't want them out, they don't leave. Looks real good in a custody battle to say your wife is loony, if you know what I mean."

He did, though when Zack's mother had been committed, custody hadn't been an issue. He'd already been well over eighteen. "See any politicians in here?"

"Sure, but they're mostly from other countries. Don't want their dirty laundry aired near home," she said breezily. She stopped and her eyes narrowed. "You were asking about a pol's wife, right? You're a lawyer for the family or something like that."

Yolanda probably didn't follow U.S. politics. And it worked to Roman's advantage that he didn't grant many interviews these days. When he did, he gave them almost exclusively to news outlets in the States. Liz handled all the overseas requests. "Yes, I'm a lawyer for a powerful man whose mother spent time here. My client wants to know more about this period in his mother's life, but his elderly father now has dementia. So I'm looking into this matter on his behalf so he can write his memoirs someday."

"Of course. Memoirs. Sounds fancy and all," she said with a grin. "Well, the good doc worked here during the time you mentioned when we spoke earlier. I wasn't, of course. I'm far too young, still a schoolgirl back then, you know."

She hadn't been, but he liked her charm. "Naturally."

Her phone rang and she answered, giving him a smile. "Sorry, duty calls. The director should be with you in a moment."

* * * *

Roman paced the too-quiet waiting room. The hospital was privately owned, and he didn't doubt its patients were all überwealthy. The lobby and waiting room were decorated in calm colors, everything elegant and plush. Actual paintings graced the walls, all artfully done, and nothing so common as prints. These were originals. Yet for all the trappings of wealth and serenity, an air of desperation clung.

Zack's father had sat in this exact room as he'd committed Constance. How hard had it been to leave his wife here? Or had it? Frank Hayes had always been an ambitious man who strove to present the best optics to the public. Their marriage had been a prearranged partnership, much like Zack and Joy's. Despite Frank's lofty aspirations, he never climbed higher than an ambassadorship. Was that why they'd splintered and she'd become a babbling alcoholic? Had the unfulfilled promise of success rotted their marriage from within?

He bet Frank and Constance had rarely fought. Likely any arguments between the two had been cool and civil—until the day Frank had his wife committed. If Joy had fallen apart, Roman knew Zack would have handled the situation with more compassion and humanity than his dad. Roman tried to imagine himself institutionalizing Gus the way Frank had Constance and he cringed. Of course, she would only laugh in his face before she beat him with her stiletto and told him to go to hell.

That image spread a smile across Roman's face. He loved that his girl didn't put up with shit.

Feeling antsy, he sat to wait. Quiet smothered this place. Of course Homewood had patients, but it felt empty, as if bodies lived here but their souls had checked out long ago.

The silence gnawed at Roman. And he knew Joy would have appreciated the complete sense of calm.

If he'd ever truly started his own relationship with her, how would that have worked? Would she have ever adjusted to his organized chaos...or would her placid façade finally have grated on him? For years, she'd seemed like his ideal, but now he wondered. No woman turned him on like Gus, and no one would ever accuse that woman of being quiet or inspiring peace.

The only time he'd ever seen a hint of assertiveness from Joy was on the final leg of the Midwest campaign bus tour. Roman had wanted to shore up a couple of states that might slip away, but she'd insisted on pushing through a handful of others they were almost sure to lose. She'd been so upset, so adamant. Roman had given in.

And gotten her killed.

Maybe the shooter would have turned up in Virginia. Or Colorado. Maybe her political death had merely been inevitable, but Roman felt as if he'd done something terrible.

And he hated that Gus had to hear about his flirtation with her friend right after they'd made love for the first time in a dozen years.

I'm not his type. Never have been. Never will be.

He'd overheard her say that to Liz the night before. How could she feel that way? He couldn't seem to stay away from her, keep his hands off her...

Maybe because you told her that over and over in the past. Yes, he'd likely spewed that litany so many times the words were burned into her brain. Roman frowned. What the hell did he know about his own damn type? He realized now that he'd given into Joy's pleading about the final stretch in the campaign not because he'd wanted to make her happy, but because he'd liked that assertive side of her and wanted to encourage it more.

His cell phone trilled, saving him from troubling thoughts. He glanced down at the screen and cursed softly. Not Gus. Darcy Hildebrandt. He thought about letting the call go to voicemail but if he didn't answer, she might go looking for him. When she didn't find him, she might run into Gus and ask why he wasn't at Downing Street. Then he would be in hot water—the kind already boiling because Gus wouldn't bother to slow roll him.

Roman reluctantly answered his phone. "Hello?"

A feminine sigh sounded in his ear. "Oh, there you are. I was a bit worried you were avoiding me today."

He planned on avoiding her for the rest of their official visit. Maybe now that he and Gus were together, he could sic his girl on Darcy. It would be fun to watch Gus dish out an ass kicking. Maybe they'd even let him make popcorn and have a ringside seat.

"I've just been very busy. The president can be demanding." That wasn't entirely untrue.

"I haven't seen you here in any of the meetings. I've been looking all over for you."

"I must have missed you." The key to lying was to not commit to too many details. "I've been running all over the place. I'm currently dealing with background issues, so we've had to divide and conquer in order to handle everything. I won't be around much today. Tomorrow, I should be with the president. I'm sure I'll see you then."

"Actually, I was hoping you would join me for lunch today. Or perhaps dinner tonight."

Oh, god no. "Sorry. I won't have time. Shame... And my schedule is tight for the rest of the week. You know how intense these meetings can be. It's almost as if the fate of the free world rests on our shoulders," Roman tried to joke.

But he didn't intend to be alone with Darcy again. The next time they were in public, he would use Gus like a shield. He would lay on the PDA, and his British counterpart would get the point.

Outward affection didn't bother him the way it used to. As a kid, he'd hated when his parents kissed in front of him. It had never been a peck. They'd constantly made out. Friends and family always remarked how in love they were, but they had never seen his parents snarl like cats and dogs, watched them scratch and claw as they did their best to tear each other apart.

He'd decided that affection was a lie. They'd used it to convince everyone else their marriage didn't have an ugly side. But last night had him rethinking that conclusion. Holding Gus's hand had felt damn good—honest and necessary. With that gesture, he hadn't been fooling anyone, least of all himself. His feelings for Gus were real and so damn complex.

But they were making progress. After pulling Gus away from Liz last night, Roman had expected a fight. Instead, she'd taken the news that Connor would be watching Kemp in stride, then curled up beside him in bed and given him comfort. Next to her feminine warmth, he'd slept better than he had in years.

"I think you can sneak away for a bit," Darcy insisted with a flirty laugh. "I would hate for the week to end and you to go home before experiencing some true British hospitality. After all, it could be a long while before I travel to the States."

Zack was right. He was going to have to make himself plain. "Darcy, I think you're under the impression that I'm available for relations that extend beyond the office. The truth is, I'm involved with another woman and I don't think she would appreciate me spending time with you that isn't business related."

Darcy fell silent. "You never mentioned a girlfriend. In fact, you told me before this visit that you had no significant woman in your life."

"I don't usually talk about my personal life with work colleagues. And frankly, it's a complicated relationship. She's been in my life since I was a kid. We're very close. We've had our ups and downs over the years, but last night we decided to give us a real try. I'm sorry if you feel I've misled you."

"Misled me? Taking me to the theater with the president and a supermodel, and not correcting me when I told the bloody press we're dating is more than misleading."

So she wasn't always sunshine and light. That made things easier. "I never indicated that we're dating. You assumed. The purpose of our outing was to accompany the president. He likes to have someone to talk to in public. Better photo ops. It's awkward if I'm tagging along as the third wheel. I never considered our outing as anything more than one colleague helping another."

"Well, then. Absolutely my fault." She forced the sunshine back in her voice, as if she hadn't just growled at him in a harpy tone he'd never heard her use before. "Please forgive me. We do have a few details to cover for the formal state dinner, but if you would prefer to work with someone else, I can arrange for another colleague to take my place."

Why was he constantly surrounded by touchy women? He sighed and deliberately softened his voice. Other than her unwanted flirtation, she'd been extremely competent, and he didn't want the tongue wagging that would accompany him asking for another liaison to affect her position. "Not at all. Let's talk tomorrow. I'll find you at Downing Street later so we can coordinate details."

"Excellent. Thank you, Mr. Calder. I look forward to it, and thank you for the pleasant evening."

Thank god they were back to being polite. "Thank you, Ms. Hildebrandt." As he started to hang up, it occurred to him that Darcy might have information about the manor house the president and his entourage were using. Connor had spoken to the ambassador, but Darcy had helped with the legwork for this trip, including securing their accommodations since the usual digs were under reconstruction. "Wait. While I have you on the phone, can you tell me anything about a series of secret passages we've discovered in the manor?"

"Of course," she replied readily. "That particular house was built nearly three centuries ago. Those passageways were quite common in homes of the wealthy in that period. The servants utilized those paths to come and go without disrupting the household or its guests. Some were even used to move rebels in and out of houses during the Jacobite rebellions and other social upheavals. But you don't need to worry. A renovation about a decade ago closed off most of the entrances to those passages. They left one for historical purposes. We often give tours there."

"Ah, that's interesting. We stumbled onto the

entrance and were quite surprised."

"Really? No one has gotten lost in the passages, I hope." Darcy sounded concerned. "We supplied the Secret Service with a complete map of the estate in part to avoid that possibility."

"Not at all," he assured. But it was interesting to know the Secret Service was well versed in those passages. They would also know what common areas of the house the security cameras captured and how to evade them. "One of the doors merely opened and it surprised a staffer. I was curious. Thank you for explaining. I'll let them know it's nothing to be concerned about."

"Now if you want to see secret passageways, I could..." She sighed over the line. "Well, I could recommend several lovely tours for you. There are so many interesting things to see while you're in London."

"If I get back for a vacation, I will. Thank you. I'll see you later, and we'll settle our schedule for the rest of the week."

She hung up, and Roman glanced at the device's screen to check the time. He had a few hours yet before he absolutely had to get on the road. But he needed to wrap up his visit quickly if he wanted to visit the site of Constance's accident. It wasn't far, and he could also chat with the local police. If he really hurried, he might even be able to talk to some of the inhabitants of this sleepy village. Maybe someone remembered what happened the night she died.

"Mr. Calder?" A tall, thin man wearing a dark suit under his white lab coat emerged from the hallway.

"Dr. Billings?" He rose to shake the man's hand.

"Yes, I'm sorry for the delay. I had an unexpected

guest," the doctor explained.

Roman had to smile. The doctor was a man in his sixties who didn't look at all like the sort to eschew his normal schedule for a flirtation. The woman must have been spectacular. "So I heard."

The doctor tossed a glance at Yolanda, who grinned. "The gossip mill is running perfectly, I see. I don't get a lot of unscheduled appointments. We're a business that thrives on privacy. Most of the public doesn't even know we're here. I had to know for certain if she was a reporter sniffing about for a story."

Roman hadn't even considered that. Usually he was much more paranoid, and if he'd been spotted that would have been a disaster. Gus was making his brain mushy. "So is she with the press? Because I definitely insist on keeping my visit private."

The doctor waved off his worry. "Not according to her, and she didn't mention your name. But just in case, I thought it smart to send her out the back so she doesn't see you entering. I'm sure she'll have cleared the building in just a moment. Surprisingly, she wanted to discuss the same patient you've inquired about. That certainly doesn't happen often, especially in an old case where the patient is deceased. She didn't have the proper paperwork from the family, so of course I couldn't say much."

Roman's every sense went on high alert. "Someone else came today to ask you about Constance Hayes?"

The demand in his tone had the doctor's eyes widening. "Um, yes. Another American, like you. As I said before, I suspected she was a reporter or perhaps a biographer working on a book. I explained to her that I couldn't disclose any information without a release from the family. And good luck with that." His voice went low. "As you know, we're talking about the mother of the president of the United States."

"Could you describe this woman to me?" Roman had suspicions. Gus had been too bright this morning. Far too happy and more than willing to talk about anything except her investigation. He should have known her mood was far too good to be true. And his Augustine was precisely the type of woman to turn a scholarly man into a blushing teen with a smile. "Was she gorgeous, tall, have a ridiculous amount of pretty hair? Did she look a bit like a Valkyrie wearing designer clothes and a pair of Louboutins?"

The doctor's expression turned loopy. "So you know her? She's beautiful. And charming. I felt bad having to tell her that even if I were allowed to show her the files, they went missing ages ago."

Roman forced a smile on his face and tamped down his scalding fury. "I see. Did she say where she was going?"

"No. She asked for the loo. I let her use my private toilet. The only other one is out here, and I wanted to avoid her spotting you in case she was a reporter. She didn't say anything about where she's headed next. If she hasn't left yet, you might be able to catch her in the car park."

"I assure you she's still here. She's searching your office even as we speak. And you're quite right—she doesn't have the proper clearance from the family to obtain Mrs. Hayes's medical records. If you'll lead me to your office, I'll help you save the sanctity of your files because she's smart. If she hadn't been born into one of the wealthiest families in the States, she might have made an excellent con artist." He withdrew his phone and touched the number that dialed Augustine's cell. "Come to think of it, con-artistry is a hobby for her."

"What do you mean? She merely asked to use the loo," the doctor sputtered as he darted back down the hall.

Roman followed. Sure enough, as the phone started to ring in his ear, he heard a faint corresponding ring down the hall. The closer he hustled to the doctor's office, the louder the noise sounded.

"Roman, I can't talk right now," Gus said over the line, her voice hushed.

He bet she couldn't. Thankfully, the carpet beneath his loafers muffled the sounds of his footsteps. He kept his voice intentionally low. "Why, baby? Are you in an important meeting?"

"Very. I'll have to call you back."

"Is Liz with you?"

"Um, yeah, but she's busy, too. You know how it is on these trips. I have to go. See you tonight." The line went dead.

Gus was probably panicking now. She had to know the doctor would be back at any moment. She must be hurrying to find anything of value in his filing cabinets.

Roman gnashed his teeth together. How the hell had she escaped the manor without his knowledge? He intended to have someone's head for this lapse.

The doctor stopped just short of his door with a frown. "I left that open."

"And she closed it."

"Oh, dear. Should I ring 999?"

He grasped the doorknob, hoping she hadn't locked herself in. He wouldn't put it past her to buy herself a little extra time, then plot to wiggle her gorgeous body out some tiny window to escape. "I'll handle her. No need for the police."

Damn Gus. Roman was one hundred percent certain he could feel his hair starting to gray, and it was all her fault. But even though she'd defied him, he felt oddly eager to clap eyes on her. He frowned. It made no sense.

The doorknob turned easily and he barged into the office.

Gus was stepping out of a door to his left and turned, wearing a bright smile. "Thank you so much, Doct... Roman?"

Her smile fled. A startled expression accompanied the whoosh of her breath. Anxiety lit her eyes next, proving to him that she did have a lick of sense. She should be afraid.

"Hello, dear. Is Liz in the bathroom, too? I had no idea you had a meeting so far from London."

At least she had the decency to blush, her cheeks turning a hot pink. "I was just... Wait." That sensible fear fled, and she narrowed her eyes at him. "What are you doing here? I thought you were going to be glued to Zack's side all day. In London. Meetings with the prime minister, I believe. Did you forget those? Or get lost?"

He pointed a finger her direction. "You are not turning this back on me."

"Excuse me, but I'm confused," the doctor said. "You clearly know each other, but you didn't come here together?" He glared at Roman. "Was your appointment a ruse so she could search my office?"

"Of course not. I don't need to resort to such drastic measures. As you know, I have a release from the family." He reached into his suit pocket, ready to pull out a copy of the paperwork.

"So you were snooping of your own accord, young lady?"

Gus sent him a look that could have frozen an active volcano. "Of course not. He was kidding. He's quite a practical jokester." She sidled up to Roman, sliding her arm through his. He felt her claws digging into his forearm through his suit coat. "He has such an odd sense of humor. I have no idea why I date him. Maybe you should think about keeping him for observation."

The doctor looked between the two of them. "You have a romantic relationship?"

Gus leaned against him. "We do, and the truth is, we must have gotten our schedules mixed up today. I thought he was far too busy to come here, so I tried to save him the trip and surprise him. And because I'd like to spend a day shopping and sightseeing before we fly back across the pond. But as Roman pointed out, I don't have the proper paperwork. That detail completely slipped my mind." She touched a hand to her forehead with a trilling laugh. "Zack gave it to this guy here. I'm sorry, I mean the president. We're both lawyers in his employ and we've known him since we were kids, so it's weird to call him anything other than his name. Or Scooter, of course." Gus smiled brilliantly before she slanted a glance his way. "Come on, babe. We've taken up enough of the doctor's time."

Roman thought his head might explode. He was so going to... He wasn't even sure what he intended to do to her, but in that moment he wished like hell he could toss her over his knee and spank the sass out of her. Still, she was right. They needed to leave before the doctor got any more suspicious.

He forced a smile. "Sorry, Doctor. I didn't mean to imply that she's a criminal. Though what she'd like to do with our spare time would be a crime against my credit card."

She leaned her head against his shoulder with an airy laugh. "One little trip to Harrods."

The doctor smiled indulgently and murmured something about his wife doing the same. No one could turn around a bad situation like Gus. She could get caught with a gun standing over a dead body and residue all over her hands, and still manage to craft a charming story the police would probably believe.

But Roman refused to be charmed. Not this time. His stern lecture would have to wait, however. Now he had to play the indulgent boyfriend.

"Glad you understand. I actually came here today, rather than tomorrow, so I could surprise her. Pray for my credit card, Doc." He smiled. "Oh, before we go, what can you tell me about Constance Hayes? You said the files we're looking for are missing?"

The doctor frowned for a moment, as though trying to figure out if he was being had.

Gus nodded and started back into the doctor's office, tugging Roman along. "I was asking the doctor about any records he might have on Constance, but he told me they'd gone missing some time ago. He tried to pull them recently, probably for you."

The doctor settled himself behind his impressive desk. "Yes. I looked for the records when Mr. Calder called to inquire about reviewing them. As I told Ms. Spencer, I wasn't Homewood's director at the time of Mrs. Hayes's stay, but I worked here."

He was still suspicious and somewhat reserved, but

Gus seemed to have kept the situation from going incredibly south. Not that it would save her later.

Roman slid into the chair beside her. When she tried to inch away, he caught her hand and wrapped her arm around his. She'd started this game, so no, he didn't mind taking advantage of the situation. Since their two investigations had crossed over, that meant he could keep an eye on her while he completed his. "Did you work on her case at all?"

"I did, but I'd prefer not to say more. Privacy laws." The doctor glanced Gus's way.

"The patient in question is deceased and her husband has dementia. Zack Hayes has his father's power of attorney and I represent the whole family. I can show you my paperwork again, if you'd like. Or would you prefer for me to get my client on the phone?"

Gus sighed and leaned toward the doctor. "Don't mind his growl. That's how he talks. But we really do need some answers. We're here for Zack...President Hayes. He can't come himself, obviously. Privacy is a deep concern—his and yours. If the president comes, we have to bring a large security detail and shut down most of your operations for the day. I assure you, it's a hassle. And then there's the press. Once they're on the scene, I fear they could learn about your celebrity patients, perhaps even catch an unauthorized glimpse of them. It's in everyone's best interest not to stir up that kind of attention."

The doctor shuddered. "I see your point, yes. And you did send the proper paperwork. Can we talk in front of Ms. Spencer?"

"Please do."

"All right. I was a secondary doctor on Mrs. Hayes's

case. Her primary physician died a few years back, and somehow we've lost his records."

"All of them?" Roman asked.

"No, that's what's strange. Only Mrs. Hayes's records are missing."

Gus squeezed his hand. Clearly, she didn't believe for one moment the records had simply been misplaced. Neither did Roman. Though nothing had really changed, Roman sensed this excursion had become far more serious—and potentially dangerous.

"Do you have any idea when the records went missing?" she asked.

"I honestly can't tell you," he began, but then he seemed to have an idea. He stood, pushing his chair back. "But…let me check something. I'll be right back. I might be able to at least give you a time period, if my theory is right."

He stepped outside, leaving his door open.

Gus immediately turned on him. "I knew you were lying to me. You never meant to take me along. Your promises and your 'deal' were just one big manipulation."

She wanted to do this here? Now? Fine by him. "I lied? That's pretty hypocritical, baby, since you're the one who sneaked in here to illegally search a doctor's office. You know, you're lucky he didn't call the police. How would that have looked?"

"He wasn't going to catch me. You're the one who made it a close call."

Roman gritted his teeth. "Why the hell are you here?"

"No, you go first."

He clenched his jaw even tighter, lips pressing into a

grim line. He couldn't admit here all the things he'd been keeping from her all along. He couldn't drag her any deeper into this conspiracy and put her in more danger.

She pointed a finger his way. "See, there you go with the stonewalling. You're not going to say a word, are you?"

But he didn't have to admit anything. Gus knew he was investigating. She was a smart woman and no matter what he did, she would put two and two together all too soon. "I'm here because Zack thinks something was…odd about his mother's death. He'd like answers."

"Okay, I'll be the one to say it. She was very likely murdered." Gus sat at the edge of her chair as though she might jump up at any moment. Her eyes were alive with suspicion. "You don't look surprised at all. I think Constance was murdered, just like my father. I've thought a lot about this. My dad must have known something, Roman. I know what all the police reports said, but I think someone covered up his murder, too. I want to know what happened and why."

Roman's breath caught. Damn it. He'd always thought she was brilliant, but damn… She was even smarter than he'd given her credit for. He couldn't not tell her why her father had died. Dax might kill him later, but in that moment he knew he couldn't lie. "Yes, I'm here because I believe your father knew something about Constance Hayes's death…and that's why someone in the Russian mafia paid your father's aide to first discredit him. They later leaned on Holland's uncle to rule that the admiral's death had been suicide."

Color leeched from Gus's face. Suddenly, her hand was in his again. The way she squeezed him, seeking comfort, tugged at his heart.

He stood and pulled her into his arms. "This is why I've lied, baby. I don't want you involved. I can't stand the thought of you getting hurt or... I can't lose anyone else. Not after everything."

She clung to him. "But I need answers, Roman. This is far more my fight than yours. I won't let you keep me out of it. Whatever's going on has cost me dearly. I lost my father and two of my closest friends. I have to know why."

True, and he felt guilty every time he thought about the enormity of what they were keeping from her.

"I also know you're angry with me," she went on. "And I'm angry with you. But I won't let you send me back to the manor and put me under house arrest."

He was fairly certain that would be impossible now. Roman sighed and held her closer, letting her scent wash over him.

Funny how it used to merely arouse him. In the past when he'd inhaled her, he'd thought of nothing except getting her into bed. Now being this near Gus calmed him surprisingly.

No, he didn't want her in danger. But she had come here of her own free will. He could hardly make her unlearn anything she'd discovered on her own. What point was there in keeping these deep, dark secrets from her anymore...and potentially driving a wedge between them?

"No, you can stay, but we're doing this together. And we're going to have a long talk first. I'm going to know everything you know."

"Yes, it was just as I..." The doctor stopped short, cleaning his throat. "Oh, sorry to interrupt."

Gus started to break away, but Roman merely shifted

his body so he could keep his arm around her.

"My apologies, but when my girl is this pretty, I'm afraid it's hard to keep my hands off her," Roman quipped. "You were saying?"

He helped Gus sit before joining her.

The doctor stepped behind his desk, finding his chair once more. He adjusted his glasses as he paged through a file. "Here it is. It's as I suspected. You see when we move the paper forms to our archives, we have to sign them in and out. Mrs. Hayes's form was signed out to be scanned, but it was never signed back in. The lad who did our scanning services no longer works here. He was a college student interning for us. I can certainly get you his name, but it's been six years and he's back in India now, as far as I know. You'll have to look him up."

That would be hard. Connor might have some contacts. "So why wasn't the file in the computer system?"

"I suppose our intern didn't actually scan it. Or he did and someone mistakenly deleted it. Normally, I would suspect her son of arranging that mishap, but you're here on his behalf."

"My boss had nothing to do with it," Roman assured.

"Wait, the files must have been in your system at one time because when I ran oppo research during the campaign, Constance's stay here was one of the things we easily uncovered. Despite the fact that she registered under an alias, her records had to be kept under her real name. I dug that up over three years ago, so the file must have been deleted and stolen since then. Can anyone in your employ look through your computer systems to find out if you've been hacked or if any purging of files has occurred?"

"A firm that handles our computer systems now should be able to answer your question. Should I advise our legal department of this?" The doctor looked wary again.

Roman leaned in, adding a hint of menace to his tone. "You lost complex and valuable information about the mother of the president of the United States."

It never hurt to have leverage.

Gus laid a soft hand on the doctor's desk. "Doctor... Charles, I don't think that's necessary. Please excuse Roman. He forgets about manners sometimes. We all want to keep this situation quiet. Is there any way you would allow our computer experts to talk to your company? Perhaps we can find some answers together. We don't want to read the sensitive records of your other patients, but we might be able to assist with technical issues. If you'll agree to that, we can all handle this matter discreetly. I'd hate for the public or press to catch wind of this snafu."

The doctor nodded, obviously having no idea he'd been subtly threatened. "Perhaps that's the best solution. I'll let them know you'll be calling and that they should give you their full support. I hope the president understands the hospital did its utmost to preserve the integrity of those files and that we're committed to restoring them. We take our patients' privacy seriously. This has never happened before. I can't apologize enough."

"Is there anything you personally remember about Constance's case?" Gus asked.

Roman sat back. She had this guy eating out of the palm of her hand. And staring at her breasts, but then if he was in the doctor's position, he would be staring at them, too. Augustine's breasts were a national treasure. Actually, they might qualify since he was fairly certain the sight of those gorgeous things had bought the country an enormous amount of goodwill with world leaders.

"As I explained to Mr. Calder, I was secondary on her case. I only really checked in on her when her primary physician was on leave. I recall she was normally a model patient. She was quiet. She liked to spend her time alone, reading books and magazines."

"Exactly what ailments was she diagnosed with? Alcoholism?" Roman couldn't remember a time when Zack's mom hadn't had a glass of wine or a martini in her hand.

"She was treated for a chemical dependency, yes. But her main diagnosis was paranoid personality disorder," the doctor explained. "Constance always thought someone was trying to kill her. And if I recall, she had trouble with hearing voices in her head, specifically a baby crying. She believed she'd accidentally killed a child, but according to everything I recall, that never happened. She attended intense therapy sessions, and we tried to relieve the guilt she had no reason to feel. But nothing changed her mind. As far as I know, she believed people were coming after her, seeking vengeance for the child, up until her untimely death in that car accident."

Roman sat back as the information rolled through his brain. He didn't want to think about the implications. Wouldn't think about them until he learned what was true and what had merely been a delusion in Constance's mind. "Do you know if her primary doctor had transcripts of his sessions with her in that file?"

"Of course," Doctor Billings replied. "We record all our sessions and save them with the rest of the files."

So if the files had been stolen, rather than misplaced—a terrible likelihood—Zack's enemies could have documented proof that his mother believed she'd murdered a child.

The conspiracies began to spin in his head. Had Constance Hayes killed her own child? Had Frank Hayes, conscious that Constance couldn't bear another, replaced that child with another? Maybe his Russian nanny's?

Was Zack actually Sergei?

"Do you remember anything else?" Gus asked. "Why was she driving the night she died? How did she escape the facility?"

"I don't know all the details. I wasn't there that night. Her death was a heavy weight on Dr. Richards for the rest of his days. But Mrs. Hayes didn't escape. We maintain strict security standards so that our patients aren't a risk to themselves or others, but there are several ways a patient can be temporarily granted limited freedom. Most of the time it's because they've been declared low-risk and have completed the initial mandatory lock-in period, so an approved person could sign them out for up to six hours. Family visits and fresh air often cheer these people up, you understand."

"But according to everything the family heard about the accident, Constance was alone in the car, rented in her name. How is that possible?" It didn't make sense to Roman. How would a woman on lockdown have managed that? There was no evidence that Frank had been in the country. His passport records showed he hadn't left the US until a full twenty-four hours after

Constance's death. That trip had been only long enough to retrieve his wife's body for burial.

So who had signed her out that night?

Doctor Billings shook his head and set his glasses aside. "I'm afraid I can't shed any light on that. Much of those records were sealed away because of the lawsuit. You need to talk to Franklin Hayes. I understand he's in no state to explain, but if you ask the right questions, you might learn a thing or two. With dementia patients, it's all about setting a proper stage and finding the lucid moments. But I can't give you those records. They're sealed."

All of this was news to him. "There was a lawsuit?"

"We paid the Hayes family an undisclosed amount of money and they signed a nondisclosure agreement. Your client should have mentioned that."

"Frank Hayes signed that NDA," Gus tried. "Zack didn't."

"You'll have to talk to our legal department. I'm not authorized to help you. Now, I have a hospital to run. I've given you everything I can." The doctor stood, his decision obviously made. "I think your best bet is to deal with our technology department and talk to the president's father."

Gus stood, too, holding out a hand to the doctor. "If there's anything else we can think to ask, we'll call you. Thank you so much. We'll be sure to tell the president how cooperative you and your staff have been."

The doctor seemed to breathe a sigh of relief. "Thank you. And yes, please feel free to call me with further developments. If I can help you, I will."

Roman took Gus's hand and headed for the door. The minute they were out of the doctor's earshot, he turned to her. "I still had questions to ask."

"He was done," she said with a shake of her head. "He got spooked when we asked about her death. He wasn't going to touch that lawsuit. We need to find another way."

"I never heard a word about that lawsuit. I'm not convinced it's real. If that's the case, we can force him to talk," Roman insisted.

At the time of Constance's death, he'd already assumed responsibility for most of the family's legal issues. They would have told him about such a lawsuit, right? Yes, and let him handle it. Even though the suit would have been filed in England, he would have been the one to vet the British solicitor and advise Franklin.

But if it was real...why had he been left utterly out of the loop?

"Not without some legal pressure. The minute we apply that, we run the risk of our investigation becoming public. The press will ask questions."

She was right, but that didn't mean they couldn't keep quietly digging. He might know someone else they could interview.

He stopped at the desk where Yolanda was once again doing her nails. "Hey, can you tell me if any of the nurses still working here were around ten years ago?"

Yolanda looked between him and Gus. "Did the good doctor pause treating the 'stars' long enough to play matchmaker?"

Gus grinned. "No, my boyfriend and I had a mix-up in our schedules. I was trying to surprise him by getting some of his errands done. You know men can't multitask."

Yolanda waved a hand. "Don't I ever! There's a

reason there aren't many male nurses. Men couldn't handle being a nurse, if you ask me. Trying to remember all those tasks while handling the emergencies. Well, this place would fall apart if it was all run by the docs."

"Yes, the nurses are important." Roman didn't want Yolanda to get off topic. He got the feeling she could talk forever if he let her. "I'll be honest, the doctor wasn't as helpful as I'd hoped. He doesn't recall much about our patient. I thought talking to one of the nurses who was here at the time might be beneficial."

"We have a small staff and a lot of turnover. I think it's because they're tight fisted with the cash, if you know what I mean. We get these bright-eyed young nurses who come here thinking they'll make a fortune and meet a man, then realize that village life ain't as charming as those romance novels make it out to be. The doctors are all old and married, and most of our young men leave here for London. So they find out that their real choices are between slow Jimmy and Alfie, who's a bit too close to his mum, if you ask me. Now Jimmy ain't slow in the traditional sense, so don't throw your political correctness my way. He's just lazy as pie and I'm fairly certain he talks to his sheep."

Gus snorted, a sound she somehow made adorable. "So you have a lot of turnover?"

"Oh, yeah. If those doe-eyed girls last a year, we count it as a win. They run right back to London, they do. Marjorie House was the director of nursing for the longest time. Now she was a local. Went to university and come right back home. 'Course she came home pregnant, which was a scandal at the time, but she was here for some twenty-five years."

"Did she retire?" Roman asked.

"Yes, but she died two years ago." Yolanda's words killed Roman's hopes. "Such a shame. Only murder we've had in this town in fifty years. Police think some punk was looking for drugs and shot her when she couldn't give him any money and ran off. We were all scared for a long time after that."

Naturally his only witness was dead under suspicious circumstances. Roman knew he'd have to hunt down her police report, too. Frustration welled inside him. Every turn seemed to lead to another dead end.

"I'm sorry to hear that." There was nothing left to say here, and they were losing daylight. No, he didn't have to hurry back to London now, but his gut told him every minute that ticked by only made this tangle more dangerous. He glanced down at Gus. "You ready to go?"

She nodded, slipping her phone back into her purse. "Yes. Thank you so much."

Yolanda gave them a little wave and picked up the e-reader near her elbow.

As he led Gus to the parking lot, the stiff set of her shoulders made Roman suspicious. "How did you get here? Do you have a car?"

He intended to return hers to the nearest facility because there was no way he was allowing her to drive all over the countryside, not when Constance had probably been conveniently murdered here. Marjorie House, too. Yolanda was most likely wrong about the cause. The nurse had died for no other reason than she'd tended to Constance Hayes.

"I took the train," she murmured as the gray afternoon enveloped him. It had rained earlier and the clouds above suggested storms yet to come. "Then I caught a cab here. Apparently the only one in the area, according to the cabbie."

"Then you can ride with me. I rented a car." He gently took her elbow, steering her toward the Benz he'd driven up in. "Are you going to tell me how you knew to look here? I told you what you wanted to know."

"Well, I knew Mrs. Hayes had died in this area. But when I was searching Kemp's room, I spotted a notepad. He'd pulled off the top sheet, but I found this address left behind as an impression. When I looked it up, it led here."

"And you didn't bother to mention that to me?"

"I was going to, but then you told me you'd turned everything I'd already given you over to Connor. Sure, you promised me updates, but I wanted in. This is my fight, too. And I knew if I gave you the address, you'd only cut me out of this excursion."

He stopped in the middle of the parking lot. "I wasn't cutting you out. I was protecting you."

"It's the same thing. And have you considered that leaving me completely in the dark puts me at risk? I realize now that I could have screwed up everything by talking to the doctor today. I had no idea you were coming here, much less had a meeting scheduled with him. If he had been the suspicious sort, he could have easily had me arrested for trespassing."

"Yet another reason for you to trust me to handle this. I'm taking care of it."

"You're still not listening." She huffed and shook her head as she approached the car. "You want me to just give it all up and sit back at the house like a good girl and forget how many people I've lost. That's the sort of woman you want, isn't it, Roman?"

"Don't make me sound like some kind of caveman. I'm worried. Everyone who has touched this case is dead. Doesn't that strike you as suspicious?"

"It certainly does now. How are these events connected to Mad's death? I don't get it. Had he figured something out? He must have, but I don't understand what he would have seen or learned that would have led him to uncover a conspiracy like this. Mad didn't care about politics."

"Mad didn't care about much except getting laid and his next party," Roman muttered.

Gus stopped, fists clenching. "That's not true. He cared about many things, but politics wasn't one of them. He wouldn't have gotten mixed up in Zack's campaign any further than to write him a check and show up at his victory party. Although he had an alternate plan. He called it a consolation bash and asked me if it would be poor form to offer Zack his choice of hookers if he lost."

Roman couldn't help but laugh at the thought of Mad trying to figure out how to buoy his friend's spirits after losing a presidential election. It probably would have involved a shit ton of liquor and likely made *The Hangover* look like a kiddie film. "Yeah, I can see that."

"Naturally he stopped talking about it after Joy's death. He said that attending a closed casket funeral for the wife of one of his dearest friends took the party right out of him."

Roman unlocked the car with a beep but didn't get in. Instead, he opened the passenger door for her. "I'm sorry I said anything negative about Mad. I have complex feelings for him, but I miss him every single day. I wish he was here because things never seemed as grim when he was around."

She glanced away, but not before he saw the haunted look in her eyes. "Yeah, Maddox Crawford made even the worst things seem a little better."

God, he hated the jealousy that snaked through him every time she said Mad's name. Neither one of them deserved it. They'd been adults and single, and Roman had been plain when he'd ended things with Gus. But it still fucking hurt that Mad had never once asked him if touching Gus was okay.

Not that he'd asked Dax. As far as Roman knew, whatever developed between him and Dax's sister was going to come as a hell of a surprise.

He held out a hand, blocking the open door so she couldn't get in the car. "I wasn't trying to hurt you by sending Connor here. I was simply worried. There's more you don't know. I want to tell you, but, damn it, Gus, you can be so reckless. I'm worried if I let you in on everything, you'll try to fix this on your own. You've always broken off from the pack and done your own thing. But the implications are bigger than just Mad's death or Constance's, or even your father's. And now that whoever is behind all this is trying to blackmail Zack, I'm sure you've figured out this is serious. I can't let you go rogue."

She laughed, the sound tinged with bitterness. "Roman, I've never broken off from the pack to go it alone intentionally. I didn't have a pack to run to, and I was never one of you. Even when I was sleeping with one of you. At the time I thought no woman ever would be included in the inner circle, but I was wrong. You've accepted Everly and Lara, and Holland fits right in. Joy was on the inside, too. I know if Mad had lived and married Sara, she would have been included with you all.

I'm the only one who gets shut out."

Because she'd picked the wrong gentleman. She'd picked the one who couldn't love the way the others did. Roman frowned, but that didn't stop his hard truths. He'd been handed someone amazing at a young age and he'd kicked her to the curb because she hadn't been who or what he'd thought she should be. She hadn't fit the ideal in his mind of whom he should love.

He stood frozen as she sat and buckled her seatbelt.

She wouldn't look at him, and he didn't blame her.

With a long sigh, Roman closed the door. Gus was here with him, but she still felt alone. That much was apparent. He couldn't ignore the fact that he was, at least in part, responsible. And the only way to fix the situation was to betray his best friends and potentially put her in danger.

CHAPTER THIRTEEN

Gus took a calming breath and again surreptitiously read the text message she'd received while Roman had been questioning Yolanda. She prayed he didn't pay her any notice now.

If you want the truth about Constance Hayes, meet me in the village cemetery at midnight. Come alone or bring the Hitman with you. I don't care, but you're the only one I'll give the information to.

Deep Throat

The message sent a thrill through her. Sure it was ninety percent abject terror, but she felt the adrenaline rush, too. Maybe this person had answers, like the Deep Throat of Watergate, the source who'd led reporters Woodward and Bernstein to the truth about the break-in at the Watergate Hotel. The information had blown up Nixon's presidency and forced him to resign.

Sure, she'd considered sharing the message with Roman, but then he'd reminded her once again that she was outside the Perfect Gentlemen's circle and she always would be. And if this source could tell her something useful, it might put her back in this game. After all, if she got answers, Roman and the others wouldn't be able to shut her out anymore.

Then, after this mess was unraveled, she could walk away on her own terms.

But if she shared the meet time and place with Roman now, she would likely find herself surrounded by armed escorts, being hauled back to London. Connor would take her place. Roman would throw a wig on the former CIA agent and style him in her Herve Leger bandage dress rather than letting her go to the cemetery.

So now she had to find a way to persuade Roman they needed to stay in the village tonight, instead of returning to London. They'd retire early because she was so exhausted, of course. Once he'd drifted off, she would slip out.

Roman emerged from the small law enforcement office he'd insisted on visiting. "That was a complete waste of time. They have the same police report I've read a hundred times. Constance's blood alcohol level was five times the legal limit, etcetera, etcetera. But when I asked the cop how he thought she could have possibly driven even a mile that intoxicated, he shrugged and said he's seen worse."

It must be super frustrating for Roman not to be able to use his powerful position to force people to follow his orders with the snap of a finger. He was so used to it.

"Were you able to talk to the officer who wrote the report?"

"He retired last year and now lives in Aruba, believe it or not," Roman replied. "Come on. Let's drive to the site of Constance's crash. I didn't notice much when we drove past earlier, and it probably won't tell us anything since it's been years, but I feel as if we should see whether the police might have overlooked anything relevant about the road or the surroundings. I owe it to Zack to be as thorough as possible. Then we can head back to London before it gets too late."

"Or we could talk to some of the locals," she suggested. "Villages like this are similar to small towns back home. Their residents have long memories about events like these. I'll bet someone remembers that night. Going to the site might even give us an idea about who we should talk to."

He opened the car door for her. "I thought about questioning the locals myself. That's not a terrible idea."

It was a brilliant idea, thank you very much, but she was used to his faint praise. "I know you need to head back to London tonight, but I could stay for a while. I saw a B and B on the edge of town. I'll see if I can get a reservation. Tomorrow, I'll shop in the village and have lunch at the local pub, see what I can find."

Roman shut the car door and before she knew it, he was sliding in beside her. He had the engine purring and they were making their way down the road that connected the village to the sanatorium again for a closer look at the crash site. "What are you up to, Augustine?"

"The same thing you are, trying to investigate without drawing too much attention," she replied carefully. "If you're worried about me being up here alone, call in Everly. She's worked security and she's nonthreatening. We'll say we're having a girls' trip. People will talk to us."

She could deal with Everly. Gabe's wife was perfectly reasonable and would treat Gus like an actual adult.

"Yes, I'm sure Gabe would love me for that." Roman turned the car right and kept his eyes glued on the narrow, hilly road. Still, she felt as if his attention was weighing her down. "I can hear the conversation now. 'Hey, buddy, my girl wants to draw yours into a shit ton of trouble and danger. What do you say?'"

"You don't have to be an ass about it." She should have known exactly how he'd respond. All these men seemed to think their women were made of glass.

Gus held in a sigh. Could she return to London and find a way back here before the meeting? She wasn't missing this opportunity. If someone wanted to play Watergate, Gus would happily play along.

"I'm sorry. I didn't say it wasn't a good idea. I just don't think Gabe would be all right with me luring Everly into a situation that might require body bags. As it happens, I have a room at that B and B tonight. If you're intent on doing this, I'll go with you. I'll keep my mouth shut since you think I scare people away. You can say I'm your mute boyfriend or that I speak no English. Hell, half the time I'm in Britain I'm sure I don't. I asked someone where the PCSO was and I was told the bizzies lived on Main."

"It's a slang term for the police." Gus had spent a lot of time in England over the years. She'd come to know a bit of the local dialect. "Though that's usually used more north of here. Don't you have to be back in meetings with Zack in the morning?"

"He'll survive a few hours without me. He thought I was staying overnight in the first place. That was the plan before…" He fell silent, the thud of the tires against the road and the gentle rap of the rain as it began to fall the only sounds in the car.

Before…what? Then the truth clicked in her brain. Naturally he'd had to change the rules of the game when he'd realized there was a new player. "You needed to get back to London so I wouldn't know you'd been gone."

"We've been over this," he said, tone grim.

They had—about a million times. There was nothing left to say.

She turned the focus back to the case. "Did you get the police report on the nurse's death?"

"In my briefcase. You're welcome to look, but I didn't see much information. The police didn't have much to go on. The nurse lived by herself in a cottage on the edge of town. No nearby neighbors to witness anything. She was known to take a walk every evening when the weather was nice. She was found dead just off the roadside two days after her daughter reported that she wasn't answering her phone."

Gus thumbed through the file. "No CCTV cameras out here in the country. And it's a charming little village that relies on tourism, so it's not as if any single stranger would stand out. That must have been a frustrating investigation."

"I don't know. It seems like a fairly thin one to me. And that doesn't surprise me at all. Here's the site of Constance's crash." Roman nodded in the general direction. "There is absolutely nothing out here. I'm not sure anyone would have seen the accident unless they happened to be coming or going from the hospital. The village is a mile back and the accident happened after midnight."

The road definitely wasn't a main thoroughfare. And Roman was right. Nothing about it looked particularly dangerous or remarkable. "My main question is who would have signed her out? And why would the hospital allow her to leave so late at night? I can't remember... How long had she been at Homewood?"

"Almost nine months," Roman replied. He stared out the windshield as though contemplating exiting the car and wandering out into the rain. "I remember Zack worrying..."

Of course he had. Gus's heart ached for him. She knew exactly what it was like to lose a parent under mysterious circumstances. "It wasn't her first time in such a place. There were two other stints in rehab, as I recall. But she stayed here the longest."

"Yes, her previous stays in facilities in both the States and France were far shorter, maybe a month." She could figure out why, given when the stays had occurred. "Did Franklin shove her in rehab so she could make campaign appearances for Zack?"

No one had really talked about it. It had been the dirty little secret of the Hayes family. But she wondered if Constance's problems had run much deeper than her love for vodka.

He sighed. "Yes. If Franklin cared about her alcoholism at any other time, I never saw it. And I spent a lot of time with Zack, so I should know. The two short stays occurred during Zack's runs for the senate. Franklin would sober her up, and she would be okay for a few months. Then once the election was over and Zack was victorious, she would go right back to the bottle."

"No one really knew what a problem she had."

"Franklin kept her at home so she didn't embarrass anyone." Roman stared out straight ahead. "I advised him to, especially after the spectacle she made at Zack's wedding. We couldn't have her in public, making waves. And yes, I know that sounds harsh, and you're probably thinking I'm some kind of a monster."

Gus watched him carefully. He got a tic above his right brow when he was really upset. It surfaced now. She wondered if he'd had it all those years ago. She'd only noticed it once they'd begun to work together. Now when he was angry, he didn't yell. No, Roman went deadly quiet. That vein in his forehead would twitch as if he was reining in an imminent heart attack.

It looked as if Roman had dealt with too much for one day. If she wanted to go it alone tonight, it would be so easy to start a fight with him now. If she got him good and mad, he would let her have her own room, and she wouldn't have to sneak away. All she had to do was plunge in a few well-placed knives, and freedom would be hers.

He dragged in a deep breath, jaw clenched. He gripped the steering wheel like a lifeline, trying so hard to keep his shit together. Gus couldn't stab him.

Instead, she leaned in and slid her hand over his. "No. I see a man who was doing his job, one he's been obsessed with since he was a kid. You're extraordinary, Roman. What you and Zack have accomplished is nothing short of legendary. You are single minded, something you must be to achieve the things you have. She wasn't your mom."

"But she was a human being." He fell quiet again. "I

haven't talked to my own mother in months."

"You have a complicated relationship with your parents," she allowed.

"We don't all get the perfect parents," he replied, flipping his hand over to hold hers. He brought it to his lips and then held it to his chest. "Or even good ones."

"Mine weren't perfect." Though she'd loved her dad, she'd eventually learned about his flaws. "But if there's one thing I've learned over the years, it's that there are always two sides to a story. Don't make yourself out to be the bad guy. You were there to protect Zack's interests. Joy tended to Constance's. Joy watched out for her, spent a lot of time with her, even when she and Zack were just dating. So Constance had someone in her corner."

"There's something I have to tell you. Maybe I shouldn't but..."

She gripped his hand tightly. "What is it?"

"One of the things we've uncovered is that Joy's death was no accident."

Gus froze. "What do you mean?"

"Whoever pulled the trigger that day wasn't trying to kill Zack. He didn't miss. The assassination wasn't botched." Roman swallowed. "He was trying to kill Joy."

"How can you know that?" she asked, feeling cold all over.

"One of Lara's friends dissected video of the last three rallies we attended. He managed to isolate the appearance of a laser sight on each one. To most, it would have looked like a blip on a screen or a temporary camera malfunction. But all three marks occurred at the same time in Zack's stump speech, and every time they were pointed directly at Joy's chest."

The implications crushed Gus. Someone had planned to kill sweet, selfless Joy? "So...I was right. All these deaths *are* related. And you're saying that whoever is behind them killed Joy, too."

His hand squeezed hers. "Yeah. We didn't know until recently."

"Why would anyone want Joy dead?"

Roman frowned, hesitated as if he debated the wisdom of answering. "We think they killed Joy to swing the election. It was close, but we were going to lose. I knew it. Zack knew it. The honest to god truth is, there was something almost freeing about that. I had made plans for my life after the campaign. Zack was going to finish out his term in the senate, then we'd talked about practicing law together. It sounds stupid now, but I was almost happy."

Of course he had been. Because if he'd lost, Zack likely would have divorced Joy to pursue Liz. Gus had always felt the attraction and the bond between those two. That would also mean Joy would have been available to become Roman's ideal wife.

What would the world look like now if that had happened?

"Augustine, are you ever going to forgive me for our past?"

"You're forgiven." She watched out the window because she couldn't look at him; she couldn't stand knowing that he'd been thrilled to hustle Joy to the altar. The only place Roman had ever been thrilled to hustle Gus was to bed.

She squashed the thought, looking out at the landscape, so hazy and lush and green. There was no green quite as verdant as the land here in England. She'd thought often that when she retired, she might move here and write her memoirs, adopt cats, and drink tea. And watch the rain.

He released her hand and made a U-turn. "I wish I believed you."

"I forgive you, Roman. I just don't know where we go from here," she said sadly, pivoting her thoughts back to Joy again. So fucking complex. Joy had been her friend...and her rival. She'd been soft and sweet, and yet on those rare occasions when she dug her heels in, there had been a whole other side to the woman.

He turned to her, looking weary, almost lost. "Let's go have dinner and a drink. In the morning, you'll talk to some of the villagers, then we'll return to London. Right now, I can't think past that."

And that was one of their problems. He could never see a future with her. But they had a few more days together until she had to let go of their past.

* * * *

"I expected you to fight me more," Roman said as he locked the door to the room they would share tonight.

Gus set down the small bag of items they'd purchased before the shops closed. They'd spent the early evening in the village. Since she'd planned to head back to London, she hadn't come prepared to spend the night.

She certainly hadn't intended the rest of the evening to be so pleasant. They'd had tea and talked to a few locals. They continued on to some of the stores, poking about and asking members of the community subtle questions while they shopped for a few necessities.

"About spending the night with you?" Gus asked, pulling out the toothbrush she'd bought.

"Staying in the same room. And yes, spending the night with me."

She could guess what he was really saying. "No, we've done that plenty of times. What you really meant was having dinner and shopping in public while holding your hand."

He'd done the latter incessantly. He'd told her it was best if everyone in the village saw them as a couple—less suspicious—but he'd done it even when no one was around. Roman's mixed signals were making her crazy.

"All right...I guess so. Yeah. It was nice. Spending time together without talking business felt surprisingly good."

It had felt good. They'd talked about their past—not the heartbreaking parts, but some of the good times. He'd reminded her that before their falling out, they'd had a lot in common, shared a similar sense of humor. They also shared a lot of memories—the teenage antics of the Perfect Gentlemen. Gus had managed to get her brother's friends out of a scrape or two, as well.

"You may not see it, but I always thought of you as the original girl in the gang." A smile played at Roman's lips as he crossed to the small desk and laid his briefcase on it. "You know we were all kinds of intimidated by your big attitude in the beginning. Well, everyone but Connor."

"Connor spent summers with me. He viewed me as a big sister, nothing else. The rest of you were horny boys, and I was just the queen of all of your teenage fantasies."

"I will not deny that." He opened the tiny closet and hung up the slacks and blouse they'd found for her. Not her usual designer stuff, but it would do. She should be able to sneak into tomorrow's afternoon meetings without raising brows. "But I like to think we were also friends."

"I was your bail-out girl," she corrected, trying to keep the conversation light. "You know I charged Dax interest, right? Ten percent. It was a good business model."

Roman eased out of his suit coat. "You did not."

"Oh, I did." The memories played through her mind. "I also charged him mileage. It wasn't an easy trip from my university to wherever the hell you guys got caught. And then I usually had to bribe someone to keep your stupidity out of the press." She gave a little gasp. "Holy shit, Roman. I was already working publicity for Zack, even back then."

He chuckled, the sound warm and inviting. "You were, and you were absolutely the person we called when we were in trouble. I think we all missed you during our years apart."

She placed the toothbrush and other sundries in the small and thankfully private bathroom. The B&B was a charming old English manor house. It looked like Roman had rented out the Lord's suite since it was much larger than she'd expected.

But once she was done arranging her temporary things, Gus had nothing left to do but stare at the clock and try not to think about why they'd missed her. Because she'd been foolish enough to give her heart to one of them. He'd merely thought of her as a fuck buddy.

Gus sighed. "It's been nice watching the guys finally get their shit together. I never thought Bond would find a woman who could handle him."

The air of sadness that had briefly loomed over Roman evaporated, and he smiled again. "Oh, Everly can. When we first met her I couldn't believe Mad had hired her as his security chief. I thought it had to be one of his jokes. Or hookups. Of course, at the time, we didn't know she was his half sister."

"I would love to have seen Mad handle his sister falling for his best friend."

"You know what you really should have seen? Everly basically handed your brother his ass when she decided she wasn't taking Gabe's shit anymore. Unfortunately, she nearly walked into a sea of reporters, so Dax had to force her back inside. She did not accept their manhandling well. Connor had to take her down."

Oh, she wished she'd been there to see her big Navy captain baby brother get a verbal smacking down by Everly. "I like her. I like Lara, too, and Holland is everything I could have wanted for my brother. He just handled their relationship like a dumbass when he first met her."

"He did. But even when your brother was at his stupidest, you watched over her. You knew how much he cared about her and you sent someone to protect her," Roman mused as he fiddled with the big fireplace. He found a switch and it *poofe*d into life.

That embodied Roman's whole existence. No taking hours to start a roaring fire. He merely found the right switch and it stoked to life for him. It was why she sometimes forgot that he was merely a man, with all their insecurities and troubles. "I knew something was going on, that Holland had put herself in a bad position. I merely sent in backup."

"You're a remarkable woman, Augustine Spencer. I

don't know if I really understood that until recently." He found the crystal decanter of Scotch the hosts had left for them and poured two drinks.

Gus sank to the comfy couch, the fire already warming her. "You're larger than life yourself, Roman." Now was the time. She didn't want to fight with him, but he'd bent a lot this evening. She should probably return the favor. Since they were warm and getting along...and she only had two more hours before she was supposed to meet Deep Throat. If she didn't tell Roman about the meeting now, it would be too late. "You handle everything that gets thrown at you with reason and intelligence."

Gus hesitated. If she told him about the meeting now, how fast could he get a helo up here? Zack didn't have Marine One at his fingertips in the UK, but Gabe had some pretty serious connections in the aeronautics field. And he knew lots of billionaires.

Roman stood over her, two glasses in his hand. He'd chucked his tie and opened the first two buttons of his dress shirt, giving her an intriguing glimpse of what she knew to be a spectacular chest. He looked yummy and sexy. And very suspicious. "Reasonable? That is not a word you usually use to refer to me."

"An oversight on my part." She took the glass from his hand and wished she wasn't about to ruin the companionable state they'd found. The old Gus would have blurted it out, ripped the bandage off, and told him what she was doing. Her younger self had been a bit of a reckless bitch. Now she wanted some peace with this man. "What do you think about the lady who said she remembered Constance and a woman hanging out at the pub?"

He stared for a moment, then sank down on the couch beside her. "Is that what she said? So hard to tell…"

He really did struggle with English country dialects. "Yes. She said she remembered seeing Constance in town a few times because she was always dressed up."

"Posh," Roman recalled. "She said Constance was a posh snob."

"Nob," she corrected. Seeing powerful, always-in-control Roman out of his Beltway element was almost cute. She wished they could go to Paris so she could watch him depend on her to order food and navigate the city because he didn't speak a lick of French, which she'd mastered long ago. "It's slang for a wealthy person. And for a tiny penis. But I think we can safely say the elderly lady we were talking to was using the word in the former sense, not the latter."

"Probably," he allowed. "She said she'd seen Constance with a man and a woman at different times."

"The man was probably Franklin. But the woman…" Gus shook her head, replaying the conversation they'd had with the local workers behind the counter at one of the shops. "She said Constance was with a younger woman, right? But she didn't remember much except that she'd been a blonde whom Constance appeared to know well. Did Joy take any trips here to visit Zack's mom?"

Roman's jaw tightened momentarily, the way it always did when she brought up Joy. "I'm sure she did. You know she and Constance were close. And I think she viewed dealing with Constance as one of her roles as Zack's wife. When we get back to DC, I can probably find Joy's calendars. She kept them. I think Zack boxed them up after she died and had them moved into storage, along with all her other things, since he couldn't bring himself to give them away. And I don't think he wants to deal with them now."

"Well, some of her things should be preserved for his presidential library. When we get back, I'll recruit Holland and Sara to help me go through her things."

Roman shook his head. "How do you do it? How do you compartmentalize like that? You offering to do that makes you one hell of a saint."

"Because you loved her, and now we're involved again? Why would I throw out the friendship I had with her and view her purely as the enemy? You didn't do that with Mad."

"Didn't I? We weren't close again for years, and never the way we had been. Honestly, when I found out you were sleeping with him again, I…"

Gus frowned. "You what?"

He stared into the fireplace as if he couldn't look her way. "I don't know. I'm starting to wonder how much of my flirtation with Joy was to get back at you for Mad. Gabe told me about it. He said you'd shown up in Vegas while he and Mad were partying and that you'd spent the night with Crawford. A couple of days, too. He laughed about it, said how nice it was to see you again. And how funny it was that Mad laid off the hookers because he claimed you were better in bed."

That had been a wild weekend, and there had been more to it than even Gabe had known. "I was there because Mad asked me to come. His father had passed away. Yes, we slept together, but mostly I held him while he cried, Roman. He was my friend. He didn't know how to show that vulnerable part of himself to you or any of the other guys. So when it got rough for him, he turned to me. It might surprise you to know that we often didn't have sex at all. We would sit in bed and eat room service and watch movies and talk."

"If you got along so great, why didn't you marry him?" he bit out.

Gus turned to glare...and saw Roman's hurt. She was starting to see through his knee-jerk responses, which made it so much easier not to take his bait. He might not even be aware he was tossing out the juicy line on purpose. Because he was emotionally dumb. Smart as a whip about everything else, but in this Roman was behind the curve, like a lot of men she'd known. Men like Mad, whom she'd always tried to help. But she'd avoided sifting through the emotions of the one man she'd truly cared about because he had the power to hurt her.

That realization made Gus terribly sad.

"I didn't love him that way and he didn't love me." She didn't tell him that Mad had offered once, that she'd turned him down because she'd been so in love with Roman she couldn't envision herself married to anyone else.

She tried not to admit to herself that was still true.

"I don't understand," he admitted.

"That's because women are infinitely more reasonable than men." It was true in most cases. At least the majority of her friends were reasonable about the high-powered, single-minded men in their lives who rarely saw anything in life but the goal in front of them. "I need to find out if and when Joy came to see Constance."

"But you said I was reasonable." He raised a brow at her. By the firelight, on the sofa with one arm around the back of the couch, lightly touching her shoulders, he looked so handsome, a little devilish, as he poked at her.

Gus melted. Roman rarely teased. He was so serious, so focused on his goals and the future, on climbing new pinnacles. She hated to intentionally end his mood and drive a wedge between them but time was ticking away. She was going to have to tell him about her upcoming late-night adventure. And the more she'd thought about it, the more she'd realized that sneaking out of the room alone would be difficult. And reckless. It would definitely piss him off if he caught her—and he almost certainly would. The floors creaked, and Roman was a light sleeper.

"You can be very reasonable…when you want to be. I would very much like you to be."

Those intense dark eyes of his narrowed. "Why would I need to be reasonable, Augustine? If you're going to tell me you want your own room, I won't be reasonable about that. Kemp is going to be coming this way in the morning. Hell, might already be on his way now. Connor is going to be on his trail, but I'm not risking you. If you don't want to sleep with me, I'll stay here on the couch."

How to handle him? Ease him in. Yes, that was the best path. The one thing she didn't want to see was that vein above his brow start to throb again. Because he took things far too seriously, he could easily be on his way to an early heart attack. Tonight could be a great adventure, something they'd look back on fondly. If she pitched it right, maybe she could get him to see it that way.

"What if I said I want to sleep with you…but I also want to visit a cemetery tonight, see who we run into?"

His forehead crinkled in pure confusion. "What?"

She downplayed her suggestion with a shrug and took a nice sip of Scotch. Not as good as what Zack would have served, but she wouldn't complain. "I've heard the cemetery here is extremely romantic at night, and there's a full moon."

"You want to make out in the cemetery like a couple of horny teenagers? Have you ever seen a horror film? Even one?"

So no to the adventure. "I just thought it would be nice to take a stroll."

"When would we take this stroll, Augustine?" His voice deepened as his suspicion returned.

She gave him a weak smile. "Midnight might be fun."

"Just say it. What horrific and terrible plan have you concocted?"

"I didn't concoct anything. I was contacted by someone who claims to have knowledge about how and why Constance Hayes died."

Roman stood, slamming his glass on the side table. "Are you kidding me? When did he call? What did he say? Did he call himself Deep Throat?"

It was Gus's turn to be surprised. "He didn't call. He texted. The number was blocked. He told me to meet him in the cemetery at midnight. And yes, he called himself Deep Throat. I know that's a cliché, but something tells me you're not commenting on how passé his moniker is."

Roman grabbed his cell phone with a curse and pointed her way. Accusation tightened his face. "He's a menace, is what he is. I swear I'll beat the shit out of him. He always goes for our women. He went after Everly, then Lara. He's never brave enough to show his damn face to one of us, merely puts our women in danger."

"Maybe he contacts the women because we're the reasonable ones. You look a little crazy pants right now, babe."

And that damn twitch was back.

"Did he say he would only give the information to you?"

"Yes."

"Fuck him." He hit a single button on his screen and put the phone to his ear. "Connor, Deep Throat's back and he's all over Gus. Yeah. The same old stale play. I need you to shave your legs, get a long, dark wig, and heels. No, make that flats. When Gus wears heels she's almost as tall as you so flats should work. Tell Lara to do your makeup. Sometimes Gus does those smoky eyes, I think they call it."

He'd gone off the deep end.

Gus plucked the phone from Roman's hand. "Connor, it's Gus."

"Please tell me you're going to save me from doing a one-man drag show," Connor all but pleaded. She could practically see him standing there with his mouth hanging open.

Because Roman didn't lose control. He was always cool and confident.

"Yes. Forget the flats and the smoky eyes," she promised. "Deep Throat did contact me, but his invitation included a plus one. He knows I'm going to bring along Roman. Everything will be fine."

"Everything will not be fine," Roman insisted. "And since you get a plus one, maybe Lara can stand in for you. Or Everly."

"There isn't a heel tall enough to make either one of them look even slightly like me." What had happened to him not risking his friends' wives? She clicked his phone over to speaker. "Connor, Roman is going with me. Contrary to what Mr. Optimism here thinks, we'll be fine. I'm not doing anything but talking to this person, and the cemetery is an easy walk to the police station."

"It's an easy setup for murder, you mean," Roman ground out. "It's a freaking cemetery, Gus. It's possible he's already dug our graves."

"He's watched way too many horror films," she told Connor.

"Roman, calm down. Every time we've come up against this guy, he's given us information we needed and gone on his way. It was total coincidence that the crazy chick from Everly's office tried to kill her while she met with him, and Lara didn't realize she had a couple of Russian assassins on her tail, which she would have known if she'd been as reasonable as Gus is being right now. You win the medal for best girlfriend because you actually told Roman instead of sneaking behind his back like the others."

"I took Everly with me." Lara's protest came over the line.

"Still haven't forgiven either of you for that," Gabe complained.

Roman shot her a pointed look.

"Hey, Gus, it's Everly. Can you try to surreptitiously take a picture of this guy because Lara and I are pretty sure our Deep Throats were actually two different men."

Roman gaped. "She is not taking a damn picture."

Gus would try. Maybe if she hid her phone in her jacket pocket and managed to maneuver it at exactly the right angle.

"Absolutely not," Roman barked, just in case they hadn't all heard his first edict.

"Fine," she replied, mostly because unless she used her flash, the image wouldn't look like anything except a black blob in the dark. "But when we come back to London, we'll all sit down and compare notes. I'll try to remember as much as I can."

"Roman, are you okay with this?" Connor asked. "I don't think I can pass as Gus, but I might be able to hop on that helo and pass as you. I know from experience this guy is serious. He won't talk to anyone but her. For once, he's giving a little by letting you come along. I'm surprised. Maybe he learned his lesson from forcing Everly and Lara to come alone."

"No." Roman sighed. "I'll go with her. I'll take care of her."

He sounded resigned, but he'd clenched his jaw so hard it looked ready to break. That vein over his brow was thumping double-time.

She needed to calm him down. "I'll text and let you know when we're done. Then we'll debrief when we get back to London."

"I'll be on Kemp's trail, but you can fill me in later," Connor replied. "And Gus, you carrying?"

"Of course." She had a small pistol in her purse.

"Don't be afraid to use it."

The phone clicked, and Roman stared at her.

"What are you carrying? Please tell me it's a rape whistle."

The poor man had no idea how to deal with her. Luckily, she was catching on quickly how to handle him. It all came down to bending a little. He was arrogant, but he did care about her. He was scared to care too much, of course. But he was here beside her. No, it likely wouldn't be forever...but how would she know for certain if she never tried? She'd never told him in the past how she'd felt, just lashed out in hurt when he hadn't felt the same. As he'd pointed out, they were older, wiser. More tempered. Maybe with honesty and communication, they had a better shot.

She set the phone down and took his hand. "A rape whistle would only annoy the man. My Ruger, on the other hand, will take care of him. I have a license to carry. I'm trained and everything. My dad started taking Dax and me to the shooting range when we were tall enough to see over the counter. I got it into the country by having the Secret Service carry it for me."

"Damn it, Gus. It's illegal for you to carry that here. England is serious about their gun laws," he insisted.

He was right, but he'd also forgotten a few things. She smoothed her hands up his shirt, all the way to his broad shoulders. Telling him about the midnight meeting hadn't gone as bad as she'd feared. With some maneuvering and help from his friends, he'd agreed to go with her, and he'd only had a little fit. "That's why I travel with a super-hot lawyer. He'll get me out of whatever mess I land in."

"That is not how it works, Augustine," he argued. But he wasn't putting distance between them.

"Are you saying you won't save me?" She softened, looking up at him. She'd kicked off her shoes and was well aware that now he stood a few inches above her.

"You don't need me to save you." His hands encircled her waist. "You never have."

"Everyone needs a little help now and then. I wasn't

going to sneak out on you. I admit, I considered it, but I'd rather have you with me." She smoothed her thumb over that angry vein popping along in his forehead. "Stop worrying. Everything will be okay because we'll be together. Besides, I would rather have you watching my back than Connor. He's too sneaky for my taste."

He took a deep breath and pressed his forehead to hers. "I know what you're doing. You're placating me."

That wasn't all she was doing. She was seducing him, too.

Gus raised her hands to his hair, running her fingers through the normally coiffed strands, and breathed him in. She loved how he smelled. He still wore the same aftershave he had in college. She knew if he didn't pay someone to buy his suits, he likely wouldn't have changed those either. He was a rock...and she'd been a hard place. What if they could manage the feat they hadn't been able to all those years before? What if they could actually stay together and make them work?

"I'm calming you down so we don't have to fight and you don't have to have a stress-induced heart attack. Sit down for me."

His hands tightened on her waist. "I don't want you to go out there."

Because he cared. Maybe more than a little?

"I'll be fine. You'll be fine. We'll get whatever information Deep Throat has and we'll be one step closer to untangling this mess." Not to mention discovering who had killed her loved ones.

"You have to promise me something."

She groaned inwardly. Was he really going to ask her to step back after tonight? Yes, he probably would insist she give him all the information she collected, so he could take it to Zack. Then he'd cajole or bully her into keeping her pretty nose out of the rest. She was doing her best to understand and accommodate him. Couldn't he at least try to reciprocate?

He wasn't there yet, and she had to accept that getting Roman to change his mind about anything wasn't a quick process. So if he asked her to back off, she would give in. It would hurt, but this was likely all Roman could give her now if she wanted a tomorrow with him.

"What is it?"

"Promise me when we find out who did this to our friends that you won't do anything rash. You won't go after them by yourself. You'll let me hire someone to make them die terribly and painfully while we sit back and watch."

Gus smiled. That was more concession than she'd expected from him. It told her that he really was trying. "I will let you arrange the appropriate violence. But I get a front row seat."

"How long before we have to leave for this crazy clandestine meeting we really shouldn't take?" Roman asked, his lips touching her forehead, skimming down her nose.

"Long enough," she murmured in a husky voice. "Why don't you sit down?"

"I don't want to talk anymore. I want to kiss you and touch you, forget we're doing something reckless that may end badly."

At least he no longer considered kissing and touching her in the reckless category. Another mark in the win column. "If you'll sit down, I promise there will be very little talking, babe. I can't talk with your cock in my mouth."

He fell to the cushion below in an instant, spreading his legs wide with a groan. "Do you have any idea how many times I've fantasized about this in the last thirteen years?"

Her body hummed with energy, brimmed with desire. They didn't have to be angry with each other to feel burning passion. That realization eased something deep inside her. She'd always been afraid they'd brought out the worst in each other, but this…this was different. They were different. She'd given him some trust, and he was repaying her with his own.

"Really?" she drawled. "Tell me exactly what your fantasy is. Do you want some hot secretary to come in and take care of your needs?"

She could role-play. It might be fun.

He shook his head, his stare focused and serious. "My fantasies aren't about some random woman. They're about you, Augustine. They're always about you."

His words melted her, and she banished the tears that threatened. She didn't remember him being so sweet, so open. Then again, they hadn't talked much back then. If she'd challenged him by suggesting a midnight stroll with a potentially dangerous informant years ago, they would have moved immediately into the screaming-match portion of the evening. Now, they were able to have a non-confrontational negotiation. Maybe they were more equipped to deal with each other—and have a future together—after all.

"Tell me your fantasy about me, Roman."

She started to unbutton her blouse, slowly, one button at a time, watching as his eyes flared, turned hot. They'd had so much fast and furious sex, so much raging passion without a lot of thoughtfulness or ease. Going slow and easy now seemed almost forbidden.

He reached for the Scotch, his body relaxed—with the single exception of his erect cock. It tented his slacks and made him look so masculine. Money and power and sex rolled off him, all directed her way.

"I'll sit in my office and watch you walk by," he confessed. "Sometimes, I leave my door open because I know what time you'll pass. Every morning you grab a latte and walk to the press office at a quarter after nine, and every morning I think about calling out and asking you to come inside and shut the door."

When she freed the last of her buttons, she shrugged her blouse from her shoulders and let it drop to the ground, gratified when his stare clung to her breasts. "And what do you intend to talk to me about, Mr. Calder?"

"Who said anything about talking? I'll have you lock the door, and even though you're a little surprised, you know that some of the work we do is important and requires secrecy. You are a bit surprised when I insist you strip naked for me."

Now they were getting somewhere. She felt her lips curl up. "Do I comply? Do I strip for you, Mr. Calder?"

"You're hesitant at first, but I explain how stressed I am and the only thing that can possibly fix my problems so I can help the president is for you to take off your clothes and get on your knees. I inform you this is a new part of your duties."

"And I do it for my country?" The grin stretched into a wide smile. To have Roman both playing with her and sharing his thoughts filled her with a lightness she hadn't been expecting. In their past, sex had been an outward expression of lust and some weird power struggle in which neither of them had been willing to bend. This was something more. This was fun. This was Roman telling her his fantasy and her playing it out for him.

Give and take. No struggle. No war to see who came out on top. This was two people who cared about each other finding middle ground so they could make it work.

Hopefully, just like their relationship.

"You're a patriot, Augustine." Something warm dominated his expression. Affection and lust wrapped up in a killer smile.

She eased the slacks off her hips and drew her lacy panties down with them. She didn't need to draw this out unnecessarily. They were on a clock, but she was already looking forward to getting back to DC where she would absolutely be fucking the chief of staff in his office. She would show him exactly how patriotic she could be.

"Damn, but I'll never get used to how beautiful you are. And how the hell did you wrap me around your finger? I should be fighting to get you home and safe, but all I can think about is how much I want that sinful mouth of yours on my dick."

She dropped to her knees. "I would rather be in danger with you than safe without you, Roman." The words slipped from her mouth without thought. Immediately, she looked for ways to walk them back. Yes, she and Roman were getting along better. And yes, he did seem more reasonable. But just because she wanted a future with him didn't mean he felt the same. She couldn't want it enough for both of them. Making herself vulnerable only made the risk to her heart more perilous. So she plastered on her brightest smile. "I mean, you're such a big strong man, Mr. Calder, that I know you'll protect me if the press finds out what we're doing."

He frowned and sat upright, leaning in just enough to cup her face in one hand. "That's not what you meant. We'll play tonight your way because I can't stand the thought of not being with you. I know I'll hate myself if you get hurt, but I can't not take this chance with you. I was an idiot in the past, and it cost us years. Don't pull away from me now."

Sincerity warmed his dark stare, and she shuddered in his grip. God, Roman was always sexy, but even more so when he was being open and honest with her. She braced her hands on his knees. "I don't know that I could if I wanted to. I'm afraid, too, Roman. You have always scared me, but I can't stay away. I'll be honest, though. I worry that we're trying to reclaim our youth or find something we lost long ago."

He'd been her whole world for that year, and she'd been so certain they were meant to be. Assuming he shared her feelings, then showing him her sass rather than her honest vulnerability, had been fuel that sparked their destructive fire.

"No, we're finding something new, something better. We're not the same people. We've lived more...and hopefully learned which battles are worth fighting and with what weapons. We've both learned to value the connections that are important. Let's find out how we are together now—this Roman and this Augustine. No looking back."

She wasn't sure the shambles of their past wouldn't always be a barrier between them, but she wanted to believe what he was saying. She wanted to give them her all so badly. "Is this anything like your fantasy?"

She slid her palms up his muscular thighs to his belt buckle.

"You're better than any fantasy. I think that's been the trouble my whole damn life. I preferred fantasy to reality." When his belt came undone under her ministrations, he moaned. "You're going to drive me crazy, aren't you?"

"Only in the best way." She eased the zipper down, carefully separating the front of his slacks so she could see his boxers. That eager cock of his was straining against the fabric. "It looks like you don't mind my kind of crazy."

"If you don't touch me soon, you'll see my crazy, baby. It won't be pretty. I'll start to beg, then the fantasy of you on your knees doing my bidding because I'm the all-powerful White House chief of staff will go up in smoke." His fist curled around the Scotch. "You see in my dream world, you do this twice a day. You show up in the morning and set aside your coffee and spread yourself on my desk so I can have you any way I like. It's my morning exercise."

She grinned at that. "And at night?"

"At the end of a long day, I pour myself a glass of ridiculously expensive Scotch and you suck my cock until I can't see straight. Then we go home and get into bed and I make love to you until we can finally sleep, and we start all over again the next day."

She peeled back his boxers, his cock bouncing free. It was a thing of beauty, the head a lovely shade of red and purple and already shiny for her. "That sounds like a schedule I can appreciate."

"You know I believe in keeping a rigorous one," he murmured as she stroked him softly. "You're killing me, baby. I'm going to beg any minute now."

Gus couldn't have that. She leaned forward and licked at the head of his cock, gripping him with one hand, holding him upright so she could explore him with her lips and tongue all over again. Roman enjoyed a firm hold. He demanded it. One of the things she could never forget was how he'd always loved to sink his hands in her hair and clench, insisting she suck at the pace he set. Now, he let her have free rein to explore him at will. Eventually he would take control, but now he seemed content to let her exercise her own.

Subtle changes, more evidence that they were, in fact, different people. But Gus appreciated them.

If they'd managed to be a little more tolerant when they'd been younger, where might they be now? Married? With children? Happy? The thought of all those missed years made her heart ache.

No. Roman was right. She had to focus on the future, not the past. It was done, and nothing could be gained by what-iffing all that. She had the now, and it was a pretty good place to be.

Gus dragged her tongue down the thick stalk of his cock, loving the way he hissed at the sensation. She sucked him into her mouth, lightly playing and teasing, before she eased back to nip at his sensitive crest with her teeth. He shuddered. And all the while she could feel her body heating, softening. The very act of pleasing him aroused her.

She explored his silken length with a moan, flattening her tongue and trying not to miss a single inch. He expressed his appreciation for her thorough efforts with a curse and a groan.

The sound of the glass clinking against the table

resounded right before his big palms enveloped her head, his fingers tangling in her hair. "Do you have any idea how good you feel?"

She certainly hoped she knew. To be sure, she swirled her tongue all around him, lowering her head again before sucking her way back up, hollowing her cheeks with an appreciative wail.

Glancing up at him through her lashes, Gus caught Roman staring down at her. His whole being seemed focused on her. He wasn't thinking about anything now except the sensation she laved all over his dick and the pleasure jetting through his body. And that was a feat because shutting down Roman Calder's always-whirling, considering-a-thousand-problems brain almost never happened.

When she lowered her mouth on him again, taking him in inch by slow inch, he watched, gripping her tightly. "Hmm. Yes, I should have my secretary put this on my daily schedule."

Loving his smoke-and-sin voice, she tilted her head up and pulled free with a grin. "I'm sure Sandra will love writing that in. 'Your nine a.m. blow job has arrived, Mr. Calder.'"

"No. All she'll say is your Augustine is here."

His Augustine. Her Roman. Still, there were some problems with his fantasy. "If I'm in your office every morning, people will talk, especially if they hear moaning coming from behind closed doors."

"They'll talk about how fucking lucky I am. They'll wonder why I get the hottest girl and the best office and all the damn perks. If they say anything else, I'll show them why they call me the president's Hitman."

"I don't care what any one of those assholes say, as

long as I get to do this to you." She swallowed him down in one long gulp.

Above her, he hissed again, his hands tangling in her hair. He'd been gentle up until this point, as though he merely wanted the connection with her, was enjoying their banter and playfulness. But now she felt the intent in his grasp.

His fingers twisted in her hair, lighting up her scalp. "You will. Suck me, Augustine."

She picked up the pace. This was what he needed. What she needed. The emotion between them was real and tangible when they were making love. Maybe if they did it often enough they could transform that feeling into a bond that couldn't be broken, one that would stand the test of time—and whatever shit came their way.

Maybe they really could use it to start over.

Gus laved Roman's cock up and down, lips and tongue working together to make his toes curl. He set a hard rhythm and she followed, shuttling him in and out of her mouth and cupping the soft sac of his balls. They were swollen and desperate in her palm. She gave them a gentle tug, and a growl tore from his throat. He couldn't possibly last long. She could feel it. His orgasm was evident in the way his balls drew up and in the stiffening of his cock.

Any minute now he would groan and surrender to the pleasure. He was so far gone, it was inevitable. She would suck him hard and he would come in her mouth and be gratified that she had given him ecstasy. All she had to do was let him find that soft place in the back of her throat where she swallowed him whole, and he couldn't resist her a second more.

Instead, his fingers tightened in her hair, forcing her

up and off his cock.

"No. Not tonight. I might have my office fantasies, but they don't work now. I want you up here, riding my cock. I'm not coming until I'm deep inside that hot pussy of yours."

When he tugged her up, Gus straddled his lap, resting her knees on either side of him. She wanted him inside her so desperately. Her whole body pulsed with pure arousal. She could feel her blood thrumming through her system and her clitoris beginning to throb in reaction.

Even more, she needed him—the connection, the closeness. The promise of their future.

She positioned herself over his thick erection, letting her palms skim over her breasts and down to her waist.

"Fuck, you're sexy. Yes, this is what I want." His grip tightened on her as he positioned his cock against her intimately. "If I could, I would keep you naked all the time, always ready for me."

It was a nice fantasy. She didn't mind entertaining that one, especially if Roman remained dressed and did all kinds of dirty, unspeakable things to cajole her complete surrender.

With a gasp, Gus lowered herself down, sliding his massive length inside her inch by inch. Slowly. God, she wanted to feel every second of his penetration, so she moved as if she didn't have a care in the world, as if they had all night to simply feel each other.

He filled her completely. No one ever had filled her quite the way this man did. She was deliciously stretched and feeling thoroughly adored by his unyielding grip on her hips and the blistering heat of his stare.

"You feel so damn good. Kiss me," he growled.

With pleasure... She lowered her mouth, brushing her lips against his as she found a rhythm, her hips moving in time with his. He held her so close, as if he would never let her go.

The tension built with every thrust, his cock and his tongue working in tandem to drive her out of her mind. Heat balled in her belly. Tingles snaked behind her clit. Gus held onto him, letting him take over because she was so close to finding that perfect place where nothing mattered except the wild pleasure she found in his arms.

It burst over her and she shook. Only his arms around her kept her from falling apart. He held her even tighter as he ground out his own pleasure with a chest-deep groan.

Once the sweet pleasure had subsided to a delicious little pulse between her legs, she slumped against Roman, breathless, heart about to burst with joy and something that felt a lot like love.

"Next time my pants come off," he murmured.

She managed a laugh. "And I probably should put mine back on."

He shifted, rolling her on to her back across the long sofa. "Not yet. We still have time, Augustine."

Then he lowered his head to her breast, laving the starkly sensitive tips and igniting the heat inside her all over again. It looked like he meant to make the most of whatever time they had together. Gus hoped it was a long while.

CHAPTER FOURTEEN

Roman glanced around the cemetery, watchful and tense. What kind of twisted fuck planned a meeting at midnight in a place where everyone was dead?

Unless the informant meant the setting as a warning Augustine was too stubborn to heed.

"Stay close to me." He reached for her hand. If someone was getting brutally murdered here, it would be him. Gus's punishment would be going through life knowing he'd valiantly saved hers and that she would never find another lover who could satisfy her the way he did.

Three times in an hour and a half was practically a record for him these days. Not that he felt old—especially when he was with her—but lately he'd been considering how the years were passing. Lately, he'd spent far more time chasing down reluctant votes on the Hill than women.

Maybe because, despite it all, he really only wanted one.

"You're too nervous, babe," Gus said with a nonchalance he wasn't sure could possibly be real. "It's just a conversation. It's going to be a piece of cake."

Right...

He'd satisfied her far too well. That was the problem. She had the look of a well-loved woman, one who didn't care that she was about to die because she'd already had the best orgasm of her life, and everything else was downhill from there. He should have held something back. Then maybe she would have rethought her whole let's-meet-a-potential-killer-in-the-dark-of-night plan.

There was a reason he'd gone into politics. The backstabbing in the Beltway was figurative...usually.

Except what had happened to Joy—as well as Constance, Mad, and the admiral... He shoved his thoughts of the string of bodies aside. Life was fleeting, and he'd lost so many years with Gus already. He couldn't let his idiocy continue to come between them.

"Pretend it's a simple walk in the moonlight," she went on, squeezing his hand.

"More like a walk in the mud," Roman grumbled. At least the rain had stopped, but his Louis Vuitton loafers were sinking into the soft earth. Every time he pulled them free with a squishy sound, he winced.

"You are determined to be Eeyore," she shot back. "You know some men would think this is sexy. It's very *Mission: Impossible*. Connor does stuff like this all the time, and I bet when he gets home from an assignment he has incredible sex with his wife."

There were a few things wrong with her scenario.

"Connor was trained to do this stuff, and I assure you he wouldn't be thinking about sex if Lara was in danger."

"Bet you're wrong."

Maybe he was. After all, he was still thinking about sex. Roman couldn't help it. His whole body felt languid, loose, as though his muscles hadn't yet caught up with his paranoid brain. His cock couldn't think about anything but how good it had felt to have Gus's mouth wrapped around it, sucking, licking, and lavishing it with singular affection.

Damn it, he needed to get his head out of the sack and into the present.

He paused, glancing around the cemetery. "This place is surprisingly more expansive than I imagined. Any idea where we're supposed to meet this guy? Did he give you instructions? Third gravestone from the left or something?"

In the silvery moonlight, he could see her biting that sexy bottom lip of hers as she considered the question. She scanned the area, her eyes lighting on something in the distance. "Well, if I was going to hide, I'd do it there." She pointed. "If you stand under that awning, no one would be able to see you since the moon's behind it."

He followed the direction of her finger. Up a small hill rested what looked like a damn crypt at the edge of a copse of trees. The darkest, nastiest, best-place-to-be-horrifically-murdered spot on the grounds. Unfortunately, she was probably right.

"Son of a bitch."

Gus started up the hill. "So Everly and Lara have met this guy? Back in DC?"

He knew what she was doing, keeping him talking

so he didn't flip his shit, throw her over his shoulder, and run for the hills—not the literal hills. The killer was likely lurking there, but at the least he would run back to the B&B and call the "bizzies." Instead, he gripped her hand and marched up toward the freaking crypt—and likely his death. "Everly met him in New York shortly after Mad's funeral. Lara encountered him in DC a few weeks later. Now he's hopped the pond and come after you."

"But he never talked to Holland. Don't you find that interesting?"

Roman had never thought about that. "I don't know why."

"What kind of information did he give the others?"

"Complete shit." Roman had no idea why they were giving in to this pot stirrer. "He talks in fucking riddles. Whoever this asshole is, he's seen way too many movies. Lara's crazy friend Freddy has been way more helpful. He's completely insane but the dude can weave a really tight conspiracy theory that holds together. And he's good with PowerPoint presentations."

When they reached the top of the hill, a shadow peeled away from the wall of the crypt. "I'm so sorry to have disappointed you, Mr. Calder. I'll try harder this time to give you information that's not complete shit."

Roman frowned because that wasn't the deep voice of a man. It was on the low side and definitely strong, but it sounded female. That made him stop in his tracks. He pulled Augustine back. "Who are you?"

"Deep Throat," she said as if the answer was obvious.

Gus stopped a few inches short of the stone stairs at the bottom of the crypt. "Hello."

"Hello, Ms. Spencer." Yes, the deep voice was definitely female. "I see you decided to bring along the Hitman. I rather thought you would be alone."

"Why the hell would I let her come alone?" Roman ground out the question.

The shadow paused briefly. "Well, you *have* left her alone for years. I extended her invitation to include you, but didn't really believe you would change your modus operandi."

What the fuck was this asshole talking about? "I thought you were a man."

"Sometimes you have problems with perception, Mr. Calder." She stepped just out of the gloom, only enough to discern a hint of her features. She wore a long black coat and a jaunty cap on her head. He couldn't tell if she had short hair or if she'd merely shoved it all under the hat to disguise its length and color. "I believe that's why you're in your current predicament."

So it was all his fault? He was so sick of the subterfuge. "How the hell do I know you're legit? That you know a damn thing? I thought I was meeting with the same person who contacted our friends previously. That's obviously not true."

"Those ladies didn't meet the same informant, either. But they were given credible information. It wasn't our fault the Russians followed Lara that night. Nor did we have anything to do with the woman who tried to kill Everly with her car." There was an amused satisfaction to the woman's voice. "Is that enough detail to satisfy you that I'm 'legit,' or do you need more? Just because the face changes doesn't mean the purpose does. If you'll let me, I'll guide you in the right direction."

He couldn't argue that she knew what had happened

at the past meetings, as well as things that hadn't been in the police reports. "Get to your point. I'm not standing out here all night."

"Of course. You're always in a hurry. I wouldn't want to keep you. If you need to get back to your work, I'll speak to Ms. Spencer alone. She's used to being without you, after all."

Those words rubbed at a wound that had barely begun to heal. "You're talking as if you know her."

Gus laid a soothing hand on his arm. "Calm down, babe." She looked to the woman. "Do we know each other?"

"We've never had the pleasure, but I know of you. In fact, I know about all of you. I've studied and done my homework," the woman explained. "It's rather like watching a soap opera play out in front of the nation. How well do I know you? I certainly know the two of you had an affair over a dozen years ago that ended in tragedy. It's why I was so surprised to see you sharing a room."

Gus went utterly still. "Tell me why you're here."

Roman wasn't sure why Gus had suddenly become less amenable to idle chitchat with Deep Throat. Did she feel as if her privacy had been invaded? Did she object to the woman calling their breakup a tragedy? He did. Stupidity on his part, yes. It had been shitty, in fact. But no one had died. He would have dismissed the woman entirely...except he didn't like how tight Gus's expression had become. How still her body had gone. Something the woman said had set her off.

"I'm here because you're close to the truth, but I suspect you're going to give up before you find the real prize."

"And what is the prize?" Roman asked.

"The tapes, of course," the woman replied. "You're almost there. Those tapes could explain so very much. If you find out what happened in Russia all those years ago, you'll understand what's happening today."

"If you're talking about the tapes of Constance Hayes's therapy sessions, you're out of luck. They're missing. The hospital has no idea where they've gone," Gus replied. "They were stolen along with the files."

"The hospital is part of the problem," the woman confided. "They think if they bury their heads in the sand, no one will discover exactly how complicit they were in Constance Hayes's death. I know they have a professional, clinical demeanor, and perhaps they do good work from time to time, but they're also infamous for handling the 'problems' of the world's wealthiest men. Many a wayward wife or mistress has found herself locked up and drugged so she wouldn't cause trouble during a delicate merger or political campaign. Often, she finds herself tossed into the hospital and not released until the doctor is satisfied. And by doctor, I really mean her husband or lover. I think even a couple of embarrassing daughters and sons have found their way here, as well. Don't think because the world has changed that the wealthy have. They still rule the world, and Constance Hayes threatened everything her husband—and by extension, her son—had worked for. Ms. Spencer, did you know your father tried to visit her at Homewood?"

"I know he was in London before he died. It was his last trip, but Constance was dead by the time he flew over, so he couldn't have seen her."

"This was before her death, roughly three months

into her treatment. He'd been in Paris for some meetings and took an extra day to stop by Homewood."

"It doesn't surprise me that he would try to see her while he was here," Gus said. "He and Constance weren't friends, per se. But they were friendly."

"And yet the hospital refused to allow the visit. You won't find Admiral Spencer's name on any of the visitor logs. In fact, your father was on the list of people who weren't allowed to see Constance. Don't you find that unusual?"

Roman certainly did. "Who *was* allowed to visit? Are you sure it wasn't simply a matter of her father not being on a list of approved visitors?"

"That's not what happened, Calder. Stop trying to fix the optics and look at the truth instead. Constance Hayes didn't have a short list of people the staff or family thought might help her progress. They cooked up a list of personae non gratae. The admiral was one. In fact, if any of the Spencer clan had shown up, even you, Augustine, they would have been denied access."

"Why? I don't understand." Gus shook her head. "What did my father know about Constance?"

"Why don't you ask your boyfriend? He knows. He's been in on the investigation from the beginning, the one that proved your father was killed by a man working for the *Bratva*. In turn, I believe the *Bratva* is working for the Russian government. Strange bedfellows, I know, but not unheard of. All the Brotherhood wants is to make money and have influence. They don't care who pays the bills. In this instance, the partnership will bring them both."

Gus looked up at him. "Do you know something I don't?"

Roman sighed. "You know the Russians have their fingers all over this conspiracy. I might not have gotten into all the details, but I did tell you that your father's death was wrapped up in this mess." He looked to the woman. "Are you trying to put a wedge between us? It won't work. I won't leave her vulnerable."

"She's more vulnerable than you can imagine, Calder. You've been looking in all the wrong places. Find the recordings and you'll understand why Constance Hayes had to die. Figure out who's leaking White House information and you'll know who's betrayed you. Who betrayed Maddox Crawford."

An icy shiver went through Roman. "Are you telling me you know who killed him?"

A chuckle left the woman's mouth, a humorless sound. "No singular entity killed Crawford. It was a group effort. But the reason he died is what's important. He saw something, knew something, had started to put the pieces of the puzzle together. That threatened the group. These are powerful enemies. Think. Who could have acquired that bomb and put it on his plane? Who knew that Maddox Crawford was even flying that day? After all, he hadn't planned in advance to do it."

Zack had known. Zack had an argument with Mad over the phone. Roman assumed it was about Sara's pregnancy. They'd both spoken to Gabe that day. It had been dramatic, then tragic because hours later Mad was gone forever. "It wasn't Zack. He wouldn't have killed Mad."

"Are you sure about that, Calder? Or do you have some niggling questions?"

"I have questions," Gus admitted, her voice low.

In the moonlight, he saw the woman grin. So broad.

It was a Cheshire cat smile, and he worried for a second that the informant would fade away now that she'd shaken everyone's faith. "Of course you do. You're the smart one here."

"But why would Zack hurt Mad?" Gus asked, her chin raised stubbornly. Her stance worried him, despite how bravely she'd asked the question. "What could he possibly know about Constance—or anything else—that would threaten not only their friendship, but Zack himself?"

"That's the question of the day," the woman replied. "And precisely why someone needs to find those tapes. Someone who desperately wants to know the truth, not hide it. I have to take every opportunity possible to get those tapes in the right hands."

"Yours, I presume," Roman shot back.

"Of course you presume. That's what you do. You think the world is black and white, but I'm here to tell you, Calder, it's definitely not. Life would be so much simpler if it was. I wouldn't have to plot and plan and have contingencies for my contingencies if the world was that simple."

So he was dumb? This woman seemed to have it in for him. "Do you have something you want to say to me?"

"Just that our lives are all complex. Isn't that right, Roman?" the woman asked. "I'm trying to figure out who to trust. I'm not sure I should trust someone so close to the presidency. That's why I have redundancies in place. But I do trust Ms. Spencer. She's above reproach. If she found evidence of the president's wrongdoing, she would do whatever necessary to protect your country."

"Yes, she's an amazing woman," Roman snapped. "I

think you want to get her killed."

"Not at all, though I think you'll find she's in a precarious position and she has no idea. And you're the one who wants to keep her right where she is. But you're pulling us off the point. You wanted information that isn't complete shit. Here it is: someone at the White House is feeding the *Bratva* information."

Gus started to open her mouth, but Roman reached for her hand. If Kemp worked for the Russians, he didn't want to reveal that they knew he was the likely traitor. The agent was still a possible lead, so they couldn't do or say anything to tip their hand yet. And she'd talked about redundancies. Kemp might not be the only treasonous bastard.

"Can you give us a name?" Gus asked, her mouth a flat line.

"I don't think you'd like the possibilities I would throw out," she said. "But I don't have anything concrete. I only know that someone is leaking intel, someone very close to the heart of power. Zack Hayes knew about Maddox Crawford's flight. He wasn't the only one."

"I knew," Roman admitted. "But I certainly didn't kill Mad. Neither did Zack."

"So you say." The woman turned directly to Gus. "Follow the trail. Constance Hayes was shoved into this hospital to shore up perceptions and shut her up. Her loving family ensured she couldn't leave until she was 'better.' But she didn't bounce back the way they thought she should. When she would no longer hide the truth about her past, she became expendable. And she was terminated. The truth is on those tapes."

"Her stories about the dead baby are true?" Gus

asked, horror all over her face.

"I believe so. I suspect the incident goes back to when the president was merely an infant."

"Do you know who Sergei is?" Roman asked. Even forcing the question out of his mouth made him a little ill.

"Sergei?" Gus looked up at him.

Damn it. This meeting would end with one pissed-off girlfriend if he wasn't careful. He hadn't mentioned the name because he hadn't been ready to drag her that deep into the danger, not until he knew something more concrete.

Through the shadows, the woman looked his way. "Isn't that the question of the day? I wish I knew who Sergei was. I believe that's the code name for the traitor in the White House."

"Natalia Kuilikov talked about Sergei. She loved Sergei." He couldn't stop thinking about that woman. According to Connor, she'd talked about how Sergei would fix everything. Had she been talking about a sleeper agent? Or her child, taken to replace the one Constance Hayes had inadvertently killed?

He had to consider the possibility that she'd been talking about the man the world knew as Zachary Hayes, president of the United States.

The woman shrugged. "I can't give you more on that. We need to listen to those tapes."

"How do we find them?" Gus asked. "How can we be sure they still exist?"

The woman in black took a step back. "We can't be, but I believe they're still here in this village. Nurse House had a daughter. Talk to her. See what she knows, and don't let her shrug you off. I suspect she's got those tapes. Her mother took them as collateral, then found out the *Bratva* didn't appreciate her demands. I think her daughter knows where the tapes are. She lives a few minutes away. Get her to give them to you. Then you'll learn the truth."

Did he want to know the truth? If that meant having one of his friends implicated? His illusions stripped away? He wasn't sure. He wasn't sure of anything except he hated this.

"If these recordings are so important, why don't you retrieve them yourself?" Roman challenged.

"Unfortunately, my reach doesn't extend everywhere, and it won't be as easy as simply asking. Alas, I don't have Ms. Spencer's charm."

"You're obviously not the same contact who met with Lara and Everly."

"It's best to spread the information around, not to leave too much in the hands of any one person," she explained.

Roman frowned at her. He'd been so focused on this woman and her yarn-spinning that he hadn't been paying attention to their surroundings. Suddenly, he had the uncomfortable feeling they weren't alone. He couldn't explain the instinct, but he also couldn't deny it. Someone was in those nearby woods, watching. Waiting.

"How many of you Deep Throats are there?" Gus demanded.

There was a small pause. "As many as required, Ms. Spencer."

Now that he thought about it, there had been small pauses before the woman's every response. As though she was waiting on something—or someone to coach her on the proper reply.

"Are you wearing a wire?" Roman was done playing games. If she knew something, she'd better damn well stop talking in riddles. And if she had some Oz behind her curtain, it was time to rip that sucker back. "Is there someone else out here?"

He couldn't stand the thought that someone was watching their every move. It worried the hell out of him.

The woman stepped back. "Be careful, Ms. Spencer. Calder will always choose Zack over you. Always. Even if it means your life. Haven't you lost enough because of this man?"

With that, the informant disappeared, darkness swallowing her up.

Fuck. He was sick of this crap. He would catch that woman and haul her back to London, let Connor find out what she really knew.

Roman lunged, but he'd already lost her in the shadows. Worse, he was more convinced than ever that they weren't alone. His heart pounded in his chest. She could have a gun or a partner. Either could be deadly.

It didn't matter anymore. He wanted more than riddles. He wanted the whole tangled mess of this conspiracy over, and that meant quitting the bullshit and getting down to actual business.

"What are you doing?" Gus reached for his arm.

He sidestepped her. He wasn't going to allow her to sway him. This was precisely why the bastard who was running the show chose to approach the women. They wouldn't take drastic measures. He was sure Gus wanted to talk to this infuriating woman more, but Roman already knew it wouldn't get them anywhere.

He followed the informant deeper into the darkness. As he reached the top step, the door to the crypt closed.

He growled and gave it a mighty shove, but it wouldn't budge.

Anger flashed through his system. It pulsed and snaked around him. He pounded a fist on the stone door. "You think I won't stay here until you come out? I will. Hell, I'll go get the police, and we'll have a long talk."

"She's gone," Gus said, her voice resigned.

"How? We have to get inside that damn crypt. Then she'll tell me every goddamn thing I want to know."

"There's a tunnel inside." Gus stared at him, her face as blank as a doll's. "Just like the house we're staying at in London. I read a pamphlet in our room about the ghost tours the cemetery gives during October. One of the highlights was this crypt and the secret passage the Brits used to move spies around during World War II."

She'd known that and not mentioned it before now? "Where does it lead? We can catch her if we're fast enough."

Gus shook her head, her arms encircling her middle as though she was cold. "I didn't read that far. But she's gone. I can't believe you scared her off. I had questions. This was *my* meeting, Roman, and you took it over, like you take over everything. The Hitman. You killed my chances to get answers, all right."

He didn't have time for this. If they couldn't find the woman, then he wanted to search the woods to see if he'd been right. Had her accomplice been here, watching them all along?

He jogged down the steps and stared into the tree line. "I know you're out there, you motherfucker. You think you can mess with me? You think I won't find out who you are?"

He heard a pinging sound. A whoosh of air passed

his ankle. The ground to the left of his foot shifted, vibrating under his loafer.

Someone was there. Someone was firing a gun at him.

"Roman!" Gus yelled.

A red dot appeared in the center of his chest. Roman stood stock-still, utterly frozen. A laser sight. He'd seen them used before but never had one pointed directly at him. His heart sawed with fear.

Suddenly, Gus threw herself in front of him, her arms spread wide as though trying to indicate she was harmless...or making herself their target. "Please don't kill him. We can't do what you need if you take him out."

That red laser dropped immediately, vanishing as though it had never splashed across his chest.

What the hell had she done? She'd stepped in front of a maniac with a gun.

Rage boiled up inside Roman. He reached for her and shoved her behind him. The cemetery was completely silent. Not even a breeze broke the still. He stood for a long moment, waiting for something more to happen.

Nothing.

It occurred to him that they were vulnerable out in the open. He had to get moving, to get Gus out of here. Then maybe he could return and comb the place for evidence.

"How could you do that?" Gus asked, her voice a hushed, angry growl.

"What? Because if we're going to argue, I could ask you why the hell you put yourself in danger. I was trying to find out what in the hell is actually going on. What's your excuse?" He wasn't the bad guy here.

Still gripping her hand tightly, he hauled them both back to the relative safety of the crypt's shadows. At least their backs were protected here. Could he figure out how to open the door?

"Don't turn this on me. I tried to save you from your hot-headed stupidity. We were on our way to figuring this mystery out when you pulled your macho-asshole BS," she hissed back. "She wasn't leaving. She would have stayed and answered our questions. Well, my questions since mostly you acted impatient and insulted her."

"Gus, you have to see that she was manipulating us both. And she wasn't alone."

"You don't know that. She could have gotten out of the tunnel and found a perch. That laser sight would allow her a good range. If she ran and then managed to hear you screaming that you intended to chase her, she might have wanted to make you think twice about it."

"No, there was someone else." He knew it. He'd felt eyes on him. "That's why there have been three different contacts—because one person is pulling all the strings. I need to find out who that is. These Deep Throats are just pawns. I want my hands on the mastermind. I want to know what's really going on."

Tears streamed down her face. "All right. You go do that. I'm going back to our room." She walked down the steps before turning back to face those woods. "He's all yours! Take him quick, though. He's a baby when it comes to pain, and I don't want to hear his screaming."

"Augustine! Get back here right fucking now."

In the moonlight he couldn't mistake the way she lifted her arm and extended her middle finger. And she kept right on walking.

She was going to get them both killed. He had no choice. He ran after her, wrapping a hand on her elbow.

"How dare you walk away like that. Do you know what that bastard could do to you?"

She pulled her arm out of his grip. "Whoever was out there didn't want to kill anyone. That shot was a warning. You're the one who turned a perfectly polite meeting into a potential bloodbath. You couldn't hold it together for thirty minutes, could you? You couldn't sit back and let me handle it."

"You weren't handling it. You were letting that woman manipulate you. She was pointedly trying to drive a wedge between us."

"Yes, and we could have used that to find out information about her. We could have played into her hand and she likely would have told us something. Like what was different about this Deep Throat meeting. Like, if every time the mastermind sends out this informant character he tries to get the woman he's contacting alone, why did he invite you this time?"

"Because she knew I wasn't going to be stupid enough to let you slip away."

"Oh, you've been stupid enough for everyone tonight, Roman. Are you going to call Connor and let him know about this clusterfuck of a meeting or should I? I assure you if I do it, you won't like how you come off."

"I'm not calling anyone. We're getting in the car and driving back to London tonight." He wasn't letting her anywhere near the danger again. No way. No how. She'd been every bit as reckless as he'd feared. He'd known she had that tendency, but he had hoped that age had brought her wisdom and tempered her recklessness. But no. She'd thrown herself in between him and a potential bullet.

She turned on him. "What?"

He hated the way she was looking at him, like he was an idiot. No, like a stranger. He hated that all their easy intimacy from earlier tonight had vanished. There was nothing he could do about that, but he could damn well take her in hand. If he didn't, things could spiral out of control. What the hell would he do if Augustine got it in her head that Zack was the bad guy? She had a strong sense of justice and she would do something about it. That would put him squarely between his best friend and the woman he loved.

He loved Augustine.

Falling for her wasn't the smart play, but then again this wasn't a game. This was their life. He'd fought these feelings for too long.

Be careful, Ms. Spencer. Calder will always choose Zack over you. Always. Even if it means your life. Haven't you lost enough because of this man?

Had he picked Zack the first time? Back then, he'd been sure he was merely a prisoner to his past. Had he wrapped all his problems up in one neat package he could understand? One in which he could assign appropriate blame? His parents had a rotten marriage and subsequently miserable lives, so he would have one as different from theirs as possible. Or had he really put distance between them because she distracted him? Had he chosen Zack and his ambition over her and his heart the first time?

He approached her, wishing they were already back at the B&B, that they'd never left their cozy, romantic room tonight. If putting a rift in their relationship had been the plan, that woman had done her job well. "Gus, it's too dangerous to stay here."

"I'm not going anywhere. If it's gotten too rough for you, feel free to leave. I'm not giving up. I'm finding those recordings."

"No. Someone was in those woods." He pointed to the tree line. "They nearly shot us."

"You. They nearly shot *you* because you were a massive asshole. There are rules to this game Deep Throat is playing and you broke them. I'm going to figure this out, then we can stop wondering who's playing these terrible games with us and stop worrying about our safety. Once we've unmasked this person, we can be done with all this and finally move on."

What the hell was she talking about? Not an hour before he'd been sure they'd gotten past that whole fuck-you-out-of-my-system nonsense he was pretty sure she'd decided on. "This isn't a game I'm playing and I'm not letting you get hurt. And I have no plans to move on."

She turned and started walking again.

At least they were moving in the general direction of their room. He didn't want to have this insane argument in the middle of a cemetery where someone was likely still watching them.

He hustled beside her as she turned down the path toward their little cottage. "I'm sorry if I didn't handle that as well as I should have, but can't you see how manipulative she was being?"

"You didn't have to give in to it. Don't you think some of the things she said bothered me, too? I ignored them to get to the information we needed."

"What if finding the nurse's daughter is a trap?"

"Did Deep Throat lead Everly or Lara into traps before?"

He could answer that one. "Absolutely. They both almost died."

"But they got the information promised, right?"

Roman went silent. She wasn't listening to him. "We'll find the information we need without being pawns."

She scoffed. "I was your pawn tonight, wasn't I, Roman? You never meant to let me take the lead. You always planned on taking charge because you protecting Zack is way more important than me finding out why my father and two of my best friends are dead." She refused to look his way, simply kept on walking. But he heard the tears in her voice. "Like I said, you go right back to London. I'll handle it from here."

"If you think I'll let that happen, you don't know me at all."

"I should know you, shouldn't I? After fucking everything you've done to me, I shouldn't be surprised by this. But I am. I'm that idiot who still thought sex with you meant love, who thought you could actually care about me."

"Baby, I never said I didn't. What is going on with you? I'll admit I went too far back there and I'm sorry for it. But I don't understand why you're bringing our personal relationship into this. Gus, please stop and talk to me. I don't want to fight with you." He was at a loss. Something was going on inside her head. For the life of him, he couldn't imagine what. He'd lost good friends, too. He had grieved Joy's death. Mad's death. She wasn't the only one with a stake here. But there was more, something he didn't understand. This anger was something much stronger, a deeper ache he could feel but couldn't comprehend.

She stopped at the cottage, stepping back to let him get to the door.

The innkeeper had given them one key, and he'd taken it because it had felt like the natural thing to do. The reservation had been in his name. But he would have taken that key even if it had been in hers.

Because he always had to be in control. In charge.

Frowning, he shoved the key in and opened the door.

"I'm not going anywhere," she said, her voice tight. "If you believe I'm giving up now and letting you return me to London, you're wrong."

The accusation in her voice put him on edge. She was the one who waited until the last minute to tell him about the meeting she should have shared with him the instant she'd received that text. She was the one who'd snuck away from the safety of London and nearly gotten herself arrested for searching the doctor's office. But all fucking night he'd been the bad guy.

"You'd be surprised at what I can do, Augustine. I can have you out of this country altogether if I choose to." It might be for the best. He couldn't think when she was around, and this conspiracy was a problem that required all of his attention.

"Because you're the one who chooses. Always." Tears had sparked in her eyes.

He hated that. She was Augustine Spencer. She didn't let any man make her cry.

Except him.

He took a deep breath. "I don't want to fight with you."

She sighed and turned to him. "Don't you think I

feel the same way? I'm tired of fighting you, Roman. Honestly, I might be tired of fighting, period. I think when we return to the States, I'll take a friend up on her job offer and move to New York."

He closed the door and locked it, feeling as if she'd yanked the floor out from under him. "You have a job offer?"

She hesitated. "Sara asked me to come and head up Crawford's legal department. She'll need a lot of help once the baby comes."

"Are you serious?" He had no idea she'd been talking to Gabe's sister about a job. But then, she wouldn't share something like that with him. She didn't share much except her body.

"Why does that surprise you?"

He was quiet for a moment because once more they were on delicate terrain. For years, he'd been walking on eggshells around Gus. The last few days had been the exception, and he'd hoped that meant... Well, it didn't look as if their relationship was going anywhere now.

"I assumed Sara knew about you and Mad. That doesn't bother her?"

She rolled her eyes and sighed, letting him know that he'd missed the point again. "Of course she knew Mad and I had a past. Everyone knew. We didn't try to hide it because we were adults who weren't ashamed of our sexuality. Sara also accepts that we were really nothing more than friends, human beings who sometimes needed comfort beyond a hug."

"Naturally I'm the one who was ashamed," he said with a bitter bite.

"I don't think you were ashamed of your sexuality, Roman. I think you were ashamed of me."

God, they were back to square one. Him trying to make things right, and Gus putting the worst spin on his words.

Then again, she had an interesting point. Why hadn't he been okay back then with his buddies knowing about her? About them?

"It wasn't like that. I didn't want to upset Dax."

"I don't buy that bullshit." She ran a hand through her hair, shoving it away from her tense face. "And why would Dax be upset that I was dating one of his best friends? He trusted you. He considers you to be one of the smartest, most honorable people he knows. So why would he have a problem with you dating his sister? Unless, of course, you never intended to have anything but sex with me. Unless I was merely a way to pass the time until the demure June Cleaver of your dreams came along. Until you met Joy."

"I wish you hadn't heard any of that," he said quietly. "I don't know what would have happened with Joy, but I don't think it should affect what's happening between you and me now. I don't see how talking about her helps us at all."

"It doesn't help, but it does put things into perspective. Roman, have you ever once thought about sending me a flirty text? How about pouring out your feelings to me on the Internet? Those must have been pretty impressive e-mails to her since someone wants to blackmail the president of the United States with them."

Frustration welled inside him. Why were they doing this? They had more important things to talk about, not some semi-emotional affair that had gone nowhere physically. "They weren't, and I wouldn't have thought about sending any to her if she hadn't approached me first. I didn't just start writing her love letters on a whim. I'm a guy and I don't think to do those things. If you want the truth, I ignored her the first few times."

She kept on poking him. "Why? You liked her from the beginning, didn't you? Did you fall for her a little on that very first double date with Zack? Did you want to switch places with him that night?"

Damn, why did Gus never listen to a thing he said? She had some stubborn, compulsive need to be right. But in this case, she was so fucking wrong. He might have been a shit in the past, but he was trying to protect her now. And she kept bringing up the past. Every time he thought they'd moved beyond what had happened years ago, she circled right back, like a dog with a bone.

He stopped in the middle of the quiet hallway. "The truth? I didn't notice her at all. I can't remember the name of the woman who was my date that night. I sat there that whole evening and wondered what you were doing."

He waited for her snappy comeback, but she'd fallen silent. Gus did that when she knew she was wrong. Or she'd done something wrong herself. "I've told you what I was doing that night. I gave you the truth. Quid pro quo. What were you doing right after our breakup? Or maybe the better question is, *who* were you doing, Augustine? Did Mad give you 'comfort' that night, too?"

She flushed, her skin flashing bright red and her eyes narrowing. "You want to fucking know what I was doing that night, Roman? I *was* with Mad. I was with Mad all night."

He felt sick. He'd known it. Deep down he'd known the woman he'd been crazy about and one of his best friends had started their years-long fling that night. That was why she hadn't returned his calls. She hadn't been hurt, merely busy. And it also explained why Mad hadn't spoken to him privately for a very long time. Yeah, he'd known she'd left his house that night looking for a little revenge.

"Well, that doesn't surprise me."

"Of course it doesn't, Roman. You always knew what kind of a woman I am. You knew it then. Except I wasn't in Mad's bed that night." Tears welled in her eyes, and she tossed back her head as if trying to will them away. "I was in the fucking hospital because I miscarried our baby."

She froze, eyes wide as she clapped a hand over her mouth as though she could somehow shove the words back in.

Roman stared, time seeming to stop. He knew it hadn't, but everything seemed to slow until the world narrowed to one thing and one thing only.

Gus had been pregnant? She had lost their baby that night?

Oh, god. "It was the stairs. You tumbled down the stairs because I grabbed you too hard and…"

It all fell neatly into place. He'd known something was wrong that night, something that went beyond the emotional pain he'd caused her. He'd wanted to follow after her, but he had ignored the impulse. Instead, he'd started drinking with Zack.

While she'd been losing their baby.

"I-I'm sorry, Roman." The words came out of her mouth on a stutter. "I didn't mean to tell you like that."

He didn't know what to think, how to feel. The bombshell had smashed him. His brain raced, and he couldn't move his body at all.

"I don't think you meant to tell me at all." He'd done his best to sound steady, but he couldn't stop his voice from shaking.

He'd done that to her. He'd known he could hurt her with his words, but he'd been determined not to let her walk out of that house with the upper hand. He'd been so furious with Gus and he hadn't thought about anything but continuing their fight.

She'd paid the worst price imaginable.

The whole fight flashed through his head as if it had happened yesterday. And he knew precisely why she'd done and said things that started the argument.

But if I stay in DC, we don't have to split up.

"You wanted to take the job with Kleinman and Horne so we could stay together. So we could be a family," he said as he realized the truth.

Tears shone in her eyes, making them bright even in the low light. "I wanted you, Roman. Not only the baby. I wanted us to be together. I was in love with you. I didn't tell you about the baby because I needed to know if you wanted me, too." Her lips pursed as she seemingly collected her thoughts. "What would you have done if you'd known?"

She thought he would have told her to take care of the "problem." Of course she thought that. He hadn't given her any reason to think otherwise. He'd actually told her that night that he didn't want children. Yet he knew exactly what he would have done if Gus had divulged her pregnancy to him. He hadn't changed that much. Yeah, he'd talked a good game back then, but he would have done the right thing. "I would have asked you to marry me."

"Yeah, I was worried about that, too. I thought we

needed more time, and I hoped me taking the job in DC would give us that. But I saw quickly that you didn't want me the way I wanted you."

"Don't presume to understand what I would have wanted." The younger Roman might have said he didn't want kids...but the man now wanted that baby deeply. Finding out they'd conceived and miscarried all in the same sentence was a kick in the gut. Gus had borne the pain and carried it all these years alone.

No, she'd had Mad.

Roman closed his eyes. More than anything, he wished he could go back to that night, wished she would tell him right then and there that he was behaving like an asshole and it was time to grow up because they were having a baby.

He wanted to hold her, like he should have that night. He ached to go back and embrace her, never pick that fight...maybe save their baby. But if it had been doomed regardless, then he wanted to be the man who took care of her, who held her hand and eased her pain.

Goddamn it, what had he done?

"Roman, are you okay?" She was suddenly standing in front of him, her hands wrapping around his arms. "I really am sorry I blurted that at you."

"How far along were you?"

She hesitated. "I think I was about nine weeks along. I was in denial at first. For a while, I convinced myself I was stressed about the job situation, and that was the reason I'd missed a couple of periods."

His head was reeling, and all that anger he had inside twisted and blew back at him. "And I didn't notice. But then again, an asshole like me wouldn't have. Why would I notice something like my girlfriend being pregnant? I would never have noticed you having morning sickness because I tried to make sure no one ever saw me leaving your bed, so I rarely stayed the whole night. Did you go through nausea alone, too?"

"There were a couple of queasy mornings, but I thought it was a touch of flu or something. Roman, it's ancient history."

"It just happened to me." He took a step back. How had he not seen it? "I would have married you, Augustine. If you'd said no, I would have gone straight to your family and gotten them on my side. We would be married."

"Or divorced," she said sadly. "I don't know what would have happened if I hadn't miscarried. I only know that I did."

"Because I lost my temper and made you fall down the stairs." In his mind, he could see her falling even now, see his hand reaching for hers, watch her slip through his fingers. He'd been a second too late.

Gus shook her head, her mouth firming with conviction. "It was an accident. The doctor told me he wasn't even sure my fall was the cause. Women miscarry all the time in the first trimester. The baby was tiny and well protected. It could have been a coincidence."

He knew better. Pretending he believed otherwise or spewing meaningless platitudes weren't going to change a thing. "It wasn't. I did that to you and our child."

"Stop, Roman. Stop taking all the blame. I was there, too. I ran down those damn stairs and I knew I was pregnant. I wasn't careful. All I thought about that night was getting away from you so you wouldn't see me cry. So maybe you should blame me, too."

"No."

Roman couldn't say more now. Right in the back of his throat sat a sob that he couldn't release. It nearly strangled him. He had to keep it inside. He had to shove it down because he had to be stronger. Anger was fine. Anger he understood, but the emotion he wrestled with now threatened to take him apart. If he gave in to it, he didn't know if he'd be able to come back. He would be shattered, and right now, he wasn't sure he was strong enough to put himself back together.

"Don't," she said, rising up on her toes and leaning into his space. "I didn't want to hurt or upset you. Forgive me."

"Forgive you?"

"For not telling you. For not being honest until now. For lashing out in anger over a truth you didn't even know. For letting my pride hurt us both." She stroked his arms, palms gliding over his skin like a benediction. Soothing. Her words were calm and measured, meant to ease him.

Why was she touching him softly? Asking his forgiveness? He didn't deserve either, not when this was all his doing. He started to pull back.

She held on to him. "Don't walk away. Don't leave me. Stay. I don't think about what happened a lot, Roman. I try not to obsess about the baby we could have had, but when I do think about him or her, I'm almost always alone. Don't make me be alone tonight."

She'd mourned by herself. She'd been alone all these years—with the singular exception of Mad, who'd kept her secret.

No wonder every time Mad had looked at him after that, his eyes had held contempt.

The anger he used to feel whenever he thought of

Gus with Mad? He couldn't summon it anymore. Mad had been there for her. The man should have called him out, but he never had. He'd just shouldered the responsibility Roman should have.

Once, they'd been the best of friends, but Mad had chosen Gus. Thank god someone had been smart enough to.

Tonight's Deep Throat had been right. He'd always chosen Zack. He'd placed Zack, and more importantly their quest for the White House, above everything else. Above Augustine. Above his own heart.

He wrapped his arms around her as she began to cry. "I'm so sorry, baby. I'm so sorry. I'd give anything to change that night."

She clutched him in return and sobbed in his arms. And Roman felt something inside him open, some door that had always been closed and locked up tight.

When he felt his own tears come—tears for the child they'd lost, for the years they'd missed out on—that sob he'd been trying to hold back came. And he knew he would never be the same again.

CHAPTER FIFTEEN

Gus looked across the small, sparse cottage and found Roman staring out the window as the rain began to fall again.

"Do you take milk with your tea?" Ellen House asked, setting the tray on the coffee table between them.

Gus smiled her way. "No, thank you, but I will take a sugar. And we both thank you for your hospitality. I know talking about your mother must be hard."

Ellen House was a petite woman in her early fifties, though she looked significantly older. Her hair was a steely gray and cut into a pixie style that didn't at all suit her face, but was likely simple to keep up. Her house was neat if a bit sparse when it came to human furniture.

It was far more crowded with cats and items to amuse them.

Gus had counted ten different felines so far, and those were merely the ones that had sauntered in and out of the living room while Ellen prepared the tea.

One of them slunk up to Roman, rubbing its long-haired body against his thousand dollar slacks and making him jump.

"Why don't you come and sit with me?" Gus offered. "Do you want some tea?"

Grim-faced, Roman turned and joined her on the tiny couch.

"I want some Scotch," he muttered under his breath. "And whatever repels cats. This one won't leave me alone."

Ellen smiled and poured another cup. "Ah, that's Mr. Darcy. Don't mind him. He's a lover, not a fighter. Never did have any kids of my own so I adopted these fur babies. I'm as much of a mother to them as I would be to a human, and I love them like they're my children."

Roman suddenly folded his hand into hers, palms sliding and fingers connecting. His mouth was flat, his body rigid. The mention of kids now was still a sore spot for him.

Gus leaned against him, offering him her silent support. "You certainly treat them well."

They'd spent the previous evening wrapped in each other's arms. After they shared their initial sorrow and tears, Roman had stripped her bare and settled her in bed. She'd been sure he would make love to her. She'd had mixed feelings about that, but sex was often how they coped when emotions overwhelmed them.

Instead, he'd doffed his own clothes and climbed in next to her. He'd drawn her close and turned off the light. There, in the warm darkness, wrapped up in one another, they'd talked about the child they'd lost. They'd shared how broken they'd both felt after they'd split up. She'd admitted that she'd kept the job in DC because she hadn't been able to go home and face her parents, so she'd thrown herself in to work. He'd done the same.

They'd confessed how much they'd regretted letting pride, immaturity, stupidity, and fear come between them. Gus felt lighter than she had in over a dozen years.

Roman was quiet this morning, but not at all distant. When she'd awakened, he'd rolled her over and kissed her before making slow, sweet love to her. Afterward, he'd held her, feeling their hearts beat together. Over breakfast, he caressed her arm before tangling her fingers with his. She would miss this easy affection when they got back to London and had to behave professionally.

On the drive to visit Ms. House, he'd made her promise she would be careful. In exchange, he'd promised he wouldn't take over the interview. Communication and compromise, not recriminations and demands. She felt the progress between them—a bit slow and tentative. It wasn't second nature to either of them, especially in dealing with the other. But it gave her hope.

Then why was she, somewhere in the back of her mind, waiting for the other shoe to drop? For the anger and accusations to spring up between them again?

Ellen passed Gus the teacup. "I certainly do. As well as me own mum ever treated me, and she was a wonderful woman."

"We actually wanted to talk to you about your mother, and more specifically about a patient your mother treated," Gus explained.

The teacup shook slightly before Ellen passed it over to Roman. "You want to talk about her time at Homewood?"

Gus was well aware that she'd crossed onto shaky

ground. Ellen had paled visibly. She had to be careful. "Yes. The patient's name was Constance Hayes, though she was registered as Jane Downing."

Ellen took a sip of tea, then reached down to lift the nearest cat, hauling a pretty tabby into her lap. "My mum was good at her job. If you're here to start a lawsuit…"

Gus shook her head. "Not at all."

"Really? Because that one has the look of a lawyer."

Roman was trying to gently disengage from the very affectionate Mr. Darcy, who seemed intent on rubbing his ears against Roman's loafer and marking him with his feline scent. "What does a lawyer look like?"

Ellen's lips pursed as she looked him over. "Uppity and very intellectual. Someone who probably doesn't like cats."

"I know lots of lawyers who have cats." Roman defended his profession while trying to look comfortable with a cat purring loudly and rubbing against his leg. "And obviously cats love me, so there you go."

He was trying. It was kind of adorable.

"I know a female named Darcy who does the exact same thing whenever you're around. I think you're irresistible to Darcys of all species." Gus winked his way before turning back to Ellen. "He is a lawyer, but not the kind who would sue a hospital. He's into politics, which is absolutely worse."

Roman frowned her way. "That's very hypocritical of you."

It was since she'd gone to the same law school and worked in the same place, but she was rolling with it. "We're here on behalf of Constance's family, but they have no interest in suing Homewood or its employees. Constance's son just wants a few of his questions answered about his mother's illness since she's deceased now and his father has dementia."

Ellen stroked the cat, seeming to take comfort from the fur ball resting contentedly in her arms. "I always knew someone would come around someday and ask questions."

"No one else has ever questioned you about your mother's job at Homewood?" Gus asked.

"A few have over the years," she admitted. "But they wanted to know if Mum treated this actress or that pop star. I don't know much about the celebrities, but I know she didn't treat any of her patients differently than she would a normal person. She believed everyone should be treated equally. And some of them were the kind to throw fits and to pretend like Homewood was a five-star hotel, not a mental facility. They learned real fast, they did."

"So you don't consider Homewood to be a good hospital?"

Ellen pondered that for a moment. "As good as any, though my mum always said the administration cared more about money than patients. It's like that in the private pay facilities. I didn't like the place at all. Oh, it might look nicer on the outside than the public hospitals, but once you get past the shiny exterior and all the suites and such, it's nothing but a place that cashes in on misery. You know, sometimes she couldn't find a sitter, so she would take me with her. I would hear patients screaming. She would tell me to read or nap in one of the offices, but I could still hear wailing. I hated that place. I hated how sad it often made her."

"Did she ever talk about Constance?" Gus didn't want to think about how long the poor woman had been left to rot in that place.

"Sure. She talked to me about all her patients. That weren't no crime at all," Ellen insisted. "I was her daughter. Who else could she talk to?"

"Of course she needed to talk," Gus allowed, noting a second cat had joined Mr. Darcy in finding Roman endlessly fascinating. This one jumped up on his lap and began kneading at his thighs with claws. Roman winced, and it was a testament to his promise to behave that he didn't leap up and shoo the cats away. "Do you recall anything she said about Constance?"

Ellen stroked the cat, her hands still shaking a bit. Her complexion now looked sallow, and Gus didn't think that had anything to do with the lighting in the room. "She felt bad for the woman, being so far from home. Her husband had dumped her at Homewood and left. Everyone knew why. She was a terrible drunk, an embarrassment to her family. I suspect he thought she'd never really sober up, so he'd decided that shoving her in a facility outside of the States would at least be a good way to keep her off the radar."

"She was there for nine months. That seems like a long stay," Roman commented as one of the cats swished a tail under his nose.

"Oh, quite a few stayed longer. Years…or until some lawyer would visit. Once they signed papers, the hospital would suddenly declare the patient cured." Ellen scoffed. "My mum used to say there were some good doctors at Homewood, but most could be bought."

"Do you know if lawyers ever visited Constance?" What would Frank have wanted from his wife? A divorce? She doubted it. That would have been a family scandal Zack didn't need while running for president.

"Not that I know of. Mum seemed to think Constance was waiting for some event to pass," Ellen replied.

"I'm sure she would have been released after the election cycle." Roman stared down at Mr. Darcy, who had leapt up on his lap and nudged his feline sibling aside. Then the big orange tom plopped down on Roman's ridiculously expensive slacks and curled up for a long nap. "It wasn't the first time Constance had been tucked away to avoid embarrassment. Frank didn't want her at Zack's wedding. Zack had to put his foot down."

"I remember." Gus had been one of the bridesmaids. During the reception, Dax and her father had calmed Constance down. She'd had far too much to drink and talked in ravings they'd all thought were insane—at the time. "Was she placed in Homewood's rehab wing?"

Ellen reached for her teacup. "Not according to Mum. She was brought in and diagnosed with paranoia of some sort and locked in an isolation ward. Apparently, she had terrible nightmares. Mum thought the drugs the doctors pumped her full of made her see things that weren't there."

Or things from her past. "According to one of the doctors, she talked about a child."

Ellen nodded, her eyes lighting with sympathy. "Oh, yes. Terrible tales. Mum would say that when she was lucid, she was an interesting woman to talk to, but when she went dark… Well, she could tell some tales. I think it was because the poor woman had to spend so much time in Russia. Those are some shifty people."

"What would she say about the child?"

"She talked about killing a baby," Ellen said, her voice going low. "I don't know if it was an accident or something she intended to do. I mean, this was probably all a fever-induced dream, something her mind made up to torment her. My mum always said no one can torture you mentally as well as you can yourself. However, given things that happened later, I might be wrong."

"Things that happened later?"

Ellen took a long sip of tea. "Lots of bad things happened with that family. I'm not foolish. I know who we're talking about. I know that man's wife died, took a bullet that was meant for him. At least that's what the news programs said. Constance believed something different. Apparently, she'd always said they would kill her daughter-in-law one day. When Mum would ask her why, she would only say it was all her fault. Everyone would die, and she was to blame."

Gus fought back a shudder. "Did your mother ever say she was worried about Constance?"

"Oh, yeah. See, Constance was fragile, and Mum didn't like some of the doctors. Thought they knew everything, they did. And they would leave the nurses to do all the dirty work."

"What kind of dirty work?" Roman asked.

"Forcing people to take meds they didn't want. Sometimes restraining 'em for days. Dr. Richards was the worst of them all. His father left him the hospital, but he didn't run it the way his dad had. He wanted to do everything all new and the like, and he thought the older nurses knew nothing. It was him who decided to let Constance go off with the woman that night. Said it would do her good, but Mum didn't think it was for therapeutic reasons at all. She said she saw money change hands."

"Do you know the name of the woman who

persuaded him to let Constance out that night?" Roman asked while trying to shrug yet another cat off his shoulder.

Ellen shook her head. "Mum said it was some member of her family. But she didn't have to sign in or out like other people. Everything was kept real quiet. Given who the son turned out to be, I suspect the family is still keeping quiet."

"Actually, her son desperately wants the truth," Gus said.

"Did he have my mum killed?" She kept stroking the cat absently, but raised her pale stare.

Roman turned to her. "Absolutely not. Her son has suffered greatly as a result of this accident, too. He wants to find out if it was actually a murder."

"I know we're talking about President Hayes. You can say his name." She cocked her head. "I was wondering if you'd come to kill me. It doesn't matter. The cancer will get me soon enough. It's why I'm not screaming or calling the police. When you showed up, I realized I might get some answers of my own."

"I'm sorry to hear that." Gus reached out to the woman, laying a hand over hers. "And I'm sorry your mother got caught in this, but we're not the bad guys. We're trying to figure out who did this and why. We were hoping you knew something about the recordings of Constance's sessions that disappeared. Maybe your mother told you who took them or where they might be stored. Whoever took those tapes is trying to use them against her son. We need to know what's on them."

"Don't know what's on them, but whatever it is, I'm sure it's something that could be used against him. Mum knew it, too."

"Can you shed any light on where they might be now?"

"Of course. Mum took them," Ellen replied readily. "Said the docs had gotten rich enough and it was her turn. She said she'd earned the money that information would fetch, and she expected that it would be a lot. I don't know who she thought would give her the money. I told her the plan was insane. And then she was mysteriously killed. I never did believe her attack was a random thing by some punks wanting drugs. Whoever she blackmailed wanted those tapes, and they were willing to kill for them."

Gus sat back, alarmed...but not surprised. She'd known for a long while these people were willing to kill to further their cause, whatever that was. Still, she and Roman needed to listen to those recordings. They needed to hear Constance Hayes in her own words. If they couldn't, Gus wasn't sure how they could move forward in their investigation. And Roman would have become a human cat lounger for nothing.

"So your mother died and they took the tapes she'd secreted from the hospital?"

"Yes," Ellen replied. "Well, the ones she hid in her house. Not the two in storage. Those are still in the box Mum packed them in. I don't want them. If I'd been smart, I would have destroyed them long ago. Never listened to them." She paused, then admitted, "I wanted to know why she died, but I was afraid to find out."

"Are you saying some of those tapes are somewhere in your keeping?" Roman asked.

Ellen looked him over, her lips firming to a stubborn line. "Yes, but I want something, too. I lost my mum over those blasted things. So I want to make sure I get something out of this deal."

"What do you want?" Gus was ready to pull out her checkbook.

"A good home for my cats."

"Done." Gus would find homes for every single one of these purring, affectionate felines if it meant she got her hands on those tapes.

Ellen relaxed, her whole body slumping back into her comfy chair. "Good. Don't want them going to a shelter. Nasty places. They're too often euthanized, particularly special-needs babies. Cats need homes." She sent Roman a little smile. "I think Mr. Darcy knows who he wants to go home with."

Gus turned to find Roman now surrounded by cats.

"Can we have the tapes now?" The cat on the sofa back batted a paw at his hair, messing up his normally perfect do.

He gritted his teeth and took it like a man.

And Gus fell in love all over again.

* * * *

"I'm not taking those cats. You can't make me." Roman stood outside one of the village shops, where they'd paused to ask for directions. And buy a lint brush. Gus rolled the adhesive contraption over him, saving his suit from becoming a casualty of the catpocalypse.

She brushed over his shoulders, peeling the cat hair off his precious Hugo Boss. "I said I would help find them all good homes and ensure they were fed and taken care of. I didn't say they were moving into your condo. Even if we could get them back to the States, I don't think your building allows pets."

"I was thinking of moving." He watched as she knelt, since it appeared Mr. Darcy had left half his fur on the cuffs of his charcoal slacks. "Not that I want twelve animals, but maybe one would be nice. I also want a place with more room. Maybe something in the suburbs."

Her eyes widened as she looked up at him. "You? Somehow I can't see you out of your high-rise."

He shrugged. "It could happen."

Lots of things could happen.

"Well, I'm sure you'll find someplace lovely." She went back to working on his slacks.

He'd never once thought about leaving the city until the night before. He didn't spend enough time in his condo to warrant buying a damn house, but sometime in the middle of the night he'd had a vision of a house he actually occupied more often than never. A house where he had breakfast and rushed home so he could have dinner. A house in which he didn't live alone, where he could do stupid things like host a barbecue for his friends or raise a couple of kids.

A house with Augustine.

Of course, first they had to pray those tapes were where Ellen House claimed her mother stored them. Then they had to ferry them back to London and hear whatever ugly truths they held.

"Did the shopkeeper know how to find the place Ellen told us about? Did we take a wrong turn?" Roman asked as he held out his hand and helped her stand upright again.

Damn but she was pretty, even when she was holding a fuzzy lint brush.

"We didn't go far enough. It's another mile north, and then we'll turn left onto a country road. He warned me, though, that no one's lived at the Farrington Farm for a few years," Gus explained. "I told him we wanted to look at it because we were thinking about buying it. It's not such a crazy idea. If he looks into it, I even gave him the name of my real estate agent."

"Why do you have a real estate agent?" How seriously had she looked at taking the job with Sara? He wasn't about to let that happen.

She didn't meet his gaze. "I've thought maybe I would get a place here if something irresistible came on the market. I love England."

She wanted a getaway house. He liked that idea. As long as it wasn't full of furry, shedding creatures, he could embrace that. He only wanted one pussy in his life. "That's nice. I thought you were talking about finding a place in New York."

She stopped briefly. "No, if I go to New York, I'll probably stay with Sara until after the baby arrives. Maybe a while longer so I can help her."

She'd lost her own baby, and it had filled her with such pain. But she still wanted to help her friend. He'd always been so intimidated by her moxie and her complete willingness to go to the mat for the people she loved. He needed to stop being intimidated and start working so she directed all that blustery affection and fierce loyalty his way.

"I don't want you to leave DC, but I'd be willing to help out, too. Sara will need a lot of it," he said quietly.

That turned her head. "You willing to change a diaper?"

He stood a little taller. "Hey, I've run votes on the Hill. Nothing dirtier than that. I can handle a diaper or two. I think I'll have to do that a lot in the near future.

After all, most of my pack has settled down and is looking to procreate. Maybe it's my turn."

She nodded, but didn't say anything.

"Do you think we'll ever tell them we were first?"

She eased into his arms, wrapping him up in a hug. She laid her head over his heart, resting it there for one beautiful moment. "If you want to. I've never talked about it. No one knew except Mad."

He embraced her tight and breathed her in, loving how perfectly she fit against him. "I think I'd like to talk about it, if it's okay with you. I want to have a long talk with Dax when he gets back."

Her face turned up, lips forming a heart-stopping grin. "I want a front-row seat for that fight."

"Hey, I thought you said Dax would be thrilled."

"Only after he beats you up a little. He's my brother after all." She shrugged and broke away from him. "We should get going. I know the farm is supposedly abandoned, but I think it's best if we get in and out as quickly as possible."

"If no one's there, we shouldn't find ourselves in jail for trespassing." At least he hoped.

Roman jogged around the car and opened the door, settling Gus inside. Then he dashed around to the driver's seat and eased the vehicle onto the road.

"Ellen told me this place used to be her grandfather's farm. It's where her mum grew up, but it went under long ago since it's too small to truly be lucrative. Her mother hadn't lived there in years, and then Ellen held on to it for sentimental value. Now she's leaving her cottage and the farm to a pet rescue society." Gus turned to him and teased, "What if Ellen's already turned the farm into some feral cat sanctuary. Maybe we'll get a rousing chorus of hungry meows."

He shuddered at the thought. "Why don't you go into the barn first?"

She grinned at him. "It's good to know you have weaknesses, Calder. You're terrified of affectionate felines." She sobered slightly and looked back out the window. "I hope those tapes have survived the years. At least her mother claims to have put them in a locked tack room and boxed them to keep the elements at bay."

He hoped that was true. "It's sad that Ellen never even listened to them because she realized those very tapes had likely gotten her mother killed. I understand she was too scared to try. Might be the most common sense she's shown. She seems like an otherwise odd bird."

"She just wanted to be left alone with her cats," Gus replied, her tone sympathetic. "I think she was tired of fighting, too. She'd seen her mom do too much of it, and knowing now that she's dying herself... I suspect she just doesn't want any more turmoil. Can you imagine what would have happened if we hadn't listened to our Deep Throat and gone looking for Ellen? According to what the doctors told her, she's only got another month to live. All of her property and belongings would have been put up for auction. What if someone else found those recordings?"

He grimaced. He didn't want to think about how close they'd come to that happening. "It would depend on whether they realized who was talking. If they figured out the psychiatric patient was the president's mother, we might have been facing a media nightmare. We could have been blindsided, and likely right before the election cycle."

"Do you think Zack will run for reelection? I know it's ridiculous to think about not running. He's popular and has a great approval rating, but it might unravel this whole conspiracy if he announced that he's going to be a one-term president."

"Maybe. Or maybe whoever is behind this mess gets pissed and accelerates the timetable for whatever disaster they have in mind. Or they start offing the rest of his friends to show they mean business. After all, they threatened to blackmail us. Murder might be the next step." Roman had lost a lot of sleep these last few months considering this exact problem. "These people have already killed at least four of Zack's loved ones. I don't think murdering a few more would bother them."

It was precisely why they had to find out what the Russians wanted…and what dirt they had.

"You're right. Constance, my father, Joy, and Mad." Gus shook her head. "We have to find these tapes and help solve some of this riddle or the Russians will always have a hold on Zack. And if they don't get what they want, they've already identified his weak spot."

"His friends." He glanced across the cabin at her. He needed her to understand why, despite wanting her back at the White House, he'd maintained distance between them. Last night had brought them closer than ever, and there would be no hiding that in the future. Her admission explained so much for him—why she'd avoided him for years, why she'd seemed somewhere between hostile and resentful so often. Now he needed her to understand where his heart had been. "This is a big reason I've kept distance between us lately, Gus. I wanted to keep you out of it. I didn't want you too closely associated with me."

She crossed her arms over her chest. "Well, you didn't think through that strategy. You've said before that you want to protect me, but it feels a lot like you're coming up with another excuse to push me away."

"What?"

"Seriously. Your reasoning is ridiculous. You didn't want me too closely associated with you? Fine. Let's pretend that no one's ever noticed how sparks fly between us when we're in the same room. Let's go with the idea that if you ignore me, you obviously don't care about me." She snorted. "That doesn't take into account that I work for Zack and I was a damn bridesmaid at his wedding. I guess we could fix that by you firing me and banishing me from DC, but then we come to the final problem with your argument, the one tie you can't cut. How exactly do you plan to fix the fact that I'm Dax's sister? You going to convince him to disavow me, too? Seems to me that the Russians always knew."

She brought up valid points, but that wasn't the one he'd been driving toward. "I could never convince him to do that. And I'm absolutely not going to fire you. But I think we need to talk about what happens when we get back to DC."

"I know what happens."

His cell phone trilled. He glanced down at the screen. Connor. He couldn't ignore the guy, even if his friend's call was inopportunely timed. "Oh, I seriously doubt that. It's something we will absolutely talk about later. Can you answer that call for me, baby? Put Connor on speaker."

Gus did as he requested. "Hey, Roman and I are on the road. We can both hear you, so watch what you're going to say because tender female ears are listening."

Roman rolled his eyes. "Gus…"

Connor whistled over the line. "Damn, she sounds pissed. I thought you were supposed to be soothing her, not riling her up again. We have to talk about your technique."

No, he needed the damn chance to finish explaining what he'd meant. But it could wait until Connor wasn't listening in because some things should be private. "Don't mind her. And don't listen to her, either. You can say whatever you like. I'd just tell her later anyway. What's going on, brother? Where did Kemp lead you?"

"That's the problem," Connor said, his tone turning serious. "I think the fucker managed to ditch me."

Roman tightened his grip on the steering wheel. "Tell me you're joking."

"I wish I could. It's hard to tail someone on these country roads. If I don't give him a little space, he'll make me in a heartbeat." There was a sigh over the line. "I think he must have turned off somewhere a few miles before we reached the village."

"But you knew where he was going. We told you he'd written down Homewood's address. This is his only day off," Gus argued. "If he doesn't go today, when would he?"

"I don't know, but I'm here at the hospital and I have been for an hour. He never showed, and he left London maybe five minutes before me. I'm going to drive around town," Connor said. "Maybe I'll spot his vehicle somewhere."

"Don't bother." Roman would rather have backup. Roman knew he was a hell of a lawyer, but he wasn't some ninja warrior. He wasn't a trained CIA agent. If Kemp somehow got the jump on them, Roman knew he and Gus would be in serious trouble. "It doesn't matter if Kemp somehow met with the staff at Homewood. He wouldn't have found any information there."

But if Kemp was, by chance, out searching for them, they could be in danger.

"Agreed."

"Her doctor at Homewood recorded her sessions. We know the location of those tapes. They're hidden in a barn off the main road. We have to beat Kemp there, get in and out and gone. You're looking for a tiny place called Farrington Farms." He recited the address. "You're about twenty minutes away. Get over here. Once we locate what we came for, we'll head back to London together. And if Kemp shows his face again, we bring him in for questioning."

"Roman, why don't you stop where you are, get back to London now? Let me go in," Connor said, his voice deeper than usual.

"Because I'm sure Kemp is nearby, and if he's figured out what we're on to then he's heading this way, too. We can't let him have this evidence. We've lost too much and have too much at stake to give him any opportunity to grab those tapes. From what we've gleaned, this information falling into enemy hands would be catastrophic." Gus sat up in her seat, pointing to the dirt road up ahead. "We just found the turnoff. We're not far now."

"I don't like this," Connor said. "I don't like the fact that he's suddenly missing and you two are out there alone. Something's off. Deep Throat sent you here?"

"Deep Throat sent us in the right direction. By the way, she was a woman this time. I think she was wearing a wire and getting her cues from someone else." She'd also said she had redundancies in place. What had she meant?

"Really? We suspected they were different, but I did not see that coming."

"I'll give you a full debrief when we get back to London," he said.

Connor sighed. "I still don't like this. Even less so now that I know where you're getting your intel."

"This character hasn't led us astray so far," Roman pointed out.

"I think it's worth the risk if she's right about where these recordings are stored," Gus argued. "But hurry up. We'll be here. If we can find the tapes and get out before you arrive, I'll text you a location to meet up."

"Be careful, you two." The line went silent.

"You have the key Ellen gave you?" With every mile they drew closer, tension had begun flooding his system. Was he making a mistake? He knew Augustine was a deeply capable woman, but she wasn't trained for stealth or combat. Neither was he. If she got hurt, he wouldn't be able to live with himself.

"I've got it. Why don't you keep the car running? I'll dash into the barn and grab the tapes."

"No, Augustine," he protested.

"I can do this without you holding my hand. The place has been abandoned for years. It should be an easy in-easy out. We'll do the whole debrief thing in London—the mission and us. There's the farm, up ahead."

Yes, he could see that. Well, he spotted a couple of dilapidated buildings that looked as if they could be used as the set of a horror movie. Still, she was probably right. The faster they got out of here and back to civilization, the better he would feel. The sooner they could discuss their future.

"Be quick. If you aren't back in five minutes, I'm coming in after you."

"She told me exactly where to look, so it shouldn't even take that long." Gus clutched the key. "If I can't find it, I'll come back, but we can't go back to London empty handed. I just wish like hell that Kemp hadn't managed to ditch Connor."

Every instinct inside him told him that he needed to turn around and get her out of here now.

He backed off. He didn't want to be the interfering douchebag he'd been last night. She was smart and brave, and he believed in her. And if she needed to finish this quest she'd started to understand Mad's death, as well as the murder of her father and the others, then he would let her try.

"Okay."

"Okay?" Gus stared at him like he'd grown two heads. "I thought I would have to jump out of the car."

Roman wouldn't be surprised if she still did exactly that.

He slowed and pulled into the long earthen drive that led to the house. The grass was muddy from the rain the previous night. "I'm not going to be able to get you much closer. I'm worried about getting stuck in the mud."

"I'm glad I switched to flats. And for the record…" She sent him a long, earnest glance as he pulled the car to a stop. "I love you, Roman."

She was out the door before he could say a word, slamming it behind her. He watched as she ran toward the barn. He hadn't said it in return. He hadn't had the chance to tell her that he loved her, too.

372   Shayla Black and Lexi Blake

Those were some of the sweetest words he'd ever heard. She wouldn't say them in an attempt to wheedle something out of him. She was never coy. Not Gus. She would only say those words if she meant them all the way to her soul.

He had no idea what he'd done to deserve a woman as amazing as Augustine Spencer. He only knew that he was never going to let her go.

He rolled down the window, trying to get a better view of her. She opened the barn door, pushing it against the thick grass that had grown there. At least it would keep the thing open so she would have some light.

"I love you, too, Gus," he murmured. No, she couldn't hear the words now, but he'd needed to say them.

"Well, isn't that sweet," a voice to his left said.

He whipped his gaze around and found himself staring right down the barrel of a gun. When he glimpsed the person holding it, he realized who the dangerous villain really was.

Gus was never going to let him live this down. Heart revving, Roman raised his hands and prayed they both lived long enough to see her one last time.

CHAPTER SIXTEEN

Gus pulled open the heavy barn door, flooding the place with light.

One glance made her shudder. She could have pretended the barn was way less creepy in the dark. The interior was filled with dusty, cobweb-covered farm equipment and empty stalls where the animals were once penned. The remnants of rotting wood from the crumbling loft above littered the floor, mingling with the years-old straw. Everything smelled old, dank. It felt still and abandoned. Forsaken.

She stepped inside, holding the tack room key in one hand and reaching in her purse to pull out her gun with the other.

I love you, Roman.

Stupid girl.

Why had she opened her mouth? She hadn't planned on telling him. Ever. She ached with the thought of him planning some new life out in the 'burbs when they returned to DC. Why would he mention it to her? Had he been giving her a heads-up that when they got Stateside again, he'd be splitting off to find his glorious future? Or because he now wanted to include her? He'd left her once because he didn't see her as capable of bringing him peace. Had that changed after last night? They'd shared honesty, along with their bodies. To Gus, it sure felt as if they'd shared their hearts, too. She had felt peaceful in a way she hadn't in years.

Had Roman felt it, too? Or was she kidding herself?

Gus crept forward. The boards beneath her feet squeaked. She paused, listening, before breathing a sigh of rueful relief. She was letting Roman's fears about this simple retrieval job creep into her head. She understood his worries. Kemp was wandering the area. For all that he was pretty, he was definitely dangerous. But without talking to Ellen House, how could he possibly know to come here? How could anyone?

A moment later, she heard a faint scratching a few feet to her right and nearly jumped out of her skin. Stifling a scream, she saw a little rodent scurry across the floor and dart back into the shadows.

Damn it. She could handle mice. Mostly. Rats...not so much. But she had to keep her cool. If she screamed, Roman would come running to save her. The notion was chivalrous, if outdated. She was capable. Still, Roman cared enough to want to save her, and that touched her more than she wanted to admit. She simply didn't need rescuing.

Gus scanned the room again, doing her best to look past the eeriness. Where was the damn tack room? Ellen had said it was to the right, past the last stall. So she strode deeper into the barn, every step taking her farther from the sunlight trickling through the open doors and into the shadows.

She hadn't expected Roman to react as he had. When she'd blurted out that she'd lost their child, she'd expected anything from a shrug to anger from him, not the deep and seemingly fathomless sorrow that had welled up. He'd pointed all his blame inward, and she hadn't been able to stand that.

Emotionally, he'd isolated himself in that moment. She'd realized that if she didn't do something, he might always be alone. And in forgiving Roman, she'd found a place where she didn't feel quite as alone, either.

She caught a glint of metal in the otherwise darkened recess of the barn. Hopefully the lock to the tack room, but if she wanted to know for sure she had to exchange her pistol for her cell phone so she'd have a flashlight of sorts.

Once Gus eased the gun inside her purse and pulled the device free, the light from the phone illuminated the dark spaces she hadn't been able to see previously. Unfortunately, that didn't make the visual less creepy. Farm tools were terrifying things. An entire wall where rusty scythes, hoes, and rakes hung in front of her almost made her squeal. A stiff breeze blew, rattling the loose wallboards, making the tools clatter and ping.

Think happy thoughts, she told herself.

At the moment, she couldn't think of a single one.

Instead, she'd focus on what would happen when she returned to the car. Maybe Roman would tell her that he loved her, too. Probably not, but a girl could dream. More likely, he'd focus on the fact that they had the tapes in hand now. On the drive back to London, they might discuss what was on those recordings and how to use them to protect all they held dear.

No, he would call the guys and they would discuss their next moves. Or he might take that time alone to gently let her down.

Gus just didn't know.

Last night was messing with her head. When they'd lain together and talked about the child they'd lost, she'd felt a deeper bond form. But maybe Roman hadn't felt the same connection.

None of that mattered right now. She just needed to retrieve these tapes, get out of here, and hightail it back to London as soon as possible. Roman's horror-movie anxiety had rubbed off on her. Getting out of the creeptastic, probably-a-serial-killer's lair became the thought uppermost in her head.

She flashed the light of her phone toward the back of the barn where she'd seen the glint of metal and caught sight of a doorknob. *Score!*

Picking up the pace, she moved toward the tack room. Her hand shook as she raised the key to the jagged opening. This had to be the right place. Gus had no idea what she would do if she found the location but the tapes had been destroyed. She had to pray enough evidence remained on them for a super-smart techie to extract.

The lock was rusty. She was able to force the key in but it wouldn't turn all the way. She needed two hands, damn it. She set her phone on a nearby shelf, the light peering down so she could see. The knob felt cold in her hand as she held it steady and turned the key.

The door creaked as she opened it. Gus grabbed her phone, lighting up the inside the dilapidated tack room. There it was, a single box marked *PRIVATE* and sealed with duct tape. It was the only item left inside the room, so she was going with it. The box even fit in her oversized bag.

As Gus slipped it in, she breathed a sigh of relief.

And then she tried to scream because a hard arm snaked around her waist and a hand clapped over her mouth.

"Hush, Augustine," a deep voice whispered in her ear as a hard body blanketed her from behind. "We're not alone and if you walk out that barn door, I'm afraid someone's going to die."

Pure fear sliced through her. She knew that voice. Matthew Kemp was holding her immobile, trapping her. Silencing her.

"Drop the phone. If they see the light, they'll know our position."

Yes, Roman would find her, and that seemed like a good idea. She clutched the source of the light. Kemp could either let go of her waist or her mouth if he wanted to make her drop the phone. Then she would run or scream.

"Don't fight me. I'm not the bad guy," he whispered. "I was sent here by my boss to watch out for you. I've had a tracker on your phone for days. Unfortunately, I think my competition has had a tracker on Roman's, but I couldn't get to it without someone figuring out I'm working this problem from a different angle. Drop it, Gus. They're going to come in here any minute."

She held fast.

He sighed. "We don't have time for this... I suspect Darcy Hildebrandt is working for the Russians, and if I'm right, she's out there with Roman right now. She'll use him to force you to give up the tapes."

Kemp knew way more than Gus had imagined. If Darcy worked for the Russians, who was his boss? Zack? Maybe the president had been using his own detail to do some dirty work and kept it quiet for discretion. Gus hadn't considered that...but it was logical. And his accusation about Darcy suddenly helped her understand the woman's bizarre behavior. No one smiled that much. Ever.

Unless it was all BS.

She let the phone drop into her purse, the flashlight still on, but hidden by the heavy leather of the Louis Vuitton bag.

"Very good. We need to move out of here. I've got a way out the back, but we have to be quick."

Dropping her phone a few inches from her reach was one thing. But letting Kemp haul her away from here—away from Roman when he might be in danger—was not happening. She kicked back at his shin.

Kemp groaned. "Hey, stop. We have to move and fast. I told you Darcy is here, and she won't be alone. She'll have at least two men with her. I've got to get you to safety. That's my main job, along with recovering those tapes."

She shook her head. She wasn't leaving Roman. If that crazy bitch had him, Gus had to save him.

"Come on." The agent started dragging her back, into the dark.

Gus kicked at him, fighting and writhing in an attempt to break his hold.

Something large banged into the barn door, and Kemp shifted with a curse, forcibly hauling her with him into the deepest shadows.

"Be still," he hissed.

"Keep moving, Roman. Don't make me tell you again. I know she's in here. I saw her." Darcy sounded nasally and arrogant.

Gus stopped struggling in Kent's grip. So, he'd been right about Darcy. It looked as if he might be right about everything else. But there was one thing only she and Roman knew: Connor was on his way. She had to somehow keep Roman alive until Connor could get here. He would handle things for sure. She just needed more time.

How did she buy them some?

"I don't know what you saw, but Augustine told me she was going to the house. That's where the tapes are." Roman's voice was strong and perhaps a bit too loud, as though he was trying to ensure that she heard him, despite wherever she might be hiding.

"I sincerely doubt it," Darcy replied. "But just in case, Gene, go and check the house. Once you're done, get the car ready. We'll need to leave here in a hurry. Leon, stay with me. I still think she came in this way."

"Excellent," Kemp whispered in her ear. "We should still be able to get out, but we'll have to ease back very quietly. There's an exit in the opposite corner we can get through."

She shook her head.

"Don't be stubborn. Calder will be fine."

She shook her head more adamantly.

"See, she's not here," Roman insisted. "You'll find her at the house."

"I'm sure you'd like me to believe that, but that whore of yours is hiding here. How does that make you feel? You know, I did my homework on the whole nasty lot of you. I was rather surprised to see a man like you would accept Maddox Crawford's seconds."

Gus wanted to punch Darcy's pretty, uptight face. She would do it exactly the way her father had taught her, too. He'd told her to envision her fist plowing straight through the object she was punching. Yeah. Gus would love that about now.

Because Darcy was doing some punching of her own, albeit verbally. The woman knew exactly where to hit Roman—right in his considerable pride.

"I was definitely surprised you were willing to tell me—or anyone—that you're sleeping with her," the bitch went on. "I admit, I thought the way to get this deal done was to have sex with you myself. You have a reputation for being a finicky lover, so I did my best to be cheerful, if a bit reserved and compliant at times. But I should have known that every man loves a whore."

Gus winced. Darcy's words would hit Roman in the gut because he saw them as true. It would surely make him blow, since image was very important to him. And if he lost his cool, they would all be in trouble.

"First of all, Mad took care of her when I couldn't, and if he got some comfort out of it, then who the hell am I to blame him? She's the most beautiful woman in the world, and I'm damn lucky Mad wasn't smart enough to put a ring on her finger. Second, the reason I'm so finicky about women is that I've already had the sexiest one I know. So why would I want anyone else, especially you? That was never going to happen. I could barely remember your name when my Gus was around. And third, if you call her a whore again, I swear to god I'll forget I'm a gentleman who doesn't hit females."

Of all the words she'd expected to come from Roman's mouth, that speech was the least likely.

There had been no shame or doubt in his voice, only pride and anger directed at the woman taunting Gus. Roman hadn't sounded like a man who wanted to keep his lover under wraps. He'd sounded like a man in love.

He'd sounded like a husband.

Darcy scoffed. "I expected better from you. Leon, check the barn. She's hiding in here somewhere. And be careful. Women like her tend to know where to hit a man."

A shaft of light blinked into existence. She could see the stream emanating from a flashlight. It began a slow rotation around the space.

Kemp's arm clamped tighter around her as he tried to huddle as far from that light as possible. "They'll kill us all once they get those tapes in their hands. If I let you go so I can get to my gun, will you promise to behave?"

If Kemp was willing to take out a few of the enemy, she would play along—as long as he didn't lump Roman in that camp. Then if Kemp decided to cross them and possibly to blackmail the president, Connor could put his skills to good use.

"Yeah," she breathed.

"Why are you doing this, Darcy? You have to know my government won't look kindly on yours trying to blackmail the president of the United States."

There was the shuffling of feet and a slight wobbling of the floor as that light continued to move around the room. Leon was being very thorough in his search.

"I'm sure my government would be horrified, but MI6 doesn't pay what it used to," Darcy replied. "That's right. I am a spy sent to make a general report on the president and his team. Nothing out of the ordinary, really. Except I serve two masters, and the one in

Moscow pays so much better. Once I hand over whatever you've been looking for to my contacts, I'll never have to work again."

"No, you won't," Roman shot back. "Because you'll be dead. Everyone who's gotten into bed with the Russians is. Follow the yellow brick road and what you'll find is a trail of bodies, many of whom thought they were going to Oz. I assure you, your contact will take the package you hand him and put a bullet in your head. It's the way the *Bratva* deals with outsiders, even helpful ones."

"Not a sound." Kemp lifted his hand from Gus's mouth slowly, as though waiting and ready to pounce again if she screamed out.

But she knew better. Shrieking now would only have bullets flying everywhere. Roman would be in the middle of that. Besides, she didn't want Kemp's tight hold again. She wanted her arms free so she could find her own gun. Then she'd feel better.

Gus knew that might not be enough to save this situation, though. She might have to make a choice whether to save the incriminating recordings of Constance Hayes that could bring down an entire presidency or Roman.

She would choose her man in a heartbeat.

Kemp moved so slowly, not making a single sound as he carefully released her.

"Somehow I think I'll take my chances. They won't want to lose such a valuable asset," Darcy insisted. "Speaking of losing, Augustine Spencer, do you know what you're going to lose if you don't come out and give me what I want?"

Gus tensed at the words but held her tongue. She

could certainly guess what—or who—the bitch was referring to.

"Give me whatever you found in this bloody barn. I'd rather not put a bullet through Roman's skull," Darcy threatened in a nasty snarl. "It's such a shame to waste a man like him. He's so pretty, isn't he?"

But she would do it, whatever happened. Now that she'd tipped her hand and admitted she worked for the Russians, Darcy couldn't afford to keep him alive.

Kemp shifted to her right, inching his way out from behind her. The thud of Leon's shoes against the wooden floor coming ever closer masked the sound. The flick of his flashlight darting back and forth made Gus's heart race.

"But he won't be quite so lovely when I'm done with him. In fact, he'll be a bloody corpse if you don't stop hiding like a coward and save him."

"Even if she was here and not up at the main house, she would be far too smart to trust you." Darcy might think Roman's words were directed at her, but Gus knew who he'd really been speaking to. "We both know you're going to kill me anyway. You have to. There's no way out, so it would be so much smarter for Gus to run as fast and far as she can because she can't change the outcome. She can only get herself killed and lose the evidence."

Kemp crouched lower as the light zipped closer to their hiding spot in the dark.

"Why would that crazy cat lady store anything here?" Darcy's voice had gone from menacing to eager in an instant. "Of course. She's the daughter of the nurse who looked after Hayes's mum. That's what the Russians want—her mental health records."

"The *Bratva* didn't get rid of the files?" Roman

sounded confused, which he rarely was. But he was likely buying them time, too. Every second he kept Darcy talking was one more she wasn't shooting him.

Gus refused to even consider running. She wasn't leaving him, either. And she definitely wasn't above using the recordings to bargain for his life. He'd called her too smart to give into Darcy's emotional blackmail, but she was far too in love not to give into it.

And if their roles were reversed, Roman would never leave her.

At that realization, she knew exactly what he'd meant when he'd said he wanted a house in the suburbs. He hadn't been rattling off some passing notion. He hadn't been randomly kicking around some ideas for his future because they'd had nothing better to talk about. No, he wanted a house in the suburbs for a family. *His* family. This was his "too scared to openly talk about his feelings" way of asking if she might want to have a family with him. If she might want to live with him in that house.

If she would marry him.

She had to save him first—now more than ever.

"I don't know anything about the files, but I would assume if my contact had stolen them in the first place, they would have been smart enough to take any other evidence, too," she mused. "Unless the Russians didn't realize something else existed."

Or if Marjorie House had swiped the recordings before anyone else could. The physical files had been subject to the hospital's storage and privacy policies until they'd been added to the database. What if automating them had tipped off their enemies about the files' existence?

None of that mattered as Kemp gripped her shoulder and urged her back against the wall, switching their positions.

He was putting his body in front of hers? She could see the light from Darcy's goon coming dangerously close, stalking them with ruthless certainty. She supposed Kemp wouldn't take her bag and run if he was working in Zack's best interest. But why did it matter to him if she lived?

It would be so much easier to create some chaos, grab the tapes from her, and run. He didn't know that she had a gun. He didn't know she'd taken self-defense classes. He was far bigger and stronger and could probably crush her. But instead, he was being protective. Why?

"Who do you work for?" she breathed the question so softly, she was almost certain he hadn't heard her.

"I'll tell you everything when we get out of here. Stay behind me."

So, Kemp really wasn't the bad guy. An agent working on Zack's behalf to catch another traitor in their midst? Or maybe the redundancy Deep Throat had talked about? That was an interesting possibility. But then what about Mad's plane and the fact that Kemp had been there before Mad had taken off?

Gus was still looking for an answer, her head whirling with implications, wrapping itself around the problem. She came up with an impossible solution.

Oh, my god.

In the distance, a loud crack split the air. She jumped at the sound. The stray beam from the flashlight almost caught them before flipping up and back at the noise, then Leon ran toward the front of the barn.

"What the hell was that?" Darcy asked.

"That was Gus," Roman lied. "My baby's packing, and it sounds like she took out your guy at the main house. I told you she was there."

"Did Sparks come?" Kemp asked quietly. "I caught someone following me and figured it might have been him. If so, we may have a chance to come out on top."

"Yes, but we can't leave Roman," she whispered back.

"We have to run. Sparks will save him."

That was not happening. "I won't leave him."

Kemp cursed under his breath. "Well, I heard you were a badass bitch. Guess that means you're stubborn, too. All right, we'll fight. Keep your head down and don't lose those tapes."

Kemp didn't wait for her confirmation before uncurling from his crouched position silently. Then he popped up like a cobra.

Suddenly, gunfire split the world around Gus. So close. So loud. *Rat tat tat.* She couldn't see anything more than Kemp's outline as he loomed above her and intermittently pulled the trigger. She didn't know who was firing and when, but she knew she had to get in the battle and make sure they won.

As she reached into her purse and curled her fingers around her own weapon, Kemp grunted and looked down at his chest. He coughed. Then his body went slack and he crumbled to the floor beside her.

"Damn," he managed to eke out, sounding weak and wheezy. "Lucky shot."

She scrambled to her knees, but it was so dark. She couldn't see exactly where he'd been hit. It didn't matter now. She had to find her weapon and defend herself or she'd likely end up with a new hole or two, like Kemp. And what about Roman?

She reached for the gun in her bag again, but she had so much crap inside that she fumbled to grab hold of it as footsteps thudded in the outer part of the barn. Who was that?

She had no idea how many of Darcy's goons were left. Had Kemp managed to hit anyone? Who had been shooting up at the main house? Connor? Or had Gene gotten in his own lucky shot? If so, Gus would have to explain to Lara why she no longer had a husband. And what if she'd lost the man she loved, too?

She felt sick.

"Move it, Calder," Darcy ordered.

Gus almost sagged in relief that Roman hadn't been caught in the crossfire—so far.

"You're going to leave Leon lying in a pool of his own blood?" he asked, giving Gus the information she needed.

So Leon was down. She only had to kill Darcy and Gene, if he'd managed to survive the firefight at the main house.

"Shut up," Darcy snapped.

"You're hell on henchmen."

"I think it's time I take you with me and see how much the president values his chief of staff."

Gus's eyes widened in horror. That couldn't happen. She felt around for Kemp. She still couldn't see anything, but he seemed frighteningly still.

"Matthew?" she murmured somewhere near his ear.

No answer.

Trembling, she groped him until she found his wrist. Frantically, she laid her fingers over his pulse point.

Nothing.

Oh, god. He really was dead.

Her heart threatened to pound out of her chest. She didn't know if Connor was even on the property yet. She might be completely alone in trying to save the day. But somehow she couldn't let Darcy have Constance's recordings while ensuring she didn't take Roman away.

Otherwise, she feared she'd never see him alive again.

How was the property laid out? With her head whirling, Gus couldn't remember much. Where would that crazy bitch have parked? She had to think, had to get there before Darcy managed to shove Roman in a trunk and leave.

She managed to feel Kemp's FN Five-Seven lying beside his slack hand. She didn't have time to hunt through her purse for her own gun, so she grabbed it and began feeling her way around the back of the barn for the hidden hole in the wall he'd mentioned.

"I'm moving," Roman grumbled. "You don't have to poke me. I understand you'll shoot me so everyone should remain calm and do what they need to do."

Gus got his message. Stay right where she was until Connor showed up, then let him handle everything. She discarded that idea. She wouldn't wait to save Roman. She had to act now.

"Where the hell is Gene?" Darcy's voice was growing more distant, but Gus couldn't miss the tension in her voice. The woman was scared now.

It seemed she'd come with two men—and one was definitely down. She couldn't possibly have thought she would be up against a Secret Service agent *and* a pissed-off woman in love. If Connor had arrived, add a former

CIA guy to the mix, and Gus didn't see how Darcy could win.

Once Roman and the recordings were safe, she would figure out if her wild theory about why Kemp had been here and who'd sent him could be true. At the very least, she would tell everyone he'd tried to protect her, as well as keep the tapes away from Darcy and her Russian contacts, so he'd be given a hero's burial.

But for now she had to move.

Since she no longer had to be inconspicuous, Gus continued to grope the wall until she found a hole that had been disguised by someone propping up a few spare boards against the opening. Wincing, she forced herself into the jagged space, a nail tearing at her slacks. Wedging her tall frame through the opening was a tight fit, but she made it.

Then Gus took a deep breath and reached back for her purse, securing it over her shoulder. Those tapes weren't going anywhere. She was going to get them to safe hands and save her man.

"Get up!" Darcy shouted. The sound carried from around the corner of the barn, somewhere to Gus's left. She wasn't sure where Darcy had parked her car. Or how the woman had found them unless what Kemp had said was true about their phones being traced.

"Stop!" Roman yelled back. "I need a minute. I rolled my ankle."

Gus flattened her back against the barn wall and crept to the corner, peeking around to get a line of sight on Roman. He lay on the ground. Sure, he might have fallen, but Gus would bet he'd tripped on purpose. He was trying to give Connor time, a chance.

But she didn't see the former CIA agent. That made

her Roman's only chance at survival.

"Get up or I'm going to shoot you," Darcy promised. "I won't wait any longer."

Gus heard the desperation in Darcy's tone. She was panicking, and that was bad for Roman.

He wouldn't leave with Darcy willingly, not until he knew Gus was safe. But without that assurance, he would fight and he might well lose the battle—and his life.

Hell no.

Gus pivoted, raising the gun as her father had taught her. He was with her in that moment, though he'd left the earth years ago, and she could hear him patiently advising. *Safety off. Target in sight. Don't rush the shot.*

Dax was with her, despite being an ocean away. *The gun is an extension of your hand, your will. See where you want the bullet to go. Take a deep breath. Steady.*

Roman jerked his head up suddenly. Their stares met. He was with her, too. While Darcy yelled and moved in behind to give him a kick, he sent Gus a simple nod.

Do it.

He trusted her. He needed her. He believed in her.

Gus took a deep breath just as Darcy caught sight of her. The woman's eyes widened. Time seemed to slow as Darcy yanked her pistol up. But Gus was way ahead and released the breath she'd been holding as she pulled the trigger.

Then time accelerated, and Darcy's head suddenly slammed back. She collapsed to the grass in an unmoving heap.

"Damn it, Gus!" A masculine voice yelled across the yard. Connor jogged over from the main house, his shirt torn, his gun at his side. "I wanted to question her. You couldn't have injured her or at least left her with a damn brain?"

Roman slumped to the grass, rolling onto his back, splattered with blood. Had he been hurt?

Gus ignored Connor utterly. Still clutching Kemp's weapon, she rushed to Roman's side and dropped to her knees. "Roman? Are you okay? Do we need to call an ambulance?"

When she gripped his wrist and began searching for a pulse, he pulled her down, wrapping his arms around her. "I love you, too, Augustine. I love you so much. Thank you."

She breathed a sigh of relief and hugged him back.

"Get a room, you two," Connor said with a rueful shake of his head. "You have to get back to London and I have to deal with all these damn bodies. I left the CIA so I wouldn't have to deal with bodies anymore, damn it."

"There are two more in the barn." Roman managed to sit up. "Unless Kemp somehow survived the bullet he took."

"Kemp's here?" Connor peered through the doors.

"Yeah, but he didn't make it. He was trying to protect me. He probably saved us." Her mind was still working. "Guys, was he possibly working secretly for Zack?"

"Not for Zack. I would have known about that. I would have told you," Roman insisted.

"How about Deep Throat?"

Roman shrugged. "That's possible. We may never know."

Gus wouldn't stand for that. That wild hunch of hers was looking more possible... She wouldn't rest until she had answers.

Connor holstered his weapon. "Get those tapes to Zack pronto. I assume you have them?"

"Of course," Gus confirmed.

Roman stood, offering her his hand. "Don't you know there's nothing my girl can't do?"

"Excellent," Connor returned with a smirk. "Then she can drive back to London, and you can help me get rid of the bodies."

Roman thumped a hand over his chest. "Nope, I've had a harrowing day. I might have a heart attack, you know. I need to keep Gus close. She can perform mouth-to-mouth."

Rolling his eyes, Connor pulled out his cell. "Go. You're useless to me. I know a firm in London I can call. The CIA uses them from time to time. They'll help me clean up and figure out who the hell the two men are."

"You can't leave Matthew here," Gus insisted. He'd given his life in the line of duty. She wasn't sure precisely why he'd been working outside of the Secret Service, but there was no doubt in her mind he'd been trying to protect the president in his way. "He should have full honors."

Connor nodded. "I'll figure out how to make that happen. His service record might have to be confidential, but his family will know he died in the line of duty. Now hurry and get out of here. I don't want this to hit the press. And Gus, you did good."

Roman hauled her up and into his arms, holding her close. "You were fantastic, and I knew you wouldn't listen to me. I knew you would show up and save the day. I love you. All I could think about was the fact that I hadn't said it back. Let me say it every day for the rest of our lives."

She rested her head against his chest, hearing the soothing beat of his heart. "I think I can handle that, Calder."

"Roman," he corrected. "Or maybe husband?"

Gus smiled. They would finally be together. "Yes."

CHAPTER SEVENTEEN

"What exactly do you mean when you say you're going to marry my sister?" Dax scratched his head, staring at Roman as though trying to figure out if he was joking or not.

Roman glanced around the large parlor in the East Wing of the White House, hoping for some backup. Dax was making him crazy. He'd tried to explain the new situation to his friend about ten times already.

Dax's new bride, Holland, slid an arm around her husband's waist and cuddled close. "I think he's trying to tell you what everyone else has known for years. He's in love with Gus. It's about damn time, Calder."

It was, in fact, far past time.

Dax frowned. "Is this like an April Fools' joke no one told me about?"

Roman groaned. "No, but we're thinking about getting married in April, buddy."

Gus claimed she needed at least that long to properly

plan her wedding. Since he was the reason she'd waited all these years to get hitched, he was willing to give her anything she wanted. The only thing he'd insisted on was that she move in with him the minute they'd gotten back to DC. He'd refused to wait another second to start their lives together.

They'd flown home yesterday morning. He'd had her in his bed that night. And he planned to every night from now on.

Life was looking up.

But this evening was likely going to be a rough one. Zack had asked them all to gather in the parlor, and Roman was almost certain the news wasn't good. Zack had waited until this afternoon to listen to the tapes, unwilling to chance that anyone could overhear while still in England. How hard had it been for Zack to finish up his meetings with the prime minister as if nothing had happened? Hell, it had even been hard on Roman, but at least he'd had Gus by his side.

Dax nodded. "So you're going to have a fake wedding then and that's the April Fools' joke. I'm going to be honest, I don't get it."

Dax seemed determined to play dumb. That or all the Maui sunshine on his honeymoon had damaged his brain. "No. We're having a very real, very legal wedding next April."

"And *you're* marrying *my* sister?" Dax said the words slowly, as though they would make more sense that way. "Roman and Augustine. Married. Okay, maybe that's funny to someone, Roman. But since you've never had a sense of humor, I think yours is probably just lame. You should stop with the jokes."

"Oh, my god, Dax. Stop tormenting him. I've

already told Mom, and she's really excited for us." Gus joined Roman, wrapping her arms around him. "The truth is, Calder and I have been banging off and on since college. I finally agreed to make an honest man of him. Get with the program. Everyone else knew."

While Dax stood gaping at her, the French doors behind them clicked open. Gabe, Everly, and Lara walked in, all dressed for dinner. Gabe cleaned up nice in his suit, while the ladies looked lovely in their sparkling cocktail dresses. But no one could match his Gus.

Dax frowned as if Roman and Gus's news was finally sinking. "Gabe, did you know something was going on between Roman and my sister?"

"I know they had a white-hot affair back in the day and Roman's been bitter about it ever since." Gabe smiled their way and gave Gus a thumbs-up. "Thanks for letting him crawl back. He's so much easier to deal with when he's getting laid."

"I did not crawl." Well, not entirely. But he did like the part where he got to sleep with the most beautiful woman in the world every night. It was a definite perk.

Gus winked up at him. "It took him a while, but he learned."

Yes, he had. He'd learned never to argue with his gorgeous, too-smart-for-him wife-to-be. He leaned over and brushed his lips against hers. "I take my time, but I get it right in the end, baby."

Dax was back to frowning. "Roman, that's my sister. Do not kiss her around me. Don't kiss her at all."

Gus rolled those pretty eyes of hers. "Maybe he'll settle down after we're married. Or have some children. I'm taking the ladies to the next room. I've set up appetizers and a bartender. Don't be too long."

He took hold of her hand and pulled her closer as Holland started trying to explain to Dax why it was all right for him to kiss Gus. "Hey, you don't have to leave. Zack wants to talk."

She gave his hand a squeeze. "I know he does and he'll feel better if he talks to his best friends first. I don't have to be in this room to be part of the group. You five need a few minutes. It's been a long couple of months, and Zack doesn't have Liz, so he needs you guys more than ever."

The ones who were left. Gus didn't mention Mad, but it was as if crazy Crawford was in the room. Hell, he should have been.

"You're right," Roman murmured.

"Besides, you'll tell me everything later, and I'm okay with that."

He needed her to understand. "I choose you, Augustine. If you want to stay and listen, I'll keep you by my side or I'll leave, too."

Gus flashed him one of those brilliant, world-warming smiles that lit up his days. "And that was all I needed." She rose up on her tiptoes and kissed him. "I love you. Now talk to your friends. I think it's time to show whoever these Russian assholes are that they can't mess with the Perfect Gentlemen."

Oh, but the Russians were messing with them. Whoever had ordered that file clandestinely delivered to Liz's room back in London definitely had the upper hand. Still, he took her words of encouragement to his heart. "I love you."

It was so nice to say the words and know what she would say next.

"Love you, too." She kissed him again, then leaned

close, her voice going low. "Any word on the Deep Throat front?"

Gus was obsessed with finding the man. Not the informant, but the mastermind behind them all. She was absolutely certain it was a man—a man they never thought they would see again. He hated to let her down, but she must be wrong. That wasn't going to happen.

"The private investigator I hired found absolutely nothing to support your theory. He also couldn't find hide nor hair of the woman you described meeting in the cemetery. I'm sorry. I can keep looking, if you like." He would hire another investigator and look into it if it made her feel better.

Exhaling a deep breath, she shook her head. "No, he'll show up when he's ready. We need to be patient. He's out there. He has his reasons for the subterfuge, I'm sure. I'm going to have faith."

He wouldn't show up at all because he was dead, but Roman wasn't about to state the obvious to his fiancée. Maddox Crawford was gone, and no conspiracy theory was going to bring him back.

Another click of the doors, then Zack and Connor strolled in.

"That's my cue to leave," Gus said. "Take care of him. He looks tired. I'm trying to be patient because I know how hard the last week has been on him, but he needs to start treating Liz better. She wasn't even invited tonight. I asked if she was coming to dinner and she had no idea what I was talking about."

He leaned over, letting his forehead rest against hers. "I can't force him to see the light, baby. I don't want to hurt Liz, either, but including her in his life has to be Zack's choice. I'll talk to him, but I can't promise anything."

She sighed, a contented sound. He knew the feeling. Being able to touch her, to connect with her, soothed him, too. They hadn't stopped being passionate. They still argued, but always with the knowledge that, more than anything, they were passionate about each other.

She straightened up. "Ladies, I've got a bartender ready for us next door and some of the most delicious canapés you've ever had. Also, the bartender is an aspiring model. He's got some very funny stories for us."

The women perked up, laughing and talking as they strode out of the room.

"Model?" Roman asked.

Gus shrugged. "Hey, we're taken, not blind. You should see what I have planned for our girls' night out."

Gabe stared after the women. "Gus is a bad influence."

Connor put a hand on his friend's shoulder. "You hadn't figured that out yet? She's a terrible influence, and I'm so glad she's here with us."

"Everly and Holland like to shoot people. Lara runs a political tabloid, and Gus eats reporters for breakfast," Roman pointed out. "We have a type, guys. They're all troublemakers."

"I just want something clarified," Dax said. "Why, exactly, was my sister kissing you? And why would she mention having your children?"

He was going to murder Dax.

"Because she loves him and she's finally where she belongs," Zack said. "And I'm very grateful to her for stepping in and handling some of the duties that traditionally belong to the First Lady. I can't ask Elizabeth anymore. And thank god Gus knows us well. I believe she arranged a very nice bottle of Scotch tonight. I could use a glass."

His woman was kind. "Gabe, please get a glass for Dax, too. He looks like he needs it."

Zack addressed Connor. "Are we good on the dead body front?"

Connor took his seat. "Absolutely. I worked with a completely trustworthy London firm, and they even got me dossiers on the two henchmen. Both known associates of the *Bratva*. No big surprise there."

"And Kemp? What else do we know about him?" Roman asked.

"I managed to ensure his record will say he died in the line of duty. His body was found outside of the house in London, on the grounds where he was keeping a lone wolf terrorist from reaching the president. It's all classified, of course, but that's what we're telling his family." Clearly, Connor had been working his ass off. "As for who he took his marching orders from, I've got nothing so far. I checked through all of his personal things. I even went through his apartment this morning. His phone and his financials are clean. If he was doing this for money, he hid it impeccably well."

"Why else would he do it?" Dax asked.

Loyalty. Duty. Honor. Country.

The why wasn't the question, but rather who. Who could convince a Secret Service agent to chase Russian coverts through England without telling his boss? It would have to be a smooth-talking son of a bitch who'd known how to properly motivate Kemp.

Roman shrugged. "You can guess. We have to consider that Deep Throat will target another agent. He'll want to stay close to the president."

Because he seemingly wanted to help.

"And Darcy Hildebrandt?" Zack asked.

"Is of no concern to me." Connor shot back. "If the Brits knew she was a double agent, they can bite my ass. If they didn't, then they should have. She flew under the radar. Spies do that. It's the way the game works. If they find the grave, they'll discover that she was buried with two known members of the *Bratva*, and the Brits are smart. They'll realize someone did their dirty work for them. It's the way our friendship survives. They help us. We help them."

Roman was willing to let it go, though Gus still teased him every day that he kind of, sort of dated a double agent who'd tried to kill them. "Then it sounds as if we have cleared up as much as we can from the trip."

"Yes, especially since I hear there's a new charity serving the English countryside's cat population," Zack said with a sly smile. "The Roman Calder Society for Felines."

He groaned. "Gus did that. Though she funded it with my cash. She's already got all my passwords and access to my accounts. Your sister is going to cost me a fortune."

Dax finally smiled, his face lighting up. "Excellent. Now I feel so much better about you sleeping with her. Wait until you get her bill from Neiman Marcus. That woman loves good shoes."

He loved how she looked in them. He wouldn't complain at all as long as she wore them for him when they were alone and she was naked. It was probably best to not say that out loud.

Roman turned to his best friend. "How are you holding up, Zack?"

Gabe started handing out drinks and they all sat. The five of them. There was an empty seat to Connor's left. A seat that would never be filled again, despite Gus's conspiracy-filled daydreams.

Zack accepted the drink. "Besides the fact that I gave in to blackmail and should likely be impeached? I'm great."

"You simply didn't mention a project that's years away." They'd been over this a hundred times. It wasn't the right time to push back. They didn't have enough information. They needed to gather more intel before they moved on the forces working against them.

"It's a slippery slope, and you know it." Zack took a long swallow. "And now they know they can control me. The good news is I think I know why."

"You listened to the tapes?" Gabe settled in.

"Of your mother's sessions while she was in that psychiatric hospital?" Dax asked.

"Yes, I listened to them. So has Connor." Zack sat back, crossing his right leg over his left. "I asked him because he's got some experience with psychology."

Damn straight he did. The CIA had taught him well. Roman was glad Connor had been willing to do it because he certainly hadn't wanted to listen in. It would hurt too much to hear the pain of a woman he'd known since childhood. He couldn't imagine what absorbing and analyzing those sessions had done to her son. "What did you find out?"

Zack took a deep breath, as though steadying himself. "My mother talks about accidentally killing a child while she was in Russia. She was drunk one night and she stumbled around. The problem is even when she talks about the incident, she sounds like she's drunk. She picked up a baby. Her baby. And she dropped him."

Connor leaned in. "That is not what she said. She said she *thought* it was her baby. Never once did she confirm the baby was hers, merely that she thought it was. We know there were at least two infants in the house at the time. You and Natalia's child. She said she was so sorry and she couldn't ever make it up. I do not believe she killed her own child."

Zack's jaw formed a stubborn line. "I think you're wrong. She accidentally crushed her infant's skull, and my father knew she couldn't have another baby. I believe that child, the real Zack Hayes, was switched for Natalia Kuilikov's son." He paused. "Me. I'm Sergei and that's why the Russians think they can use me."

Roman refused to believe it. "Zack, your mother's ramblings might not mean anything. Your theory... It's all supposition. I believe you are Zack Hayes. You were raised to be Zack Hayes. You're the best man I know."

"But if I'm correct, I was born on Russian soil of a Russian mother. I'm a Russian citizen," he replied, his voice softer. "I'm not only ineligible to be president, I'm the ultimate sleeper agent—the one who has no idea he's in place. I think I should step down immediately."

"And send the entire country into chaos?" Gabe asked. "Do you know what that would do to the stock market? Your VP isn't exactly the brightest bulb."

"That's why they picked him." Dax scrubbed a hand over his hair. "Franklin wanted someone he could control easily, but if you step down, the speaker will likely control him, and we all know that son of a bitch doesn't care about anyone but himself. No. You can't step down now."

"This is not a democracy," Zack said.

Connor laughed. "Of course it is. It has been ever since Mad brought us together and we first voted on whether to study for our chemistry final or sneak out to watch the girls' school swim practice."

They had not studied that night.

"He's right. Let's vote," Dax insisted.

"Guys, this is not only dangerous for me, but for you and all your wives," Zack pleaded.

"I know how my wife would vote," Gabe said. "Roman, organize this sucker. That's always been your job."

Because he'd understood parliamentary procedure at a very young age. "I call for a vote of the Perfect Gentlemen. All for staying the course and standing behind our friend and our president say aye."

"Aye," said Gabe.

Connor nodded. "Aye."

Dax gave his commander in chief a salute. "Aye."

"Aye." There was no way Roman would let him step down. "We fight."

Zack sighed. He sounded tired, but he looked damn relieved to have his friends on his side. "All right then. We fight."

Roman took a long swig of Scotch and vowed they would do whatever it took to win this fight, come hell or high water.

* * * *

Zachary Hayes straightened his dress shirt and looked in the mirror. When the hell had he gotten those gray hairs at his temple? They'd seemingly popped up overnight.

I didn't mean to do it. I wanted to hold him. He was

my baby. My sweet baby. I hated what Franklin had planned for him. I wondered if it would be better if I put him out of his misery then and there.

He shivered at the insanity in his mother's voice. Was that why his father had shoved him in a boarding school? Because he'd been afraid to lose the replacement? How much had he paid Natalia Kuilikov for her baby so he would have a new Zack Hayes?

"Are you ready to go, sir?" Thomas asked.

He depended on the massive Secret Service agent. Thomas had been with him since his first day in office. "Yes. I already sent my bag along."

"It's good that you're taking a weekend to yourself, sir. I can't remember you relaxing for even an afternoon in years," Thomas said.

He needed to get away or he might do something he shouldn't. Couldn't. But the temptation to wrap his hands around Liz's graceful throat and strangle her was strong. What else was he supposed to do after discovering that the incriminating e-mails indicating he'd stifled the FAA investigation had come from her office? Her desk. Her laptop. Oh, she'd made a good attempt to cover it up, but she'd been the one to leak critical information to the press. She'd been the one privately communicating with Darcy Hildebrandt. He had proof. Connor had even found an e-mail from Liz telling Darcy that she'd managed to tag Augustine's phone.

Liz, who had the clearest bluest eyes. Liz, who had always taken such good care of him. Liz, who he dreamed about at night. Liz, the woman he'd yearned for more than any other, even his own wife.

Liz was the snake in the grass. Liz was in bed with the Russians.

How long had she been plotting against him? How long had she been planning to sell him out? Had she done it because she hated him? Because she didn't care about her country? Because she sought power? Or had she stabbed him in the back simply for the money?

He'd been such a fucking idiot, suckered in by her halo of pale hair, her sweet expressions, and that body he'd kill for.

Hence this trip to Camp David. He intended to get his head right. A guys' weekend. His best friends and no one else.

Well, except a security detail because he was hardly allowed to use the bathroom without them.

He and Connor would lay out all the details for the rest of their friends. Together, they would help him decide how to deal with the beautiful traitor he'd been in love with for years.

No. He lusted after her. It wasn't love. It couldn't be. He didn't deserve love. Power and money and a father who ranted and raved about his demons, yes. But not love.

"The car is ready when you are," Thomas said, stepping back out of his room.

How the hell had he gotten here? His problems were pulling his friends away from their wives. Did he have any right to do that? Did he have any right to drag any of them down with his sinking ship?

Hadn't his ambitions taken enough from all of them already?

He glanced at his cell and thought about calling the whole weekend off. He could shut himself up at Camp David and...

I don't know anyone at all who broods quite like

you, Zack.

He could hear Liz's soft Southern voice teasing him. She was the one who often pulled him out of his broody moods. She was the one who made him look forward to waking up in the morning. She was certainly the one who'd made him look forward to the future. For so long, he'd been looking forward to formally dating her. After the campaign for his second term, he'd planned to do just that. He'd even thought about how nice it would be to have a White House wedding…and maybe a baby.

Now everything had changed. He was running away so he wouldn't kill her.

No, he was running away because once Connor had brought the incriminating evidence to him, his first thought had been to drag Liz to his bed and teach her that she couldn't betray him without consequences. He ached to tie her up and make sure she understood exactly who was in charge and that she would never be allowed to betray her country—or him—again. He'd thought about marrying her so he could remind her every night that she served at the pleasure of the president—and no one else—and always would for the rest of her life.

That would be a terrible mistake.

She was somewhere in the West Wing working with Gus, who thought Zack was the worst human being for mistreating her friend.

He was going to have to tell Gus to be careful of the people to whom she gave her trust.

Zack grabbed his cell phone, then pocketed it. Maybe he should call this weekend off, but he wasn't going to. He needed this. And he owed his friends. They had elected to fight with and beside him. That meant getting all their ducks in a row before the Russians came at them again. Maybe they'd even mount an offense of their own.

He strode out of his room, nodding at people he passed down the hall. He moved quickly, not wanting to be drawn into conversation. He needed a glass of Scotch and the company of his pack.

Would they still be his friends if the worst about his past and his parentage proved true? Maybe it was silly to worry, but he did.

Thomas waited at the limo. "I'll be driving you today, sir. And for the record, it's been a pleasure to serve you. Don't get the car too bloody."

"Bloody?" Zack shook his head as he peered inside the open limo door to climb in. "What are you talking about?"

But Zack instantly saw that the backseat wasn't empty. The lights from the car door illuminated a pair of expensive loafers and designer slacks in the otherwise dark car. Someone was sitting inside his limo.

A chill raced through him. "Thomas?"

"I hope you don't fire me, sir. But respectfully, I insist you talk to him. It's time."

So Thomas was in on this conspiracy, too. He had wolves all around him—the kind in sheep's clothing. They wouldn't kill him, not today. They had plans for him, after all…

Better to get this over with. Maybe he would finally find out everything he needed to know. Information would certainly help him decide how best to fight back.

Zack climbed into the limo and sat, then turned to face his enemy, still sitting in shadow.

The outline of the face seemed eerily familiar. The shape of the nose. The piercing color of those eyes.

But that was impossible. Wasn't it?

"Hey, buddy. Do you have any idea how good it is to be back in civilization? I'm done with the prepper shit, and no matter how hard I tried, there was nothing glamorous about glamping." Maddox Crawford leaned forward, light shafting across his face. He held a crystal tumbler filled with Scotch and wore a jaunty smile. He looked a little older than he had a few short months ago, before his "funeral." But he also looked utterly alive. "I've been living on freeze-dried crap, and Lara's friend Freddy makes this rotgut whiskey that's truly horrible."

Zack blinked. "Mad?"

"In the flesh and even more handsome than before I died," Mad shot back with a wink. "I've had time to perfect my skin care regime. You need some, buddy. You look like shit. Now let's get down to business and talk about who's trying to twist your balls and ruin this country because you have fucked this up terribly."

Zack stared at his not-dead friend as the car pulled away from the White House. He grabbed Mad's arm to make sure the guy was actually real. "I can't believe it's you. Where have you fucking been? How could you let us think you were dead? Why the hell—"

"I know. I know. But it's all part of the conversation," Mad assured. "Settle in. This won't be easy."

Zack's mind whirled with possibilities and implications, but he grabbed a Scotch and sat back to listen. It was going to be an interesting, informative ride.

Zack, Liz, and the entire Perfect Gentlemen family (including Mad) will return in *AT THE PLEASURE OF THE PRESIDENT* in Fall 2018!

MORE THAN WANT YOU
More Than Words, Book 1
By Shayla Black
NOW AVAILABLE!

A fresh, sexy, and emotional contemporary romance series by Shayla Black...

I'm Maxon Reed—real estate mogul, shark, asshole. If a deal isn't high profile and big money, I pass. Now that I've found the property of a lifetime, I'm jumping. But one tenacious bastard stands between me and success—my brother. I'll need one hell of a devious ploy to distract cynical Griff. Then fate drops a luscious redhead in my lap who's just his type.

Sassy college senior Keeley Kent accepts my challenge to learn how to become Griff's perfect girlfriend. But somewhere between the makeover and the witty conversation, I'm having trouble resisting her. The quirky dreamer is everything I usually don't tolerate. But she's beyond charming. I more than want her; I'm desperate to own her. I'm not even sure how drastic I'm willing to get to make her mine—but I'm about to find out.

This book is the first in the More Than Words series. The books are companions, not serials, meaning that backstory, secondary characters, and other elements will be easier to relate to if you read the installments in order, but the main romance of each book is a stand-alone.

This book contains lines that may make you laugh,

events that may make you cry, and scenes that will probably have you squirming in your seat. Don't worry about cliffhangers or cheating. HEA guaranteed! (Does not contain elements of BDSM or romantic suspense.)

* * * *

"This will be our last song for the set. If you have requests, write them down and leave them in the jar." She points to the clear vessel at her feet. "We'll be back to play in thirty. If you have a dirty proposition, I'll entertain them at the bar in five." She says the words like she's kidding.

I, however, am totally serious.

Keeley starts her next song, a more recent pop tune, in a breathy, a capella murmur. "Can't keep my hands to myself."

She taps her thigh in a rhythm only she can hear until the band joins during the crescendo to the chorus. Keeley bounces her way through the lyrics with a flirty smile. It's both alluring and fun, a tease of a song.

Though I rarely smile, I find myself grinning along.

As she finishes, I glance around. There's more than one hungry dog with a bone in this damn bar.

I didn't get ahead in business or life by being polite or waiting my turn. She hasn't even wrapped her vocal cords around the last note but I'm on my feet and charging across the room.

I'm the first one to reach the corner of the bar closest to the stage. I prop my elbow on the slightly sticky wood to claim my territory, then glare back at the three other men who think they should end Keeley's supposed sex drought. They are not watering her garden, and my snarl makes that clear.

One sees my face, stops in his tracks, and immediately backs off. Smart man.

Number Two looks like a smarmy car salesman. He rakes Keeley up and down with his gaze like she's a slab of beef, but she's flirting my way as she tucks her mic on its stand. I smile back.

She's not really my type, but man, I'd love to hit that.

Out of the corner of my eye, I watch the approaching dirtbag finger his porn 'stouche. To stake my claim, I reach out to help Keeley off the stage. She looks pleasantly surprised by my gesture as she wraps her fingers around mine.

I can be a gentleman…when it suits me.

Fuck, she's warm and velvety, and her touch makes my cock jolt. Her second would-be one-night stand curses then slinks back to his seat.

That leaves me to fend off Number Three. He looks like a WWE reject—hulking and hit in the face too many times. If she prefers brawn over brains, I'll have to find another D-cup distraction for Griff.

That would truly suck. My gut tells me Keeley is perfect for the job.

Would it be really awful if I slept with her before I introduced her to my brother?

LOVE ANOTHER DAY
Masters and Mercenaries, Book 14
By Lexi Blake
NOW AVAILABLE!

A man born to protect

After a major loss, Brody Carter found a home with the London office of McKay-Taggart. A former soldier, he believes his job is to take the bullets and follow orders. He's happy to take on the job of protecting Dr. Stephanie Gibson while the team uses her clinic in Sierra Leone to bring down an international criminal. What he never expected was that the young doctor would prove to be the woman of his dreams. She's beautiful, smart, and reckless. Over and over he watches her risk her life to save others. One night of pure passion leads him to realize that he can't risk his heart again. When the mission ends, Brody walks away, unwilling to lose another person he loves.

A woman driven to heal

Stephanie's tragic past taught her to live for today. Everything she's done in the last fifteen years has been to make up for her mistakes. Offering medical care in war-torn regions gives her the purpose she needs to carry on. When she meets her gorgeous Aussie protector, she knows she's in too deep, but nothing can stop her from falling head over heels in love. But after one amazing night together, Brody walks away and never looks back. Stephanie is left behind…but not alone.

A secret that will change both their lives

A year later, Stephanie runs afoul of an evil mercenary who vows to kill her for failing to save his son. She runs to the only people she trusts, Liam and Avery O'Donnell. She hasn't come alone and her secret will bring her former lover across the world to protect her. From Liberia to Dallas, Brody will do whatever it takes to protect Stephanie from the man who wants to kill her, but it might be her own personal demons that could destroy them both.

* * * *

"Somehow I think the subs at The Garden took care of you. It's all right, Brody. We weren't together. It was one night and it didn't change anything."

One hand tugged the band out of her hair, spilling it across her shoulders. "I think the baby sleeping in the next room is evidence that night changed everything. And I'm trying to tell you that I haven't had another woman since I left you. I wasn't off gallivanting around and forgetting you. I spent every moment of our time away from each other miserable as hell. So let that towel drop and give me what I've only seen in my dreams for a year. Let me see you."

She wasn't sure why she did it, but her feet moved. She stepped back, putting a small but critical distance between them as her hands floated up and she dropped the towel.

The offering of a submissive to her chosen Dominant.

The towel hit the floor and she felt herself flush. She wasn't as pretty as she'd been the first time. Now she had stretch marks that spoke of her pregnancy. Her belly was still rounded, her breasts not as firm.

"Stop it," he said. "Don't you think about anything but how the air feels on your skin. Don't you think about how you look. I'll tell you what I see. I see the most beautiful woman I've ever known. I see that my dreams of her were nothing compared to the real thing. She's stunning and my heart aches at the thought of her not understanding how beautiful she is."

"Brody, I still haven't lost the weight I gained with Nate," she said, trying not to let his words affect her too much. She was already on the verge of tears, and she'd cried enough.

"You get one," he said, his voice deep. "One time I'll let you get away with saying something like that, but now you know the rule. You are beautiful and thinking or saying anything else about yourself will end in discipline."

"You can't control my thoughts." But she could feel her lips curling up at the very arrogance of him thinking he could. This was the Brody she'd fallen for. She'd known his larger-than-life, damn the torpedoes attitude had been half truth and half cover, but she'd adored it when he would walk in, take control, and do something or say something ridiculously over the top to make her day better.

"Watch me," he replied. "After I've spanked the hell out of that gorgeous arse a dozen times, you won't think that way again. I'll tie you up and torture you until you agree with me that you're the most gorgeous woman on the earth."

"Fine, I'm gorgeous." She didn't believe it, but standing here felt weird. "Shouldn't you get undressed? Or did you change your mind?"

His eyes roamed over her body, not missing an inch. "I didn't change my mind at all. I told you how this is going to be. The first time we did this, I let you push me."

"The first time we did this, you didn't want to."

His eyes narrowed. "You know damn well that's not true. Turn around and put your hands on the side of the tub."

"Why would I…" The answer hit her with the force of a steam engine. "You want to spank me?"

It should have come out in that horrified, I'm-a-feminist, shocked tone she often used when a random asshole told her she was cute to think she could be a doctor but they would prefer to see a man for their medical needs. Nope. It came out all breathy and porny. The porny part might have been because when she watched porn—rarely—she gravitated toward the movies where the big, dominant man spanked his lover to orgasm.

Which likely was a myth. Like most porn.

"Yes, and every second you make me wait is another smack to that pretty arse of yours." His hands were on his hips, his jaw squared as he looked her over. "If you push me too hard, I'll find a way to clamp your nipples and *then* I'll spank you."

What was she doing? She was standing here naked with a man who'd broken her heart once already.

"Tell me you don't want to know what it feels like." His voice had lost its harsh edge, sliding into silky smoothness. "Tell me you don't want to try it once.

You're the woman who was brave enough to get on your knees and present yourself to me like the sweetest treat I've ever been offered. Do what I'm asking. You can always stop me. One word will work tonight. No is all I need to hear. If you say that, then I'll get you dressed and I'll sleep beside you so you know you're safe. But I think you're braver than that. I think you're still a woman who knows what she wants."

ABOUT SHAYLA BLACK

Shayla Black is the *New York Times* and *USA Today* bestselling author of more than fifty novels. For nearly twenty years, she's written contemporary, erotic, paranormal, and historical romances via traditional, independent, foreign, and audio publishers. Her books have sold millions of copies and been published in a dozen languages.

Raised an only child, Shayla occupied herself with lots of daydreaming, much to the chagrin of her teachers. In college, she found her love for reading and realized that she could have a career publishing the stories spinning in her imagination. Though she graduated with a degree in Marketing/Advertising and embarked on a stint in corporate America to pay the bills, her heart has always been with her characters. She's thrilled that she's been living her dream as a full-time author for the past eight years.

Shayla currently lives in North Texas with her wonderfully supportive husband, her teenage daughter, and two spoiled tabbies. In her "free" time, she enjoys reality TV, reading, and listening to an eclectic blend of music.

Connect with me online:
Website: http://shaylablack.com
VIP Reader Newsletter: http://shayla.link/nwsltr
Facebook Author Page:
   https://www.facebook.com/ShaylaBlackAuthor

Facebook Book Beauties Chat Group:
  http://shayla.link/FBChat
Instagram: https://instagram.com/ShaylaBlack/
Twitter: http://twitter.com/Shayla_Black
Google +: http://shayla.link/googleplus
Amazon Author: http://shayla.link/AmazonFollow
BookBub: http://shayla.link/BookBub
Goodreads: http://shayla.link/goodreads
YouTube: http://shayla.link/youtube

If you enjoyed this book, please review it or recommend it to others so they can find it, too.

Keep in touch by engaging with me through one of the links above. Subscribe to my VIP Readers newsletter for exclusive excerpts and hang out in my Facebook Book Beauties group for live weekly video chats. I love talking to readers!

ABOUT LEXI BLAKE

Lexi Blake lives in North Texas with her husband, three kids, and the laziest rescue dog in the world. She began writing at a young age, concentrating on plays and journalism. It wasn't until she started writing romance that she found success. She likes to find humor in the strangest places. Lexi believes in happy endings no matter how odd the couple, threesome or foursome may seem. She also writes contemporary Western ménage as Sophie Oak.

Connect with Lexi online:

Facebook: www.Facebook.com/AuthorLexiBlake
Twitter: www.twitter.com/authorLexiBlake
Website: www.LexiBlake.net

Sign up for Lexi's free newsletter at
www.LexiBlake.net/newsletter/

ALSO FROM SHAYLA BLACK

CONTEMPORARY ROMANCE
MORE THAN WORDS
More Than Want You
More Than Need You
Coming Soon:
More Than Love You (February 13, 2018)

THE WICKED LOVERS (COMPLETE SERIES)
Wicked Ties
Decadent
Delicious
Surrender to Me
Belong to Me
"Wicked to Love" (novella)
Mine to Hold
"Wicked All the Way" (novella)
Ours to Love
"Wicked All Night" (novella)
"Forever Wicked" (novella)
Theirs to Cherish
His to Take
Pure Wicked (novella)
Wicked for You
Falling in Deeper
Dirty Wicked (novella)
Holding on Tighter (February 7, 2017)

THE DEVOTED LOVERS
Coming in 2018!

SEXY CAPERS
Bound And Determined
Strip Search
"Arresting Desire" (Hot In Handcuffs Anthology)

THE PERFECT GENTLEMEN (by Shayla Black and Lexi Blake)
Scandal Never Sleeps
Seduction In Session
Big Easy Temptation
Smoke and Sin
Coming Soon:
At the Pleasure of the President (Fall 2018)

MASTERS OF MÉNAGE (by Shayla Black and Lexi Blake)
Their Virgin Captive
Their Virgin's Secret
Their Virgin Concubine
Their Virgin Princess
Their Virgin Hostage
Their Virgin Secretary
Their Virgin Mistress
Coming Soon:
Their Virgin Bride (TBD)

DOMS OF HER LIFE (by Shayla Black, Jenna Jacob, and Isabella LaPearl)
Raine Falling Collection (Complete)
One Dom To Love
The Young And The Submissive
The Bold and The Dominant
The Edge of Dominance
Coming Soon:
Heavenly Rising Collection
The Choice (Winter 2018)

THE MISADVENTURES SERIES
Misadventures of a Backup Bride (October 17, 2017)

STANDALONE TITLES
Naughty Little Secret
Watch Me
Dangerous Boys And Their Toy
"Her Fantasy Men" (Four Play Anthology)
A Perfect Match
His Undeniable Secret (Sexy Short)

HISTORICAL ROMANCE (as Shelley Bradley)
The Lady And The Dragon
One Wicked Night
Strictly Seduction
Strictly Forbidden

BROTHERS IN ARMS MEDIEVAL TRILOGY
His Lady Bride (Book 1)
His Stolen Bride (Book 2)
His Rebel Bride (Book 3)

PARANORMAL ROMANCE
THE DOOMSDAY BRETHREN
Tempt Me With Darkness
"Fated" (e-novella)
Seduce Me In Shadow
Possess Me At Midnight
"Mated" – Haunted By Your Touch Anthology
Entice Me At Twilight
Embrace Me At Dawn

ALSO FROM LEXI BLAKE

EROTIC ROMANCE

Masters and Mercenaries
The Dom Who Loved Me
The Men With The Golden Cuffs
A Dom is Forever
On Her Master's Secret Service
Sanctum: A Masters and Mercenaries Novella
Love and Let Die
Unconditional: A Masters and Mercenaries Novella
Dungeon Royale
Dungeon Games: A Masters and Mercenaries Novella
A View to a Thrill
Cherished: A Masters and Mercenaries Novella
You Only Love Twice
Luscious: Masters and Mercenaries~Topped
Adored: A Masters and Mercenaries Novella
Master No
Just One Taste: Masters and Mercenaries~Topped 2
From Sanctum with Love
Devoted: A Masters and Mercenaries Novella
Dominance Never Dies
Submission is Not Enough
Master Bits and Mercenary Bites~The Secret Recipes of
Topped
Perfectly Paired: Masters and Mercenaries~Topped 3
For His Eyes Only
Arranged: A Masters and Mercenaries Novella
Love Another Day
At Your Service: Masters and Mercenaries~Topped 4,
Coming November 14, 2017
Nobody Does It Better, Coming February 20, 2018
Close Cover, Coming April 10, 2018

Lawless
Ruthless
Satisfaction
Revenge

Masters Of Ménage (by Shayla Black and Lexi Blake)
Their Virgin Captive
Their Virgin's Secret
Their Virgin Concubine
Their Virgin Princess
Their Virgin Hostage
Their Virgin Secretary
Their Virgin Mistress

The Perfect Gentlemen (by Shayla Black and Lexi Blake)
Scandal Never Sleeps
Seduction in Session
Big Easy Temptation
Smoke and Sin, Coming September 26, 2017

URBAN FANTASY

Thieves
Steal the Light
Steal the Day
Steal the Moon
Steal the Sun
Steal the Night
Ripper
Addict
Sleeper, *Coming October 17, 2017*

CPSIA information can be obtained
at www.ICGtesting.com
Printed in the USA
FSOW02n1110031117
40381FS